COMMANDING ROYAL

CLUB ROYAL, BOOK SEVEN

ELOUISE EAST

Publisher: Elouise East
Cover Design: Design By Tina Løwén
Editor: Maria Vickers
Beta Readers: Emma Brown

COMMANDING ROYAL

Andrew has suffered through a loss he would never wish upon anyone. Louisa had been the light of his life and at his side for too many years to count. When she was killed, he promised to do better by his family, to stick by their sides no matter the consequences to himself. He owed that to Louisa, to fight for those who cannot fight for themselves. When he finds himself wanting to be in the presence of two people who should stay far away from him, he tries to step back, but will they let him?

Kean loves his family, but he doesn't particularly like them. They push him to be someone he's not and towards people completely wrong for him. Although, the people he chooses himself haven't worked out either. How can they when one is a king and the other has been hurt too much. He expects to live his life as their friends, nothing more. But when he gets the chance, he grabs it with both hands.

Kendal plans to stay alone for the rest of their life. They've stopped trusting their instincts after everything that had happened to them before. What they choose to do instead is to live their life as if it never happened, creating a sanctuary. But when their needs become too much, who can they turn to? How about the two men who've come to mean so much to them?

Three people with entirely different needs come together in the unlikeliest of situations, but is the weight of the crown too much for them all to handle?

This is an MMM book containing BDSM scenes and D/s dynamics in all forms. It also has lots of loving, friendships, family drama, a large age gap and, of course, a HEA.

CONTENTS

List of characters   xi
Bodyguard list of characters   xiii
Author note   xv

1. Andrew   1
2. Kean   12
3. Kendal   23
4. Andrew   34
5. Kean   45
6. Kendal   56
7. Andrew   67
8. Kean   80
9. Freddie   91
10. Kendal   94
11. Andrew   106
12. Kean   117
13. Kendal   129
14. Andrew   141
15. Kean   153
16. Kendal   164
17. Andrew   176
18. Christian   188
19. Kean   191
20. Kendal   203
21. Andrew   215
22. Kean   227
23. Henry   239
24. Kendal   242
25. Andrew   253
26. Kean   260
27. George   271
28. Kendal   274

29. Andrew — 286
30. Patrick — 298
31. Kean — 301
32. Kendal — 313
33. Andrew — 325
34. Douglas — 336
35. Kean — 338
36. Kendal — 349

FREE! — 361
Protecting his Past — 363
About Elouise East — 365
Books by Elouise East — 367

DEDICATION

To my entire team
You've made this series possible, and I thank you from the bottom of
my heart.

LIST OF CHARACTERS

(ALPHABETICAL ORDER)

Andrew, King of England
Brady, Police Commissioner, Andrew's friend
Charles, Andrew's nephew, Charlotte and
    Ernest's child
Charlotte, Andrew's sister
Christian, Andrew's nephew, Oscar's boyfriend
Clarice, Club Royal's receptionist
Damon, Frederick's fiancé
Daniel, Christian's friend, works with Neil
Dante, Kean's father
Douglas, Andrew's son, Mav's boyfriend
Eddie, George and Timothy's boyfriend
Elizabeth, Andrew's niece
Ernest, Andrew's brother-in-law
Frederick, Andrew's son, heir to the throne,
    Damon's fiancé
George, Andrew's son, Timothy and Eddie's
    boyfriend
Gia, Christian's friend, works with Neil

Henry, Andrew's nephew, Robert's fiancé,
Victoria and Patrick's son
John, Andrew's brother, Christian's father
Kean, Henry's best friend
Kendal, friend of family
Kieren, Patrick's boyfriend, security consultant
Louisa, Queen Consort, Andrew's late wife
Maverick, Douglas's boyfriend
Miranda, Andrew's sister-in-law, Christian's
mother
Neil, Christian's boss
Oliver, Club Royal bartender
Oscar, Christian's boyfriend
Patrick Snr, Andrew's brother-in-law, Patrick
and Henry's father
Patrick Jnr, Andrew's nephew, Victoria and
Patrick's son
Pierce, Quinn's partner
Portia, Randall's assistant
Quinn, Kendal's friend
Randall, Andrew's assistant
Robert, Henry's fiancé
Simon, Kean's late brother
Timothy, George and Eddie's boyfriend
Victoria, Andrew's sister
William, Andrew's brother
Xan, Kendal's friend

BODYGUARD LIST OF CHARACTERS

(Showing royal member assigned.)

Brett = Christian
Colt = Andrew
Des = Henry
Dominic = Andrew
Eric = Douglas
Felix = Oscar
Ford = Kendal
Gerald = Andrew
Greg = Kean
Isaac = George
Jade = Patrick
Jared = Andrew
Landon = Andrew
Locke = Frederick
Matt = Robert
Nick = Andrew
Nina = Kieren

Owen = Frederick
Rae = Mav
Sam = Eddie
Selena = Andrew
Simon = Andrew
Van = Timothy
Viola = Andrew

AUTHOR NOTE

If you would like to see any potential triggers for this book and any other books I've written, please go to this link on my website: https://elouiseeast.com/triggers

COMMANDING ROYAL

1

ANDREW

$\mathcal{A}$ndrew Alexander Charles Sutcliffe, King of the United Kingdom of Great Britain and Northern Ireland, stared at the bathroom mirror, seeing the deepening lines on his face. He wasn't one to notice these things usually, but he was feeling every hour of his age of late. The lines seemed to have sunk to craters this past year, but it was no surprise. Stress and grief could do that to a person.

That day was no different. It would take every ounce of strength he had to get through the hours to come. Not only because it was the first anniversary of his wife's death but also because it was a security nightmare. If he hadn't believed they needed a show of strength, he would never allow his family to have targets on their backs. Unfortunately, sharing the weight of the crown with his sons was the only way they might be able to retain it.

He sighed and rubbed a hand over his chin, his beard scratching audibly, and set about washing the weariness from his face.

Far too soon, he stood in front of the suit hanging innocently in its place. The black-on-white had never looked so bleak, but maybe that was just his outlook on life. Louisa hated the dark colours they were forced to wear in their grief, and if the media wouldn't have crucified him for wearing a purple shirt, he would've done so. It was her favourite colour, after all. Instead, he slipped the white shirt over his shoulders and fastened the buttons, sliding the jacket over the top and pinned a purple flower to his lapel. It was the best he could do, and he hoped she forgave him for it.

A knock sounded, and he sighed. The time had come.

He opened the door and smiled at Simon, his head of security. Simon had his work cut out for him, managing Andrew's eight personal guards, but he'd been steady as a rock, even with the issues they'd had from within their circle last Christmas. Simon had taken it upon himself to recheck and audit every member of his personal guard after the attack. There was only so much he could do, though. People were good at hiding their goals if they wanted to. As Andrew well knew.

"Morning, Your Majesty," Simon said with a head bow.

Andrew returned the greeting, grateful Simon hadn't said "good" morning. There was nothing good about that day, and he doubted there ever would be.

They strode down the hallways towards the exit, one other guard falling in line beside him and two guards settling behind him. His final four guards would be positioned by the exit doors, waiting to spread out around him as they walked the distance to the chapel.

His heart clenched when his sons came into view, waiting just inside the doors. With them were their partners, and an immense well of love filled him at the sight. Louisa would've loved to see them all happy, and as Freddie always said, she must've been psychic with how much of what she predicted had come true. Her final prediction would be a failure, though. But that was something to think about another day.

"Father," Freddie said, clasping him.

Andrew was too choked up to reply but smiled when they pulled apart. He repeated the action with Douglas and George, then hugged each of their partners: Damon, Mav, Timothy and Eddie.

"It's time, Your Majesty."

Andrew nodded and gazed around him. "Chin up, boys," he whispered. He hoped the reminder of their not-so-secret action of tilting the other's chin up before they departed would help bolster them.

"You, too, Father," George whispered.

Andrew nodded towards the guard by the door, and several of the security team left the building before the royal family did, fanning out to ensure they covered the family as much as possible. It wasn't like it had been—even a year ago —when they could have one or two guards surrounding them. With everything Charlotte and John had put them through, they'd increased the guards at all events, and although there had been no sight nor sound from either of them recently, they had highlighted this event as the last hurrah, so to speak. He wasn't sure what to expect, but he'd given his guards and the security team an order they had initially refused to obey; if something happened, his children and their partners were their first priority, not him. It had taken a lot of persuading and explaining before they would even consider it.

Andrew heard the roar of the crowd, shouting and screaming to them, but he shut it out, unable to distinguish what anyone was saying. He focused on the walls of Windsor and the rhythm of his footsteps as he drew closer to the chapel, where he would give a speech about his late wife before closing the curtains on his grief for good. At least to the public. Internally, she would never be gone.

They climbed the steps at the front of the chapel, shaking hands with the Dean of Windsor, who would preside over the service. They wandered down the long aisle, nodding at the guests already in place, the music low and sombre. Andrew took the spot he usually sat in, and Freddie settled beside him in what used to be Louisa's seat. The toll that knowledge took on his son lined his already drawn face, and Andrew rested a hand on his shoulder and squeezed before staring at the space on the floor where Louisa's coffin had stood three hundred and sixty-five days ago before being taken to her final resting place.

The Dean of Windsor started the service, talking about Louisa and her charity work, and then led them in a hymn. Then Andrew stood and, followed by two guards, took his place at the lectern. He had prepared a speech for the guests and the viewers who watched the service through their TV screens, but he couldn't bring himself to take it from his jacket.

"My wife...was one of a kind. I've never known anyone with a bigger heart, a warmer embrace or such gentle words. Even when I was in trouble with her, she never raised her voice. She stated her reasons and made me see sense." He gave a small smile, remembering how she had taken him to his knees when he'd demanded things of Douglas that no father should. As soon as she'd made him see he was following in *his* father's footsteps, he'd acquiesced and changed his ways. She would always be the conscience on his shoulder whenever he had a decision to make, or he needed to reply to something.

"Her wisdom was beyond her years, leading us all to believe she was psychic." He chuckled. "But I know, from having loved her for forty years, she would prefer to be where she is now than for the same thing to happen to her children. As would I. Louisa's love will never leave us. We'll feel it in every interaction that brings a memory with it. We'll feel it in every place we scent honeysuckle. We'll feel it every day when our hearts beat because she was the beating heart of this country."

He swallowed the lump in his throat. "When her heart beat for the last time, she sent that love into all of us. Yes, I may be the king. Yes, my family are the heirs to the throne. But in every one of us, she lives, and therefore, her heart beats within us. She would not want us to falter in our belief of how amazing our country and the commonwealth could be, but she would gladly hand over the reins if that was what the public deemed in the country's best interests.

"So, I stand before you today, hoping your hearts still beat for us. That your love for your late queen still lingers within you. That you trust in *love* itself, no matter what form that love comes in. I, for one, know Louisa would have been over-joyed to be surrounded with as much love as my family has recently brought within it. I hope you can be, too."

He stepped back, closed his eyes and breathed for a second before going back to his seat. The rest of the service was a blur, but he followed the motions of his family and his guards until it was time to leave. They walked the distance back home but headed for the receiving room they had begun using as a meeting room. There were too many of them to fit into the rooms they'd used previously. His family often used it for their parties and get-togethers, too, which was what they had decided to do now. A small party for those who couldn't attend the service, this time away from the prying eyes of the media and the public.

He greeted his nephews, Patrick, Henry and Christian, the

latter of who he saw more as a son than a nephew after what his family put him through. No child should ever be disowned because of who they loved. Other guests had arrived while the service was in progress, and he spent a few minutes with each before he found himself faced with a man he wanted to spend more time with but couldn't.

"Your Majesty," Kean Seymour said with a bow and sympathetic smile.

Andrew hugged him, closing his eyes for a brief moment and inhaled, trying to borrow some of Kean's strength to keep him going. "Kean. Thank you for coming."

"You're welcome. If there's anything I can do…"

Andrew squeezed his shoulder. "I appreciate that." He exhaled. "How are you? How's the studying?"

Kean rolled his eyes, making Andrew smile. "It's okay. I still don't understand why I need the qualification, but my father insists I have it if I want to be part of the business. It's keeping me busy if nothing else."

"And is construction where you want to be?" He asked the question he'd been wanting to for a while because he could see something inside Kean. Something that appeared to want something other than following in his father's footsteps.

Kean's eyes widened. "Maybe," he said finally, his gaze never wavering from Andrew's.

Andrew pushed down the need to pull him into his arms again and soothe whatever worried him. Kean wasn't his, and he needed to remember that he never would be. After all, it was okay to be out and proud about being the first bisexual king, but if he were ever to take a partner, it couldn't be someone the public would crucify because Kean was thirty years younger than Andrew. He was younger than his sons.

"You know I'm here if you need to talk about your options," he said instead.

"Thank you."

A hand appeared on Kean's biceps, and they both turned to see the other person who had a piece of Andrew's heart. Kendal Lawson. An amazingly resilient person who was a ray of sunlight whenever they were in the room, and a sub who had been abused by a Dominant who'd been part of Club Royal. Andrew didn't take too kindly to people hurting others, especially those under his care. In the aftermath, Andrew had taken it upon himself to ensure Kendal's health and safety and had checked up on them to make sure they were managing since the incident.

"Your Majesty," Kendal said, lowering their eyes and bowing to him.

Andrew wished they wouldn't. He didn't like them giving him respect when he didn't deserve it.

"Kendal, it's lovely to see you."

A flush tinted their cheeks as they rose, and they didn't meet his gaze completely, looking more at his chin. "I heard your words. They were beautiful." Kendal's voice was soft as if they were checking each word before they said it.

"Thank you. She deserved a lot more than that, but it's the least I can give her." Andrew's head ached, and he needed to get out of there despite not wanting to leave either of them. "I'm glad you could both be here, but I need to..." He paused and breathed as the ache above his eyes intensified. He pressed against it for a second and smiled at them again. "I'll see you soon, okay?"

He leaned in for a hug with Kean and paused before Kendal, leaning gently forward so as not to scare them and pressing a kiss to their forehead. Inhaling, he threaded his way through the people and towards the door. He stopped beside Freddie.

"I'm going to head out. Let everyone stay as long as they want. Well, as long as security allows them to."

"Are you okay?" Freddie's expression was tight; he was worried about him.

Andrew hugged him. "Just a headache. I'm fine."

"I'm beginning to hate that word," Freddie murmured but nodded. "Get some rest."

Andrew disappeared out of the door, his guards falling into step, and he headed for the room he used when he couldn't face the places where Louisa was imprinted in everything, like his suite, which he'd shared with her for years. It wasn't that he didn't want the reminders; it was that he couldn't deal with them at that moment. He needed…blankness. A clean slate.

He entered the room after the guards checked it and reached for the bourbon, splashing several fingers into a glass so he didn't have to keep getting up to refill it. Sinking onto the sofa in front of the fireplace, he sipped his drink, allowing the alcohol to soothe him as he stared at the unlit fire.

He had no idea where to go from here. Things with his siblings were on rocky ground, and as nothing had happened that day, as per the list they'd received from Christian's mother, there was no way of figuring out what their next move was. They were completely in the dark, and Andrew hated it.

The door opened, and he glanced over, surprised to see Kean. The man didn't say a word, just strode for the drinks and poured himself a bourbon, then settled on the opposite side of the sofa to Andrew. He peered at him, but Kean stared at the fireplace, just like Andrew had been doing. The silence between them stretched, but Andrew didn't fill it. It wasn't uncomfortable. It didn't need to be broken. And he hadn't realised how much he needed it. The company. Even when no words were spoken.

Something inside him unfurled, and his body relaxed further into the cushions. Transferring his gaze to the fireplace, Andrew let his mind wander. Kean rose several minutes later, taking Andrew's empty glass and refilling them both. The younger man handed it back to him without a word.

A knock sounded as Kean returned to his seat, and Andrew called for whoever it was to enter. Freddie stepped inside, followed by Douglas and George.

"Are you okay, Father?" Douglas asked.

Andrew smiled. "I'm doing okay. Don't worry about me." He stood, embracing his second-born son. "Has everyone gone?"

"Yes. We wanted to check on you before we headed home." Freddie glanced at Kean and back at Andrew.

"I'm good. Get yourselves home."

Douglas chuckled. "I already am."

Andrew laughed and clipped him around the head. "You know what I mean."

George stepped closer. "Are you sure you're okay?"

Andrew hugged his youngest son. "I'm positive. Yes, it's been a…tough day, but I'm fine."

Freddie sighed. "Can we ban that word from our vocabulary?"

"Sorry. I'm going to go," Kean said, moving around them towards the door.

"Are you in a hurry?" Andrew asked; the first words he'd spoken to the man since he'd entered the room.

Kean paused and faced him, a small smile lifting his lips. "Not at all."

"You're welcome to stay." Andrew *wanted* him to stay.

They stared at one another until Kean nodded once and returned to his seat. Andrew focused on his sons and found them smiling. He shook his head at them and ushered them out.

"Go home. I'll see you soon enough," he said. "We have plans to make."

Freddie paused before exiting. "I know what you told the security team." He pointed a finger at him. "Don't do that again. I don't care if you outrank me. You are just as important as we are."

"I can't promise that. I *won't* promise that."

Freddie stared at him, then shook his head. "Don't do anything I wouldn't do," he said, nodding towards Kean.

Andrew clipped his head, too, laughing. "Go away." He shut the door, smiling. His kids were incorrigible. "Sorry about that," he said to Kean, striding back to his seat.

"It's okay. They're worried about you."

Andrew sighed. "They are, but they don't need to be."

"Don't they?"

Andrew glanced at him, taking in his messy brown hair, sparkling eyes and the long nose with a slight bend to the left at the end. He refused to focus on his lips, not wanting the temptation he always felt when he did.

"No, they don't. I'm—"

"Fine. Yeah, I heard." Kean's mouth quirked, and Andrew huffed and shook his head.

"Maybe we *should* ban that word around here. Everyone seems to be fine when they are and when they're not." Andrew sipped his bourbon. "I suppose I'm hoping she agrees with what I'm doing. I'm trying to...fill her shoes. Do things the way she would want them to be done, but I don't know." He sighed again. "I wish I knew if I was doing it right."

Kean twisted in his seat, bringing his knee onto the cushion. "You are. You're supporting those that need it. You're supporting your family. And yet, you're still trying to give the country what they want. You're between a rock and a hard place, but you're still standing."

"For how long?" Andrew glanced at him, not wanting to voice his concerns but seemingly unable to stop. There was something about Kean that made him want to be vulnerable, to be seen. And it wasn't a good idea, but he couldn't stop.

2

KEAN

ean's heart skipped a beat at Andrew's words. He didn't want to think of a time when the king wouldn't be around. It was inevitable, but that didn't mean he had to enjoy thinking about it. "As long as you need to be," he said instead. "You won't give up."

"I might not need to. The country could easily take me from the throne. The country votes...and we follow."

Kean huffed. "You know that's not always how it works."

Andrew glared at him. "That's how it's *supposed* to work. When I have the option, I choose whatever the public wants, as long as it won't hurt them."

"And losing you and your family will hurt them. The grass certainly isn't greener on the other side."

Andrew chuckled and sipped his drink, and Kean withheld his smile at cheering him up a little. They lapsed into silence again. He couldn't remember anyone, apart from Henry, he'd been able to sit with like this. Saying no words and not needing to. It was far too comfortable, and he had to end it. Andrew would not take a chance on them with so many obstacles in their path. Kean knew that, but it didn't stop him from wanting his company when he could.

"I need to go," he said, standing.

He replaced the glass on the table with the bottles and faced one of the people he loved. "I'm sorry for your loss," he whispered. He lowered his eyes and headed for the door, unsure if he wanted the man to stop him or not and trying not to feel upset when he didn't. When the door closed behind him, he continued walking, not wanting the guards to sense his turmoil, but the moment he rounded a corner, he leaned back against the wall and exhaled. Whoever said love wins had never been in his situation. There was no winning there.

He blew out a breath and continued down the hallway, almost to the exit, when someone called his name. Freddie stood with his hands in his pockets, looking every inch the prince.

"Is everything okay?" he asked as he moved closer.

Freddie nodded slowly. "Are you okay?"

Kean nodded and forced a smile. "I'm good."

"It won't be easy," Freddie said. "Being with him. He'll want to do what's best for everyone else rather than himself. But if you love him like I think you do, you need to keep at it. Wearing down his walls is the only way to win him over."

Kean swallowed hard. "He's still grieving."

Freddie nodded. "He is, but I can see how he looks at you. He's keeping himself away because he thinks you deserve better." He shrugged. "Maybe you do. This life isn't what everyone thinks it is, and though I know you could cope with it, it's different for a monarch. Worse. Heavier. I'm not trying to talk you out of it. I know you can do it. I'm trying to explain him."

"I know him," Kean said. "He won't take the chance when the other options are better for the family or the country."

"He may not have a choice."

Freddie stared at him, and Kean's stomach rolled. He wasn't sure if it was excitement or fear, but either way, there was something Freddie was trying to tell him. Kean needed to be honest to show Freddie the problem.

"He's not the only one I love," he whispered.

Freddie smiled. "I know."

Kean frowned. "Damon told you."

"No. Never said a word. I see the way you are together. The three of you. I think if anyone else saw, they would see one person comforting the other two, but I know my father, and I know you. Kendal, not so much, but I'm getting to. I see you together, and there's something intangible between you. Something that cannot be brushed aside." Freddie stepped closer and sighed. "I think *you* need to be the one to bridge the gap. I think *you* are the only one who can make this happen. It won't be easy, and you need to be sure, but if you want this, you have to be the one to get it."

"I'm worried about Kendal," Kean said. "After everything they've been through, I don't want to mess with them."

"That's why you need to be sure. You need to make up your mind once and for all, then never turn back. They both need something solid, something real to hold on to, and if you change your mind halfway through, you'll destroy all three of you." Freddie squeezed his shoulder. "It's all or nothing. When you've decided, let me know. I'll support you —we'll support you every step of the way."

Kean swallowed back the tears that wanted to fall. "Why are you doing this?"

"Because you both make him smile like he did when Mother was around, and no one should live without that."

Kean lost the battle with his tears, and they trickled down his face as Freddie dragged him in for a hug. He swallowed repeatedly to get himself under control and pulled back.

"Thank you."

Freddie smiled. "No, thank you. I honestly don't know what would've happened to him if he hadn't found you."

"It was nothing I did."

"Just being there, like you were tonight. When he shouldn't be alone, even if he says he wants to be. You're doing everything right, Kean. Keep going."

Kean cleared his throat. "What about what happened with Henry?"

Freddie chuckled. "No one else knows about the three of you that I'm aware of, but they're not stupid. They probably have figured something out. It might be wise to talk to Henry, but you don't need to if you don't want to. As for what happened *with* Henry, well, that's your story to tell." Freddie turned away. "I'd love to be a fly on the wall for that conversation, though," he murmured over his shoulder.

The words startled a laugh out of Kean, and he cursed the man as Freddie headed down the hallway. Kean watched him disappear, then aimed for the exit, needing to get home. As he drove away from Windsor, he thought through everything that had and hadn't been said that night. He wanted to head to Henry's straight away, but it wasn't the best time to do so. He might come across as insensitive in broaching the subject on Queen Louisa's anniversary. Instead, he headed home, knowing his father would be waiting for him.

The ten-minute drive wasn't long enough, and as he pulled up through the gates and into the driveway, he wished it had been an hour and ten minutes. Or even two hours and ten minutes.

He switched off the engine and stared at the enormous

house that was far too big for just three people. It looked fantastic, and his parents had bought it at a good price and then added on to the property over the years, but it had too much space and never felt like home. It was more of a show home for the clients his father brought back. Climbing out of the car, he braced himself, not knowing what mood his father would be in. He wasn't so worried about his mother. She would either be asleep or slipping into her alcohol-fuelled thoughts.

"I'm home," he called, sliding his keys into his pocket rather than the porcelain shell on the foyer table, as his father did.

"I was expecting you back before now." His father's voice came from the library, which doubled as his office, and Kean headed that way.

"I was talking to Henry," he lied. He refused to use the others' names because he didn't want his father to know exactly how close he was to them. He knew he was friends with Henry, but it was a whole other matter if he knew the higher-ups, as his father put it.

"I can understand it is a hard day for them all. Well done for being there for him."

As if he'd be anywhere else. "Did you need me for something?" he asked, trying to change the subject before his father started on about how he would never have been kidnapped if he wasn't involved with the royal family.

Dante Seymour was a formidable picture, so Kean thought. He had been a rugby player in his younger years and had kept up with the sport and training even after he decided to forgo being a professional player and become part of the construction business instead. His height and strength had never left him, though his father never used that to physically hurt anyone, only to intimidate. Although that was sometimes worse. If Kean ignored his father's muscles, they were the image of each other, though he often didn't want to acknowledge that because it made him feel too much like him, and he hoped with everything he had that he was nothing like him. He wasn't sure he had it in himself to be as cutthroat as Dante.

"No, not tonight. I have the investors coming for dinner soon. It would be an ideal time for you to meet them properly and start networking."

Kean's heart sank. "Of course."

"How is your degree coming along?"

The same question he asked every night. "Good, Father. I finished the current assignment last night and sent it straight to the professor."

"Good. Keep on top of it, and you'll be done in no time." Kean nodded. "Right, get some sleep."

"Goodnight, Father."

Kean disappeared, trudging up the stairs to his room and closing himself inside. He hated the house. He hated how his father treated him like an employee rather than a son. He hated how everyone left him on his own. His mother, although there, might as well not have been. His brother had overdosed on drugs eighteen months before. Henry had left him—granted, only for a year, but he'd still left. No one ever stayed. So, could he trust in Freddie's words of encouragement? Could he believe it would all work out with Andrew and Kendal? Or would he end up being left alone when it all went wrong?

The crucial question was, did he have the strength to take the chance?

He stared at the ceiling from where he'd flung himself on the bed and wished his path would shine enough to make it clear which route he should go. Closing his eyes, he brought

Andrew's face to the front of his mind, and his heart rate increased. He did the same for Kendal, acknowledging the same response. He was in love with them both, that was certain, and he couldn't imagine his life without them in it, even if it was only the small bits he could get now. But could he have more? Freddie seemed to think so.

Now, he just needed to figure out if he was willing to risk it all.

Nine days later, he still hadn't made up his mind fully. But he couldn't stay away from either of them. That day was the anniversary of Queen Louisa's funeral, which he was sure would be as emotional as the day she died, so he set out for Windsor Castle.

He'd thought nothing of the royal family living there until Henry had mentioned once that most monarchs chose to live in the private quarters of Buckingham Palace. Kean couldn't understand the fascination with living in something so big when there were other places more suitable. But then, he hadn't been brought up in homes like that, so maybe that was why. Windsor Castle, however, seemed large, but not excessively so, considering there were plenty of people living within it, so it made sense.

He pulled through the gates when the guards waved him through and parked to the side. Windsor Castle was open to tourists most of the year, and he was used to being gawked at by people whenever he entered or left the building. He was grateful he didn't have to deal with any of them and took every chance he could to ignore them.

Henry had messaged him earlier that day to say they were all spending the day at Windsor, having a big Thirsty Thirteen get-together. Kean wasn't included in the title group, but they had assured him he was always welcome. And he could be of help to lighten the mood if needed.

"Hey, Kean. How are you?" George said when Kean entered the room.

"All good, thanks. Is there a barbecue today, or is it just snacks?" he asked as he grabbed a drink and settled opposite the prince and his men.

"Barbecue, of course," he said.

"You do know it's going to rain, don't you?" Robert said as he and Henry entered.

George shrugged. "Don't care. We'll get an umbrella over it if we have to."

"I don't think that's quite safe," Timothy said, pressing his lips to George's temple.

"No matter what, we're having a barbecue," George argued.

"Of course we are. We love barbecues." Eddie slid his arm around George and kissed him.

Kean glanced away and focused on Henry, not wanting to intrude when he could see George was emotional. He could understand it. He often focused a bit too much on George and his partners, being the triad they were. They made it work.

"Hey. How're things with the history lessons?" he joked. Henry had lost himself down the rabbit hole of the royal family's history and, from what Kean could gather, was enjoying it immensely. He'd already found that one pertinent piece of information about the law that Andrew's father had never passed, even though the paperwork said it had been. Which reminded him that he needed to speak to Andrew about it.

Henry rolled his eyes. "It's good. I've not found anything

too incriminating, but that doesn't mean I won't. There's just so much to go through. Douglas has been helping as well."

Kean sipped his bourbon. "I can imagine it would take a lifetime to go through all the history tomes for this family."

Henry nodded. "Without a doubt. We're focusing mainly on the previous two monarchs to ensure no more surprises are lurking around the corner."

"Anything to make you think there's something amiss?" he asked.

"Nothing else so far. It all seems pretty much standard, thankfully."

"Glad to hear it."

He diverted his attention to the door when more royals entered. Soon, the room filled with the sound of laughter and conversation, reminiscing about things they'd done in their childhood and the punishments they'd received. Damon and George went outside to sort the barbecue, and everything was great.

But there was an underlying buzz flowing through Kean, and when Henry went for another drink, Kean followed.

"Hey, can I have a word?"

Henry grinned. "Of course." He glanced over at Robert and motioned between him and Kean. Robert smiled and turned back to his conversation with Timothy. Henry wasn't asking permission; he was letting Robert know what he was doing.

They moved towards the window in the corner of the room and settled into two chairs. Kean wasn't sure where to start now he was there. "This might sound strange," he said. "I'm not in love with you anymore." Henry tilted his head like Kean had seen his pup self do before. "I haven't been for a while. I..." He licked his lips. Why was it hard to tell him?

"I'm in love with two people, and I wanted you to know so there's no weirdness between us."

"Unlike the weirdness you're displaying now, you mean?" Henry said with a smirk.

Kean huffed a laugh. "Yes. Sorry. What I'm trying so inelegantly to say is that I love..." He inhaled and let it out. "I love Andrew. And Kendal."

Henry blinked at him, not saying anything, and Kean bit his lip. What was Henry thinking? Was he upset?

"You're in love with Uncle Andrew?" Henry murmured.

Kean nodded, then jumped when Henry snorted. "What?" Kean asked.

"You don't make things easy on yourself, do you?"

Kean smiled and shook his head. "You wouldn't like me any other way."

"Bloody hell, Kean. So, what's your plan?"

"Yeah, I have no idea."

Henry sipped his drink. "You're going to have a fight on your hands. Uncle Andrew won't want you dragged into this."

"I know." Kean shrugged. "I can't help it, though."

Henry sighed. "Thank you for telling me. You didn't have to."

"You're my best friend. Of course, I did."

"Let me know if I can help with anything."

Kean stood and pulled Henry into a hug. "I will. Thanks." He exhaled. "I'm going to head out."

"Not staying for food?"

Kean shook his head. "I need to...do something. I'm too antsy."

"Call me if you need me, okay? You don't need to do this alone."

"I will."

Kean said goodbye to everyone else and headed to his car. He maybe should've stayed a little longer, but he had too much on his mind. He waved to the guards and drove, his thoughts going off on tangents all over the place. When he parked the car, he peered around him, realising he wasn't at home. He glanced at the two-storey house and bit his lip. Should he go home? He hadn't asked them if he could visit. But the longer he stared at the house, the more he wanted to see them.

He climbed out of the car and strode for the door. If they answered, he would apologise for just turning up. And if they didn't answer, he would apologise in a message instead. He just needed to see them. Needed to check with his own eyes that they were okay. Nothing had happened recently, but he still couldn't fight that need. He'd never thought himself extremely dominant, but when it came to them, he couldn't help feeling protective.

He wanted things from Kendal that he wasn't sure they could give him, but he couldn't help but try, anyway.

3

KENDAL

Kendal Lawson froze when a knock sounded. They hadn't been expecting anyone, so who the heck was it? They grabbed their phone, their heart pounding, their breath choppy, and checked the cameras Prince Christian had installed for them. It was the only thing that made them feel safe being alone, and they would be forever grateful to the entire royal family.

Ever since the attack, they had been jumpier and prone to panic attacks at the most inopportune moments. It was better now that they had moved into a new house. They couldn't face the old one and had never been back. They had needed to rely on their friends to move their belongings for them, which rankled because they had never been the helpless person most people assumed they were.

They released a breath when they saw Kean on their doorstep. Taking a few seconds to calm their breathing, they wandered to the door, double-checking the peephole first, then unlocking and opening the door.

"Hey. I wasn't expecting to see you," they said.

The slightly messy hair, which looked like he had been running his fingers through it constantly, the hazel eyes and that crooked nose all merged to make a fine-looking man. One who was the complete opposite of the beast who hurt them. But that night, Kean looked weary.

"Sorry. I didn't mean to show up unannounced," Kean said. "I just drove and ended up here. I wanted to check on you." He shook his head. "I can go. Sorry."

He turned to leave, but Kendal stopped him. "I was just going to sit down and watch a movie. Would you like to join me?"

Kean looked torn, so Kendal opened the door further and tilted their head, waiting for Kean to decide. When he stepped inside, Kendal ignored the butterflies swarming in his stomach. Kean bit his lip, making him look a lot younger than his years and experience. Kendal slid the phone they still held in their hand into their pocket and stopped in front of their visitor. No second guesses plagued them as they reached for Kean, wrapping their arms around him and holding him.

"What's wrong, Kean?" they asked, and Kean seemed to tighten his hold a little more.

"I'm okay."

Kendal pulled back and smiled. "No, you're not. But it's okay. I'm here if you want to talk."

Kean smiled sadly, and Kendal's heart broke for him. Something was bothering him, and it made Kendal physically hurt for him. They grabbed Kean's hand and tugged him to the sofa, pushing him to sit down.

"Do you want a drink?"

Kean shook his head. "I've already had one, so I better not. I won't be able to drive home if I do."

"You can get a taxi," Kendal said, wandering over to their

tiny bar area. They weren't a huge drinker, but now and then, they liked the taste of bourbon before bed.

"Okay, thanks."

Kendal poured bourbon into two glasses and took them both to the sofa. They tucked their legs beneath them as they settled into the cushions and handed the second glass to Kean before pulling their long slimline jumper over their knees.

"What do you fancy?"

An expression Kendal couldn't decipher crossed Kean's face, but then it cleared, and Kean smiled, small though it was. "Anything at all."

"Okay, I think *Pride and Prejudice,* then." They reached for the remote to hide their smirk. When they glanced back, Kean tried to school his expression, but Kendal laughed. "Just kidding. That'll teach you to give a blanket answer."

Kean chuckled, a genuine laugh that had Kendal warming inside. "Duly noted. Are there any recent book adaptations you recommend? I know you like to discuss the differences between the book and the film."

Kendal beamed that Kean had remembered what they'd mentioned randomly during their conversation a few weeks ago. "Well, I still haven't seen *The Time Traveller's Wife,* even though it's been on my list for years. What about that one?"

Nodding, Kean said, "Sounds good. Go for it."

They lined up the film, and while the title sequence ran, Kean said, "I saw Henry and everyone today. They're upbeat, which is good." Kean frowned. "I didn't see Andrew, though. He's been really sad. Understandably. I wish I could do something to help."

Kendal rested a hand on Kean's shoulder. "I'm sure just being there helps."

"Maybe, but it doesn't feel like it does."

"Tell me this, when you stayed with me after the kidnapping," they said, refusing to tiptoe over what happened, "did we talk all the time?" Kean shook his head. "And did just being with someone help?" Kean hesitated, then nodded. "Then I'm sure it's the same for him."

Kendal understood what it meant to lose people. Their family might not be dead, but they might as well have been. When Kendal finally figured out who they were at fourteen years old, they decided to change their image to portray how they felt inside. With all the confidence their parents had built inside them growing up, they didn't care what other people thought. But wearing what their parents deemed "feminine" clothing and shoes and growing their hair had tested their parents' limits. And though Kendal saw it coming, the vehemence their parents portrayed surprised them when they threw them out at sixteen.

Luckily, they had some amazing friends who supported them during the trying time. Kendal had refused to back down and become something they weren't, so they pushed their family to the back of their mind and continued with their life.

It wasn't the same as someone dying, but it was pretty close. And on top of that, Kendal had lost themselves for a while after the attack. They were stronger now, thanks to therapy and their friends, but during that time, it had felt a lot like grief.

"I hope it helps," Kean said.

"I'm sure the king is grateful for your time and support. The loss he's feeling won't ever go away, but it will hurt less as time passes."

"I know," Kean murmured.

Kendal closed their eyes and inwardly cursed themselves.

"Sorry. I know you've been through it as well. You don't need to hear this from me."

"Actually, I think I do. I don't know." Kean shook his head, staring at the TV but seemingly lost in memories. "Losing Simon pained me, definitely. But there's something about the idea of losing the other half of you that seems… more debilitating. It's probably the same, and I know everyone deals with it in different ways. It feels like he's holding everything inside him when he needs to let it out."

"You're right. Everyone is different, but unless he tells you to leave him alone, I'm sure he's fine with you being there."

Kean smiled across at them, and Kendal's heart galloped off early at the races. They shut it down, returning the smile, then paused the film, which had barely started.

"I've decided we need a change of drink. Hot chocolate with the works. My speciality." They grinned and headed for the kitchen, blowing out a breath once they were out of sight. There was something about Kean that sent Kendal's pulse into overdrive, but he could see what Kean was trying to hide. Kean liked Andrew. There would be no place for Kendal in Kean's heart.

Which was probably a good thing because they weren't sure what they could offer someone. After Talon took his anger out on them, Kendal had kept to themselves and was only just going back to the club and other social gatherings. It had to be with people they knew, though. Too many people and too much noise were overwhelming.

Who would want to put up with someone who had to deal with that?

They heated the milk and mixed the hot chocolate powder with it, added squirty cream, marshmallows and grated chocolate to the top, and set them both on a tray with two spoons. They carried them into the living room and, once again, calmed their heart as Kean smiled their way.

"One hot chocolate with the works for Mr Seymour."

Kean huffed a laugh, taking the large, overflowing mug. "Please don't. That reminds me of my dad." He shuddered.

Kendal chuckled. "Sorry. I'll have to settle for calling you sir instead."

They hadn't meant for the words to sound flirty, but the alternative meaning hung in the air. Kendal focused on the mug, tucking their legs beneath them again.

"I love that jumper," Kean said, garnering Kendal's attention.

They glanced down at themselves to the purple, thigh-length jumper, their cheeks heating. "Thanks. It's one of my favourites. I'm always pulling it out of shape, though." They snorted. "Maybe I need to get some looser ones."

Kean shook his head. "No. I think it looks great."

Kendal swallowed and tried to meet his gaze, but they struggled. They didn't take compliments easily. "Thank you," they whispered.

They set the film playing again and settled back against the cushions, cradling their mug and determinedly not looking at Kean. It wasn't easy, especially when they could see him out of the corner of their eye whenever Kean lifted the mug to his lips. It was torturous. And they noticed the moment Kean fell asleep during the last few minutes of the second film.

Kendal glanced across at him, tracing Kean's lips with their gaze, his fuller bottom lip protruding slightly more than his upper. The stubble coating his cheeks and jaw only made him look more refined. Kendal's gaze dragged down Kean's body until they made themselves look away. They waited until the end of the film, then clicked off the TV. Rising, they grabbed the blanket from the back of the sofa and carefully draped it across Kean, hoping to ward off any chill that might occur during the night.

Taking the empty cups to the kitchen and setting them in the dishwasher wasted a few minutes, but they needed to sleep, too. Double-checking the locks on the doors and windows throughout the downstairs, they avoided Kean for as long as possible. Standing over the man like a creeper, Kendal watched him sleep, noticing how young he seemed. It wasn't the first time Kean had fallen asleep on their sofa, but it was getting harder and harder for Kendal to continue thinking of him as a friend.

Kendal shook their head and strode for the stairs, flicking all the lights off but one in the hallway, leaving Kean a muted glow so he wasn't confused about where he was when he woke. Setting the front door alarm with their phone was as easy as pressing a button, and luckily, Kean knew about it, so he wouldn't try leaving without letting Kendal know.

They showered, dried and wrapped their dressing gown around them before settling at their table to go through their skincare routine. Because Kendal wore makeup occasionally, they had to make sure they removed it, and when they'd started getting dry skin, it had turned into a big routine overhaul. They now refused to go to sleep without cleansing and moisturising. It was a good time to give themselves a pep talk, too.

Every morning, they spent the first half an hour doing some mental preparations for the day, then another half an hour of yoga before feeling like they could even face exiting their bedroom. A similar thing happened at night, minus the yoga. They needed to destress before being able to sleep. Kendal climbed into bed and lay on their back, closed their eyes and concentrated on their breathing. The meditation-style relaxation helped, but they often found their mind wandering to other things. Most of the time, it wasn't a problem, but times like that night, where visions of Kean floated in their head, were more difficult than others.

They brushed the thoughts aside, and their mind drifted to the king. Andrew. He'd told Kendal to call him that, but it was difficult to change years of using "Your Majesty" to something so personal.

As they pulled the covers to their shoulders, they tried to ignore the same bubbling, fluttering sensation in their stomach that they had when they saw Kean. They couldn't have feelings for the king as well, even if the man had been so kind and careful with Kendal. However, they could do everything in their power to help Kean get Andrew if it was possible. It was the least they could do after receiving so much love and support from them all.

Kendal checked the cameras and security features on their phone before descending the stairs, needing to make sure the house was secure before leaving their room. It had become easier to work through their feelings and reflexive actions before they caused issues, but they still needed that gentle push that everything was okay. They knew Talon and Harvey couldn't reach them from prison, but it didn't stop the thoughts from encroaching on them now and then.

They could hear Kean in the kitchen and followed the sounds and the scent of toast. "Good morning," they said, heading for the kettle to make their first cup of tea for the day. "Did you sleep okay?"

Kean nodded as they buttered the toast. "I'm sorry I fell

asleep. I meant to leave you in peace after the second movie. Guess I was more tired than I thought."

"It's okay. I don't mind. Besides, you've stayed with me before. It's not like I don't know you." Kendal smiled over their shoulder. "Coffee?"

"Please." Kean placed a plate beside Kendal. "I made this for you when I heard you start moving around."

Kendal's chest warmed at the thought. "Thank you." They took a bite of the toast and hummed. "Just the right amount of butter. I have you trained well." They glanced at Kean, a telltale blush darkening his cheeks, though he was smiling. Kendal finished the drinks and set Kean's beside him.

"It's the least I can do."

"You don't have to do anything. I've told you that before. You're welcome to stay whenever you need to. In fact…" They set their mug down and rummaged through the one drawer in their kitchen that held potentially anything a person could hope to find—all those weird items they found around the house that they couldn't figure out where they belonged got thrown into this drawer along with random tools and stuff. They grabbed a key and put it on the counter next to Kean. "Take this. You already know the security code. If you ever need to come by, whether I'm here or not, please come." They paused. "Just send me a text before you enter so I don't freak out."

Kean shook his head and pushed the key back in Kendal's direction. "I can't take this. You deserve your haven to be your haven. I refuse to ruin that. Thank you for the offer, though."

Kendal pushed it back towards him. "I insist. Everyone should have a haven, and this can be yours, too." They stepped closer to him. "I can share."

Kean's eyes widened, and something akin to heat flared in

those orbs. Kendal wasn't sure what had caused it, but they couldn't look away. They weren't sure how long they stayed locked in his eyes, but eventually, Kean cleared his throat and blinked, breaking the haze that had fallen over Kendal. Kendal turned back to their mug and toast and picked them up, heading for the dining table.

"Thank you," Kean said. "I appreciate it."

"You're welcome."

Kean settled on a chair nearby and sipped his coffee. "Some of us are heading to the club tonight to celebrate Mav's birthday. Would you like to come with us?"

For a second, they were thrown back to the moment they'd met Talon at the club, unsure of his intentions but enjoying the attention, then to the time when he started raining down lashes on them in their old house. They closed their eyes and exhaled before smiling across at Kean.

"That would be nice. I'm getting more comfortable being there now, even though I haven't made it into the club proper yet."

"You don't need to do anything or go anywhere if you don't want to, Kendal. Don't force yourself."

Kendal gave a small smile. "But that's what I need to do, remember? Part of my therapy. Facing old demons and whatever." They huffed a laugh. "It seems to be working, so I can't complain."

Kean nodded slowly. "It does work. Therapy, I mean. I've spoken to Timothy a few times, but having someone outside of them is helping, too."

Kendal leaned forward and rested a hand over Kean's. "And you know I'm here if you need anything at all."

Kean rolled his hand until they were holding hands, and Kendal's heart picked up its rhythm. They tried to ignore the heat transferring from Kean to themselves, but it was such a pleasant feeling to be holding someone's hand. Someone they knew they could trust. Someone they knew wouldn't hurt them.

"Thank you. That means a lot to me."

Kendal didn't want to let go—either the hand holding or Kean's gaze—but they needed to. There was no use hoping for more when they could see Kean wanted Andrew. Slowly, they removed their hand, pretending they were reaching for their breakfast.

"Who's going to the club?" they asked.

"All the Thirsty Thirteen, me, you, and maybe Quinn, though I've not asked yet. The entire inner circle, as I call it." Kean grinned.

Kendal chuckled. "I don't know if I'm glad or saddened that George doesn't need to think up any more names."

Kean threw his head back and laughed, the sound lifting Kendal's spirits as it always did. "I know what you mean."

4

ANDREW

Andrew dropped his head into his hands, his elbows resting on his desk. He exhaled, trying to remove all the tension and anger he held inside him. It wasn't easy. Even after the events of the past two years or more, he couldn't believe his own family would do this to him—to them. Trying to kill them off, one by one, to gain access to the supposed power the crown would give them. The grass was definitely not greener, as Kean had told him.

The king smiled and leaned back, the thought of Kean doing what his meditation attempts hadn't been able to. He closed his eyes and thought back to how much comfort Kean had given him on the anniversary. Just by being there, Andrew had calmed and felt a little less grief-stricken. And that was something he knew Louisa would've been happy about, even if it hurt Andrew's heart a little.

A knock sounded. "Come in!" he called.

Randall entered and bowed his head. "Good morning, Your Majesty. I have your calendar updates for today if you're ready for them."

Andrew waved him to a seat. "Of course."

Randall was the extra limb Andrew needed to ensure he didn't miss things and kept on top of everything he needed to. The man was exceptional at his job, though he refused to drop the title whenever he spoke to or about Andrew. If Randall ever left his service, Andrew didn't think he'd find anyone as competent.

While Randall ran down Andrew's appointments and phone calls, Andrew found himself drifting back to Kean and everything he'd done to help them. It had come at a price Andrew had never expected Kean to pay. The young man had been kidnapped along with Damon when Charles, Andrew's nephew, had taken it upon himself to remove them from the equation because they were getting too close to finding out what Charlotte's plans were. In the end, they'd rescued both Damon and Kean, and Charles and Elizabeth, Andrew's niece, had been arrested and sent to prison without the chance of bail until the Commissioner had investigated. Elizabeth hadn't survived the experience because an inmate had stabbed her not long after her incarceration. Andrew had been heartbroken despite everything she had done or been privy to. No matter what anyone else thought, he loved his family, even if their choices weren't the best thought out.

"Your Majesty?"

Randall's voice brought him back. "I'm sorry, Randall." He rubbed a hand over his mouth.

"It's fine. Are you okay?"

Andrew sighed. "I've just been trying to make sense of all the information we have. What are they going to do next because every piece of the puzzle we had pointed towards the anniversary being the last event? But I don't believe it's over, even if they are being extremely quiet now."

"Would you like me to call Prince Christian or Prince Frederick? I know they don't have any official events today."

Andrew contemplated the question, then decided he might as well see if they could figure it out, even though they'd tried many times over the passing weeks. "Yes, please."

Randall stood. "I'll rearrange your morning appointments. Let me know if you need me to do the same for this afternoon."

"I will. Thanks, Randall."

"You're welcome, Your Majesty."

Randall disappeared, and Andrew once again felt bad for making more work for his personal assistant. It was Randall's job, but it didn't stop Andrew from not wanting to overtax him.

Half an hour later, Freddie, Christian and Damon arrived, and after their greetings, Freddie got right to the point. "What did you want to talk about?"

Andrew settled on the uncomfortable sofa. "To be honest, I don't know. I want to go through everything we know and see if we're missing anything. I know we've done it a thousand times already, but something's niggling at me."

Christian scooted forward in his seat and opened the folder he'd brought with him. "We can go through it a thousand times more if it'll help." He dragged a wad of paper onto the small coffee table between them.

"Thanks for not thinking I'm crazy."

"He wasn't saying that, Father," Freddie said with a grin.

Andrew chuckled. He was so glad Louisa had made him see what he'd been turning into when Douglas had found Mav because, otherwise, he didn't think he'd have the same relationship with his children and extended family as he had now.

"So, we have three companies that have been proven to be funnelling money into Charlotte's plans, which we're in the process of shutting down. Kletti Pazo has been closed down completely. The company can no longer do business with anyone, and we have access to their accounts, so we can see who they worked with."

"I'm currently auditing those businesses to see if they knew what was happening or if they were oblivious," Damon added. "So far, it looks like most of them didn't."

"I've not had any luck in finding more information about Ernest yet," Andrew said.

Freddie shook his head. "I don't understand what Ernest would get from being a part of this. With Charlotte, he would become Prince Consort, but siding with John? I don't get it."

"Me either," Andrew said. "There has to be another connection we're missing."

"Neil has been working with Gia and Daniel, but they're coming up blank on everything they've tried so far," Christian said. "The properties that Damon had been refused access to when he'd been visiting are still impenetrable by us. I'm wondering if it's a ruse to get you to go to them." Christian stared at Andrew. "Which obviously you won't be."

Andrew's mouth lifted at the corners at the thinly veiled threat from his adopted son. The man had been through too much, but Andrew had decided he was now his son instead of belonging to John. Andrew's brother didn't deserve someone so kind and caring.

"So I've been told," Andrew retorted.

"What about the club?" Freddie asked Andrew.

Andrew crossed his legs, linking his fingers together in his lap. "The club has...issues. We have cameras in certain places, and I have the go-ahead to have someone review them for any security breaches, but some of the board members are stonewalling us."

"Are they in on it?" Damon asked.

Andrew shrugged. "They could be. I wanted to ask who you think would be the best person or people to review the videos. We have to be careful, naturally."

They were quiet for a moment until Freddie said, "I think Kieren would be ideal, and maybe Patrick could help. He might know the people that were flagged up."

"I'd prefer it if they were people who didn't know who was who. It would be easier to have them look at it through a veil of separation." Andrew didn't want anyone to be dissuaded because of who they saw.

"I agree," Christian said. "What about Kean?"

Andrew raised his eyebrows, about to deny his involvement, when he realised he was a good choice. "He might know some of them, but he hasn't spent as much time at the club as others have. Good idea."

"Maybe we can add a bodyguard into the mix. What about one of the newer ones?" Christian said. "They will have been researched deeply when they first came on board, but they won't have been here long enough to get too comfortable with others."

"Agreed," Andrew said. "Christian, can you arrange it with Brett? I'll speak with Kean about it."

Andrew caught Freddie's and Damon's shared smirk, but he ignored it. Freddie had voiced his opinion of him and Kean being together, but it wasn't going to happen. Andrew enjoyed Kean's company—more than he probably should—but he couldn't let him shoulder the burdens of the crown.

"We'll see how they go with the videos, then add more people to it if it needs to go faster," Andrew said.

"Sounds like a plan," Freddie said. "We're going to the club tonight unless you need us for anything?"

Andrew shook his head and waved his hand before standing. "Go. Have fun."

"You should come." Andrew glanced at Freddie, eyebrows raised. "Kean and Kendal are going to be there."

"I'm too old to be going there now, Freddie." Andrew turned his back, but a knot of churning mess began in his stomach at Kendal being exposed to the club, even two years after what had happened to them.

"You're not too old," Christian said.

Andrew chuckled. "I notice you said *too* old. Does that mean you think I'm old?" he teased.

Christian laughed and gathered his paperwork. "On that note…" He stood and hugged Andrew. "You're not old. You need company. See to it," he whispered in Andrew's ear.

Andrew squeezed him closer for a long second and let go. He didn't answer him, but the knowledge in Christian's eyes was plain to see. The man knew he wouldn't do anything about it.

"Have a good day and evening, boys."

Andrew waved them off. As he settled behind his desk again, he couldn't help but focus on that niggle of something he couldn't catch hold of, but it was being overshadowed by the concern for Kendal. He picked up the phone.

"Hello?"

"Kendal, it's Andrew. How are you?"

"Oh! Your Majesty…um, Andrew. Hello."

Andrew smiled at the fumbled words, Kendal finding it troublesome, even with permission, to call Andrew by his given name. It was cute.

"How are you, Kendal?" he asked.

Kendal cleared their throat. "I'm good, thank you. How are you—?"

He heard the bitten-off words as if they'd been spoken but held in his laughter. "Not too bad, thank you for asking. I hear you're going to the club tonight."

"Yes, sir. Um, Andrew. Kean told me everyone was going and invited me. It's nice to see everyone."

"It is. How are you managing being there, might I ask?" He didn't want to step over any boundaries Kendal set.

Kendal was quiet for a moment, then said, "It's difficult in the beginning, but then I focus on my friends, and it's a little easier."

"I'm glad." Even though he had been the one to call them, Andrew wasn't sure what else to talk about, but he didn't want to end the call.

"Do you have a busy day today?" Kendal asked.

"Truthfully, every day is busy, but yes, I do have a few phone calls and one meeting, though if I could, I'd wipe my day clean." He chuckled.

Soft laughter sounded. "And what would you do with a free day?"

That stumped him. "Um, I don't know, to be honest."

"What do you do for fun?"

"I read."

"Me, too. What do you read?" Andrew's cheeks heated, not sure if he wanted to admit what he read. His pause must've told Kendal he didn't want to say because they chuckled in his ear. "That good, huh? Let's see... shifters? No. Hmm." Andrew held his breath, not sure if he wanted Kendal to guess or not. "Romance?" Andrew closed his eyes, trying to keep his breathing steady so he didn't give anything away. "Yes, romance, I think. Is that right?"

Andrew let out a breath. "Yes, okay. I read romance. It's

Louisa's fault for getting me into it. And then she gave me..." He stopped, his throat drying up.

"Did she give you some gay romance, Your Majesty?" Kendal's voice had lowered, and Andrew felt it deep inside him, but he refused to admit where.

"Yes," he murmured.

"And what did you think, Andrew? Did you enjoy them?"

"I did. More than I imagined I would."

"I'm glad. Reading should offer joy and solace in a turbulent world. It's why I read as much as I do. To escape reality."

Andrew's heart broke. "I hate that you need to do that."

"I don't. I like living in a fictional world for hours on end. Think of all the different places I can go without having to move from my sofa."

Andrew chuckled, despite the emotional heaviness of the situation. "Plenty of worlds around for you to visit."

"Exactly."

Andrew leaned back in his chair, closing his eyes and enjoying the moment. "I don't read as much as I wish I could."

"You have to make time," Kendal said. "It's an excellent tool for relaxation. I'm sure you're stressed enough."

Andrew swallowed past the lump in his throat, not denying it. He changed the subject. "How are you getting to the club tonight?"

"Kean is swinging by to pick Quinn and me up. I told him we could drive, but he wouldn't have it."

"That's good. I wouldn't want you to have to be there alone."

Kendal chuckled. "I am a grown person, you know."

Andrew winced. "Sorry. I didn't mean for that to come out as it did. I know you are more than capable of taking care of yourself. I just like you having company."

"I knew what you meant. I'm teasing. I'm glad to have someone with me. In fact, I prefer it. I doubt I could go somewhere that busy without having a partner in crime."

"In crime? Oh my, Kendal, what *are* you planning?"

Kendal laughed again, and Andrew smiled at the sound. "I plead innocence."

"Innocent until proven guilty. Is that what you're saying?"

"Of course." There was a noise on the other end of the phone, and Kendal said, "I'm sorry, Your...Andrew. I have to go. Work calls."

"I'm sorry for keeping you talking. I'll speak to you soon, okay?"

"You don't need to be sorry. I've enjoyed talking with you. Maybe...we can discuss gay romance the next time we talk."

Andrew huffed a laugh. "I'm sure that will be embarrassing as hell, but sure. Take care, Kendal."

"You, too, Andrew."

Andrew ended the call and sighed. His stomach fluttered, and his heart pounded. He kept his eyes closed and tried to calm himself. He knew exactly what he was feeling, but he couldn't act on anything. What would the country think if he took not one but two people as his partners? It was enough of a problem that he'd admitted he was bisexual. If he showed up with anyone who wasn't female on his arm, the media would destroy them, and he couldn't let anyone go through that.

Kean and Kendal were better off without him. But maybe he could see them getting together.

He sat up straighter. That would work. They were perfect for each other. Kean had the dominant streak, though he didn't let it out often, and Kendal was submissive. But more than that, they had both been through something traumatic and were working through it to find themselves at the other end. They could help each other.

And Andrew could help them get there.

He lifted his phone and sent a message to Freddie, letting him know he would make an appearance at the club that night. It wouldn't be for the reason Freddie thought it was, but it wouldn't matter. He'd clue his sons in on his idea at the right time. Whatever they thought in the meantime could wait.

His desk phone rang, and he answered. "The Foreign Secretary is on the phone, Your Majesty."

"Thank you, Randall. Please put them through."

The rest of the afternoon was spent putting out fires, working through legislation, giving opinions he knew would be ignored and signing paperwork. And everyone thought being a royal was glamorous.

For once, he left his office at six o'clock and had an earlier dinner than usual in his suite. It was quiet, but he didn't mind because he worked through his plan. When a thought occurred to him, he paused in chewing. What if his being there would stop them from being together? Would they feel more comfortable without him there? He brushed the thought aside. If he saw anything that made him think that, he could leave, citing tiredness. No one would doubt him because he *was* tired. He'd been tired for years.

After showering and changing into fresh trousers and a black shirt, he advised Simon he was ready to leave. Four guards joined him as he climbed into the car; two guards in the front seat and two in a car behind them.

It had been far too long since he'd visited the club. It would be nice to see the place again, even if he never intended to use all the facilities. He was too old to join in any of the scenes, and besides, most members would feel uncomfortable having him around while they played. He intended to stay for a short conversation, then head home again.

Simon climbed out with him once they arrived, and they both headed up in the lift. When he stepped into the foyer, Clarice stood and curtsied.

"It's lovely to see you, Your Majesty," she said,

"Thank you, Clarice. How are things here?" He pressed his thumb to the sensor, confirming his attendance, and Simon did the same.

"No problems to report so far tonight. I'm hoping it stays that way."

Andrew smiled. "Me, too. Are my children here yet?"

"Yes, Your Majesty. Princes Frederick, Douglas, George, Patrick, Henry and Christian are all here with their partners, though Prince Patrick will be working."

"Thank you, Clarice. Have a good evening. I promise not to cause any problems." He chuckled.

"That would be appreciated, Your Majesty."

They headed for the main doors, not bothering to put anything in the lockers because they didn't have anything with them to lock away. The bar area was half full, mainly with his family, and he smiled when laughter rang through the air. It was louder than the subtle music they piped into the room.

"Good evening, everyone. Happy birthday, Mav. Are you all having a good time?" he said as he reached the group.

Freddie stood and embraced him. "I'm glad to see you."

Andrew smiled and glanced around the group, seeing some stunned expressions, including those on Kean's and Kendal's faces. Hopefully, it was a pleasant surprise.

5

KEAN

ean's jaw dropped when Andrew appeared at the club. From what he knew, Andrew had not visited for months. Years, even. The shock would wear off, but Kean could admit he was glad to see him. A smile crept across his face when Andrew glanced at him, and Kean took a side look at Kendal to see the same surprise on their face.

"I don't need to introduce Simon, do I?" Andrew joked and settled into the seat beside Kean. Simon, however, nodded and moved away from them to the wall.

Kean's smile dimmed a little, not because he didn't like Simon, but because he had the same name as Kean's brother, and it was difficult not to react when someone said the name. Instead, he focused on the conversation.

"Hello, Xan. How are Oliver and Griffin treating you?"

Kendal's friend, Xan, had recently begun a relationship with Club Royal's bartender, Oliver, and Oliver's husband, Griffin. The triad's relationship was something Kean secretly wanted for himself. Everything would fit together beautifully —if only they felt the same way he did.

Xan flushed. "They're treating me very well, Your Majesty."

"And I expect you to tell someone if it was any other way," a voice said. Kean glanced over Andrew's shoulder to see Oliver handing Andrew a drink.

"I would," Xan stared at Oliver, his bottom lip caught between his teeth.

Kean's heart thumped at the pure love he could see and feel in the exchange. That was what he wanted. He took a sip of his drink, lowering his gaze to his lap and trying to push down his feelings.

"And Quinn, how are you?" Andrew asked.

"Very good, Your Majesty. Master is in the club teaching at the moment," Quinn replied. He had always been more at ease in the presence of royalty than others were. "I thought I would spend some time with my friends."

"Sounds wonderful. Kendal," Andrew said. "How are you faring?"

Kean heard Kendal's shaky breath, but they answered sure and steady. "Well, Your—Andrew. Thank you. It's getting easier."

"I'm glad. You know we're all here to help you. You just need to ask," Andrew said.

Kendal nodded. "I appreciate it..." They rubbed one hand over the knuckles of the other, which was holding their drink. "Actually..." They glanced around the circle of friends, making Kean do the same. Most people weren't looking at them. "I do have something to ask you and Kean." Kendal glanced at Quinn, who nodded and squeezed their forearm.

What was going on?

"Whatever you need, Kendal. You know that," Andrew said.

Kendal rolled their lips inwards, staring at the drink in their hands. "I...would very much like...to get closer to who I was...before. The club was a large part of my life, and I want it back." They glanced up at Kean. "I need someone I can trust to help me, and I wondered if you would."

Kean's mouth gaped. "Me?" He glanced at Andrew. "But wouldn't someone else be better at it?"

He ignored the way his brain kicked his ass for trying to stop what Kean so desperately wanted. It needed to be what was best for Kendal, not what Kean desired.

"I think he's a worthy choice," Andrew said, resting his hand on Kean's shoulder.

Kean's heart skipped at Andrew's compliment. "I—"

"I trust you, Kean. That's what I need." Kendal paused. "But...I also need someone else who can be there, just in case." They glanced at Andrew.

Andrew leaned forward, scooting to the edge of his seat and putting his drink down. "I meant what I said, Kendal. Whatever you need. But I need you to be clear so we all know what's what."

Kendal licked their lips and glanced at Quinn again, who nodded. They must've discussed this with their friends first. Understandably.

"I would like Kean to flog me, but I need you to be there in case something happens." Kendal flicked their gaze to Kean. "I trust you, Kean. I truly do, but where I am at the moment, I can't trust that I trust correctly. Does that make sense?"

Kean held out his hand, palm upwards, and waited until Kendal rested their hand in his. He squeezed gently. "It makes complete sense, Kendal. I understand where you're coming from. Are you sure I'm the right choice? There are better people than me."

"There's nothing wrong with you, Kean," Andrew said.

"I need someone I trust, and I trust you. I can't imagine anyone else helping me," Kendal said.

Kean exhaled, locking gazes with Kendal. "Then, if you are truly certain, I would be honoured." And extremely aroused. He locked that thought behind the cage he would ensure all his feelings stayed in during the event. "Whenever you're ready."

Kendal swallowed. "Tonight?"

"Are you sure you don't want to think about this some more first?" Andrew asked.

Kendal shook their head. "I think this might be as courageous as I will ever be. My only concern is what people will say when the three of us go into a room."

Andrew smiled and stood. "I'll sort that. Don't worry. I'll be back." He stepped towards Simon, and they both disappeared back into the foyer.

Kean realised he still held Kendal's hand, and he rubbed his thumb over their knuckles, meeting their gaze. "You're so bloody brave," he murmured.

Kendal's cheeks flushed, and their bright green eyes filled a little. The first time it happened, Kean had apologised because he thought he'd upset them, but Kendal had quickly explained that their eyes watered when they were embarrassed, something they wished wouldn't happen.

He couldn't believe Kendal had been strong enough to ask for what they wanted. Kean wished he could be that strong, but there was no way he had the courage to ask Kendal and Andrew for what *he* wanted. It would be too easy to lose what he already had with them, so that would have to be enough for him.

The sound from the main area of the club rose as the door opened, and Patrick stepped through. He wandered over to them, leaning down to kiss Kieren and whisper something in his ear before heading over to Kean and Kendal.

Patrick crouched between them, lowering his voice. "You can make your way to the teaching room whenever you're ready. Are you okay going through the main club, or would you prefer not to?" he asked Kendal.

Kendal inhaled, tightening their hold on Kean's hand. "I think I can manage the club."

Kean leaned forward. "Don't force yourself. Only if you can."

"It's the first step in the right direction, right?" Kendal straightened their back. "I'll be fine. I'll have Kean with me."

Pleasure swept through Kean at the sheer trust Kendal placed in him. "I won't let anything happen."

"Kieren and I will escort you to the door. No one will touch you, Kendal. I promise," Patrick said.

"Thank you."

"Take your time," Patrick said. "Let me know when you're ready."

He rose and stepped back to where Kieren stood, waiting for him. They wrapped their arms around each other, smiling.

"They're an amazing match," Kendal said, breaking Kean's attention.

"They are. They all are," Kean said, glancing around the group.

Kendal blew out a breath. "Are you ready?"

Kean squeezed their hand. "I should be asking you that."

They shared a laugh, and Kendal murmured something to Quinn before standing. Kean followed suit and rearranged their hands, linking their fingers as they wandered towards Patrick and Kieren. Kendal didn't complain about the handholding, so Kean didn't mention anything either. He'd let go if Kendal wanted him to, but until they asked…

"Ready?" Patrick asked. Kendal nodded. "I'll go first, and Kieren will be behind. If at any point it's too much, reach a hand back for Kieren, and we'll get you out of there."

Kendal nodded again. Kean tightened his hold for a second, and then Patrick opened the door to the club, the noise rising once more. It wasn't loud enough to miss the hitch of Kendal's breath, and Kean hoped they would be okay. The sounds of skin slapping, moans and groans grew louder as they weaved through the club members. Kendal kept their head down, and Kean followed Patrick, leading Kendal along the way. Kendal's free hand crept to Kean's biceps, tucking themselves into his side, and they rested their head against his shoulder.

Once again, Kean wanted to have five minutes alone with Talon. That asshole had hurt Kendal, and they were suffering for far longer than Talon had been. Despite the man—and Kean used that word in its loosest possible meaning—being in prison, he deserved so much more shit for what he did.

They stepped through an arch and headed right, doubling back on themselves until they reached a teaching room. It wasn't the only one in the building, but it had a lot more space than other rooms. Patrick glanced behind them, then knocked, and the door opened a second later, revealing Andrew's bodyguard. Simon opened the door further when he saw who it was, and Patrick ushered Kean and Kendal through.

"Radio us when you're ready," Patrick said.

"We'll take them out the other way, so don't worry about it," Simon said.

"Okay. Tell Clarice to let me know when the room is free."

Simon nodded and closed the door, leaving the four of them in the room together. Kean frowned.

"How did you get in here?"

Andrew chuckled. "Secret entrance." He winked.

"Seriously?" Kean shook his head. "Why am I surprised?" he asked Kendal.

"You s-shouldn't be." Kendal's voice wobbled a little, but they stayed strong.

"I'll be right outside the door, Your Majesty," Simon said.

"Thank you, Simon."

Kean's eye twitched, but he shoved it aside. Simon left, closing the door behind him, and Andrew locked the door and faced them.

"Right, Kendal. Are you sure about this?"

"Yes."

Kean was glad to hear no hesitation in their voice, even though their hand was shaking in his.

"Okay, then." Andrew stepped in front of Kendal, lifting their chin to look into their eyes. "I'm going to sit over here, out of the way. If you need anything at all, tell me." Kendal nodded. "What's your safe word?"

"Hairspray." Kendal's cheeks darkened, and they sniffed.

Andrew smiled and wiped at their eyes. "Perfect. Thank you." He leaned down, and for a second, Kean thought he would kiss Kendal, as did Kendal if the widening of their eyes was any indication. But Andrew only whispered in their ear. "Enjoy yourselves." It was loud enough for Kean to hear as well, and Andrew met his gaze with a smile, reaching to Kean's nape. "You're going to be fine."

Kean swallowed hard and nodded. He was out of his depth. Not because of the flogging—that he'd done before—

but with having such a role in helping Kendal get through their first scene since what happened with that asshole. Kean was glad Andrew was there, not only because he got to share this with the two people he loved but because if Kean made an error in judgement, Andrew would be there to stop him from hurting Kendal.

Andrew moved to the corner of the room, where a chair rested, and settled in, reaching for something from the shelf. A book. Kendal snorted beside him, making him jump.

"Are you going to read while we get into it, Your Majesty?" Kendal asked, a smirk on their face.

"Yes," Andrew said, winking. "I'm only here as backup. You don't need to worry about me."

Kean chuckled, glad for the lightening of the atmosphere. He stepped in front of Kendal, squeezing the hand he still held. "Are you ready?" He wasn't sure *he* was.

"Yes, sir."

Warmth gathered in Kean's stomach, but he ignored the arousal those words sparked. "Is there anything I should know before we do this?"

Kendal exhaled shakily. "I have scars," they whispered.

Kean brushed his knuckles against Kendal's cheek. "They show how strong you are. And anyway, so do I." He waited to see if Kendal would say anything else, but they stared at Kean, need darkening their usually bright green eyes to an emerald colour. "Undress for me, then lean over the bed. I won't be restraining you for this."

"Yes, sir."

Kendal stepped back, the cool air replacing the heat from their body against Kean's. Kean couldn't watch them undress because it would make him far too aroused, and this wasn't about him. Moving to the cupboard that held the equipment, he stared at the floggers, trying to decide which would be the best one to use. The rabbit flogger was softer and caused less pain, but it was more for sensation play than impact. The deer leather was a slightly higher pain level, but not too harsh. He grabbed that one, hoping he'd chosen correctly.

Turning around, he swallowed his moan when he saw a naked Kendal leaning over the end of the bed. He inhaled, then exhaled and moved closer. "Is the deer leather okay to use, Kendal?"

"Yes, sir."

Kean sucked in a breath and reached a shaky hand forward to rub against Kendal's back. Kendal startled, but Kean ran his hand over their back, ignoring the silvery lines crossing the skin and getting closer and closer to his ass cheeks. "I'm going to warm your skin first."

When he received no denial, Kean rubbed his palms over Kendal's ass, squeezing gently to begin the warming process. Kendal had not been flogged or spanked at all since the incident, so Kean was going to go easy on them. He gave a sharp smack to the fleshy part of Kendal's ass on both sides, eliciting a hitch of breath from Kendal. It sent a shiver of need through Kean, but he pushed it down yet again. This wasn't about him. He was glad he'd kept his jeans on when he'd arrived, so they held down his erection more than the trousers he sometimes wore.

He spanked them again, then rubbed over the skin, soothing it. He lifted the flogger, clenching it in his hand. The strips of leather caressed Kendal as Kean ran it over their skin, getting them used to the sensation. Across their back, over the ass, down their thighs and in reverse, over and over, until Kendal's breathing increased further.

"I'm going to start slowly, Kendal. Stop me if you need to."

"Yes, sir."

Kean flicked the strips against Kendal's skin, not enough to cause any type of pain but to allow Kendal to get used to it. Certain areas of the body were off limits when it came to impact play, and Kean knew them all, so he wasn't worried he would inadvertently hurt Kendal in that way, but he didn't want to cause emotional or mental pain either.

Pushing aside his worries, he continued, flicking slightly harder each time and soothing the skin in between. He paused after the third strike, checking in with Kendal.

"I'm good, sir. Green. It's… I'm good."

Kendal's breathing was faster than normal, but they didn't seem in distress, and from the glimpse Kean caught of their cock, they were enjoying it. At least, he hoped they were.

"Okay. Do you want a little more?"

"Yes, please, sir."

Kean swallowed and exhaled slowly, bringing the flogger down onto Kendal's skin harder than before. Kendal bucked forward, then moved back again.

"Sorry, sir."

"You have nothing to be sorry for. Move if you need to."

Kendal's hands gripped the covers of the bed, and they braced their legs. "I'm good, sir."

Kean let the flogger fly again, and Kendal only moved a little that time. Dragging the flogger along Kendal's skin again gave them both the chance to calm down. Scenes like this were sometimes for getting off and reaching orgasm and sometimes for just the pain itself. This, however, was neither. Although if Kean could make Kendal come, he'd be happy about it, but he didn't think Kendal was in the right frame of mind to orgasm.

The flogger flicked through the air, smacking against Kendal's skin, and Kean rubbed at the area.

"Colour?"

"Green, sir." Kendal's voice was softer than it had been, so Kean crouched to look at their face. Tears overflowed, and Kendal's cheeks were flushed, their lips bitten until they were ruby red.

"I need you to be honest with me, Kendal. I won't go any further if I believe you're not being truthful."

Kendal glanced at him, and Kean stared into their eyes. "I'm good. I promise. This is helping, but..." Kendal licked their lips.

"But what, Kendal?" Kean's voice shook. Had he hurt them?

"I need more, but I don't..." Kendal shook their head.

Kean waited, but Kendal didn't continue. "What more do you need?" He was lost. He wasn't giving Kendal what they needed, and it crushed him.

"Andrew."

Kean frowned, and then he swallowed. Kendal wanted Andrew. Was that what this was all about? An excuse to get Andrew here? Kean slapped himself mentally. Of course, it wasn't an excuse. Kendal truly needed help to get through their ordeal. But maybe they felt more for the king than they realised. Kean could see it now if he was honest with himself. They were so easygoing with each other, laughing, joking, talking. It was easy for them.

Kean stood as Andrew came over, obviously having heard Kendal's words. If he could help them get together, then he would. It was the least he could do after everything they had done for him, and he didn't know more deserving people for love than those two.

6

KENDAL

endal couldn't express what they needed without sounding stupid. Instead, they caused Kean pain by asking for Andrew. Not what they intended at all. Kendal wanted Andrew in on the scene because they wanted him and Kean to get together, but now the time was here, they couldn't figure out how to do it without seeming strange. They saw the hurt in Kean's eyes when they asked for Andrew, but they couldn't explain why. What excuse could they come up with?

"I want to go over the edge, but I'm scared," they said when Andrew settled onto the bed beside Kendal's clenched hand. It wasn't a lie. It scared them to orgasm at something that had once caused them irreparable damage. Well, it used to be irreparable. Now, they were thinking these two men might just be able to help them.

No, they couldn't think like that. This was for Kean and Andrew, not Kendal.

Andrew rested his hand over Kendal's. "If that's what you want, we can help."

Kendal exhaled. "I used to be able to achieve orgasm through flogging. I want that back." They choked back their tears, their face in full-on embarrassment mode.

"Okay. Anything we need to know about how you got there before?" Andrew asked.

Kendal shook their head. "No."

"Do you need any other stimulation?"

"No."

"Okay." Andrew squeezed their hand. "Kean, keep going."

Kendal couldn't see Kean without glancing over their shoulder, but they met the man's gaze so he could see the truth in Kendal's eyes. Kean nodded, and Kendal faced forward again. Andrew still had hold of their hand, and Kendal didn't make a move to shake it off. If this was all they could have, so be it.

Kean warned him before he started, and Kendal's mouth gaped as the sting of the flogger warmed their skin. Their eyelids fluttered closed as the arousal bloomed in their body. Pleasure flowed through him with each strike.

"Please…," they said, stretching for the finish.

The flogger faltered. "It's too much, Kendal. You'll be in too much pain after," Kean said.

"Please!" Kendal wasn't going to be able to come like they used to. They firmed their mouth and unclenched their hand to stand upright, but Andrew's hand tightened on theirs. Kendal remembered then this wasn't supposed to just be about them.

"Let us help you," Andrew said. He lifted Kendal's chin, brushing his thumb over their face. "Trust us."

"I do!" they cried, feeling like they were losing something.

"Kean, put the flogger down. Stand behind Kendal. He's going to press against you so you feel the burn of the strikes, but he won't penetrate you, okay?" Kendal wished he would at that moment, but they nodded. "Kean." Andrew's gaze went behind Kendal, and he nodded. "Trust me," he said to Kean.

Kendal moaned at the feel of Kean's jeans against his sore ass as Kean shifted his hips back and forth.

"Now, reach around and stroke him," Andrew said.

Kendal felt the hesitation in the stilling of Kean's hips, but after a few seconds, his warm hand closed around Kendal's cock.

"Ah!"

Kendal hadn't come from anyone's ministrations but their own for years, and it was almost too much, over too quickly.

"That's it, Kendal. Come for us, sweetheart. Let's get you over this first hurdle."

Kendal closed their eyes and held onto their orgasm for several minutes, but when they lifted their gaze to Andrew's, their body tightened. Andrew's expression was anything but platonic. Was that for them? Or was it for Kean? Or both? Or maybe it was because he was telling Kean what to do—Andrew was a dominant, after all. There were too many plausible reasons for it for Kendal to know for certain, but the expression, along with Kean's presence, sent them over the edge. Kendal let their eyes close as the pleasure swamped them.

"Fuck," they heard Kean murmur through the roar of their climax.

Kendal's arms gave way, and they would've fallen face-first into the bed if Andrew hadn't kept hold of them.

"Easy there. We're going to make you comfortable."

Andrew's voice drifted into Kendal's ear, and they felt arms wrapping around them before they were picked up carefully. They scented Kean and snuggled closer. Kean settled them on the bed and tried to pull away, but Kendal didn't want him to go and gripped his shirt.

"Stay with them, Kean. I'll get the lotion," Andrew said from far away.

Kendal drifted, the endorphins from their climax lingering in their body and making their brain feel like it was floating. Kean raked his fingers through Kendal's hair, and Kendal hummed as their body relaxed even more. Kean reclined, taking Kendal with him until their cheek was on Kean's chest.

"Kendal?" Andrew said.

"Hmm?"

"I'm going to put lotion on your skin, okay?"

"Uh-huh." They couldn't make their voice work properly, but they knew it was important; otherwise, they would hurt more later. They gasped when the cool cream touched their skin, but more about the feel of Andrew's fingers on them. Their skin burned as the healing lotion soaked in.

"Drink this," Kean said, and Kendal opened their mouth but not their eyes. Kean chuckled, and a straw touched Kendal's lips.

They drank their fill of the sweet drink and pushed the straw out with their tongue when they were done. They let themselves float away with the sensations of Andrew's fingers on their ass and Kean's body against theirs. The bed bounced slightly, however long later, and Kendal prised their eyes open.

"There they are," Kean said, smiling down at them, his fingers still stroking Kendal's hair. "How are you feeling?"

"Wonderful." Kendal smiled sleepily and snuggled closer, resting their hand on Kean's chest. "Can you get Andrew here, please? I want to thank you both."

Kean covered Kendal's hand with his own, pressed his

lips against the top of Kendal's head and said, "Andrew, Kendal would like you to come closer."

They heard soft footsteps, and then the bed depressed behind them. "I'm here, little one. What do you need?"

"Will you lie down with us?" Kendal tried to keep their breath even, making it seem like it was their endorphins talking.

There was a brief hesitation where nothing was said and no one moved, then Kendal jostled a little as Andrew settled behind them. Doing more than they'd expected, Andrew reached over them and rested his hand over the top of both of theirs, his upper body resting against Kendal's back and pressing Kean's arm tighter against Kendal. They were in heaven, but they needed to remember their manners.

"I cannot express how grateful I am to you both. I know you did more than you intended to, but it's helped. So much." Kendal swallowed, trying to keep the emotion from their voice. "Would you...?" They couldn't ask again. It wasn't fair—on any of them.

"We would love to help you again. Whenever you need it," Andrew said.

Kendal opened their eyes and peered over their shoulder, Andrew's face closer than they'd expected. Understanding the consequences, they closed the gap and pressed their lips to Andrew's mouth. They didn't push for more, but they held it longer than a "thank you" kiss, then pulled away slightly. Andrew stared at them, eyebrows raised. Kendal kissed him again, putting everything on the line, then pulled back again. Andrew's face held the same expression. Kean moved, but Kendal snapped their gaze around, moving their hand from the bottom of the hand pile to the top, gripping both Kean's and Andrew's hands.

"No," Kendal said. When neither made a move to leave,

Kendal let go and reached up for Kean's nape, tugging him closer. They had no idea where their confidence had come from, and it could all blow up in their face, but they needed to do this. They refused to let this go on without letting Kean and Andrew know exactly what Kendal thought of them.

Kendal pressed their lips to Kean's mouth, the same way they had done for Andrew. Insistent but brief. When they pulled away, Kean's eyes were wide.

"Kendal?" Kean whispered.

Kendal swallowed hard, gathering their courage. "I'm going to possibly regret this when it blows up in my face, but I want you both. I believe you have feelings for Andrew, Kean, and I think you, Andrew, might have feelings for Kean. I don't know if either of you feel anything for me—"

Kendal stopped talking when Kean fused their mouths. He didn't dip inside like Kendal wanted him to, but he didn't move away quickly, either. When Kean lifted his head, his mouth curved. "I feel a lot for you, Kendal." He glanced over Kendal's shoulder, biting his lip. "And you, Andrew. God knows I've tried not to because I don't want to make a mess of things for you, but I can't help it."

Kendal watched Andrew. He had a good poker face, but Kendal had experience with him and could see some things that got past. He was scared. Andrew cupped Kean's jaw, brushing his thumb across the skin, and Kendal could almost feel a similar sensation on their own body.

"I care deeply about you both," he said, meeting Kendal's gaze. "More than I should. But I can't bring you into this further. You've both been hurt enough because of this fight, and I refuse to be the cause of more."

Kendal's heart broke, but they'd expected it. Andrew had the weight of the country on his shoulders. He wouldn't be selfish. It wasn't in him to be.

"We can help," Kean said, covering Andrew's hand against his cheek.

Andrew sighed. "You can, yes. But from a distance. If anyone found out about us, they would crucify you in the media. It would place you in the crosshairs within seconds. Especially because of our age difference and being the three of us. I can't do that. I can't risk losing someone else."

Kendal reached back and stroked Andrew's scratchy beard. "No one can guarantee if they'll be around for the next ten minutes, let alone the next few years. I want to spend time with you and Kean, learning everything I can."

Andrew shook his head. "It's too risky."

"Shouldn't that be our choice?" Kean said.

Andrew closed his eyes and dropped his head, dislodging Kendal's hand. They were all touching each other, and Kendal didn't want to move anytime soon, but they were running out of time. Could they entice Andrew to give them both a taste in the hopes it would stay with him and make him want more?

"Give us tonight?" Kendal asked.

Andrew met their gaze, then glanced at Kean. His answer was plain to see, and Kendal's heart broke. Then Andrew dragged Kean forward, sealing their mouths together over Kendal, and their blood heated at the sight. Kean groaned as their tongues tangled, and Kendal licked their lips. Their cock rose to the occasion, and their eyes took everything in, not wanting to miss a second.

Kean dragged his mouth free, gasping for air, pupils blown, lips bruised. Andrew turned to Kendal, letting go of Kean and sliding his hand to Kendal's cheek. "I won't be so rough with you," the king murmured.

"Yes, you will," Kendal replied, raising an eyebrow.

Andrew huffed a laugh and lowered his head. "As you wish."

Kendal thought they'd been prepared for the onslaught, but the moment their lips touched, Kendal flew. Their brain went offline, and all they could see, smell and hear were Andrew and Kean. The taste was all Andrew, though. Andrew licked across Kendal's lips, and Kendal parted for entry. His tongue dived into Kendal, and Kendal groaned. He took no prisoners as he explored every inch of Kendal's mouth. Feeling light-headed, Kendal pulled back, feeling as ruined as Kean looked.

Andrew cleared his throat. "I can't put either of you in danger. I refuse to. But I would love nothing more than to see you both happy together. You'll always have a piece of my heart, but I can't give you more."

Kendal expected as much, but it still hurt. Andrew brushed Kendal's cheek before doing the same with Kean, then rose from the bed. Kendal instantly felt the loss, though they tried to swallow it down. He pulled the covers over Kendal and Kean and went to the door, letting Simon in. When the door was closed again, Andrew faced them, and Kendal could see how much he was holding back.

"When you've finished in here, you can use this exit if you wish," Andrew said as Simon pressed against the wall and opened a door Kendal hadn't even realised was there. "It will take you to the Monitors' changing room. I'll ask Clarice to give you access as we leave."

Simon waited outside of the room in the secret passageway, and Andrew stood beside the bed, staring down at them.

"I'm sorry," he said.

Kendal's chin trembled as Andrew left, closing the access door. They burrowed into Kean's chest, and their tears fell, soaking into Kean's shirt. Kean rocked them gently, pressing a kiss to Kendal's head.

"It'll be okay. We'll be fine," Kean said, though his voice was thick with emotion.

"I hate that he's hurting," Kendal sobbed. "We can help him, but he can't see it."

"I know. But he has a lot on his plate. He's not like us, who can choose who we love without caring about the consequences. You never know; he might come around."

Kendal hoped he would, but they didn't hold out hope. "I wonder what he meant about us helping?" they said once they'd calmed a little, content in Kean's arms.

"I'm not sure. I'm already helping with some things, but it sounded like he had something else planned. I'll see if I can get it out of him or one of the others."

Kendal stayed quiet for a moment before voicing their one fear. "Do you think he'll avoid us now?"

Kean lifted Kendal's chin, gaze hot on them as his mouth quirked. "After your sneak attack, I doubt he'll be able to."

Cheeks heating, Kendal tucked their head into Kean's neck, inhaling deeply. "I hadn't planned to. I'd planned..." They stopped, biting their lips to stop their words.

"You'd planned...?" Kean asked.

Kendal sighed. "I'd planned to get you and Andrew together. I saw how you looked at him, and I thought you would be good together."

"And what about you? Where did you fit into it?"

"I didn't. I'd planned to ignore my feelings and let you live happily ever after."

Kean chuckled. "If this is a fairy tale, then you should have a happy ending, too."

"I would've been happy seeing you both happy."

"What changed?"

Kendal couldn't answer that. "I don't know. I just looked at Andrew and saw something. I took a tremendous risk. And it backfired. I'm sorry."

Kean lifted Kendal's chin again. "You don't need to be sorry. I've wanted you both for so long, but I never believed I'd have you. I was too much of a chicken to ask for it." He dropped a kiss on Kendal's lips. "You are so brave." His eyes roamed all over Kendal's face, enough to heat their cheeks again. "You deserve everything, and if you let me, I'd love to be a part of your life now. A *bigger* part, I mean."

Kendal smiled. "I'd love that." They frowned. "I can't guarantee what will trigger me, Kean. I trust you completely, even more so after tonight, but it won't be plain sailing."

"I know. I don't expect it. All I want is to spend time with you. To..." Kean licked his lips.

"To what?"

Kean inhaled so deeply, his chest lifted Kendal. "To love you."

Kendal frowned. "You love me?"

He shrugged a shoulder. "Have done for a while."

Kendal pushed themselves further up Kean's body and kissed him, bracing their hands on either side of Kean's head. "Same." They kissed him again. "I love you."

Kean blew out a breath. "Gosh. We've gone from friends to playing a scene to declaring our love in the space of... what? Two hours?"

Kendal laughed. "Does it matter?"

"Not even a little." Kean stroked across Kendal's back, keeping away from their ass. "I wouldn't trade this for anything."

Kendal bit their lip, staring down at him. "Will I be enough?" they whispered.

Staring right into their eyes, Kean said, "Definitely. We're both going to miss him, but we are just as complete with two as with three."

That wasn't completely true, but they appreciated Kean's effort to comfort them. They leaned down on Kean's chest, chin resting on their hands. "What do you want to do now?"

"Shall we get out of here? Go…home? I mean, your home."

Kendal smiled. "I keep telling you, it can be your haven as well. Your *home* as well. I'm through taking the simple, easy route. You're welcome to stay for as long as you want."

Kean bit his lip and stared off to the side. "Freddie told me not to give up."

Kendal waited, but Kean didn't expand on his words. "Give up on what?"

He blinked and glanced back at Kendal. "You and Andrew. He knows how I feel about you both. He said I would have to be the one to bring you together, but he was wrong. You did it."

"Not really. He's not here." Kendal's heart clenched. "What else did he say?"

"To keep fighting."

Kendal kissed Kean. "Then that's what we'll do. We'll stay as two, but we'll keep fighting to be three."

"You *are* enough, Kendal. I promise you. But I think we both need him with us, don't you?"

"The empty spot in my heart will be there until he's with us, but I can live with it if I need to. What I can't live with is leaving him on his own."

"Agreed."

Was it going to be as easy as they hoped? No. But they would keep fighting to have Andrew as part of their lives. It was what they all deserved.

7

ANDREW

 alking away from Kendal and Kean was the hardest thing Andrew had ever had to do after burying his wife.

"Is everything okay, Your Majesty?" Simon asked as they entered the Monitors' changing room.

Andrew sighed and shook his head. "Not really, Simon, but I can't do much to make it better, either. It'll work itself out."

"Let me know if there's anything I can do to help."

"I will, thanks."

They headed for the foyer, and he asked Clarice to add Kean's and Kendal's prints to the changing room doors. The woman was such a professional she didn't even consider arguing with him. There was a reason they paid her highly and why she had been with them for years. Simon led the way into the lift and down to the car. It was only as they were on their way that he realised he hadn't said goodbye to the boys. He sent a joint message to them all, apologising and letting them know he was going home. After that, he stared out of the window, remembering every second of the time he'd spent in that room. The sounds Kendal made. The sight of Kean's body rippling as he brought down the flogger. The bliss on Kendal's and Kean's faces when Kendal came. The kisses. It had been a culmination of months' worth of feelings that Andrew had no right feeling.

How could he bring them into his life when they were facing such dangers? How could he even consider destroying their lives? Because that was exactly what it would be. Destruction. Not only would the media run wild with the story of their triad, but they would pick apart Kean and Kendal until they couldn't take it anymore. And as for the age difference? Well, thirty-odd years wasn't a problem for normal people, but the king? No way. He'd done the right thing. Kean and Kendal could live happily by themselves without Andrew getting in the way.

Andrew sighed and brushed everything aside. He had criminals to catch, and that had to take precedence. It was late, but he needed to speak with his brother.

"Are you busy?" he asked when William answered.

"Never too busy for you. What's wrong?"

"Can you come by? I want to discuss some things."

"Sure. I'll be there soon."

Andrew ended the call without saying goodbye, but William could tell him off when he got there. It would take him around an hour, which gave Andrew enough time to shower and change before heading for his office.

Just under an hour later, William entered his office with a smile.

"So, Mr 'I don't need to say goodbye,' what's wrong?"

"Sorry, Will. I've got a lot on my mind."

"Haven't we all?" William sat on the sofa after grabbing himself a bottle of water.

"I'm concerned that we haven't heard from anyone in a long time."

"I thought that would be a good thing."

Andrew raised his eyebrows. "Why? If they're quiet, they're planning."

"They could have given up?"

"Since when have you been such a fanciful optimist?"

William chuckled. "Must be all those stories I've been reading. Makes me believe in a simpler world."

Despite the seriousness of the situation, Andrew smiled. "True." He sighed. "Charlotte would usually be heckling us or calling us out or encouraging her followers. Why hasn't she said or done anything? She's too opinionated to remain silent."

William stared at his water bottle. "Do you think they've taken over from her now we've rumbled their plans?"

"They were already the leaders. We just didn't know it."

"I know. But they don't have to hide behind her now. They can be upfront about it."

"That's what I don't understand. If they don't have to keep it a secret, why aren't they doing anything? I don't like this silence. I don't trust it."

William shook his head. "What else can we do? We've hit a wall."

"I'm getting two people to look over the camera feeds from the club. They'll see if anything stands out as strange. It's our only plan at the moment."

William stood and stopped in front of Andrew's desk. "Why are you up so late, anyway?"

Andrew stared at the blotter on his desk. "I visited the club tonight."

"And?"

"Someone asked me to help them get over their fears."

"Bloody hell, Andrew. This is like pulling teeth. And did you?" Andrew nodded. "Who?"

Andrew stared up at his brother, not saying a word.

A grin spread across William's face. "Let me guess. Kendal."

"And Kean."

William raised his eyebrows and whistled. "And how did it go?"

Andrew sighed and rubbed his hand over his beard. "Good, then amazing, then not so good."

Rounding the desk, William perched beside him. "Explain, you annoying twit."

"Hey! That's no way to speak to your king."

"Maybe not, but it is how I speak to my brother." William waved his hand, encouraging Andrew to continue.

"Kendal wanted Kean to help them get over their hurdles, but they asked me to be there as kind of a security blanket. Just in case Kean went off on one. Not that he would, but it made Kendal feel safer. It went well until Kendal struggled, so I went to help. I didn't realise how much strain it would put on me." He stood and went to the window, leaning his shoulder against the frame and staring into the darkness. "During aftercare, Kendal kissed me, then Kean. They are so much braver than anyone gives them credit for." He shook his head, remembering how his body froze when Kendal's lips met his own. Fire had licked at his skin, running down his spine, and he'd been grateful that he had set his hips back from them so they couldn't feel his arousal.

"What did you do?"

"Kendal admitted how they felt, and so did Kean. They wanted…"

"You," William said.

Andrew nodded. "I couldn't do it to them. I couldn't burden them with this life."

"But you can burden them with the thought that you don't care?"

Andrew shook his head. "I told them the truth. That I cared deeply for them, but I refused to give them this life."

"So you showed them a glimpse of happiness and then took it away." William snorted.

Anger raged, and Andrew swung around. "What did you expect? There's no happy ending here, Will! Yes, I would love to have them in my life, but I don't exactly live quietly, do I? The media would rake them over hot coals, and it's not fair to them."

William stood, shaking his head and heading for the drinks table. He poured bourbon into two glasses and brought them over, handing one to Andrew. "You didn't give them the choice, though, did you?" he mumbled.

Andrew stared at the swirling copper liquid and swallowed. "It's the best option."

"For who?"

"Everyone." He sighed and settled back against the window.

"The only people I see winning in this scenario are the public and our treasonous family."

Andrew glanced over his shoulder. "Why?"

"You're giving up your potential happiness for the benefit of everyone else." Andrew just stared at his brother, waiting for him to expand. "You're pushing away happiness because you're scared. Scared the public will refuse your relationship. Scared that our family will use them as bait or something heinous. Scared you might lose them." William stepped closer. "Scared you'll love them."

"Don't forget, I'm also scared I'm too old for them." Andrew huffed.

William's hand rested on his shoulder. "You've given this country enough, Andrew. Now is the time to take something for yourself."

"And what if they're then taken from me because I was selfish?"

William didn't answer because there wasn't a suitable answer for a question like that. Andrew had already lost Louisa to this fight; he refused to lose anyone else.

"Are you sure you shouldn't cancel this?" Freddie asked Andrew as the king pulled on his suit jacket.

Andrew shook his head. "There's no reason to. They've not done anything recently, and we don't know if they ever will again. I can't just drop all my obligations on the off chance something will happen. There has always been the chance that *something* will happen. It's what we live with daily. You know that."

Freddie sighed. "I do. Still sucks, though."

Andrew chuckled and embraced his son. "You've been spending too much time with George again, haven't you?"

Freddie grinned. "And Damon. They're both as bad as each other."

"How are the wedding plans coming along?"

"Good. Randall seems to have it all under control, and he won't let us help, so we're kind of at a loss. The only thing we're allowed to do is decide what we're wearing, but even that, for me at least, is already decided. Damon hasn't chosen yet."

Andrew picked up his phone and tucked it into his

pocket. Officially, he shouldn't have it on him in case it rang during an event, but his security team had told him, in no uncertain terms, that he was to have it on him at all times because there was an alarm on it that Andrew could press if he was in danger, and it had a tracking chip in it. He always had it on silent, though the vibration was on to let him know something had arrived and he needed to take the time to check it. The team had also arranged for a Morse code-style vibration. If it vibrated five times in a row, it meant there was trouble, and someone was coming to remove him.

"You'll look great in your military uniform, and Damon will look amazing in whatever he chooses. Is Robert doing the flowers?"

"I believe so. He's doing the flowers for his own wedding, too." Freddie snorted. "No rest for the wicked."

"He really should let someone else do it," Andrew said, heading for the bedroom door.

"You know he won't."

"Oh, I know. But maybe we can get Naomi and Finn to take over from him."

"We can try."

Andrew glanced around the living area. "I think I have everything."

"Be careful, Father."

Andrew cupped Freddie's nape. "I will be. I have enough security to keep me safe."

Freddie glared at him. "You know better than to tempt fate."

Andrew chuckled though his heart was in his throat. "Have a good evening."

He stepped out of his suite and met Simon, Jared, Selena and Landon. He nodded at them and headed for the exit. Simon spoke into his radio when they reached the door, then nodded towards Jared to open it. The other four members of his personal security officers, Dominic, Colt, Nick and Viola, joined them. Andrew always got to know his team. He found it helped them work together, and they could relax a little around him. Rarely did he cause them problems.

Simon opened the passenger door for him, and Andrew slipped inside and settled into the seat. Simon climbed into the front seat, and off they went.

The event was a dinner, raising funds for children's hospitals around the country. It was something he and Louisa would usually attend, but this time, he would fly solo. It didn't feel right to bring someone else in her place. Not yet, anyway.

Andrew didn't bother doing any work, as he would've under normal circumstances. Instead, he spent the journey staring out of the window and thinking about a truly significant event that had happened five days prior. Something he still couldn't get out of his head or get around. Having a relationship with Kean and Kendal would benefit no one but themselves. If he was honest with himself—which he could be when no one else was with him—if he could ensure their safety, he wouldn't hesitate.

Louisa's final prediction—the one he never believed would come true—could easily happen if he let it, but he cared for those two people too much to put them through what they would have to go through to be part of his life. And it hurt his heart to deny them, but until he could see a solution, it was what he had to do.

His phone vibrated against his leg, and he pulled it out, clicking on the message from George. Andrew laughed as the picture loaded. The entire group of them squashed into the frame, all pulling faces at the camera. In other words, the kind of picture Andrew would cherish for years to come. He zoomed in on the photo, focusing on two people he hadn't realised would be there. Kean and Kendal stood next to each other with Kean crossing his eyes, and Kendal turned towards him, smiling. They looked happy, and that was all Andrew could hope for.

He returned to the landscape outside of the window, his stomach aching and his chest reaching for what he couldn't have. If he thought giving up the throne to Freddie would help, he would do it in a heartbeat, but a king's life would never be out of the media. Even when he was dead, someone would bring something up about him.

It was a risky situation, especially with the club being a major part of their lives. Which took his thoughts in another direction. How had Charles got people involved with their scheme, and who was involved? Andrew needed to speak with Kean—and maybe Kendal—and see if he would go through the videos. He'd planned to ask him the previous weekend but got distracted, understandably.

As for who the moles were, were they likely to be doing more damage beneath the surface of the club where Andrew couldn't see, or were they in sleeper mode now? Maybe if Kean and Kendal were still at Windsor when he got back, he would ask them if they'd help. They said they wanted to.

"Five minutes out, Your Majesty."

"Thank you, Simon."

Andrew didn't mind these events so much because he knew a lot of the people he would dine with, so conversation wasn't awkward. But sometimes, it would be nice to have a normal dinner out, maybe with the entire family, and just relax. Not having to be "on" all the time. It would never happen, though. Having his family at Sandringham was amazing, and he was grateful for it, but he wanted to show his family off. Show what they'd achieved and who they were to the world without fear of retaliation or hurt. Which was why it would never happen.

The car stopped at the base of the steps going up to the hotel the event was taking place at. Andrew waited for Simon to exit and round the car to open his door. He was more than capable of doing it himself, but Simon would check the area to make sure it was safe, and Andrew refused to do anything to make his—their—job harder than it needed to be.

The charity organiser waited for him at the top of the steps, and Andrew shook her hand after she'd bowed. "Thank you so much for attending, Your Majesty. It means a lot to us."

"It means a lot to me, too. Shall we?"

They entered the large foyer, and several people lined the walls, bowing as he passed. When they crossed the threshold of the ballroom, Andrew inhaled and smiled, Simon at his side and Selena and Jared at his back. There were lots of guests milling around, talking to other people, and Andrew had just decided to head over to someone he knew when he saw someone—or rather two someones—he would never have expected. John and Ernest.

"Simon, do you see?"

"Yes, Your Majesty." Simon's voice grated with barely withheld anger. "Can I request we leave?"

As much as he wanted to, he couldn't. "Sorry, Simon. Not yet."

Andrew headed straight for them, wanting to get whatever they wanted out of the way before it messed with the dinner event.

"I didn't expect to see you two here," Andrew said, giving a congenial smile as people, who might not understand what was going on, surrounded them.

John chuckled and sipped his drink. "Why not? The children's hospitals are such a worthy cause."

"That they are, but I would be surprised if they were at the top of your list if you got your wish."

John's smirk never wavered. "True, but we all have to keep up appearances, don't we? Otherwise, you wouldn't be talking to us right now."

Damn the man for being right. "What do you want, John?" Andrew glanced at Ernest, seeing a steeliness in his eyes that Andrew hadn't noticed before.

John stepped closer, as did Simon. John glared at his guard but stopped moving closer, lowering his voice instead. "Well, Andrew, you see, I'm not happy with you. You blurted everything out to Charlotte, and now she's being troublesome. If you had just kept quiet..." John sighed and shook his head.

"Why would I do that, John?"

Ernest chuckled. "You always take the easy route, Andrew. Why not let us do the same?"

Andrew stared at him, wondering what he was on about. "The easy route? Since when? Besides, you're the ones who are making things difficult. If you want easy, just give up, and we'll all be happy campers."

John shook his head. "Nah, it'll soon be my time to shine. Don't you worry about that." He glanced at Ernest. "I've made my point. Let's go."

Andrew wanted to keep them, but he was aware of the people surrounding them. He smiled and said, "See you soon." He watched them leave, and then Simon leaned closer to him.

"We need to leave, Your Majesty. We don't know what they've done in the time they've been here."

Andrew nodded. "Let me give my excuses."

He made up something to do with a family emergency, and they made their way back to the foyer. John and Ernest were nowhere to be seen, sending shivers down Andrew's spine. Would they have done something drastic?

"Simon, would I be wise to evacuate the hotel?"

"It will be as soon as we've left, Your Majesty."

Simon stepped out of the door with Andrew closer behind and his other security staying in close formation. At events like these, there was always a sniper or two on the tops of the buildings, especially since everything had started going to shit, covering their backs should they need it. So when bullets started pinging around them, Andrew was confused.

Simon grabbed Andrew's nape and forced his head down while they stumbled down the steps towards the car. The shots increased, and Andrew heard more than one person drop to the floor, but he couldn't see who it was.

Simon grunted and pushed Andrew against the car, settling in front of him. The occasional bullet still hit the steps, but it slowed drastically. Had this been what John had wanted? To scare Andrew enough to leave and then open fire? What about the snipers? Were they on John's side? Andrew tried to lift his head so he could see who was hurt, but Simon kept muttering for him to stay still.

When the bullets stopped, Simon's radio crackled. "Suspect down. All clear."

Simon sighed shakily and responded, his voice cracking. "London needs cover. Only three guards are available. Held by the car."

Andrew's heart rose to his throat. "Any dead?"

"Yes."

"Who?"

"Not now."

"Cover coming up on your three," the radio said.

Simon glanced to the side and held his gun up towards the incoming guards, and then his arm dropped. "You're in…good hands…now, Your…Majes…" Simon's voice trailed off, and Andrew moved from behind him, grabbing his arm.

"Simon? Simon?" His bodyguard slumped to the side. "Shit! You fuckers!"

8

— · —

KEAN

"So, how did things go?" Freddie asked Kean when everyone else was distracted.

Kean hadn't spoken to anyone about the few hours he'd spent with Kendal and Andrew. He'd received a few looks from the members of the Thirsty Thirteen, but he'd ignored them as best he could. But he couldn't ignore a direct question, especially from Freddie, who knew what was going on inside him.

He tilted his head back and forth. "It went." He chuckled. "Kendal and I are now taking things slowly. One day at a time. I'm not announcing anything until they're ready for it to be common knowledge, so I'd appreciate you keeping it quiet for now."

"Of course. And what about Father?" Kean sighed. "Ah, that well, huh?"

"The one bright light was that he admitted caring for us, but he refuses to let us choose if we want to be thrown into the spotlight. He thinks he's protecting us."

"Sounds like him." Freddie sipped his drink. "I know I've said it before, but you need to decide if you want it and if he's worth it. If you do, and he is, fight for him."

Kean smiled. "We've already decided to. In Kendal's words, 'We'll stay as two, but we'll keep fighting to be three.' I think that sums it up nicely."

Freddie chuckled. "I put my money on you two."

"Thanks."

"If you need anything at all, let—"

A heavy-handed knock sounded, and the door opened. Brett stepped inside. "I apologise for disrupting your evening. Kieren, we need you. Patrick and Christian, too, if you don't mind. We need all hands on deck."

Freddie stood. "What's happened?"

Brett licked his lips and swallowed. "There's been a shooting. Your father is fine, but he's lost some guards. We need to get him covered again."

"Where do you need us?" Damon said, stepping towards the door.

"We're locking Windsor down for now. I have four men I'm leaving here. I need the three of them to cover for those of us who are leaving. I don't know who else to trust right now." Brett stared at Freddie. "You need to stay with Freddie." A beat passed before Damon nodded.

"What happened?" George said.

"We don't have a huge amount of information, but from what I can gather, either one of our snipers turned, or someone was pretending to be our sniper."

"Where is Father?" Douglas asked.

"He's being taken to the hospital as a precaution. They want to check him over, just to be sure."

Kean glanced at Kendal, seeing their pale face, and stood,

uncaring about outing their relationship now this had happened. He knelt beside them. "Shall we go to him?" Kendal nodded. Kean pulled them to standing and glanced at Freddie, who nodded once at him. "We're coming with you to the hospital," Kean said.

"No, you need—"

"They're coming with you, Brett," Freddie said, in a tone that brooked no argument.

Brett opened his mouth to do just that, but something stopped him. "Understood. We're leaving now."

Kean and Kendal headed out of the door behind Brett, their fingers linked so tightly, the blood couldn't reach the tips of their fingers. That Andrew wasn't hurt was a good thing, but he needed to see for himself. Andrew would curse at them for being there, but he didn't care. They needed to prove that they could make up their own minds about their destinies, not be told what to do. Andrew would learn soon enough. And this was the first step in that direction.

"You need to stay with at least one of us at all times," Brett said. "We don't know if there are more snipers around." Brett sighed. "He's going to kill me," he muttered.

They exited Windsor, and Brett guided them to the back of the car. They huddled together, Kean with his arms around Kendal, and Kean watched the scenery as the car raced down the road towards the king. Which guards had Andrew lost? Did Andrew have any injuries? Brett had said he was fine, but that could just mean he was alive.

"I hope he's okay," Kendal said into Kean's chest.

"He will be. He might rage at us for being there, though."

"I don't care. I need to see for myself that he's alive and well."

Kean smiled into Kendal's hair. "I know what you mean."

They dropped into silence as the miles continued. He had a feeling that what should've taken roughly an hour took about two-thirds of the time with how fast they were going, but he couldn't have been happier when they stopped outside of the hospital that treated most royal members.

Brett opened the passenger door for them to climb out, and they kept their heads lowered as cameras flashed.

"Who do you have there?"

"Where is the king?"

"Is he alive?"

"Can you give us an update?"

Questions bombarded them as Brett led them through the doors of the hospital and into the main foyer. It was as sterile looking and smelling as most hospitals, but that's where the similarities ended. Kean had never been there before, but he could see the benefits to it when the nurse immediately showed them to the room after Brett told them who they were there for.

"Van, Sam, stay by the entrance," Brett ordered. "Felix, Jade, Hudson, Des, take posts at the end of the corridors. Nina, Matt, Rae, you're with me."

The guards dispersed to do their assigned jobs, and Brett continued behind the nurse until they came to a door. Brett nodded at the nurse, and she disappeared down the hallway again. He waited until she turned a corner, then knocked. The door opened to Dominic, one of Andrew's guards. The man visibly relaxed when he saw Brett. His eyes flicked over the six of them before raising his eyebrows in Kean and Kendal's direction.

"Yes, he'll be pissed. I know," Brett said with a sigh. "I'll take the crap for it."

Dominic's mouth twitched, but he opened the door

further. Kean and Kendal stepped into the large room. Kendal let go of Kean's hand and moved to Andrew's side. The king sat on a bed with the back raised to support him, and although he had a few scrapes Kean could see, he'd never looked better in his life.

"Kendal! What are you doing here?" Andrew said.

Kean stayed back as Dominic and Colt, Andrew's other guard, left the room, closing the door with a quiet snick.

"I needed to see that you were okay," Kendal said. "I was so worried."

Andrew cupped Kendal's cheek and sighed. "You shouldn't be here. Neither of you should." He glanced up at Kean.

"We can decide for ourselves," Kean said, with a little more bite in his voice than he intended.

Andrew rubbed a hand over his beard, his scraped knuckles more apparent with the movement. Kendal whimpered and grabbed his hand, rubbing their fingers over his skin.

"Where are you hurt?" Kean asked, unable to stay away any longer. He stopped on the opposite side of the bed from Kendal.

"Just scraped hands and knees, and a minor bruise likely to arrive on my shoulder. Nothing to worry about." Andrew's voice was soft, yet there was a note of pain in it.

Kean rested his hand on Andrew's biceps. "Who did you lose?"

Andrew sighed and stared at him, his eyes filling right in front of Kean. "Selena... Jared... and..." He sniffed and wiped his eyes. Clearing his throat, he continued, "And Simon."

"Shit, Andrew. I'm so sorry." Kean squeezed his arm. Andrew had a close bond with Simon because they'd been together for a long time. It must hurt as much as losing family.

"Nick and Viola are being treated for serious injuries, and Landon has a few superficial ones. Dominic and Colt were in the best shape of them all because they were fetching the cars." Andrew shook his head. "This is what I meant about you being in danger. If you're with me, you could get hurt."

"Don't," Kendal said sharply. "Stop making excuses. If I was to die tomorrow, no matter the circumstances, I want to have lived my life with you and Kean. Why should we miss out on what we want because of what people might say?"

"It's not as easy as that, Kendal," Andrew said. "We could lose everything I've worked for."

"How?"

"All it takes is for the country to lose faith in us, and everything the royal family has stood for could crumble to dust."

"I think you're not giving them—us—enough credit. We know a good thing when we see it," Kean said.

Andrew closed his eyes and rested his head back. He remained quiet for a moment, then murmured, "I don't know if *I'm* strong enough to fight."

And there it was. Andrew had finally opened up to them about what his problem was. Kean wasn't going to let him take it back.

"Do you care for us?" he asked.

Andrew opened his eyes and stared back at him. "You know I do."

"Do you want to be with us?"

Andrew swallowed. "Yes."

"Will you let us help you shoulder the burden?"

Andrew shook his head. "It's not your fight."

"Do you care for us?" he asked again.

"Kean…"

"Do you care for us?" he asked in a sharper tone.

"Yes!"

"Then you have no choice. Because we're not going anywhere. It would be better if you understood that now and gave us the tools we need to survive your world. Otherwise, we're going to be floundering. Help us to help you."

"This isn't—"

"This is happening," Kean said, leaning over the bed. "When they let you go, we're coming with you. We can sort everything else out later. But for now, we're staying." He stepped back and headed for the window, staring out of the one-way glass to the dark night outside.

"I can't remember him being so bossy before," Andrew murmured.

It brought a small smile to Kean's face. He didn't let his dominant side out very often, but when he did, he meant business. He refused to let Kendal suffer for Andrew's idiocy, but he was second-guessing himself now. Did he have the right to put his foot down? He didn't know what was in store for them, he could only guess, but they would need information, and fast. He pulled out his phone and sent a message to Freddie.

KEAN: Your father is fine. Just a few scrapes and bruises. He's lost Selena, Jared and Simon, and Nick, Landon and Viola are injured. Not sure when we're coming back yet as doctors haven't been in since we've been here. FYI, I've put my foot down with him. Kendal and I are here to stay, but we're going to need help. Andrew seems determined to keep us out of harm's way, and I think he's going to keep things from us. I need you to help us get up to speed with everything. I doubt he's ready for us to go public, but I'm not hiding from family. Will keep you up to date with what's happening.

He received a message back before he could put the phone away.

FREDDIE: Thanks. I agree. He will keep things from you, thinking he's helping. I can't go behind his back, but I will back you up and try to make him see he's doing wrong by you. No guarantees. But where I can, I'll include you both. Let us know when you're on your way back, and we'll wait to see you. No one will sleep until they've checked he's okay. Chin up.

Kean raised his eyebrows at the final words. That was something usually used for those in the Thirsty Thirteen, or even just the original Scandalous Six, but he was grateful for it. He needed the reminder.

"Kean?"

He glanced to the side at Kendal's voice and saw the doctor had entered while he'd been distracted. They stayed by the window while the doctor checked Andrew over once more. They murmured low enough that Kean couldn't hear what they said, and with the glances sent their way, the doctor was purposefully keeping his voice low to stop them from hearing. He was doing a good job of not showing his surprise at them being there.

The doctor's voice rose. "You're free to go home, Your Majesty. Ice that shoulder if it gets stiff, but other than that, you're doing good. I would recommend you rest for a couple of days, though."

"Thank you, Leonard. I think I need a holiday after this." Andrew chuckled.

"Highly recommended, Your Majesty. I hear Hawaii has pleasant weather at this time of year." Leonard smiled.

"Maybe one day." Andrew glanced at them.

"Take it easy now, and please don't take this the wrong way, but I hope I don't see you anytime soon," Leonard said.

Andrew laughed. "Understood."

The doctor left, and Kean and Kendal moved back over to the bed. Andrew yawned.

"Let's go," Kean said.

Andrew reached for his hand, then for Kendal's with his other. "This will not be easy." He glanced between them. "I want this. God knows I do. Even Louisa knew." Kendal gasped. "Not about you two, but about falling in love again. She knew it would physically hurt me to put someone else in danger. Louisa knew what she was getting into when she married me, and I have to explain it to you. But not here." He sighed. "When we get back, after some sleep, I want to sit down with you and tell you everything. Only then, when you have all the information, will I allow your decision. That's my final offer. If you can't accept that, then we can't be."

Kean smiled and squeezed Andrew's hand. "I'd like to know everything."

"Me, too," Kendal said.

"So be it. Let's go home."

Andrew let go of their hands and swung his legs off the bed. Kean held his biceps as he stood, making sure he was steady first. "Dominic!" Andrew called.

The door opened and closed, and Dominic stepped closer. "Yes, Your Majesty?"

"It's time for home."

"Of course. We have everything ready." Dominic glanced at them. "Might I suggest..."

"Go ahead," Andrew said.

"I think it would be wise to go in separate cars, Your Majesty. The media are camping outside, and...if you pardon my overstepping, I don't think you want rumours to run just yet."

"You're right." Andrew nodded. "I'll go first. I want guards on them, too, please."

"Of course, Your Majesty. I'll get it organised. We'll leave in five minutes."

"Thank you, Dominic."

Dominic left, and Kean faced Andrew. "I don't like going separately."

Andrew cupped his jaw. "I know, but this is part of the royal life. You have to get used to doing what's *best* for us instead of what we want."

"Exactly why I don't like it," Kean murmured with a sigh.

"It won't take long to get home."

A knock sounded again, and Andrew called for them to enter.

"Your Majesty, it's time to go," Dominic said. "Brett, Felix and Hudson are staying with Kean and Kendal. The rest of us are with you."

"Thank you. Give me a moment, Dominic."

Dominic left again, leaving them alone. Andrew glanced between them. "I could never have imagined either of you being as brave as you have been lately. Telling me what you want and need is the bravest thing anyone could ever do. As much as I hate the idea of bringing you into this, I will stand by my words. Tomorrow, we will talk."

Andrew leaned down and pressed his lips to Kendal's mouth for a few seconds longer than Kean expected him to, then brushed his thumb down Kendal's cheek. He turned to Kean. Resting his hand on Kean's nape, Andrew drew him closer and repeated the kiss. It didn't last as long as he'd hoped, but his brain still misfired.

"I'll see you when we get back."

Andrew left, and Kean brought Kendal into his arms, holding them while they waited for the guards to tell them to leave. Were they getting what they wanted, or were they about to lose everything because they couldn't handle the truth?

9

FREDDIE

Not being able to visit his father in the hospital was one downside of being a prince. Or rather, the heir. Freddie paced the room. Forward. Turn. Back. Turn. Forward. He wasn't sure how long he'd done it before Damon had slid his arms around his waist and held him in place.

"He's okay," Damon murmured. "He's on his way back now."

Freddie couldn't relax. He didn't want to admit that he wasn't as concerned about his father as he was about trying to contain the anger that was bubbling beneath the surface. He could feel the pit in his stomach warming and growing as he remembered every infraction those so-called family had wrought upon them. He couldn't stand for much more before he blew.

"We'll get them, Freddie. I promise. We'll get them and make them pay for what they've done. All of it."

Trust Damon to understand what he was feeling without him having to say a word. He turned in Damon's arms and slid his own around his fiancé's back, gripping him and burying his face in his shoulder.

"I know we will. But sometimes, it feels like we're continually treading water instead of swimming to the shore."

"It does. But bad people always get what's coming for them. Always."

Freddie chuckled and lifted his head. "You watch far too many happily ever after films."

"Name a film that doesn't have a happy ending?"

"*Armageddon.*"

Damon opened his mouth to argue and snapped it shut. He took a breath. "Technically, it did have a happy ending because they saved the world. But I agree, it wasn't the best one. Bruce Willis should never have died."

"Exactly."

But Freddie knew what Damon was trying to do. He was distracting him and helping him through the next however long until his father returned.

"We lost so many good people," Freddie murmured.

"We did. But we will pay our respects and make sure their families want for nothing."

"Father must be heartbroken about Simon."

"It won't be easy for him, especially after losing some at Christmas, too. We'll be there for him, though. And he still has Dominic and Colt. Landon, Nick and Viola will recover as well, but whether they want to continue will be up for discussion. They certainly won't be working for a while."

Freddie sighed. "Is it worth it?"

Damon cupped Freddie's chin and frowned. "Is what worth it?"

"This life. The crown. Is it worth everything we're being put through? Should we step down?"

Damon reared back. "And give it to them? No way in

hell!"

"No, I mean disbanding us altogether. Father could do that, and then no one would get the crown."

"Who would that benefit?"

Freddie stared into his green eyes, falling into them as usual. "Us. It would benefit us. We would have a normal life."

"But would we? Just because we gave up the throne doesn't mean we would be left alone. We would never be left alone. In fact, it would probably be worse."

"We'd have our lives," Freddie stated.

Damon sighed and nodded. "We would. But do you really want that?"

Freddie exhaled. "No, I want to fight for us. I want to fight for this country because they don't deserve what would come to them should Charlotte or whoever take over."

"There's the prince I want to marry," Damon murmured.

Freddie chuckled. "I didn't go anywhere."

"But you went a little loopy for a while."

"It's just not fair, is all."

Damon slid his arms around him again. "It's not. But I can't think of any family more worthy of the crown and capable of the weight of it."

A knock sounded. "Your Highnesses, the king is home," Locke called through the door.

"Thank you, Locke."

Freddie stared at Damon. "Ready?"

"Not yet."

Damon kissed him, his lips sipping at Freddie's mouth, and Freddie cupped the back of his head, deepening the kiss until they pulled apart, panting.

"Now, I'm ready," Damon said.

Fortified by Damon's reassurance, Freddie was ready, too.

10

KENDAL

The journey back to Windsor took longer than it had to get to the hospital, but they were travelling at a more sedate speed this time. Kendal was tucked into Kean's side, although Kean was on his phone, sending message after message to someone.

"You're busy," Kendal said.

Kean chuckled. "I'm giving Freddie an update. He knows everything anyway. I messaged him earlier, telling him..." He lowered his voice. "Telling him I put my foot down with Andrew, but I'm just telling him it's not set in stone yet. They're waiting up for him to get back so they can check he's in one piece. We'll no doubt be bombarded when we get back, too."

"I can deal with that, although I'm getting tired. All that adrenaline is seeping out of me now." They yawned, setting Kean off.

"Would you like me to stay with you tonight?"

Kendal smiled up at him. "Yes, please."

"We'll head out as soon as the meet and greet has finished. We can rest until tomorrow."

Kendal wasn't sure what to expect the next day, but they doubted it would change their mind. Would Andrew stick to his word and allow them the opportunity to explore what was between them if they decided it wasn't too much for them? Would he try to persuade them otherwise? Probably. Kendal wasn't naïve. They understood a lot was going on behind the scenes that they knew nothing about. But unless it was something huge that would hurt them all rather than just cause a few hills in their relationship, they were willing to try.

When they arrived at Windsor, they were ushered through a different entrance to normal, away from prying eyes, if Kendal was to guess. Brett led them to the receiving room the princes had begun using for their get-togethers.

"Is—"

"The king is inside," Brett said with a small smile, though Kendal could see something was troubling him. Kean, too, if his next words were anything to go by.

"What's wrong, Brett?"

Brett shook his head. "A lot's happened, Kean. That's all. I'm worn out." He chuckled. "Have a good evening. I'll leave you here."

"Thanks for the escort, Brett," Kendal said.

"You're welcome."

Kean opened the door and pulled Kendal in behind him. Conversation stopped until the door closed behind them, and then Freddie headed over to them, enclosing Kean in a hug.

"Thank you for going to him," Freddie whispered, loud enough for Kendal to hear.

Freddie let go and glanced at Kendal. Kendal leaned

forward and embraced him, knowing he wouldn't do so without Kendal's permission. Freddie held them tightly, then let go.

"Would you like a drink?" Freddie asked.

"No, thanks. We're going to head out soon," Kean said, linking his and Kendal's fingers again.

"Head out?" Andrew interrupted, stepping closer. "Where?"

"Home," Kendal said, their stomach somersaulting. "We'll be back tomorrow, though."

"Stay," Andrew said. "There are plenty of rooms."

Kendal wasn't sure they could. They knew the security around the castle was immense, but they were used to their home with the security cameras they could check.

"Uncle Andrew, can I have a word?" Christian said.

"In a min—"

"It won't take long."

Christian glanced at Kendal and nodded as he almost bodily dragged Andrew away from them. They had a feeling Christian was going to explain about security, which Kendal was grateful for. They didn't want everyone to know how scared they were, but they found it difficult to explain without feeling stupid sometimes.

"So, you're coming back tomorrow?" Freddie said.

Kean nodded. "Big discussion time."

"Don't let him persuade you otherwise," Freddie murmured, looking over his shoulder. "If you want it, fight him for it."

"We intend to," Kendal said as Andrew returned.

"Would you allow me to send a guard with you?" There was something in his eyes that Kendal couldn't define, but when Kendal agreed, Andrew's shoulders lost some of their tension. "Thank you."

Kendal smiled. "We're going to head out," they said, glancing at Kean with raised eyebrows.

Kean nodded. "Sure. Let's say goodbye to Henry." He squeezed Kendal's hand before letting go and wandering off in search of his best friend.

"Oh, Quinn's still here. I need to speak to him before I go," Kendal said, staring at Andrew.

Andrew studied Kendal for a long moment before stepping aside. "Please say goodbye before you go," he whispered as Kendal moved.

Quinn stood as they got closer, gently pulling them into a hug. "Are you okay?"

Kendal nodded. "I'm fine. I have a lot to explain."

Quinn raised his eyebrows and chuckled. "You do. But it can wait. Whenever you're ready, you know I'm here."

"Thanks, Quinn. Maybe we can have dinner one evening?"

"Sure. I'll speak with Master and see what day is best."

Kendal smiled. They were infinitely grateful that Quinn had an amazing Master. After Talon had abused Kendal, they had both taken them in with no question and looked after them for several weeks until they could find a new house. They had a lot to thank them both for.

"Do you want a lift home?" they asked.

"No, Xan is taking me."

Kendal leaned in for another hug and then hugged Xan, too. "See you soon."

They glanced to see where Kean was, and he was talking to Andrew. They wandered over, not wanting to interrupt, but Kean waved them closer.

"—have lunch with me?" Andrew said.

"Sure. We can be back around twelve o'clock? Is that okay with you, Kendal?" Kean asked.

"Yes. It'll give me plenty of time to sleep."

"If you're too tired when you wake up, we can leave it until later in the day. I want you to rest," Andrew said.

"I'll be okay."

"Right," Kean said. "Let's get you home." He smiled at Kendal.

Andrew stood and tugged Kean into a hug. When he pulled back, he glanced at Kendal, who leaned in for a hug, too. "See you tomorrow," Andrew said.

"Or later, as it's already two o'clock in the morning."

Andrew chuckled and led the way to the door. He held it open for them. "Be careful."

"Always am," Kean said.

They exited the room and wandered down the corridor, Hudson, their assigned bodyguard for the evening, following in their wake. Kean held the car door open for Kendal and rounded the car before climbing in behind the steering wheel. Hudson got in his own car, flashing his lights when he was ready. Kean pulled out of Windsor and drove the few minutes to get to Kendal's house. When they pulled into the driveway, Hudson flashed again and parked the car on the street. He would stay there all night, according to Kean.

As the front door closed behind them, Kendal exhaled. "That was a long day."

Kean wrapped his arms around them. "It was."

"Do you think he's going to change his mind?" Kendal asked.

Kean pressed his lips into Kendal's hair. "I don't know. I'll try to keep him to his word, though."

They headed up the stairs after Kendal had completed their usual security checks.

"I think he's blinded by what happened to Louisa,"

Kendal said several minutes later, once they were ready for bed.

Kean sighed. "It's understandable, and I can't say I'm not worried about what we're walking into, but I can't live without you both."

"Me either."

"Are you sure you want me to stay here with you?" Kean asked.

Kendal smiled and climbed into bed. "We're just sleeping, Kean. I know we've not shared a bed yet, but after what happened tonight, I'd like to keep you close by."

"I'm okay with it. I just wanted to make sure you were, too."

Kendal held up the covers on the opposite side of the bed, and Kean climbed in. Kendal wore silk pyjamas because they liked the feel of the fabric against their skin. Kean wore a T-shirt and pyjama bottoms. It was probably more than Kean normally wore, but he was being careful, no doubt.

Kendal rested their head on Kean's chest, and Kean held them close. It was nice and something they hadn't had for a very long time. Talon had never held them like that, and it had been several years before that when he'd had someone who did. As Kean stroked his fingers through their hair, they hoped, with everything inside of them, that something with Andrew was possible. They would both be missing a piece of themselves if Andrew decided they weren't worth it. They would manage, but there'd always be something missing.

As their eyelids grew heavy, Kean pressed his lips to their head. "Goodnight, sweetheart."

Kendal wrung their hands as Kean drove them back to Windsor the following morning. They were running a little late because they had slept in, both having forgotten to set an alarm. Kean had drunk a cup of coffee, whereas Kendal had decided on tea, but neither had time for breakfast, but as it was close to lunchtime, that wouldn't matter. They'd be eating soon enough.

Kean reached across and squeezed their hands. "I would tell you to stop worrying, but I know it won't help."

Kendal chuckled at that. "No, it won't, but thanks for trying."

Hudson had told them to use the entrance they'd used the previous evening, so Kean pulled around the back of Windsor instead of the usual gate. Once he'd parked, they got out and headed inside, Hudson on their tails.

"I've been asked to escort you to His Majesty's suite," Hudson said.

"Thank you," Kean said.

They didn't say anything along the way, though Kean threaded their fingers together like he seemed to love doing. Kendal wasn't opposed to it, either. They loved the heat from Kean's hands bleeding into theirs; it made them feel less alone in the world.

Kean knocked on the door to Andrew's suite, and soon, they were inside, face-to-face with the one man they both wanted to embrace and never let go. But would he agree? That remained to be seen.

"I'm glad you're here," Andrew said, opening his arms for a joint hug from them both. Kendal kept hold of Kean's hand as they melted into Andrew, closing their eyes and enjoying the scent of whatever aftershave or shampoo he used. Andrew kissed their head and pulled back. "I haven't ordered yet because I wasn't sure what you'd want. Here's the menu." He passed them a book and waved for them to sit.

Kean led them to the sofa and settled Kendal in the centre while he took one side. Kendal hoped Andrew would join them, but he remained standing.

"Would you like a drink first?"

"Bourbon?" Kean asked with a raised eyebrow.

Andrew chuckled. "I think I can manage that. Kendal?"

"Same, please."

"Hmm. How did I not know we were all bourbon drinkers?" Andrew said as he headed for the bar.

Kendal studied the menu, choosing a panini because they didn't want anything too heavy for the conversation they were about to have. Andrew passed a glass to Kean and Kendal, then placed their food order before settling beside Kendal with his glass.

"Do you want to talk before or after food?"

"While not before, during and after?" Kean grinned.

Andrew huffed a laugh. "Okay."

"First, though, how are you feeling?" Kendal asked.

Andrew rolled his shoulder and flexed his hand. "Surprisingly fine. A bit of an ache in my joints, but I can't say that's not more about my age than what happened." He chuckled, and then his smile dimmed. "I'm scared for you."

"We know you are," Kean said. "But you need to let us make up our own minds about what we're willing to risk. Once you've finished explaining things, we might decide it's too much. But until you do, we don't know." Kean glanced at Kendal. "I don't mean to speak for you. You probably have your own concerns."

"I do, but what you said is right." They glanced at Andrew. "Will you explain so we can decide together?"

Andrew nodded and sipped his bourbon. "The media is unforgiving, as you probably know. When I made that speech about my family and came out as bisexual, I didn't expect it to become anything big. It was a statement. That's all. It was the truth, but I hadn't planned on having another relationship, especially at my age." He rubbed a hand over his beard, scratching it. "Even though, at the time, it was just words, the media went into a frenzy. They brought up every meeting or event where I'd been photographed with men who were known to be bisexual or gay. They joked about whether any of them had been my side pieces. They dragged everything right and honourable about those times through the mud just to make headlines."

Andrew swallowed the rest of his drink, then rose for some more. Kendal's heart broke for him.

"I know to ignore them. I've lived with it all my life. But it still hurt that the country I have given so much to could honestly believe I could be like that while my wife was standing not two feet away."

"It was so the papers could make money," Kean said.

"I know, but I'm human. It still hurt. Still hurts every time it happens." Andrew settled beside Kendal once more, reaching an arm across the back of the sofa. "If we go public with a relationship, the same will happen to you. They will bring your past to light. It will be twisted and moulded into something it's not to make money. To entertain. Your past, Kendal, will be there for all to see, and I guarantee they will show you in an unfavourable light instead of Talon. Because that is what they do."

Kendal's throat narrowed, and they closed their eyes. Andrew's hand rested on their nape, and Kean took their hand. They hadn't thought about the incident being brought up again. Could they survive it again?

"I'm sorry. I don't mean to upset you, but you have to understand," Andrew continued. "Every choice I've ever made will be taken and revisited and misunderstood until it fits what *they* want it to. I don't want anyone to hurt because of me."

"What else?" Kean said.

Andrew snorted. "Is that not enough?"

"Not for me."

"Well, how about what's happening with Charlotte, John and Ernest?" Andrew said, sitting forward. "How about the fact that they want us all dead?" He stood, pacing the floor. "They've already taken Louisa, Simon, Selena and Jared, not to mention all the other guards. And I'll include Miranda and Elizabeth here because, even though they were on the wrong side, they're still victims." Andrew raised his hand towards the window, though he kept his gaze on them. "Every time we step outside, there's the chance we won't come back again. I don't know if I can live with that fear for you."

"As I said last week and last night, we could die at any point. Something that has nothing to do with our relationship. If we lived in fear of death, we would never live," Kendal said. "What else?" They repeated Kean's earlier question.

Andrew shook his head. "My family might not like it."

Kean chuckled and shook his head. "They're fine about it. You know that. Freddie told us none too quietly that they were okay with us. What else?"

They were prodding Andrew to get all his worries loose, but Kendal could see he was scared. Even if they brushed aside all his worries, there was no guarantee he would be willing to try.

"What would it take for you to give our relationship a chance?" Kendal asked before Andrew could answer.

Andrew swallowed and stared out of the window, though it was too far away to see much. "Something I don't think you could give me."

"Try us."

"Secrecy," Andrew said, glancing back at them. "No one outside of my family can know. But that's not fair of me to ask. It's not that I want to hide you, but I don't want you in danger."

Kendal understood. They peered at Kean, who frowned. "I'm fine with secrecy. It's not much different from what we have now."

Kean studied Kendal, and his mouth firmed. "I would prefer to tell the world so we didn't have to hide, but if that's what it takes." He stared at Andrew. "I'm in."

Andrew raised his eyebrows. "You're serious?" Kean and Kendal nodded. "You'd keep everything quiet just to be with me?" he murmured.

"We would do anything to be with you," Kendal said. "But we're not keeping quiet where it matters, which is with your family. We can be together at Windsor, then when we're not here, we're friends." They wrung their hands and glanced at Kean. "Although, are you okay with Kean and I still being together outside of here?"

Andrew smiled and sat beside them again. He covered their hands, squeezing, and held out his other hand for Kean. "I would be more than happy with that. I wouldn't want you alone when you're not here."

"We're doing this?" Kean asked. "For real?"

Andrew sighed. "I still have my reservations, but yes. I promised you we could try if we could find a way to work, and we did. I'm just sorry it has to be this way."

"You don't need to be sorry. We can do this," Kendal said, leaning in to rest their head on Andrew's shoulder. "I'm so happy." And they were. They could have both the men they wanted, and to be honest, they were content not to announce it to the world. It would give them the opportunity to find their way through the relationship with three people and figure out how they work. They couldn't wait.

11

ANDREW

ndrew couldn't believe they were willing to hide everything just to be with him. He hadn't thought himself that much of a catch, but as long as they were happy, then so was he. He couldn't deny that the idea of them in danger made him itch with the need to shield them, but he'd get through that. He hoped. Would they really want him to touch them and be intimate with them when he was so much older than them? He wasn't a spring chicken any longer. He had wrinkles upon his wrinkles.

He swallowed the rest of his bourbon and shoved the thoughts down. They wanted him; otherwise, they wouldn't be there. They wouldn't be willing to pretend they didn't have a relationship if they weren't serious. Anyone who was after his money or his fame wouldn't be willing to do that. Besides, Louisa had always thought highly of the pair of them, which went a long way to soothing his paranoia.

"Andrew?" Kendal said.

"Hmm?" he replied, turning his head and pressing his lips to Kendal's head.

"Can we get some sleep? I didn't sleep well last night. Even though my cuddle bear was very helpful." Kean grinned at them. "I kept waking him whenever I moved. I think we could both do with a nap."

"We can definitely sleep once we've eaten. I must feed you first," Andrew said just as someone knocked at the door. Kendal lifted their head and scooted closer to Kean. "Come in!"

Darcy, one of the household staff, entered with a trolley. She pushed it to the small dining table and placed the plates and cutlery in place before bowing her head and removing the trolley.

"Thank you, Darcy," he said before she disappeared completely.

"You're welcome, Your Majesty."

Andrew sighed. "Why can no one call me Andrew?" he said when the door closed behind her once more.

"Because you're a shining star in the dull world, and people want to worship you?" Kean said, and from his tone, he was only half joking.

"Come on. Let's eat before you get too snarky," Andrew said.

Kean stood, leaning down to peck Andrew's cheek before tugging Kendal to stand. "Food!"

Kean and Kendal settled at the table, tucking into the food without waiting for him. Whether that was a conscious effort on their part to make Andrew feel more relaxed or whether they were just that hungry, he didn't care. Seeing those two people happy and eating filled a part of Andrew he hadn't known was empty. He was taking care of them in the few ways he could.

"Are you eating with us?" Kean asked.

"Yes."

Andrew rose and joined them. The conversation stayed light, with them telling him about the shenanigans from the get-together the previous evening. At least until they'd been interrupted. Which reminded Andrew of his need to speak to Brett about bringing them along. But that could wait.

When they had soothed their hunger, Andrew broached the next phase of their relationship. "This is a bit of a sensitive subject, but I need to ask so I know where your heads are at." He swallowed. "You mentioned sleeping, which I assumed meant you would like to sleep here. I have no problems with this, but I want to make sure you're okay with knowing this was also the bed I shared with Louisa. I understand completely if this is not something you want to do."

Kendal covered Andrew's hand with their own. "I can't speak for Kean, but for me, I have no problem with it. Queen Louisa will always be a part of our relationship because she will forever be a part of you. I don't ever want you to think you can't talk about her when I'm around. You loved—no, love her, and she is a big part of this world."

Andrew's throat closed up with Kendal's words.

"I second that. Louisa was a big part of my life, too. Not as much as yours, obviously, but I understand how irreplaceable she is. I don't want you to think I'm trying to take her place. I'm not. I'd love to have a place beside her, though."

Andrew closed his eyes and swallowed thickly. "Thank you," he croaked. He stood and held out both hands. "Come with me."

Kean and Kendal settled on either side of him, and he led them to a room few people had access to. His sons were allowed in, and so were some household staff, Randall and his security guards, but that was about it. As he crossed the threshold of his bedroom, he inhaled and held his breath as if waiting for lightning to spear him on the spot. When nothing happened, he exhaled.

"Are you okay?" Kean asked.

Andrew smiled. "I am." He pulled on them both until they stood in front of him, and he dragged them into a hug. He pressed his lips to each forehead in turn. "I care about you so much. Don't let anyone or anything tell you otherwise."

"Yes, Sir," Kendal said, a smile curving their lips.

"Wouldn't dream of it, Sir," Kean replied, smirking.

"I've never attempted a three-way kiss before. Shall we see if we can do it justice?" Andrew grinned to hide his nervousness. He was sixty-seven years old and felt as trembly as a teenager having his first foray into Club Royal.

Kean was only an inch shorter than he was, but Kendal was five inches shorter, making it necessary for him and Kean to lean down., but once their lips met, it didn't matter. Noses bumped, and chins clashed, but their first official kiss was something to remember. Andrew pulled back, and Kean leaned in to kiss Kendal. Andrew kept hold of their hands, but Kean's free hand slid into Kendal's hair, holding them in place. It was a sight to behold. Kendal lifted Andrew's hand to their hair, and Andrew released their hand and raked his fingers through their hair until they covered Kean's hand. Kean moaned, and Andrew slid their other joined hands around Kean's back, holding him close. He was content to watch, but Kendal drew back, panting for air, eyes locking onto Andrew's.

"Your turn while I breathe for a minute."

Andrew chuckled. "I've been told many times that breathing is overrated. However, I do appreciate oxygen."

Kean removed his hand from behind his back, though Andrew kept his there, and cupped Andrew's cheek. "Kiss me, my king." Andrew shook his head, locking gazes with Kean and waiting. The crease between Kean's eyes deepened for a second before he smiled. "Kiss me, please, Sir."

"As you wish."

Andrew joined their mouths, keeping things soft and gentle, but Kean nipped at his lower lip. Tightening his hold on Kean's back, he deepened the kiss, sliding his tongue deep into the warm cavern. His hand rose to grip Kean's nape as he plundered his mouth in a way he hadn't kissed anyone for a long time. Kean pulled back, gasping, and Andrew turned to Kendal. They smiled at him.

"I won't break," they said.

Andrew kissed them the same way he kissed Kean. Slow to begin with, then harder and deeper. This time, he pulled away, resting his forehead against Kendal's.

"Sorry," he murmured.

"Gosh, don't be sorry about that," Kendal said. "That was hot."

"You don't need to tell me," Kean agreed. "Shall we get a little more comfortable?"

Kean led them closer to the bed and stepped behind Kendal, facing Andrew. Kean pressed his lips to Kendal's nape, and Kendal's eyelids fluttered closed while Kean's hands busied with unbuttoning Kendal's shirt. They were an arresting sight, and Andrew's hands itched to join, but it seemed they were in a teasing mood.

When he exposed Kendal's chest, the itch grew stronger. Kean drew the shirt down Kendal's arms and flung it to the floor, his hands returning to skim across Kendal's pale, slender body. His fingers slid around the edge of Kendal's trousers but didn't go any further.

"Kean," Andrew said. "Undo their trousers."

Kean's gaze met his, and he smirked. "Yes, Sir."

Andrew's blood heated, and he stepped closer. Kean's fingers deftly unfastened Kendal's trousers, sliding them down their legs to pool at their feet and leaving them in their briefs. Their *tight* briefs left little to anyone's imagination.

"Gorgeous," he murmured, his cock lengthening behind his zip. "Kendal, be a dear and return the favour."

Kendal opened their eyes, and Andrew barely kept himself in check. Kendal's pupils were blown wide, and their lips bruised from being bitten. But Kendal nodded, kicked their shoes and trousers away and turned to Kean. With every inch of skin exposed on Kean's body, Kendal followed it with a kiss. Soon, Kean's shirt joined Kendal's clothes, and Kendal unfastened his trousers. Kean's boxers barely contained his erection, and Andrew licked his lips.

When they were both left in their underwear, Andrew moved closer, skimming his hands over their backs and arms, enjoying the warmth of their skin.

"Now me," he told them.

Neither hesitated. Kendal reached for the buttons on his shirt, and Kean dropped to his knees to unfasten his trousers. It was a heady experience and one he would never forget. Even if they didn't plan on consummating their relationship at that moment, he remembered how it felt to be happy with his partner, or in this case, partners. Kendal's hands smoothed across Andrew's chest and up his shoulders to push the fabric away. It bunched at his wrists, and Kendal took one wrist, then the other, and unfastened the cufflinks. Kean tapped each of his calves for him to lift his foot so he could remove Andrew's shoes and trousers.

Once they were in similar states of undress, Andrew slid his arms around them, drawing them close again.

"Let's get some rest," he murmured, leading them over to the bed.

He let go of them to pull the covers back, waving at Kendal to climb in, then Kean. Andrew tucked them in and rounded the bed before climbing in on the other side of Kendal. He lay on his back, and Kendal snuggled against his chest, with Kean tucking himself at Kendal's back and reaching an arm across to rest on Andrew's stomach. Andrew slid his arm around them both—which wasn't as easy as he thought it might be—and exhaled.

"Sleep," he commanded. Kendal relaxed almost immediately, but Kean stared at Andrew. "What's the matter?" Andrew whispered.

Kean gave a small smile. "I can't believe we're here," he whispered back. Andrew frowned in question, and Kean continued. "After you left us at the club, we'd decided to make a go of it as a couple, but we'd kept hoping and fighting to become a triad with you. We never believed you'd agree to it."

Andrew sighed, and Kendal snuffled and snuggled closer. He paused before saying, "I will be honest with you. I don't know if you'll be happy with what I can give you, but I will do my best, to be honest with you at all times. It's not as easy as saying, 'yes,' and that's it. I wish it was. But I won't go back on my word."

"We won't let you," Kendal murmured, nuzzling Andrew's chest. "Too comfy now."

Andrew chuckled and pressed a kiss to Kendal's hair. "Sleep, precious." He rubbed Kean's back. "Sleep, sweetheart."

Kean closed his eyes, and Andrew felt their bodies relax in slumber. He stayed fully awake and alert while they slept, not wanting to miss a moment of this first taste of what they could be together.

"Remember what I told you, Andrew." Louisa's voice sounded

in his head, and he returned to the conversation they'd had several months before her death. The conversation he never wanted to have. *"When I'm no longer with you, you need to allow some people access to your heart. You can't spend the rest of your time alone. You're not built that way. And if you find someone, don't shut them out with excuses. People will surprise you if you let them. In a good way. Allow those close to you to help. And for the love of god, let them love you."*

Andrew swallowed hard, blinking back the tears. At the time, he had thought she meant for him to sleep with several people, but had she meant for him to have two people in his life? Using "them" hadn't registered as strange at the time, but now, when he thought about their conversations, she had mentioned Kean and Kendal many times during the months before her death. Had she seen something he hadn't? It wouldn't have surprised him in the least. He swore, even now, that she was psychic. Having predicted too many of their families' relationships before they happened, she had been on a winning streak. Even with the prediction for him, though he hadn't wanted to acknowledge it before now. He focused on the words he'd read so many times he could recite word for word.

Andrew, my love,

I'm sorry I'm not there to see you to the end, but you know me. I'm happy to look over you and our family from wherever I am now.

Never doubt my love for you. I've always told you I felt honoured that you had chosen me when you had the entire population to choose from, and I still feel that way. Your love has meant everything to me, and I will cherish it always. But you need to live now. You need to go on, conquer the world and continue to show them who you are. Don't be afraid of conflict because there will be.

As for love…your heart is too big for one person, Andrew. I know you're scared but have faith. You'll find those people to stand by your side, and once you allow them in, live and love. I know you will put your love to good use.

But don't forget to communicate. I still swear it's the only reason we stayed married for so long.

You might not see what's coming, but I do, and I promise you, I'm happy because you're happy. Reach for your sons when you need to remember, then reach for those standing beside you, holding your hands.

With strength, stand before the world.

All my love.
Louisa. x

The meaning of the words seemed to have changed as his circumstances had. Before, he assumed she meant his heart was too big for *him*, but now, he realised she meant he had space for more than one person. And as for "reaching for those standing beside you, holding your hands," he had thought she was talking about the rest of the family. However, as good as she was at seeing deeper into things, he believed she'd seen Kean and Kendal coming a mile away. Naturally, he couldn't ask her to explain, but one day, when his time was up, he'd ask, and maybe she'd tell him.

A knock sounded on the outer door of his suite, and he glanced towards the open bedroom door—having forgotten to close it—but didn't answer, not wanting to wake Kean and Kendal. If it was anyone but his security guards or Randall, they wouldn't enter without him needing to answer. And though he didn't want them to find him in such a position, it would stop the need for explanations.

The outer door opened. "Your Majesty?" Randall called.

The suite door closed again, and Andrew heard footsteps

coming closer. Andrew glanced at his companions, making sure they were covered, and stared at the doorway where Randall would appear.

"Oh! I'm sorry, Your Majesty," Randall whispered, averting his gaze. "I'll come back later."

"Is it urgent, Randall?"

Randall hesitated but shook his head. "I just need you to go over the statement about last night, Your Majesty. It can wait."

"Leave it on the table, and I will check it as soon as they wake."

"Yes, Your Majesty." Randall turned away, then paused. "Forgive me for speaking out of turn, but I'm happy for you." Randall smiled at him, pulled the door closed and wandered off.

With the door shut, he couldn't hear the outer door close, but he knew Randall would mention it to the guards for them to not be disturbed. Andrew would get to explanations for those who needed to know as soon as he could, but right now, he wanted to luxuriate in the sensation of having his partners beside him.

Their journey wouldn't be easy. Secrets had a habit of becoming public knowledge, and Andrew had to make peace with that because he didn't think he could let them go now. Requesting them to keep things quiet had been the only way his heart had considered making them part of his life, but he knew all it would take was for the wrong person to see or hear something, and they were found out. He'd need to work on accepting that they would be in danger no matter what before their secret got out.

There were plenty of things that needed to change now Kean and Kendal were in his life. Security guards for each of them were the second port of call, though how he could get away with it, he wasn't sure. It was something he could speak to Brett about—after he'd chewed him out for bringing them to the hospital.

His priority was speaking with his sons. He wasn't sure what he'd do if they didn't accept his choices.

12

———————

KEAN

hen Kean woke, he was still wrapped around both people in the bed. It was as if he hadn't wanted to move too far away from them. Which was true.

He rolled to his back, stretching and yawning, then turned to face them. Andrew stared at him, a small smile on his face. "What?" he murmured.

"Nothing. You look more rested," Andrew whispered.

"You don't have to whisper. I'm awake," Kendal mumbled, rubbing their cheek on Andrew's chest.

"Are you feeling better, precious?" Andrew pressed a kiss to Kendal's head, and Kean smiled at the affection he easily gave.

"Much. How long did I sleep?"

Kean chuckled. "It depends on how long you laid there listening to us."

Kendal aimed an elbow back towards him but missed. "Not long. Why? Would I have heard trade secrets?"

It was Andrew's turn to laugh. "You were both tired. You slept for two hours."

Kendal lifted their head. "Two hours? Jeez. I won't sleep tonight if I'm not careful." They pushed to sit upright and yawned, making Kean yawn again.

"Stop it!" Kean complained after another round of yawning.

"What are your plans for the rest of the day?" Andrew asked, moving around to face them both.

"I don't work today, so I had no plans except to read. But that can change," Kendal said. They looked at Kean.

"Nothing, except for a dinner to attend tomorrow evening." He pulled a face. "My father's request."

Andrew opened his mouth to say something but shook his head instead. "I'd love for you to spend the day here. I'd like to speak with the boys and let them know what's going on if that's okay with you both?"

Should he tell him they most likely already know? Probably. Would he? No. He'd let Andrew find out for himself how astute his kids were.

"Fine by me," Kean said.

Kendal frowned at him but agreed as well. "Do you want us to be there?"

"I think it would be the best idea. They need to know where we stand."

"And where's that?" Kean asked. He wasn't trying to trip Andrew up, but he needed the reassurance that he was all in.

"Together. We stand together," Andrew replied, staring straight at him and helping him to understand he meant what he said.

Kean flushed and ducked his head. "Thanks."

Andrew leaned forward and reached for Kean. "No thanks necessary." Andrew cupped Kean's nape and joined their lips in a soft but sensual kiss that sent Kean's brain swirling. Then Andrew let go and reached for Kendal, who eagerly slid their arms around Andrew's neck as they kissed. Kean knelt behind them, kissing down their spine, and Kendal groaned into Andrew's mouth.

Andrew's arms slid around Kendal's back, pausing when he felt Kean, and continued around Kean's back instead, holding them together as three. Kean kissed up Kendal's neck to their ear and sucked on their lobe. Kean's cock hardened at the sounds Kendal and Andrew made as they kissed. He wanted more, but he knew Andrew wanted to wait. That didn't mean they couldn't give him a show, though.

Kean slipped his hand between Kendal and Andrew and cupped Kendal's cock. It hardened in his hand, and he gently stroked it. His knuckles bumped against Andrew's stomach each time. No way could he not tell what was happening. Andrew's hand lowered to Kean's ass, squeezing and pulling him against Kendal's back, his shaft nestling between Kendal's cheeks.

Kendal pulled his mouth away, leaning his head back on Kean's shoulder as Kean continued to stroke.

"More," Kendal breathed.

Kean slipped his hand inside Kendal's briefs, though there wasn't much room to move with how tight they were. Andrew's hands left Kean's back and slid into the back of Kendal's briefs, nudging Kean's cock in the process. Andrew tugged the briefs down over Kendal's cheeks and their dick, freeing it and Kean's hand for them all to look at.

"Beautiful," Andrew said.

Kean encircled Kendal's shaft properly, stroking up and down. Kendal bucked their hips.

"Please!" Kendal asked.

Andrew plucked at Kendal's nipples, and Kean rubbed his groin against Kendal's ass. It wouldn't take him long with how hot the scene was. "Are you close, Kendal?" he murmured in their ear.

"Yes!" They trembled a full-body shiver and gasped.

Andrew lifted Kendal's hand and kissed their palm. "Later," he said, though Kean wasn't sure why.

"Come on, Kendal," Kean whispered, biting their earlobe. "Come for your king."

"Oh, fuck!" Kendal tensed and exploded, covering Kean's hand but also marking Andrew's chest.

The streaks of white were enough to send Kean over the edge, and he gripped Kendal's hip as he came in his boxers while staring into Andrew's eyes.

"Fuck me," he breathed, resting his forehead on Kendal's shoulder.

"Andrew can. I'm too tired," Kendal murmured.

Andrew slid his arms around them both and lowered them to the bed. He left for a few seconds and returned with a cloth, wiping Kendal clean.

"Do you need attending to?" he asked Kean.

Kean flushed. "I think my boxers caught most of it." He leaned away from Kendal and raised his eyebrows. "Or maybe not."

He reached for the cloth, but Andrew evaded him, leaning between them to clean Kendal's lower back and Kean's stomach. Andrew removed Kean's boxers and cleaned his groin, too.

"What about you?" Kean asked, gesturing to Andrew's hard cock.

"Later." He kissed Kean. "You definitely won't be wearing those when we visit my children," Andrew murmured, throwing the underwear into a washing basket as he went past. He opened a drawer and pulled out a pair of boxers. "Try these. They might be too big for you, though."

Andrew gathered their clothes and deposited them on the bed, handing them out to their owners. He helped them dress until they were fully clothed. Once more, he dragged them into his arms and held them, Kean and Kendal resting their heads on his shoulder and chest, respectively.

"Thank you for that. It will give me something to look forward to later," Andrew said. He exhaled. "I have one thing I need to read through before we find where my children are."

"I can message them and find out," Kean said.

"Thank you."

Andrew kissed them both and led the way back into the main room. He grabbed a piece of paper from the table and settled into a chair to read. Kean glanced at Kendal. They had a small smile in place, but they wrung their hands. Kean covered their hands and squeezed.

"Do you want a drink?"

"Tea, please."

Kean shuddered. "You two are evil incarnate." He grinned and started on the drinks. Two teas and a coffee later, he took them over to Andrew and Kendal.

"Thank you," Andrew said. "Randall dropped this off earlier. It's the statement about what happened last night." He held it out to Kendal. "What do you think?"

Kean settled beside Kendal and read it over their shoulder. It was short and to the point, but it mentioned nothing much, either.

"Don't you want to call them out?"

Andrew frowned. "Who?"

"Charlotte, John, everyone?" Kean said.

"We don't have proof at the moment."

Kean sighed and sipped his drink. The whole situation was a shitshow, and he hated it.

"I know, Kean," Andrew said. "But I have to play by the rules because they aren't. Hear me on this, though. If I get proof it was them, *everyone* will know about it. I promise you. This will stop."

Kean nodded, but it didn't stop him from worrying. Not about himself. About Andrew and Freddie and everyone else. Which reminded him to send the message.

KEAN: Where are you all?

Seconds later, a message came back.

FREDDIE: Douglas is at his apartment with Mav, George is at Windsor with Timothy and Eddie, and I'm at home with Damon. Why?

KEAN: Your father wants to see you all.

FREDDIE: Okay. Tell him to give us half an hour.

KEAN: Will do.

"Everyone will be here in half an hour or so," he told Andrew.

"Great, thanks. It gives us time to have another quick chat." Andrew faced them. "I would like you both to review the videos of the club. We need someone who would know who's who and who might be causing trouble. You both have knowledge of the club but don't socialise much with the people there. I think you'd be perfect, but I understand if you don't want to."

"I'd be happy to," Kean said. "It would have to be around my studies, though."

"That's no problem. We have time."

"Same for me, although mine is work, not studies."

"Thank you. We need to figure out what Charles was doing to recruit all these people, and we know he was using the club to do it."

"He always appeared chummy with everyone. Maybe that was why he was so...believable? Approachable? I'm not sure of the right word, but I know many people had good things to say about him for the most part," Kendal said.

"He did have a certain charm," Andrew said. "I'm sure he's using his skills now to make his life in prison easier for him."

"Is Charlotte still campaigning to get him out?" Kean asked.

Andrew frowned. "Do you know, I'm not sure. I haven't heard anything recently about it. I'll have to call Brady and find out."

"How are you doing?" Kendal asked Andrew. "You've had a lot of changes and upset these past two days. How are you managing?"

Andrew sighed, and he rubbed a hand over his beard. "I've been better. But you're making it easier. I need to contact my guards' families to give my condolences. I know they came into the job understanding the risks, but it still hurts when their lives are taken because of their job. Because of me."

"I don't think they'd see it that way at all," Kean said. "I know Simon wouldn't." He withheld the flinch from using the name so seldomly spoken now. "He would be content to know he saved your life."

"I just wish this life didn't come with so many risks. My fear for you will never go away, but I'll try to keep it restrained," Andrew said.

"Make sure you tell us, though," Kendal said. "I want to know when you're finding it hard. We might be able to help ease the burden."

"I'll try."

"That reminds me. What did you decide to do about the law? You know, the one your father tried to pass before he died." Kean had originally advised Andrew to keep it as it was to stop Charlotte from getting the throne, but now they know John was the intended recipient, it would be better to get it passed as soon as possible.

"I have someone quietly drawing up the necessary paperwork. A loophole we found was that we don't have to put it up for a vote again because it was already signed and sealed, ready to go. We can pass the law without making any fanfare about it."

"And god forbid it happening, but if they got their hands dirty, John wouldn't get it, Charlotte would," Kean said, nodding. "But they wouldn't know until too late."

"Exactly."

A knock sounded.

"Come in!" Andrew called.

George entered, his huge smile lighting up the already bright room. Andrew stood, embracing his son.

"Where are Timothy and Eddie?"

"I wasn't sure if the invite was for them, too."

"Of course it is. They're family."

"I'll message them." George sped off a message and shoved his phone back in his pocket. "They're coming."

"Have you decided on when you want your commitment ceremony?" Andrew asked while they waited for the rest of the family to arrive.

"We've been talking about it, but with Henry's and Freddie's weddings coming up, we don't want to overwork everyone."

"Don't be silly. Whenever you want to have it, it's yours. Just let me know so I can get Randall some extra help." Andrew winked.

"I think Eddie likes the idea of a winter wonderland. We'll see."

Another knock sounded. "Come in!"

Timothy and Eddie entered, followed by Freddie and Damon.

"Douglas and Mav are on their way," Freddie said, settling into a seat while Damon dropped to the floor at his feet.

If it had been anyone else, someone would've mentioned getting another chair for him, but Damon loved sitting at Freddie's feet.

"Any more information on Kletti Pazo?" Andrew asked.

Damon shook his head. "We've been searching for the name and any company or person related to it, but nothing has been flagged yet. Unless they change their name, there is no way they can use the company again."

"Any more prisons found?"

Kean shivered, and Kendal leaned against his side. Kean smiled at them in thanks. "Nothing yet, but I can almost guarantee it won't be the only one."

Andrew sighed. "I'll make calls to get access to those houses who wouldn't let you in, Damon. I should've done it before now, but with everything that happened..."

"You're not superhuman, Andrew," Kendal said, resting their hand on Andrew's forearm.

Douglas and Mav entered shortly after, and Kean found himself getting nervous, even though he thought he knew how the conversation would go.

"So, what's up, Dad?" George said, impersonating the cartoon rabbit he had recently become obsessed with.

Andrew sat forward, leaning his elbows on his knees and linking his fingers. "I have some news."

Kean eyed Freddie, who couldn't keep the grin off his face.

"Kean, Kendal and I have decided to give a relationship a try."

"Fuck, yeah!" Douglas shouted, fist-pumping the air.

"Go, you!" George said.

Freddie winked. "I see you got your way, Kean."

"I'm determined when I want to be," he replied with a laugh.

"Hey!" Kendal said, elbowing him.

"Sorry. *We're* determined when we want to be." He slipped his arm around Kendal's back.

"Before you go announcing it to the world," Andrew said. "We're keeping it quiet for now. I don't want more targets on their backs than are already there. If they're known as being my partners, all hell will break loose."

"I think you'd be surprised at the reaction, Father," Freddie said. "Since our announcement, things have calmed down drastically."

"I am probably overthinking things, but my heart can't take much more," Andrew admitted quietly.

Kendal slid their arm through Andrew's and rested their head on his shoulder. "We've already said we'll do whatever it takes to make things easier on him. He has enough weight on his shoulders without this as well."

"And what if it's taken out of your hands?" Douglas asked. "The media are hellhounds."

"Then we deal with it at that time. Let's not borrow trouble," Kean said.

"As much as this news deserves a celebration, I don't feel right doing it now. Not with the results of last night's circus," Andrew said. "We will celebrate, though. Just not right now."

"We don't need it, Andrew," Kendal said. "We just need you."

"Same here," Kean agreed.

"I want to celebrate us," Andrew said. "And we will." He paused. "I just remembered… Last night, Ernest said that I always took the easy route. I still haven't figured out what he meant by that. What part of this life has an easy route?"

Freddie frowned. "Any other context to go with that?"

Andrew shook his head. "It came out of the blue. He was angry, though. There must be more to his story."

"Did Ernest know Charlotte or John before he became part of the family?" Timothy asked.

Andrew shook his head. "Not that I know of. Charlotte barely mentioned him before bringing him home to announce their engagement, and John is eleven years younger than him. I doubt they would've met before he married Charlotte."

"There has to be something," Kean murmured. "Did Ernest purposefully marry into the family with a plan already in place, or did John approach him with a plan and get him on his side?"

"Or did Charlotte start the plan, and John go behind her back with his own plan?" Mav said.

"There are too many possibilities, and I don't like it," Andrew said.

And wasn't that the truth? They needed more information, but where could they get it from? Charles wouldn't speak out against his mother. Charlotte's other son, Albert, had defected but had given them all the information he had.

John's children were on his side, apart from Christian, who was on theirs, but he no longer had access to insider information.

"Has anyone spoken to Elizabeth's husband? Or Charles's wife?" Kean asked. "They can't be none too happy about what happened to their spouses. Would they talk?"

"It's a possibility. Especially Elizabeth's husband, Ian," Freddie said. "Let me talk to Christian about it."

"Okay. I think we need to continue with our plans as they were," Andrew said. "At least until we have more information about the shooting." He stood. "Which reminds me, I need to visit Brett. And take this back to Randall." He faced Kean and Kendal. "Think of this suite as yours. Come and go as you please. I'll inform the guards."

Kendal's face flushed as they smiled, and Kean nodded in thanks. Andrew leaned down and kissed them both, said goodbye to his family and left.

"Well, welcome to the family, stepdads," George joked.

13

KENDAL

Kendal choked on their drink at George's words. They weren't anywhere near being stepdads, and wasn't that a mind-bending thought? He and Kean were younger than Andrew's son but could potentially end up being their stepfathers. They pushed the thought aside, not wanting to dwell on such matters.

Despite the two-hour sleep they'd had, they were still a little tired, but they wanted to spend some time with their men. They saw the paper Andrew was supposed to take to Randall still on the table.

"Hey," they got Kean's attention. "Andrew forgot this for Randall. I'm going to take it to him."

"Do you want me to come with you?"

"No, it's okay. You stay and talk. I won't be long."

Kendal rose, taking the sheet of paper, and exited the suite. They were only a few steps down the hallway when someone called their name. They turned to see Eddie rushing up to them.

"Hey, I thought you might like some company," Eddie said.

Kendal smiled. "Thanks." They continued walking. "You probably know your way better than I do, anyway."

"Are we going to Randall's office or the security wing?" Eddie asked, stepping in beside them.

"Um, the security wing, maybe. I don't know if Andrew needs to do anything with this before giving it to Randall, so I need to ask him."

"Okay, this way then."

Eddie slipped his arm through Kendal's and veered them towards an area of Windsor Kendal had never been in before. After all, he'd only been there as a visitor before, and they'd stayed within the rooms allocated to them, mainly the receiving room.

"How are you?" Eddie asked. "I mean, really. I know it can be a lot to take on a royal partner, but you've gone right to the top." Eddie flushed and lowered his head. "Not that I think you shouldn't. Sorry."

Kendal chuckled. "Eddie, it's fine. I know what you mean. I don't think I really understand what I'm getting myself into, but it won't stop me from jumping in with both feet. I've had so much taken from me; I won't let anyone take Andrew unless there is no other option." Kendal sighed. "I honestly believe I've been waiting for him to be ready. And for Kean. We've all been through so much. I think it's time we tried to heal each other."

"I understand that completely. After what T...happened to me, I didn't think I would be able to trust anyone, which was why I approached George in the first place. I'd heard many things about how he'd been so kind and generous that I thought if I could trust anyone, it would be him." Eddie chuckled. "And I ended up living a fairy tale."

"As opposed to Talon," Kendal said. Eddie jerked, and Kendal apologised. "I try to say his name because I don't want it to have a hold over me any longer. Every time I say it, it makes it easier to say it the next time. But not everyone is the same as me."

Eddie sighed. "No, you're right. I should say his name. After all, what he did to you was ten times worse than what he did to me."

Kendal pulled them to a stop. "It doesn't matter whose injuries were worse, Eddie. What matters is that we're survivors. Talon didn't break us. He made us stronger. My therapist has helped me to realise that, even if I had the option to go back and change my past, I wouldn't because I wouldn't be the person I am today if I did."

"Timothy is helping me with that. It's getting a lot better."

Kendal cupped Eddie's cheek. "I'm glad. He shouldn't have any more of a hold over us now. He doesn't deserve it."

Eddie smiled, and they continued on their way. "So, a triad, eh? Just like me. Didn't see that coming, I must admit."

Kendal laughed, throwing their head back and letting the joy ring through. "I have to admit to never believing it would happen. I knew I had feelings for them both, but I saw how Kean looked at Andrew and thought it would be a good idea to help them get together." Kendal snorted. "Instead, I took a chance and laid my heart bare to them. Didn't work out very well, to begin with."

"What? Why?"

"Andrew was concerned about everything that's happening and didn't want us in the crosshairs. He admitted his feelings, but he refused to start a relationship."

"You obviously changed his mind."

"Only after last night. When we went to the hospital, we gave him no choice."

"And I'm glad for it," a voice said from behind them.

Kendal whirled around, gasping, a hand over their chest. "You scared me!"

Andrew chuckled and slid an arm around their shoulders. "Sorry. I should've announced myself better." He pressed his lips to Kendal's temple. "Where are you off to?"

"I was looking for you, actually." They held out the piece of paper. "You said you needed to take this to Randall, but you left it behind."

Andrew took it. "Thank you, precious. I appreciate it. I would've ended up in Randall's office with nothing to give him." He glanced at Eddie. "Eddie, would you do me a favour, please?"

"Of course."

"Could you head back to everyone and ask them to join us for dinner this evening? Say, six o'clock. And I mean, everyone, if they can make it."

"No problem." Eddie smiled, then waved at Kendal. "Don't be a stranger." He skipped off down the hallway, chatting to the bodyguard beside him.

"I'm glad you have someone to talk to," Andrew said, steering them down the same hallway Eddie had just traversed.

"He's great. They all are. You've created some amazing men, Your Majesty."

Andrew chuckled. "I can't take all the credit. I was heading in the direction of my father a few years back. Louisa sat me down and made me see what I was becoming before it went too far." He sighed. "I could've lost Douglas if I'd kept going."

"Why?"

"Because I told him he couldn't have a relationship with Mav. Because Mav was someone we employed. It wouldn't look good." He shook his head. "Now, whenever I think about the conversation I had with him, I see everything my father had said to me. And I never wanted to become him."

"I'm glad Louisa was able to rein you in," Kendal said with a smile. "My statement stands, though. It wasn't just Louisa who brought up your kids. It was you, too."

"Maybe."

"Now, you're just placating me."

"Maybe," Andrew said with a chuckle. "Here we are."

He opened the door and entered, pulling Kendal behind him.

"Your Majesty," Randall said, bowing his head and standing.

Andrew glanced at Kendal. "See what I mean. No one calls me Andrew."

Randall spluttered. "I can't do that!"

"I've been telling him for years, but he won't lose the title. Same as Clarice at the club." Andrew tutted and held out the paper, his smile peeking through. "Here's the statement. It looks great. I've only changed a couple of small bits."

"Thank you, Your Majesty. I'll get this sent out to the media straight away."

"Perfect." Andrew peered at Kendal. "I usually like to make a speech when things like this happen, but I've decided not to this time."

"Why not?"

Andrew nodded at Randall and led Kendal over to an ornate door, opening it and pulling Kendal through. "Randall, feel free to tell anyone who asks where we are. I'm just showing Kendal my office."

"Of course, Your Majesty."

Andrew closed the door and waved his hand around the large room. "Welcome to my job."

Kendal hadn't been inside his office before. Whenever they'd been there, it had always been the receiving room, but this was pure Andrew. The dark wood furniture stood out against the paler wall colour. The desk stood before a large window overlooking the gardens, and several chairs and sofas waited before the desk. Kendal trailed their finger along the edge of the desk and looked at the little trinkets waiting for their owner.

"I can see you working in here. It's you all over," they said.

Andrew chuckled. "It's not perfect by any means because it still has my father's stamp on areas of it, but I can stay here for hours and not be annoyed by anything." He pointed to the sofa. "Many people complain about my sofas, though."

Kendal frowned. "Why?"

"Because I've made them purposefully uncomfortable. As I tell anyone who asks, if the furniture is comfortable, it'll make people want to stay longer. I'm a busy man. I can't chitchat all day."

Kendal laughed and stepped closer to Andrew, drawn by his cheerful demeanour. They slid their arms around Andrew's waist. "Didn't you chitchat with Brett?"

Andrew raised his eyebrows. "No, I told him off for allowing you to come to the hospital."

Kendal slapped his biceps. "Why did you do that? It wasn't his fault."

"He should've kept you safe here. Not gallivanting to my side." Andrew frowned. "What do you mean it wasn't his fault?"

"Brett denied us several times before Freddie put his foot

down and told Brett that we were coming. Brett couldn't deny an order from Freddie."

Andrew stared at him, eyes wide. "He never said a word. He just let me rant at him."

Kendal smoothed their hands over his chest, soothing him. "From what I can tell of Brett, he's a man who would admit his failings without issue, but he would also take the brunt of something to save someone else."

"So true." Andrew sighed. "I have to apologise now."

"Maybe give him some time off."

"What do you mean?"

Kendal stared up at him. "He's tired, Andrew. You just need to look at him to see that. He has a lot on his shoulders, just like you do. And he's working hard to keep you all safe. Does he have a partner? Does he have a family? What does he do on his days off?"

Andrew studied them, then abruptly covered their mouth with his own. Just as quickly, he was gone. "You're amazing. I often forget that the people who work for me are people. And I shouldn't. I try my hardest to remember, but security is twenty-four-seven for me. I forget that the same people shouldn't be here all the time."

"You're human, Andrew. But I have a feeling Brett isn't telling you how much he's working."

"He's probably been working overtime. Hold on." Andrew let go of Kendal and headed to his desk. He picked up the phone and made a call. "Kieren, I need a straight answer from you now. How much overtime has Brett been doing?" He listened for a moment. "I know all that, Kieren. Answer me." Andrew sighed. "Is it just him?" Andrew stared at the floor as he listened. "Thank you. I'll see you later."

Kendal stepped closer as Andrew leaned heavily against the desk. "What did he say?"

"Brett has been working almost non-stop for weeks. You were right." Andrew lifted the phone again. "Felix, I need your help. Meet me at the security room." He stood. "Let's go."

"Where?" Kendal asked, following Andrew.

"Back to Brett."

Kendal stayed beside Andrew as they retraced their earlier steps, coming to a stop in front of a door. Andrew knocked and waited for the door to open.

"Your Majesty," Brett said, eyes bloodshot and hair sticking up. "What can I help you with?"

They stepped inside, and Kendal watched Brett shuffle some papers on the desk he'd obviously been sitting at before they'd arrived.

"You didn't tell me you were given a direct order," Andrew said.

Brett paused and glanced up, flicking his gaze to Kendal and then back to Andrew. "It wasn't relevant."

"Yes, it was. You let me rant at you when it wasn't your fault. Why?"

"Because I shouldn't have allowed it. I should've argued."

Andrew scoffed. "You're not allowed to argue with a direct order."

There was a knock, and Felix stepped inside. "Your Majesty."

Andrew faced Felix. "Remember the time when Brett helped you after the incident with Oscar?" Felix swallowed and nodded. "I'm asking you to return the favour." Andrew pointed at Brett. "Take him home and make him sleep. I don't want to see either of you for at least a week."

"I don't need—"

"Yes, you do. I've checked up on you, Brett. You've worked more hours than you should have for too long. It's time to rest. I need you at your best for when I decide on our next plan of action. I'm sorry I didn't see it before."

"I'm perfectly capa—"

Andrew stepped closer. "You're choosing now to argue?"

Brett opened his mouth, then snapped it shut. "No, sir."

"Good. Felix, I'm leaving him in your hands."

"Yes, sir."

Kendal watched the interaction with some fascination because they'd heard the rumours from the Thirsty Thirteen about Brett and Felix but had never seen them together, apart from officially. Now, though, Brett's shoulders slumped, and Felix's cheeks reddened, and neither could look at the other. Was that because they didn't like each other, or was it for the complete opposite reason? Whichever reason it was, this next week would either make or break them. And as much as it made them a bad person, Kendal couldn't wait to see which it was.

Andrew opened the door for Kendal to pass through, then led the way through the hallways.

"They might kill each other by the end of the week," Andrew said.

Kendal laughed. "They might. Or they might find the one thing they're missing in their lives."

Andrew glanced at them, rubbing a hand over his beard. "Why would you say that?"

"Just some gossip."

"Hmm."

When they arrived back at Andrew's suite, everyone except for Kean had disappeared. With the door closed, Andrew leaned down and kissed Kean, where he sat on the sofa, and then kissed Kendal, too.

"We have an observant partner, Kean."

Kean's eyes twinkled at Kendal and refocused on Andrew. "We do?"

"Yes. They made me see the error of my ways. And what's this gossip about Brett and Felix?"

Kendal laughed and made some drinks while Andrew and Kean chatted, carrying them over when they were done. As soon as they'd put the drinks on the table, they were grabbed by the hips and deposited onto Andrew's lap, laughing. Kean pulled Kendal's legs over his lap.

"What's all this, then?" they said.

"I want to hold you both for a little while longer. Then we can take a shower and head for dinner with everyone."

Kendal settled their head beneath Andrew's chin and reached a hand for Kean. When they threaded their fingers together, they were all touching each other, and Kendal loved it. They weren't sure how long they stayed that way, but their tea was cold when they finally got up. Kean offered to make another one, but Kendal shook their head.

"Let's shower," Kendal said.

Andrew led the way to the bathroom. It was a huge cream and gold room that had an entire back wall of tiles with several showerheads overhead and a huge bath. It looked divine.

"I think if we ever want to share a bath, I might need to get a new one made." Andrew chuckled.

Kean did, too. "Yes, the three of us wouldn't fit in there."

"Shall we?" Andrew said.

Kendal wasted no time in divesting themselves of their clothes, and Andrew showed them how to work the shower. When rainfall fell around them, they laughed.

"Oh, my god. This is the best shower in the world."

They rubbed their hands through their hair, soaking it completely. Hands slid around their waist, and they leaned back against a warm body. Kean kissed their shoulder, running their hands over their body. Andrew stepped in front of them, and Kendal slid their hands up his chest, feeling the slight smattering of hair.

Andrew reached for the soap, running it over Kendal's body. Kendal returned the favour, then spun around to do the same for Kean. Kean's body was leaner than Andrew's but no less strong. Kendal didn't feel an ounce of fear despite what they knew Andrew and Kean could do with their strength if they wanted to. They knew neither of them would touch them without their consent, and that, more than anything else, made Kendal happy to give up their control.

When they were clean, Kendal dropped to their knees in front of them both, closing their eyes and lifting their chin. They reached for the two cocks they wanted so desperately, encircling them with their hands, all the while keeping their eyes closed to stop the water from blinding them.

They licked over the head of one, then the other, repeating the action several times, then brought them closer together and thrummed over the sensitive nerves of both at the same time. The volley of moans and groans and curses echoed around the room, and it made Kendal more eager to make them lose it. Despite their size, Kendal slid both cock heads into their mouth, not trying to suck them down to their throat but wanting to feel what it was like to have both inside them at once.

"Fuck, Kendal," Kean groaned, sliding his fingers into their wet hair.

Kendal used their hands to stroke them as their tongue danced across the heads. They pulled free. "Will you come in my mouth, Sirs?"

Andrew hummed and cupped Kendal's jaw. "Remove your hands and open wide, precious."

Kendal did as they were told, and the water stopped. They opened their eyes to see Andrew and Kean stroking their cocks as they stared down at them. Kendal let the thrill of being wanted flow through them.

"Ready?" Kean growled. Kendal stuck their tongue out, catching the underside of Kean's cock. "Fuck!"

Heat and a salty taste hit their tongue, but they didn't swallow it, waiting until Kean had unloaded fully before moving to Andrew's shaft. They wanted to swallow, but they wanted both loads at the same time. To share the taste.

"Bloody hell, Kendal. You're fucking beautiful," Andrew groaned, and his abdomen tightened.

More heat exploded onto Kendal's tongue, chin and cheek. They watched until Andrew stopped stroking, then took their tongue back into their mouth and swallowed. They closed their eyes and hummed in delight. There was nothing better than tasting the people who meant something to them. No greater gift.

"Thank you," they said once they were done.

"You say that like you mean it," Kean said.

Kendal smiled. "I do. I'll take that any time of day or night."

"Damn right you will," Andrew growled.

14

ANDREW

ndrew sat Kean and Kendal on either side of him at dinner, feeling a little bad for pushing Freddie further down the table, but it couldn't be helped. Due to the number of guests they'd invited, they'd used the largest dining room, and Andrew could admit to himself that he was nervous about their announcement. William gave him a knowing smile and nodded when he saw him, and Andrew would've clipped his head if he was close enough.

When everyone had sat and received their drink, Andrew stood.

"Thank you for coming. I'm not standing here for hours with a speech because you don't need that. I do have some news for you." He glanced at Kean and Kendal. "I would like you to know that Kean, Kendal and I have decided to start a relationship." He paused as a round of cheers went up, smiling when Kendal's cheeks darkened. "Thank you. For the moment, you are the only people who we're telling. I...have concerns about painting targets on their backs, so they have agreed to keep the relationship quiet for now. It's not ideal, but until we figure out what's going on, I think it's the best option. So, even though you already know them, please welcome Kean and Kendal to the family."

"Woohoo! Another triad in the mix," George shouted.

Andrew chuckled and sat down, covering Kean's and Kendal's hands and squeezing them. "Sorry for embarrassing you."

"It's fine. I have to get used to it," Kendal said, wiping under their eyes.

Andrew let go of their hands when the servers came in to deliver the food, thanking them before they disappeared again. They spent an enjoyable hour eating and drinking, and then they moved everything into the receiving room, which had become a lot more comfortable since his sons had taken over it as their en-mass social room.

"I'm so glad for you, Andrew," Victoria said, leaning in to hug him. "I wasn't sure if you'd take the step or not, to be honest."

"Neither was I. They took it out of my hands." Andrew snorted, glancing at Kean and Kendal as they chatted with their friends.

"I'm glad for it, then. They are the perfect complement to you. Just like Louisa was."

Andrew's heart skipped a beat, but he smiled. "I feel unworthy of being so lucky."

Victoria waved her hand. "Pfft. You're the most worthy man I know. Except for my husband." She smiled. "But I may be biased."

"I hate that I'm bringing them into this when everything is so...fragile."

"Stop borrowing trouble, Andrew. Let them stand by your side and support you through this upheaval."

"I'll try." A hand landed heavily on his shoulder.

"You will because, otherwise, they'll give you hell about it," William said.

Andrew chuckled. "You know them well already."

"How are things?" William asked.

"Unsteady, as always at the moment." Andrew glanced around him.

"Life in general, then."

That startled a laugh out of him. "True."

"Enjoy the evening, Andrew. Stop trying to be everything for everyone, and stop trying to shelter others from the truth," Victoria said. "Let others help you shoulder the burden."

Kendal slipped their hand into Andrew's. "Sorry for interrupting, but she's right, Andrew. Let us help."

"I'll do my best." And he would. Everything everyone said was true, but it wasn't easy to let more people in. He'd only ever needed Louisa, but now that she wasn't there, he'd been adrift. Like a boat without an anchor. He'd realised it, but he hadn't understood how much it was affecting him.

They spent the rest of the evening laughing and socialising, and Andrew couldn't remember such a good evening in the past year. The death of his wife had taken his joy, but she had given it back with her acceptance of who he was and what she believed was in store for him. One day, he might share her words with Kean and Kendal, but for now, he would keep it close to his heart.

It had been four days since he'd seen Kean and Kendal for more than a few minutes because of their jobs and the work they were doing reviewing the videos, but he had plenty of work to get done, including many, *many* meetings.

"Yes, I understand that," he said patiently, "but you need to realise that this won't help the people. You'll alienate them."

The Prime Minister straightened in his seat. "Maybe so, but it's for the good of the country. A short-term upset will allow us to thrive in the future."

Andrew sighed and shook his head. "You have my concerns, Alan. Do with them as you wish."

Alan Grey was a forty-eight-year-old man with a large family, who seemed to have the country's needs at the forefront of his mind when he initially became Prime Minister, but now he had changed his tune. Too many people and businesses were pressing down on him to line their pockets, and he was caving to the pressure. Unfortunately, Andrew couldn't do much about it. He only had a certain amount of weight with the government, even though he was the king.

After further conversation—of which nothing good came—Alan left, leaving Andrew's mood in the dungeon. He brightened considerably when Christian came through the door.

"You don't have to book an appointment to see me," Andrew said, giving his adopted son a hug.

"I know, but it's two-fold. I thought you could do with a break, and I have some news to share," Christian said, taking a seat on the opposite side of the desk.

"Personal or professional news?"

Christian chuckled. "Professional."

"Damn it." Andrew grinned. "Do you want a drink? And where's Oreo today?"

"No, thank you. He's with Oscar. Probably being spoilt rotten." Christian passed a folder over to him. "This is the information on the two households Damon could not get access to, Highgrove House and Clarence House. It appears staff turnover has been much higher than normal for those properties."

"Who saw to the hiring of new staff?"

Christian grimaced. "Charlotte."

Andrew sighed. "Should've guessed. Can we get hold of those staff who left and interview them?"

"Already working on it." Christian cleared his throat. "I've spoken with Commissioner Thomas today. They're collating information from the businesses that were involved with Kletti Pazo. From the summary he gave me, most of them seemed to have no idea who was behind it."

"And those who did?"

"Have had all their bank accounts frozen until a deeper investigation has taken place. They're also suspended from their jobs and unable to contact anyone related to it."

"That's something, at least."

"Commissioner Thomas asked for you to call him at your earliest convenience."

Andrew nodded. "Thank you. Has anything come up from the video footage yet?"

Christian shook his head. "Nothing so far. Kean, Kendal and Nina are going through the videos from before Charles was last recorded as being present."

"Before they arrested him the first time?"

"Yes. They're going to check the time afterwards as well, just in case Charles managed to get into the club without checking in, but not until they scoured the earlier times first."

Andrew rubbed a hand over his face. "When I asked them to do this job, it never occurred to me that I would hardly see them."

Christian chuckled. "That's the problem when we have to keep certain jobs within the family."

"How are you holding up?"

The news that John was part of the conspiracy to kill off members of the royal family hadn't surprised Christian in the least, but the knowledge that he was the head of the snake, or potentially the head of the snake, was a lot harder to swallow. He'd spent most of his time either with Oscar or working to find out everything he could to bring his estranged father down.

Christian sighed. "I've been worse. I feel like we're closing in on them, though. Especially after what happened to you."

"I'm hoping that is what Brady wants to talk to me about. There must be some news by now."

Christian stood. "I'll leave you to it. Make sure you rest. You've been working hard."

"Says the kettle to the pot, or the pot to the kettle. Whichever way round that saying goes."

"Just think of how bored we're going to be once this is all over." Christian hugged him and left.

"Bored is not what I think we'll be when the public and media focus on other things," Andrew murmured to the empty room.

He picked up the phone and dialled.

"Brady Thomas."

"Brady, it's Andrew. How are things?"

"Well, they could be better, but they could be worse, too. I'm trying not to jinx it."

Andrew leaned back in his chair, a small squeak accompanying his movements. "I can imagine. Christian said you wanted to talk to me."

Brady sighed. "Yes. We've got more information about the shooting."

Andrew tensed, bracing for news he didn't want to hear. "And?"

"The sniper wasn't one of yours. It was someone dressed the same as yours. They managed to sneak in when yours did, according to the CCTV footage we found. Although the team members knew how many they were supposed to have, they hadn't counted once they reached their positions, which was why he slipped through the net."

Andrew breathed a little easier. "I'm glad it wasn't one of mine. I don't think I could take another traitor in the mix."

"Your team did a good job tackling him. Unfortunately, they weren't quick enough at finding him."

"Who was it?"

"Jeremy Blatch. An ex-Army veteran who wasn't afraid to voice his opinions, especially when it came to the royal family. We're still looking into his finances, but he had no existing family ties, just a long history of family joining the Army, with him being the last in his line."

Andrew swung his chair around to stare out of the window. "What a way to end it."

"My thinking entirely."

"He had to have known where this could end. If he might die, what was the point of having money? Especially if he had no one to give it to."

Brady sighed. "I don't know. There could've been some martyr complex, maybe. Wanting to go down in history. I have no idea what he was thinking, Andrew."

"Well, at least we have some information. Thanks, Brady."

"I'm sorry it's not better news. We're still looking through his computer and online presence, so I might have more information for you soon."

"I'd love it if there was a large arrow pointing towards

John, Ernest or Charlotte. Something solid we can take them down with."

Brady snorted. "As much as it pains me to say, they're too clever for that."

"Unfortunately. We're getting there, though."

"Have you more from your end?"

Andrew spun back around to view the folder Christian had left with him. "Higher than usual staff turnover at Highgrove House and Clarence House, which was overseen by Charlotte. Christian is getting in contact with the previous staff to see if they heard or saw anything."

"They were the two properties Damon couldn't get into, right?"

"They were."

"Do you want me to get some plain-clothed police to search?"

Andrew considered the idea. "Yes, actually. I think it's about time we showed our hands. I'll let everyone know not to go near the places for now. Let me know when we get the all-clear."

"Will do. I'll get the team set up. It probably won't be until tomorrow or maybe the weekend, but I'll keep you up to date."

"Thanks, Brady."

"No problem. Let me know if anything else crops up."

Andrew ended the call and leaned back, his chair arguing again. He wished he could understand why his family felt the need to fight for the throne. If he didn't think it was a huge mistake letting them take over, he would've given it up in a heartbeat if it meant the rest of them would be safe. Now, he had added two more people to the list of targets, but he couldn't bring himself to stop.

A knock sounded, and Randall poked his head in. "Your next appointment is here, Your Majesty."

Andrew sighed and hid the folder in his desk drawer. "Send them in. Thank you, Randall."

The rest of his morning was not much better. Especially when he messaged Kean to ask him to join him and Kendal for dinner, and Kean replied he had to have dinner with his parents and their business partners, but he very much wished he could. Andrew hoped he could ease the burden by stopping Kean from making a mistake for his career, but until Kean made the decision himself about what he wanted to do with his life, there was nothing Andrew could do but support him.

Andrew had asked Kean to drop by after the dinner if he could because he'd asked Kendal to stay overnight and wanted Kean with them. It wasn't that they couldn't see one of the others outside of their triad, but he wanted them to get through the initial relationship stage together so none of them felt out of the loop. But it looked like there might be more couple dates than triad dates in their future. That was one thing he hadn't expected.

Staring at the paperwork he had yet to complete, his thoughts turned again to his treasonous family, not that they were ever far from them. Where was Charlotte, and why was she so quiet? The truth of the law was shocking for her, but was it enough to stop her from trying? Did he have the chance to sway her back to his side? Did he want to?

It certainly would be easier to keep track of her if she was helping him rather than working against him, but would he be able to trust her?

No, he wouldn't. But she didn't know that. He could be persuasive when he needed to be.

He picked up the phone. It rang and rang without even

stopping for the voicemail. Was that on purpose? He tried again. Same thing. Was she screening the calls? He tried twice more, but nothing changed.

He rubbed his hand over his beard. If he wanted to talk to her, it looked like he'd need to visit her. Not that his security team would be happy with that, but they'd have to deal with it. He needed to find out what her plans were, and if that meant going straight to the source, then he would.

But not today. He inhaled and set to finishing the paperwork that Randall needed, then strode from the office.

"Randall, I'm done today. I can't concentrate anymore. If there's anything urgent, though, I'll be in my suite."

"I'm sure it can wait until tomorrow, Your Majesty. Have a good evening."

"You, too."

Dominic settled into step behind him, but Andrew's mind settled on his lovers. It was strange to use the word lovers, even if it was true. It didn't have a strong enough connotation for him, but until he could think of something better, it would have to do.

He entered his suite, a smile immediately stretching across his face when Kendal glanced up at him. The door closed of its own accord – probably Dominic – and Andrew took Kendal into his arms, holding them tightly. He buried his face into Kendal's neck, inhaling deeply and sighing it out again.

"You're very tense today. Has it been a rough one?" Kendal asked, rubbing Andrew's back.

"It's had its moments."

Andrew lifted his head, taking in every inch of Kendal's blemish-free skin. "Thanks for being here, my sweet."

"There's nowhere I'd rather be."

Andrew lowered his mouth to theirs, pressing their warm

lips together in a chaste kiss that didn't stay that way for long. The moment their skin touched, fire burned through him in a way that hadn't happened for years. He'd thought he was too old to feel the sexual need so acutely, but he did. He traced Kendal's lips with his tongue, and when they opened to him, he explored every crevice. Every groan, moan and whimper he drew from them was another streak of fire through him until he'd thought he'd combust.

Dragging his mouth away from them was pure torture, but they both needed to breathe.

"God, Kendal. You make me burn," he murmured, clasping them as they regained their breath.

Kendal huffed against his chest. "You and Kean both make me yearn for more than I ever expected to again. It's crazy!"

"Maybe the three of us are crazy. It would make sense."

Kendal peered up at him. "We're not crazy for loving you, Andrew. We're crazy *in* love with you."

Andrew stared at them. They were in love with him? But it was so soon. How can they know… He stopped his train of thought. They knew their own minds and bodies. If they believed they were in love with him, who was he to argue? His feelings for them had stretched for longer than he wanted to admit, but he would. Because they needed to hear it. Though Kean's would have to wait.

"You stole my breath the moment you looked into my eyes at Quinn's house." Kendal's mouth gaped. "Louisa knew. When I started helping you, she knew." He huffed a laugh. "But she knew I wouldn't do anything about it. And I never would have if she hadn't…"

It was probably why she'd pushed him towards them all the time. Truthfully, he'd known exactly what she meant in her letter, but he hadn't let himself believe she could let him off the hook so easily. She knew him better than anyone, though, and she was just as selfless in death as she was alive.

"She was a wonderful woman," Kendal said, snuggling into his chest again.

"She was." He kissed their head. "What would you like to do after dinner?"

Kendal peered up at him again, cheeks flushing. "I can think of a couple of things, but I think a movie might be nice. Kean might be able to get away and join us."

"Hopefully, he will." Andrew pulled away a little. "I think what we need first is a shower."

Kendal laughed. "Why? Do I stink?"

Andrew reached for them, but Kendal danced out of reach. "No, but your backside will smart if you're not careful."

"Promises, promises."

Kendal headed for the bedroom, and Andrew followed, smiling at the light both Kendal and Kean had brought him. With them, he felt like he could do anything, even if his fear for them was just as strong. He loved that Kendal was as strong-willed and opinionated outside of the bedroom as they were submissive inside of it. And as for Kean, he could play both submissive and dominant roles perfectly.

They fit. The three of them were perfect as if they were pieces of a jigsaw. And Andrew couldn't wait for Kean to join them so Andrew could show them both exactly how well they *could* fit together.

15

KEAN

The dinner request—or rather, order—had come out of the blue. Kean had been looking forward to spending the evening with Andrew and Kendal, but his father had insisted he join them. With a heavy heart, Kean dressed in a suit and descended the stairs, pasting a fake smile on his face before he entered the room.

"Ah, there he is!" his father said, holding his arm out in invitation for Kean to join them. Dante clapped him on the back, slid his arm around his shoulder and squeezed. "Almost finished his course now. He'll be with us in no time."

The pride in his father's voice did little to stop Kean from grimacing internally. As a child, he'd always wanted praise from him, but now, when everything was so fragile, he was beginning to see what Andrew had been implying for months—Kean didn't want to join the construction business. But how could he break the news to his father?

Tonight was not the night, regardless.

"Kean, I'd like to introduce my son, Ezekiel," his father's partner, Ted, said. "I'm sure you two will have lots to talk about, what with being the next generation of construction moguls." Ted laughed, and Kean huffed a laugh, unable to muster any more enthusiasm because he'd just realised what this was.

A blind date.

Fuck!

"Zeke, please, Father," Ezekiel—Zeke—amended.

Ted held up his hands. "Sorry! Not like we didn't name you or anything." Ted sighed and glanced at Dante. "Shall we leave them to talk?"

Dante clapped Kean on the back again. "Don't spend all night talking business now, you hear?"

Dante led Ted away, laughing, and Kean sighed quietly.

"Yeah, you got that vibe, too?" Zeke said, staring after their parents.

Kean glanced at him. "Sorry?"

"I'm gay. You're gay. We both work for the same company. What a boon for them if we were to become a couple," Zeke snorted. Kean choked on nothing, and Zeke laughed again. "Let's get you a drink. I think we both need loosening up to deal with this clusterfuck."

Kean didn't say anything as they chose a different table full of drinks from where their parents were. Zeke handed Kean a glass.

"I have no idea what this is, but we need it." Zeke knocked the drink back and grimaced. "Expensive, but shit."

Kean stared at him before a bite of laughter escaped him. There was no way he would ever date that man, but he was funny if nothing else. Kean held out his hand. "Kean Seymour, nice to meet you."

"Zeke Greenfield."

"So, you're gay. I wonder why it's taken them so long to get us in a room together?" Kean said. His eyes widened as his words registered. "Not that I mean…" He stopped and held his breath.

Zeke chuckled, deepening the laughter lines around his eyes. "I know. To be honest, I've only just come out to him. I've been out and proud for years, but he either ignored it or finally sees the benefit of having a gay son." Zeke shook his head and glanced in his father's direction. "I'm betting on the latter, hence my attendance tonight."

Kean bit his lip. "Just to clear the air, as much as you seem like a nice guy, I'm not available. My father doesn't know that, though."

Zeke grinned at him. "Glad to hear it. You're not my type, anyway. No offence. The twinkier, the better for me."

"Good to know. I'll keep my eyes peeled for you."

"Thank you, kind sir." Zeke glanced over his shoulder again. "How about we play the game tonight? It'll make things easier for us, and we can get to know one another without the need to worry about later. What do you say?"

Kean smiled. "Sounds like a plan." He held out his arm. "Shall I escort you to your seat?"

"Thank you, Mr Seymour." Kean shuddered, and Zeke noticed. "Not a fan of your father's name?" he murmured.

"Not really," Kean answered honestly.

"We're far more alike than I realised."

They sat at the far end of the table, furthest from their parents, with other partners and board members between them, and as far as Kean was concerned, had one of the best "work" dinners he'd ever had. Even when his mother was carefully led away from the table, her legs barely able to hold her up, it didn't dampen his mood. If Zeke noticed, he didn't say anything.

When the evening came to a close, later than Kean had intended, Zeke approached him.

"Would it be too forward to ask for your number?" Zeke asked.

Kean frowned. Why would he need his number when they had already agreed they wouldn't be going further?

"Trust me," Zeke whispered.

Kean entered the number into Zeke's phone, and Zeke's fingers flew across the screen. Kean felt his phone vibrate in his pocket and pulled it out.

UNKNOWN: Now you have my number, too. I'm hoping we can be friends. We can 'beard' for each other if we need to. Z.

Kean chuckled and closed his phone. "Sounds like a plan."

"I'm well known for my good plans." Zeke winked. He leaned in and hugged Kean, whispering, "Nice to meet you, *friend.*"

"You, too. Safe journey home."

Zeke waved as he left with his father, and Dante stopped beside Kean.

"You two looked like you got along well. It will be good for the company."

The weight that had lifted from his shoulders during Zeke's presence fell back onto him again with added pounds.

"He's a good man," Kean said.

"You could do a lot worse," Dante said. He stared at Kean. "Don't mess it up."

"Yes, Father."

Dante studied him for a moment longer. "Get some rest."

"I'm going out."

"What about your studies?" Dante frowned at him.

"All completed and sent." Kean had busted his ass to get

the work done that day so he could spend the evening with Andrew and Kendal and, instead, had to waste time with his father's business. Although, he'd met Zeke, so it wasn't all bad.

"Okay. Don't stay out too late. You have more to do tomorrow, no doubt."

"Yes, Father."

Kean didn't wait to see if his father would demand anything else of him that evening and left the house, climbing into his car. He didn't stop for clothes or anything else. He just left.

It was almost midnight. He wasn't sure if either of them would still be awake, but he needed to see them all the same. He could sneak into bed if he had to, staring at them like a creeper before succumbing to sleep. But he couldn't spend any more time away from them tonight.

Once he'd parked the car, he entered Windsor Castle, quietly wandering the hallways until he reached the king's suite. Colt was stationed outside, and he smiled and nodded at Kean.

"Is he inside?"

"They are, yes," Colt said, answering Kean's unasked question.

"Thanks."

Kean let himself inside, closing the door behind him as quietly as possible. No one was in the living room area, so he headed for the bedroom. The door was ajar, and he peeked through before slipping through the gap and shutting that door, too.

They were both asleep. Andrew held Kendal back to chest, his arms around them, and Kean smiled at the picture. He wished he could take one to show them what they looked like, but he would never take the risk.

Instead of joining them, he headed for the bathroom, closing himself inside so he didn't disturb them during his shower. He shampooed his hair and washed the suds clear, then jumped when arms slid around his waist.

"Did you have a good evening, sweetheart?" Andrew murmured, nosing against Kean's jaw.

Kean tilted his head, giving him more access, and closed his eyes. "Sorry if I disturbed you. I was trying to be quiet."

"I'm glad I heard you. I didn't want to miss your arrival." Andrew sucked Kean's earlobe. "But you didn't answer my question."

Kean's mind pulled him back from the edge of bliss to concentrate on Andrew's words. "Um...yeah, it was good. I met a new friend. I think Father's intentions were for us to become a couple, but neither of us wanted that."

Andrew's arms had tightened, and Kean hid his smile at the possessive gesture. "Who?"

"Zeke Greenfield. He's the son of one of my father's partners. Luckily, we're not each other's type, though he's a nice guy. He made the evening more bearable."

Andrew reached for the soap and washed Kean's body. "Then I'm glad you have him."

Kean let himself be manhandled and cleaned, loving being taken care of as much as he loved to take care of others. There was nowhere else he'd rather be than there.

"How is Kendal?" he asked.

"Let their ass tell you the story of their smart-ass remarks," Andrew growled, and Kean chuckled.

"I'm sorry I missed that."

"You'll have more chances, I'm sure." Andrew kissed Kean's knees and stood, pressing his lips to Kean's for the first time that evening.

Kean slid his arms around Andrew's neck and held on for

dear life as Andrew reacquainted himself with Kean's mouth. Kean would happily let him take as long as he needed. As Andrew's tongue explored his mouth, Kean held nothing back. He allowed his king, his lover, his...boyfriend to take everything Kean offered. The groins rested against each other, their cocks hard, but they didn't go further.

When Andrew pulled back, Kean followed, his brain misfiring completely. Andrew chuckled and switched off the shower.

"Let's get you dry."

Andrew wrapped a large towel around him and dried him off, waiting until Kean was ready before drying himself. Then he grabbed Kean's hand and dragged him to the bedroom. Kendal had moved onto their stomach, and Andrew held up the covers for Kean to slide in.

"I'll go to the other side," Kean whispered.

"No. You've been without us for long enough. Let us surround you now," Andrew murmured.

Kean bit his lip, but Andrew nodded towards the bed again. He slipped between the covers and closer to Kendal while Andrew climbed in behind him. Kean didn't want to disturb Kendal, but Andrew had no qualms. He reached over Kean and skimmed his fingers over Kendal's back.

"Hmm." Kendal moved their head towards them but didn't move otherwise.

"Kendal, my sweet. Kean's back," Andrew crooned.

Kendal snuffled and rolled to their side, blinking sleepily at them. Their smile lit up the room. "Kean," they murmured. They slid closer and burrowed their head in Kean's chest, and Kean's heart skipped.

"Hey, you. Go back to sleep now, okay?" Kean slid his arm around them.

"Mmhmm."

Kean smiled and settled in, enjoying the warmth at his front and back. He hadn't realised how much he needed it, but Andrew had, hadn't he? He was more observant than most people gave him credit for.

"Thank you," he whispered to Andrew.

"You're welcome, sweetheart."

Kean had thought he'd stay awake for a while, but he couldn't remember doing so if he did. The next moment, gentle kisses on his chest woke him, and he smiled with his eyes closed.

"Morning," he murmured. He opened one eye. "It *is* morning, isn't it?"

"It is," a rumble said from behind him. "A little earlier than usual, but someone was eager for what I promised them last night."

Kean rolled his head to the side, blinking at Andrew, seeing the lazy smile curving his lips. "And what did you promise the little minx?"

"A morning of debauchery."

Kean feigned shock. "We can't! It's a work day."

Andrew's lips twitched. "We have time."

Kean rested one hand on Kendal's head, which was lowering with every kiss, and reached one up to cup the back of Andrew's neck, pulling him closer for a kiss. He gasped into Andrew's mouth when Kendal wrapped their lips around his cock. The suction was pure torture, and when Andrew sucked on Kean's tongue, he knew he needed more. He wanted them to be together, fully together. Kendal licked, sucked and stroked his shaft until Kean's head spun.

"I want us," he said into Andrew's mouth.

"Yes," was his reply. "Kendal?"

"I'm in."

Kean chuckled. "No, we're in. Or we will be."

Kendal closed their eyes and pulled off Kean. They rolled onto their back, staring at him and Andrew, waiting.

"Well done, my sweet. Kean, prepare them."

"Yes, Sir."

Kean fitted his shoulders between Kendal's thighs and lifted their legs, exposing their pucker. He wanted his mouth on it, but he couldn't do anything until Andrew told them how. He licked his lips, staring at the bud.

"Use your mouth first, Kean," Andrew ordered as he climbed off the bed.

Kean would've wondered what he was doing, but he'd received permission to do what he wanted to and licked a stripe from Kendal's pucker to their balls. Then he firmed his tongue and massaged it against Kendal's hole. Kendal moaned from above, and Kean pressed harder, letting them feel the stretch as his tongue pierced the ring. He withdrew a little, wet his tongue and did it again, this time sinking further. He loved doing this. Giving pleasure to others, but it was even better when it was someone he loved. Almost as if he was giving a piece of himself to them.

He sucked and licked and tongued Kendal's channel, loosening and stretching them for their cocks.

"Now the lube, Kean," Andrew said, dropping a tube beside him.

Kean slicked his fingers and pressed one inside Kendal's warm channel. It went in easily, and Kendal pushed back against him, so he assumed they needed more. Sliding two fingers in, Kendal whimpered and arched. Kean scissored his fingers, then added another one before Andrew halted him.

"That's enough. Here." Andrew handed him a condom, and Kean glanced up at him.

"Me?"

Andrew nodded. "Yes."

Kean swallowed, honoured at the choice Andrew was giving him. He glanced at Kendal, who nodded with a smile. Rolling on the condom took no time, and Andrew reached down to slick it. Kean bit his lip, already hard and aching for what they were going to do. Andrew cupped his chin, lifted his head and kissed him. Closing his eyes, he fell into the sensation of being with Andrew and Kendal like he'd only ever dreamt of before.

Andrew broke the kiss and leaned down to Kean's ear. "Push inside them, Kean. Make them ours."

A shiver flowed down his back, and he complied. He settled between Kendal's thighs and leaned over to kiss them. Kendal gripped his back, pulling him closer and pressing their cocks together.

"Please, Kean." Kendal whimpered.

Kean reached between them, but Andrew's hand encircled him, and his breath caught. Andrew held him at Kendal's entrance. "Push."

Kean did, and he slipped inside Kendal's heat. Andrew's hand flattened against Kean's groin, staying between him and Kendal but not stopping him from moving. He withdrew a little and pushed in again.

"Oh, god," Kendal said. "It's been so long." They moaned and lifted their legs. "Please."

Kean increased his speed, and Andrew removed his hand, leaning down to kiss Kendal. Kean watched them, his arousal rising as tongues tangled and Andrew's fingers flicked at Kendal's nipples.

"You feel so good," Kean said, gripping Kendal's hips.

Andrew rose and stared at them, and Kean's body heated further at his perusal.

"Stop," Andrew said.

Kean froze, fully buried inside Kendal. He swallowed hard at the need to move, but he listened to his Dom. "Sir?"

Andrew's mouth quirked. "Keep their mouth busy, Kean, but don't move. I have something to do."

Kean leaned down, sliding his arms around Kendal's back and holding them close. Kendal wrapped their legs around his waist. Kean smiled at them and dropped a kiss on their lips. He taunted Kendal, licking and tasting and sucking until Kean gasped.

Cool lube touched his hole, and he clenched.

"Relax for me, sweetheart. I can't wait to join us all," Andrew said.

Kendal's mouth quirked, and Kean's eyelids fluttered as Andrew prepped him. "Fuck," he breathed.

16

KENDAL

endal clenched around Kean's cock, still nestled inside of them, and Kean hissed. Whether that was because of their movement or because Andrew was fingering him, they weren't sure, but either way, Kean was enjoying himself. And so was Kendal. They couldn't feel Andrew, but wrapped around Kean as they were, every time Andrew's fingers entered Kean, Kean's hips bucked, sending delicious tingles through Kendal's body. And the sounds Kean made set their blood boiling. They were very much on the edge, and it wouldn't take much to send them over. They needed to last until Andrew was inside Kean, though. Their first time as a triad needed to be special.

"That's it, sweetheart. Suck those fingers in," Andrew crooned.

Kean rested his forehead against Kendal's, blocking their view of Andrew, but they tightened their hold.

"Are you ready for me?" Andrew asked Kean.

"Yes, Sir. Please."

"Kendal, hold him open for me."

Kendal's groin pulsed at the words. They dropped their legs to the bed and slid their hands down Kean's back to his ass cheeks. They spread their fingers and gripped his ass, pressing a kiss to Kean's lips as they did. Gaze focused on Kean as it was, Kendal heard the rip of a packet and envisioned Andrew rolling the condom down his length. The click of the tube came next, and then the bed moved as Andrew settled into place.

"Beautiful. You both look gorgeous like this."

Kendal moved their head to the side, Kean's head nuzzling into their neck instead, and met Andrew's gaze. In the limited light they had, they could see the arousal in his eyes, the flush of his cheeks and chest, and the sweat beading on his skin. He was holding back.

Andrew focused on Kean's hole and held the base of his cock. "Push out, sweetheart."

Kendal felt Kean relax completely, getting slightly heavier on them.

"That's it."

Andrew pushed inside slowly, the gentle ebb and flow of his thrusts sparking little fires through Kendal with Kean as the conduit. With every forward momentum, Kean pressed into Kendal, and with every withdrawal, he released his hold. Kendal's head swam as their climax drew closer, but they held it back, waiting for Andrew to say they could come.

"Almost there," Andrew said. He gave a harder thrust, and Kean and Kendal groaned in unison. "There we go."

Andrew's hands came to rest on the bed beside Kendal's chest, and they peered up at him. Andrew kissed Kean's shoulder, up his neck, along his jaw and to the corner of his mouth before reaching over for Kendal's mouth. He kissed him with softness and love.

"Thank you for allowing me this," Andrew whispered.

"Please, Sir," Kean murmured. "Can we move now?"

Andrew's chuckle was dark and rich and sent goosebumps across Kendal's skin. "Yes, sweetheart." He met Kendal's gaze again. "Ready, my sweet?"

Kendal nodded, and Andrew lifted off his hands, removing Kendal's hands from Kean's ass and gripping Kean's hips himself. Kendal slid his hands up Kean's back, holding him steady for the onslaught they were sure was coming.

Andrew withdrew, and Kean whimpered. He slid back in, pushing Kean into Kendal, then pulled back again. The slow and steady speed was nice, but they knew it was just the beginning. They could see the coiled strength and need in Andrew and couldn't wait to see what he did.

Without warning, Andrew slammed deep.

"Fuck!" Kean murmured and rose to his forearms, the cold air brushing over the sweat that had been gathering between them, cooling Kendal's skin rapidly.

Kean braced himself, but with every thrust, he slid into Kendal. Fire raced down Kendal's spine, pooling in their groin.

"You both feel amazing," Andrew growled, sweat dripping down his temples as his body tensed and thrust.

Kendal had never seen a more beautiful sight than Andrew and Kean losing control with them. Kean leaned down and attached their mouth to Kendal's nipple, and more heat gathered in their cock. It wouldn't take much more to send them over the edge. Andrew reached for Kendal's leg, pulling it around them both, altering the angle, and Kendal saw stars. Their orgasm slammed into them, and their shaft pulsed between them and Kean. They were distantly aware of Kean groaning and the thrusts increasing before a bellow gained Kendal's attention.

Andrew leaned over them on one hand, eyes narrowed, jaw clenched, his other hand gripping Kean's hip as he held himself deep inside. All at once, his shoulders relaxed, he blinked, and he panted.

"Wow," Kean said, resting their forehead on Kendal's chest. "That's it. Just wow."

Andrew smiled, kissed Kean's shoulder and leaned forward to kiss Kendal, which resulted in them all moaning as a fresh wave of sensitive arousal flowed through them. Andrew pulled back, reaching down to hold the condom, and Kean released a shaky exhale. Kendal kissed Kean's temple, and Kean rose, holding *his* condom and withdrew. Kendal held their breath until he pulled free, and their hole clenched at the emptiness. They closed their eyes and dropped their legs to the bed, aching everywhere, but all good aches.

They dozed, listening to Andrew and Kean moving around, then woke when Kean slid his arms beneath Kendal's body and lifted them. Kendal lazily opened their eyes and hooked their arms around his neck.

"What's this?" they murmured.

Kean carried them into the bathroom, and Kendal gasped at the bathtub that was now full of water—and Andrew. Kean carefully lowered them into the water and into Andrew's arms, which encircled and held them. The size of the bath allowed Kendal to sit sideways on Andrew's lap and snuggle their face into his neck.

"Drink," Kean said, and Kendal opened their eyes to see a small bottle with a straw poking from the top.

Kendal drank their fill and waited for Kean to join them. When he didn't, Kendal glanced over their shoulder.

"Kean?" they asked.

"Yes?" Kean crouched beside the bath.

"Are you not joining us?"

Kean smiled and stroked Kendal's hair. "No, I got to be inside you. This is for you and Andrew. I'm here, though."

"But you must be sore. Come in with us."

Andrew chuckled. "I've asked him several times, my sweet. He won't."

Why wouldn't he? "Then order him to, Sir."

Andrew opened his mouth, no doubt to argue, then he paused and glanced at Kean. "Kean, you're upsetting our sub. Into the bath with you."

Kean's jaw tightened for a second, but he sighed and rose, climbing into the water with them. He hissed when his ass touched the warmth but settled with crossed legs, facing them when Andrew widened his legs.

"Happy?" Kean asked.

Kendal smiled and reached a hand for him, resting their cheek against Andrew's chest. "Perfectly."

Andrew chuckled again. "And anyone who believes the Dom has the power needs to think again." He kissed Kendal's hair. "What are your plans for today?"

"Well, I need to go home, as I have a full day of work ahead of me. My authors need me. But I'll be back later to go through some more videos," Kendal said.

"And I have a class to attend and some coursework to do, but I'll come back when Kendal does for the videos," Kean said. "And what about you, my king?" Kean grinned when Andrew narrowed his eyes.

"To be honest, I have no idea. Randall will be here soon to talk me through my day. I don't think I have any outside events today, but I may have meetings. At the very least, I will have several phone calls to make and a pile of paperwork that would rival the Shard."

"I'm glad you have Randall," Kendal said.

"Me, too. Otherwise, I'd get nothing done."

They settled into silence, and Kendal drifted away in the comfort of their presence.

"I'm turning into a prune." Kendal held up their hand several long minutes later.

Kean rose, water sluicing off his body and making Kendal's mouth water. "Come on. Here's a towel."

Andrew helped Kendal to stand, holding them until they stepped out of the bath and into Kean's arms. Kendal watched Andrew climb from the bath and pull the plug, and Kean handed him a towel, too, and then came back to dry Kendal.

"I didn't bring any clothes with me, so I have to go home before I go to class," Kean said when they were back in the bedroom, dressing. He frowned at his crumpled shirt and trousers.

Andrew cleared his throat. "I have..." He scratched his beard and stepped to the chest of drawers. He opened one. "There are some clothes in here that might fit you." He glanced at Kendal. "You have some in this drawer," he said, pointing at the one below.

Kean stepped closer. "You bought us clothes?"

Andrew shrugged, then stood taller, meeting Kean's gaze. "Yes. I didn't want you to worry."

Kean smiled and slid his arms around Andrew's waist. "Thank you, my king."

Andrew huffed a laugh and returned the hug. "Is that your new name for me?"

"It is. Pure, unadulterated love in two words," Kean admitted.

Andrew cupped his chin and kissed him. "Thank you, sweetheart." He glanced at Kendal. "I'm sorry if I overstepped."

Kendal slid into their arms. "Not at all."

Kendal chose some clothes from the new ones Andrew had bought to show they didn't mind that he'd spoilt them, and from what Kendal could see, the clothes were things they would usually wear, anyway. They smiled as they smoothed down their new knee-length jumper.

They headed for the living room, and Andrew rang through for some breakfast.

"Won't it seem strange that you're ordering for three people?" Kean asked.

Andrew shook his head. "I often have visitors first thing in the morning." He paused when Kean coughed. "Not like that. I meant my sons."

Kean grinned. "I know." A knock sounded, and Kean frowned. "That was quick."

"That won't be breakfast. Come in!" Andrew said.

Randall entered, bowing his head. "Good morning, Your Majesty. I know we usually go through your day over breakfast, but would you prefer we did it later today? I don't want to interrupt."

"You're not interrupting, Randall. Come sit down."

Kendal listened with half an ear while Andrew and Randall discussed the plans for his day. They focused on their cup of tea and mentally flicked through their own task list for the day. When they considered heading home, their pulse increased. They hadn't checked the cameras at home at all over the previous night or this morning. They stood, putting their cup down on the coffee table harder than planned, and headed for the bedroom where they last remembered seeing their phone. It was on the bedside table, and they settled on the edge of the bed and stared at it.

What if someone had been in their house while they'd not been there? They wouldn't feel safe going back again.

"Kendal?" Kendal jumped, pressing a hand to their chest when Kean settled beside them. "What's wrong?"

Kendal shook their head, returning to stare at their phone.

"Does it not work? You can borrow mine?"

"It's not that," Kendal started. They breathed methodically, trying to calm down. "I haven't checked the cameras," they admitted.

Kean slid an arm around their shoulders. "Do you want me to check?"

Kendal stared at him, losing himself in the hazel depths, and nodded. "Please." They unlocked their phone and handed it to him before closing their eyes.

Kean was quiet for a moment. "Nothing looks amiss. The security sensors are still on and working. They haven't been turned off since you left yesterday."

Kendal blew out a breath. "Thank you. You two are good at distracting me from my anxieties, but I didn't realise they'd come back and bite me when I thought about them again."

"It's okay. Whatever you need."

"Everything okay?" Andrew asked from the doorway.

Kendal nodded. "Yes. I got a little worried because I hadn't checked on my house. Everything's fine, though."

"Good." Andrew crouched in front of them. "As Kean said, whatever you need, consider it yours."

"Thank you." Kendal leaned down and kissed him, but their stomach growled, interrupting them. "Sorry!"

"It's good that breakfast has arrived." Andrew stood, pulling them both to their feet. "Let's eat."

By the time Andrew had fed them and they'd parted ways, Kendal was already looking forward to seeing them again. They checked the cameras one last time before entering the house and locking the door behind them. Heading straight for their office, they closed that door, too, needing the barriers between them and the outside world.

They made themselves a cup of tea while their computer started up, then settled in front of the screen to check what they'd missed since they'd last logged on. Thirty-four emails and double digits of notifications from social media wasn't the worst it had been, but they needed to get to work. They started by sending good morning messages to their authors to let them know Kendal was at their desk if they needed them, then focused on the emails. Some of them were unsolicited emails that they put into a separate folder to look at later; most of them would go in the bin, but they liked to check credentials to see if any were worth looking into further. Some held information about upcoming events, and Kendal added the details to the relevant author's calendar.

They'd made a small dent in them when they received their first message from an author. And so it continued. They ate lunch at their desk, putting out fires and assisting where they needed to. Before long, their day was over, and although there were a couple of things that still needed attending to, they left them for the following day. Or maybe that night if they couldn't sleep, which sometimes happened.

They switched everything off, checked the cameras on the phone, and headed for their car. The drive back to Windsor didn't take long, and they wandered straight down to the security office they were using for their task. Kean was already there, and Kendal went straight into his arms.

"Have you had a good day?" Kean asked.

"Busy." Kendal lifted their chin, and Kean kissed him. Kendal clung to him, their blood heating more, but the door opened before they could get too lost.

"Oh, sorry," Nina said, standing in the doorway.

"No, it's okay. Just saying hello," Kean said, tugging Kendal into a chair beside him.

Nina settled into the chair on the opposite side of Kendal and set up the next video they needed to watch.

"How many more do we need to go through?" Kean asked.

Nina blew out a breath. "I think there's another half a dozen, but from what I can see from the details, they're short ones."

"We've not found much," Kendal said. Maybe they were barking up the wrong tree.

"We found that woman," Kean said. "She might turn out to be something."

The three of them had noticed the woman interacting with Charles on more than one occasion, but Charles's body language didn't seem like it was anything to do with treason.

Nina set the video going, and Kendal focused on the screen in front of them. They were glad there was no sound because it was something to see what was happening on screen but to hear it too would be too embarrassing. For them, anyway. They scanned the screen for anyone they knew and those they didn't know. It was a long time before Kean spoke.

"Wait, what was that?" Kean leaned forward. "Go back about two minutes, then focus on the bottom left corner of the screen. Charles spoke to someone, and it looks like he handed something to the other person, which they dropped."

Kendal watched the video over again, immediately seeing what Kean saw. "Is it a piece of paper? He's quick to pick it up again. Charles doesn't look back, though."

"Who is it?" Nina asked.

"I don't recognise him," Kean said.

"Are you able to get a little closer?"

"I can try, but it might blur it too much," Nina said.

Kendal scooted to the edge of their chair, closer to the screen, when Nina zoomed in and played it again. "I know him."

"Who is it?" Kean asked.

"His name's Danny. He's in the Army. I played with him years ago, but he's not there very often because of his work."

Kean stared at the video, murmuring, "Danny. Army. Holy shit!" He scrambled from the chair and flung open the door.

"Kean! Wait!" Kendal said, racing after him down the hallways to Andrew's office.

When Kendal entered Randall's office—basically, the foyer to Andrew's—Randall had his hands up, stopping Kean from entering.

"You can't go in there right now."

"It's important, Randall. Really damn important."

Randall frowned. "Wait here. I mean it. Don't come in. I'll speak to Andrew, but I'm making no promises. This is an important meeting."

Kean nodded, and they waited while Randall disappeared.

"Kean, what's going on?"

"I know who that was."

"Who?"

Kean sighed. "Someone who's supposed to be on our side."

Randall appeared again. "He needs five minutes."

Kean's jaw clenched, and Kendall rubbed his back, not wanting to ask questions until they were with Andrew. They led Kean over to the window to wait, and within minutes, Andrew's office door opened.

"Thank you, Gerald. Randall will see you out." Andrew glanced at them, then focused on the other man until he exited the room. "What's wrong?"

Kean stepped forward. "Charles has been talking to Daniel."

Andrew frowned. "Daniel?"

"Neil's second in command?"

Andrew briefly closed his eyes. "Christian's friend?" he whispered.

Kean nodded. "Unfortunately."

"I didn't even know he was part of the club," Andrew said.

Kendal stepped closer. "I've played with him before. A few years back. He told me he didn't visit often because of his work schedule. He said he was in the Army, and they sent him all over the place."

Andrew squeezed Kendal's shoulder. "It's not your fault."

"They identified him," Kean said.

Andrew entered his office, and they followed. He clicked a few buttons on his computer and pointed. "Is this him?"

Kendal glanced at the picture of three men, one of whom was Christian, and one woman. They nodded.

Andrew sighed and sank into his chair. "This is going to destroy Christian."

17

ANDREW

Randall knocked and entered. "What do you need, Your Majesty?"

"I need everyone here. William and Victoria, too. Make sure Oscar and Oreo come with Christian. And get Neil on a secure line for when they get here. Make sure he's alone."

"Are you sure he's not involved?" Kean asked.

Andrew shook his head, his stomach churning. "I'm not sure of anything at this point. Christian knows him best. I'm hoping he'll be able to tell if Neil is lying or not."

"What can we do to help?" Kendal asked.

"Just be here."

People started arriving, but Andrew wouldn't explain until everyone had arrived. They settled around the room, getting drinks and chatting amongst themselves, but it was more subdued than usual. The heaviness in the air was palpable. When Christian, Oscar and Oreo entered, Andrew smiled at them, then waited for William and Victoria to arrive.

"We have some news," Andrew started once everyone was situated.

"Personal or professional?" Christian said, echoing Andrew's question to him a few days prior.

Andrew chuckled despite the seriousness of the situation. "Professional." He glanced around the room. "We may be one step closer to figuring something out. But it's not happy news." He rose and rounded the desk, crouching in front of Christian and covering his hands. "I'm sorry for what I'm about to say." Christian frowned at him. "We believe Daniel is working with Charles."

"Daniel? My superior, Daniel?" Christian said. Andrew nodded. Christian stared off to the side, eyes bouncing around as he digested the information. "Why?"

Andrew glanced at Kean, who took over. "Kendal and I have been reviewing the video feed from the club, as you know. We watched Charles hand something to a man, and Kendal identified them as 'Danny,' someone they'd played with before. Kendal told me that Danny had said he was in the Army and wasn't always able to get to the club because of his schedule."

"There could be other Daniels."

Andrew nodded. "There could be. But I showed Kendal a photograph of you with Neil, Daniel and Gia. They pointed Daniel out."

Christian rose, hands on hips, pacing at the back of the room. Andrew let him be for a few minutes and answered the questions from others.

"Was he seen any other time on the feed?" Freddie asked.

"Not that we've noticed," Kean said. "We might have to go back over it, or maybe facial recognition might work."

"It could be something completely innocuous," Christian said.

Andrew sighed. "It could be. It's why I need you to help me, Christian. I wouldn't ask if there was any other way."

Christian paused and studied him. "What?"

"I have Neil on a secure line. I'm going to ask him questions, but I need you to listen and tell me if he's telling the truth. You know him better than any of us. If he's telling the truth, I'll tell him about Daniel."

Christian sighed, and Oreo got up and nudged his side. Christian rested his hand on the dog's head and nodded. "All right."

Andrew settled behind his desk and picked up the phone. "Randall, put Neil through, please." He pressed a button on the phone and replaced the receiver. "Neil?"

"Your Majesty. How can I help?"

Andrew rubbed a hand over his chin and sighed. "Are you a traitor, Neil?" he said, going right for the jugular.

"*Excuse me*, Your Majesty?"

"Are you a traitor? It's a fairly simple question."

"No, I'm not, Your Majesty."

Andrew glanced at Christian, who nodded his head. "One more question, then I'll get to the point of my call. How well do you vet your team?"

Neil was silent for a minute, then said, "The usual checks through the Army, then additional ones when they join this team. If certain jobs need higher clearance, we do them before people join. Is that detailed enough?"

Andrew raised an eyebrow at Christian, who nodded again. "You might need to upgrade your vetting system, Neil. I'm sorry for coming at you so hard, but we have evidence to suggest one of your team is not on our side."

"Who?" Neil's voice whipped sharp through the line.

Andrew sighed. "Daniel."

"No way, Your Majesty. I hand-picked him myself. I

double-checked the clearance results. There were no flags on the background checks at all. His psychiatric report was clear. Everything was clean."

Christian nodded, but something Neil said bugged Andrew. He followed his train of thought, then asked, "Why did you double-check the results if you were so sure about him?" Silence greeted his question, and Andrew's heart dropped. "You weren't sure, were you, Neil? Something made you hesitate. What was it?"

Neil sighed. "It felt too clean."

"In what way?"

"Many people have benign things, like stealing a crème egg from a shop when they were younger, or being in the same vicinity as something that had happened, and their name ended up on the report, or a parking ticket. Just something small. Others have a list as long as my arm. Some people have completely clean records with no evidence of any wrongdoing in their entire life. In my experience, that means they've either lived a completely clean life or they've wiped it clean."

"What made you decide one way or the other?"

Neil cleared his throat. "I didn't."

"You didn't what?"

"I had no evidence one way or the other, Your Majesty. I couldn't refuse him because he was *too clean*."

"You could've refused him because of your gut instinct," Andrew snapped. "Where is he?"

"On leave."

Bloody hell.

"When's he due back?" Christian said, coming closer.

Neil hesitated. "Two weeks."

"When did he leave?" Christian asked.

"Yesterday. Look, Christian, I'm sorry—"

"Save it. What you need to do now is find Daniel without tipping him off. Do not let anyone else know what we've just told you. We can't trust anyone right now."

"Not even me." It wasn't a question.

Christian paused. "The Army has taught me well, Neil. I can tell you're telling the truth. But if they trained Daniel as well as they did me, we might need some help."

"Whatever you need," Neil agreed.

Christian glanced at Andrew. "For now, just find him without him knowing. Tell us the minute you do."

"Okay."

"And Neil? Wasn't my check clean, too?"

Neil huffed a laugh. "No, Your Highness. You got into a fight when you were nineteen, amongst other things."

Christian closed his eyes and shook his head, smiling slightly.

"Thank you, Neil. Keep in touch," Andrew said, ending the call.

Christian settled back into the seat beside Oscar, wrapping his arm around his boy.

"Where might he go?" Andrew said.

"I don't know. We didn't socialise outside of work."

"The club," Kendal said. "He said he went to the club when he was off work."

Andrew picked up the phone again.

"Club Royal, how may I help?"

"Clarice, could you check to see if a member is present tonight, please? Daniel March."

He heard the clicking of buttons. "No, Your Majesty. He's not been present for two months."

"Can you put a flag on his account so we get notified if he turns up? He can be allowed entry as normal; we just want to know when he's there."

"Of course, Your Majesty. All done."

"Could you also send across the list of times he's been there, please?"

"I can."

"Thank you, Clarice. Have a good evening."

"What's the next step?" Douglas asked.

"Checking the videos for the times he's been there. We need to see who he interacted with recently," Freddie said.

"Facial recognition, too," Christian said. "He's capable with a computer. He might be able to override the data. Or even change it completely."

"Our systems are too good for that, surely?" Andrew said.

Christian shrugged. "It won't hurt to check."

Andrew nodded as a knock sounded. "Come in!"

Randall entered, carrying his laptop. "Your Majesty, we have a problem."

Andrew tensed. "What?"

"You need to see this."

Randall rounded the desk and put the laptop down.

TWO BOYFRIENDS FOR THE KING!
By Adelaide Thompson.

An anonymous source has revealed that King Andrew has taken two men to his bedchamber. The source would not reveal who those men were, but after some scouting, we can reveal the possibilities.

First in line is a bodyguard. Easily able to come and go, and with the king all the time. He's lost a few recently, so maybe he's grieving again. Who knows?

Second, it could be a friend of the family. My bet is on Kean Seymour, though his age may lower the chances. He's been in attendance at Windsor Castle more often than usual lately, including some sleepovers. Hmm, maybe?

The third could be a distant relative, though we've not seen any of those recently.

Fourth, it could be one of a handful of newly integrated people. Just some of the names are Quinn Lambert, who has a boyfriend he lives with, and Kendal Lawson, who we don't know much about, but he's friends with Quinn.

Fifth could be his personal assistant, Randall Hopkins. They work closely together. Why not?

Or maybe it's long-time friend, Brady Thomas, or Commissioner Thomas to you and me?

I can't wait to see what comes from this.

King Andrew, I didn't think you had it in you!

Let me know who you think are the king's bedfellows. See you next time.

Andrew sighed.

"I've already sent the takedown notices, so it shouldn't be on there much longer, but it's still long enough that others will pick up on it," Randall said.

"Thank you, Randall. Do what you can."

Mav stood. "I'll help."

"What is it?" Kean asked when Randall and Mav disappeared.

"News about my new relationship is rife."

Kean raised his eyebrows. "How does anyone know?"

"Either one of the household staff is talking," George said, "or they're just guessing. Though why they'd guess at two, I don't know."

"I supposed it could be worse. They could say I have a harem," Andrew joked, trying to lighten the mood, though he didn't feel like having fun.

"Don't you?" William said, joining in.

Kendal crossed their legs. "Can you have a harem with only three people?"

"What are you looking at me for?" George asked, flinging his hands in the air. "How would I know?"

Andrew let the banter continue while he considered the options. Denying it was the best choice, but that didn't mean it would work. If others had seen the article, it would have shone a light on them, and they would be watched more closely from now on. It wouldn't surprise him if the media were outside waiting for them. They could ignore the questions and let them die down by themselves, but that was unlikely to happen for some time. The media loved a juicy story, and as he'd said before, a king with two lovers was enough to set off the hellhounds.

The other option was to be honest with them, and Andrew couldn't do that to Kean and Kendal. Their quiet lives would be gone.

But hadn't they already?

"Yes, Father?" Kean said into his phone and moved to the side of the room. "I'm with Henry." Kean glanced at Andrew and grimaced, and Andrew held out his hand, beckoning him closer. "We've not finished—" Kean's shoulders dropped as he listened and grabbed Andrew's hand, leaning his ass on his desk. "No, I'm not—" Kean closed his eyes. "Of course, I do, Father." He sighed. "You know what journalists are like." Kean tensed, jaw clenching, and Andrew braced for what Kean had heard. Kean stared at Andrew and inhaled. "No, Father. I'll come home when I'm finished. No! I'll be home *when I'm finished.*" He ended the call and exhaled, his face pale.

"Are you okay?" Andrew asked.

Kean stared ahead of him through the window behind

Andrew. "I told him no," he murmured. "I've never done that before."

"What did he want?"

"He wanted me to go home. To distance myself from the royal family until the news dies down."

"It might be a good idea," Andrew mused. Kean glared at him, and Andrew chuckled. "I never said you had to, just that it might be a good idea."

"It's not. I'm here, and I'm staying." Andrew squeezed his hand. "So, what's the plan now?"

"Stay the course, I suppose."

"For which? The treasonous plot or our relationship?" Kean said.

Andrew chuckled. "Both."

Kean leaned down and kissed him, and cheers filled the room. Andrew grabbed Kean's head and deepened the kiss before letting go.

"I've decided on our new name!" George announced, and Andrew groaned.

"Why do we need a new name?" Patrick asked. "We haven't had any new members."

"Ah, but we have to include the king and his harem." George smirked.

Andrew glanced at Kean and Kendal, who had joined them. "I dread to think."

"You'll like it!"

"Just say it, George. Stop dragging it out," Damon shouted.

"We're now called the Sexy Sixteen."

Everyone groaned, and Andrew pointed to the door. "Everyone out!" He refocused on Kean and Kendal. "I still have a bit of work to do. Do you want to hang around here or head to the suite, and I'll get there as soon as I can? Or do you need to go, Kean?"

"We'll leave you in peace and get comfortable in your suite," Kean said. "I'm not going anywhere."

Andrew smiled. "It's your choice."

Kean leaned down again and kissed him, then stepped to the side. Andrew took Kendal into his arms and held them, nuzzling their neck. Then he lifted his head and kissed Kendal, too.

"Make sure you eat."

"Yes, Sir," they said in unison and laughed.

They exited the room hand-in-hand, and Andrew dropped his head into his hands. He should've listened to his instincts. Their relationship was never meant to be kept quiet. It was next to impossible because someone always wanted the inside scoop and had enough money to pay for it. Apart from those closest to him, no one knew about their relationship.

Except for some household staff, maybe. Kean and Kendal had sat next to him at the dining table the other day. It never occurred to him it would show the staff who attended to them that they were dear to him. Had it been one of those who had told? And if so, why hadn't they told the reporter who?

Andrew sighed yet again and tried to focus on his work. It took him a couple of hours to get it done, and when he exited his office, Randall was able to give him an update on the media.

"It's been taken down, but other sites are trying to cash in on the story. Mav is focusing on it and will work to get the sites shut down every time it's loaded. There's not much more we can do at the moment."

"Except make a statement," Andrew murmured.

"Sorry?"

Andrew shook his head. "Let me think on it, Randall. I'll let you know if I decide to do anything drastic, don't worry."

"I'd appreciate that, Your Majesty." He smiled. "Have a good evening."

"Make sure you finish quickly, Randall. I don't want you working too late."

"I'll do my best, Your Majesty."

Colt trailed him to his suite before getting his attention. "Your Majesty? We have the details about the funerals now."

Andrew's throat closed. "Thank you, Colt. Can you let Randall know, please?"

"Of course. Have a good evening."

Andrew nodded and entered the suite, leaning back against the door when he closed it. Kean and Kendal sat on the sofa, Kendal with their head in Kean's lap while they read, and Kean watched TV.

Kendal glanced over. "Hey. Everything okay?"

"It's been a long day."

"Let's get dinner ordered," Kendal said, standing. "What do you want?"

"I'm not really hungry."

"Chicken it is, then," Kendal said, picking up the phone. They placed the order and walked over to Andrew, who still stood by the door. "Come. Sit. Rest."

Andrew didn't deny them and allowed them to guide him to the sofa. Kendal pushed him down until he was in the position Kendal had been in when he entered. Kean threaded his fingers into Andrew's hair, and Andrew's eyes closed. Kendal slipped beneath his legs, and Andrew let himself float, emptying his mind of everything except how he felt.

With four hands relaxing him, he felt at home. Just like he had been with Louisa. How had these two people managed to make him feel alive again? He hoped he did the same for them.

A phone rang, and Kean cursed. "Sorry." The noise cut off.

"Do you need to go?" Andrew asked, looking up at him.

Kean shook his head. "I'm right where I need to be."

Andrew closed his eyes again. They needed to talk about how they would address the media, but it would have to wait. It's not like they were going anywhere.

18

CHRISTIAN

*H*ow the hell could he have been so wrong about Daniel? Christian had trusted him with so many thoughts and personal things that it made his stomach churn to think about what Daniel could've done with that knowledge. What he might've already done with that knowledge.

He couldn't get the thought of being deceived out of his head.

"Daddy?"

His head lifted from where it had been resting on his palms. "Yes, sweetheart?"

"Do you need Rexie huggles?" Ollie stood before him, clenching his stuffed dinosaur, and Christian relaxed.

"I would love some Rexie *and* Ollie huggles."

Ollie giggled and climbed into Christian's lap. "We can do that."

Christian nestled his face into Ollie's neck, breathing him in. The scent of the bubble bath Ollie loved so much helped to centre him, and he took several long breaths before pressing his lips to Ollie's temple.

"Thank you, sweetie. Would you like to play with the animals?"

"Yes, please!"

Christian stood, still holding Ollie, who yelped, then giggled as he carried the little boy to the playroom. As much as Ollie needed the release of being little, Christian needed the release of being his Daddy. To wipe away everything else but what Ollie needed. He set Ollie down when they entered the room, and his boy immediately raced to the animal box. Playing any game that involved animals was one of Ollie's favourites. It didn't matter if it was vets, Noah's Ark, or just having a pet; Ollie loved it all.

Christian helped him to set up the animals in a zoo, and the stress began to recede. He would never forgive Daniel for what he'd done, but it had taught him to be more vigilant. After everything that had happened, he sometimes felt like having every person triple-checked to ensure they were who they said they were, but that wouldn't help. As in Daniel. He had been checked several times, and they found nothing. It didn't take much to realise he was as good at computers as Gia was, but no one had known that because he'd hidden that particular talent.

"Daddy, it's feeding time!"

Christian turned his attention once more to his boy and smiled. "Well, I better find the fish for the penguins then, hadn't I?"

"And the meat for the lions!"

Christian chuckled and reached into the small box they had of different foods they could feed the animals. Ollie had quite the collection now, but as the number of animals had grown, so had the necessity to buy what they needed to be fed.

As they played, Christian found his attention divided, which wasn't his normal practice when Ollie was little. He refused to stop Ollie from having what he needed, though, so every time he felt his attention wandering, he brought it back again. He couldn't stop it from happening, but he could brush it away every time he needed to.

Ollie climbed into his lap and snuggled into him. "We need a nap, Daddy."

Christian smiled and cradled his boy. He carried him over to the small day bed they had, but Ollie wriggled. "What's wrong?"

"Not this bed, Daddy. Big bed. We *all* need a nap."

Christian couldn't argue, so he ignored the mess—they could tidy it later—and carried his boy to bed. He undressed them both and, wearing boxers, slipped beneath the cool sheets. He wrapped Ollie in his arms and sighed.

"Sleep, Daddy. Rexie and I will look after you." Ollie kissed his nose, and Christian smiled.

"Thank you, sweet boy."

He closed his eyes, knowing that was what Ollie wanted, but his mind was busy trying to figure out how Daniel had hidden his true nature from them all. Undercover agents were able to hide everything about themselves, so it wasn't difficult to think that Daniel could do the same, but Christian didn't *want* to think he would do that. Problem was, he had.

"Sleep, Daddy," Ollie murmured in a tired voice.

"Sweet dreams, sweetheart."

"Night, Daddy," Ollie breathed.

Christian let go of everything but the feel of his boy in his arms. Everything would still be there when they woke.

19

KEAN

None of them slept brilliantly, and in the early hours of the morning, Kendal finally broke the silence.

"We're strong enough to withstand the backlash, you know," they whispered. "Individually and together."

They were, but Kean understood how difficult it was to put a loved one in front of the world who might not accept them. Insults and mockeries rained down on them regularly would be enough to weigh on the strongest of people.

"I know you are," Andrew said. "I just didn't want you to have to withstand it."

Kean's heart rate increased. Did this mean he was thinking about it? "What are you thinking, my king?" he asked, purposefully saying his pet name for him.

Andrew sighed, but he kept up the gentle stroking of his fingertips on Kean's arm. "I'm trying to decide the best course of action. A way that no one will get hurt."

"What have you thought of so far?"

"Denying it, which hurts you both and undermines me

when it does finally come to light. Ignoring it, which does the same. Admitting it paints targets on your back and allows the public to cause an uproar. No option is the best."

"You need to do what's best for your country," Kendal said. "If it was just us three, I'd say screw the media and tell the world. But you have many people to think of, not just us."

As much as Kean wanted to argue, Kendal was right. "We knew going in this would be tricky. I won't deny that I'd love to tell the world that you're both mine, but I'm not selfish." Kean chuckled. "Not always. Kendal's right. You need to do what's best for the country."

Andrew rolled to his back, and after a few seconds, Kean climbed out of bed and slipped in on the other side of him. Kendal snuggled up to Andrew's other side, and both rested their cheeks on Andrew's chest. Kean tried to give him as much comfort and support as he could without saying anything.

After a few minutes, Andrew exhaled. "We're going to tell the world."

Kean's heart raced, and he lifted his head. "What?"

Andrew pushed himself upright and leaned over to the bedside table, clicking the light on and blinding them for a few seconds. Then he took their hands in his.

"If you are sure you want this, we'll tell everyone. I'll make an announcement today."

"What changed your mind?"

Andrew glanced at them in turn, smiling. "Your strength astounds me. With everything that has happened to you both, you should be distancing yourself from me, not getting closer. But instead, you stay by my side, willing to keep everything to yourself because you don't want to upset the balance." Andrew shook his head. "No more. I've stood up before the world supporting Henry and Robert, then coming out as bisexual along with George's triad. Taking in Christian as my own, shedding light on what was happening with Charlotte, and supporting all my children and nephews through the trials of their love. If I can be strong for everyone else, I need to be strong for myself. For you. We're telling the world how much I love you both, and we're doing it today."

Kendal sprang forward and threw their arms around Andrew's neck. "We'll be there every step of the way."

Kean squeezed Andrew's hand and smiled. "We will."

Andrew exhaled when Kendal pulled back. "I may have wobbles about your safety now and then, but don't ever forget I love you."

"I love you," Kean said, staring at them both.

"And I love you both, too," Kendal said.

Andrew leaned in to kiss them but paused. "Oh, and just so you know, this isn't an April's Fool joke."

Kean frowned, then laughed. "It's 1 April now. Far too early in the morning for these discussions, in my honest opinion."

"It's never too early to say I love you," Kendal said.

The three of them kissed like they had done when Andrew first took them to bed. It was messy, it was awkward, and Kean loved every minute.

"Okay, you two get some sleep. I need to get to the office," Andrew said, climbing from the bed.

"Why now?" Kean asked.

"I won't be able to sleep now. I have to write a speech, and I don't trust anyone else to do it this time."

"Can we help?" Kendal asked.

Andrew hesitated. "How about you two sleep for a couple of hours, then come and find me? You can help me once I have a basic outline to work with."

"It's a deal," Kendal said, laying back on the bed and pulling the covers up.

Kean and Andrew chuckled, and Kean watched him get ready. "You know where we are if you need us," Kean reminded him.

Andrew smiled back at him. "Thank you. I'll see you soon." He closed the bedroom door behind him.

"Do you think he'll change his mind?" Kendal asked.

"No. Once he sets his mind to something, he'll follow through. We might need to support and remind him now and then, but he'll stand strong."

Kean slipped into bed, dragging Kendal to him so they were snuggled under the covers.

"He loves us, Kean," Kendal whispered.

"He does." He pressed a kiss to their forehead and listened to Kendal's breathing until it softened into sleep.

Kean wasn't concerned about Andrew changing his mind. What he'd said was true. What worried him was his father. He was already going to be in trouble for not returning home the previous night, but this might tip his father over the edge. Should he tell him before the announcement or after? After would be the better option. Then his father couldn't do anything about it because the world would know. If he told him before, he wouldn't put it past Dante to lock him in the house.

He probably had a thousand messages waiting for him on his silenced phone, but he wouldn't check. He'd ignore them all until after the announcement.

Just over two hours later, they entered Andrew's office. Freddie, Douglas and George were already there, and the former stood and hugged them both when the door closed.

"It'll be fine," Freddie said in his usual supportive way.

"Do you want a drink?" George asked, moving to the drinks table.

"Water will be good, thanks," Kendal said.

"I'm fine, thanks," Kean added.

They settled onto the sofa, and Andrew joined them, holding out a sheet of paper. "This is what I've got so far. These buffoons tried to help, but I wouldn't let them."

"It's my job, remember, Father?" George said with a chuckle, handing Kendal their water.

"It is, but have I done a poor job of announcements that you haven't written for me?"

George scrunched his face and sighed. "No. I suppose."

"I'll take that as a compliment, even though it didn't sound like one," Andrew said.

Kean leaned over Kendal's shoulder, reading the words Andrew had written, and his heart broke and got stitched back together again.

Andrew crouched in front of him. "Hey, what's wrong?"

Kean frowned at him. "What do you mean?"

"You're crying. Is everything okay? Did I write something bad?"

Kean huffed a laugh, wiping at his face, and shook his head. "It's perfect."

Andrew pecked him on the lips. "Not quite, but it will be." He stood and gave the paper to George. "I'm going to ask Randall to arrange the announcement for midday. Is that enough time for you to fine-tune it?"

"Yes."

"Thank you."

"Have you decided how you're doing it?" Kean asked. "An in-person announcement or on-screen?"

"In-person. I want the media to have the opportunity to ask

questions. It's what I normally do, though this will be harder to keep under control." Andrew waved his hand. "I mean to keep the questions under control, not the people. But that reminds me of something I have to tell you. From the moment I step out into that room, you will have a bodyguard each. I'm just waiting on Kieren to let me know who so I can introduce you."

"I don't need—"

"It's not up for debate. You know my fears, Kean. This will help a little."

Kean stared at him, seeing the worry in his eyes. "Okay. Once we've finished, I need to go home and speak to Father."

Kendal squeezed his hand. "Do you want me to go with you?"

Kean shook his head. "I don't want you near him. I'm sorry to say, he's never been a fan of the royal family. I've had to fight every time I came to visit Henry, even though I was an adult. He has no idea I socialise with anyone but Henry because I let him believe I didn't."

"Why?" Douglas asked.

"Because I was concerned he would use it to help his business. A business I now want nothing to do with." He peered up at Andrew when he said it, and Andrew beamed at him.

"I'm glad. You're worth so much more than that."

Kean ducked his head. "I might need a place to stay…"

George chuckled. "Are you asking your sugar daddy to let you stay at the castle?"

"George!" Andrew snapped.

"It was a joke!"

"Get that speech sorted, then come back with your tail between your legs, please."

George huffed but stood. He stopped beside Kean. "Sorry. It *was* just a joke. I promise I don't think of you like that."

Kean chuckled. "I know, thanks."

He disappeared. Andrew turned to Freddie. "Can you check in with Randall and make sure everything's set up? My head is killing me."

"Of course."

"Douglas, could you get an update from Mav for me? I know he's been working on the leak from yesterday."

"Sure."

Both men exited the room, and then it was just them again.

"You sure know how to clear a room," Kean said.

Andrew exhaled and sat in a chair to the side of where they were, rubbing his head. Kendal rose and stood behind him, massaging Andrew's head for him. Andrew closed his eyes and groaned.

"Have you taken anything for it?" Kean asked.

"No. It only came on a few minutes ago," Andrew murmured.

"Do you have anything in here?"

"No."

Kean rose and headed out of the room. Randall was at his desk, talking to Freddie.

"Sorry to interrupt. Do you have any paracetamol, please?"

"Of course..." Randall seemed like he wanted to add something, but instead, he opened his desk drawer and handed Kean a small box.

"Thanks."

"You're welcome..."

Freddie chuckled. "In case you're wondering what's come over him," he thumbed over his shoulder, "Randall is struggling with what to call you." He grinned. "I bet it's hurting him not to acknowledge your rise in the ranks yet."

Kean frowned. "Rise in the ranks?"

Freddie's expression cleared and softened. "You're about to be announced as the king's consorts. What did you think would happen?"

Kean stared at him as the words penetrated. "Holy shit," he breathed.

"Damn, I think I broke him." Freddie grabbed his shoulders and led him back into Andrew's office. "Sorry, Father. I assumed you'd told him what would happen after the announcement. I might've said the wrong thing."

Andrew settled beside Kean on the sofa Freddie had deposited him on. "Bloody hell, Freddie. You've been here the entire time they have. When did I have the chance to tell them?"

"How about when you told them you were going public? That would've been a good time," Freddie snapped.

It brought Kean out of his head, and he faced Andrew. "It wasn't Freddie's fault. It never occurred to me, but it should have."

Andrew sighed. "Let me get you a drink of water, and I'll explain to you both."

While Kean sipped a glass of ice-cold water, Kendal settled beside him, and Andrew sat on the coffee table, Freddie having gone back to Randall.

"Freddie is right. I should've mentioned this before agreeing to announce it all. I'm sorry." He sighed. "So, when a king or queen takes a lover-slash-spouse, they're usually given the title of consort. Louisa was Queen Consort, though most people just called her Queen Louisa. However, with you two, it needs to be slightly different. It can't be King Consort, unfortunately. I was thinking of a compromise, but I want your honest opinions." Andrew scratched his beard. "I was considering for you, Kean, Prince Consort, and Kendal,

Princex Consort. If you'd prefer different titles, we can discuss it."

Kean glanced at Kendal, who seemed as shocked as Kean had been a few moments earlier. "I don't really need the title, but I understand why I need to have one. It sounds fine to me. Whatever you think is best."

"I'm good," Kendal squeaked.

Kean chuckled and slid an arm around Kendal's back. "Breathe, Kendal."

"I'm breathing. I'm breathing." The more they spoke, the more normal they sounded. They inhaled. "I'm back. Holy crap. This never occurred to me."

Andrew smiled. "And that makes me happy because it means you're not here for the titles and prestige."

"Not even a little," Kendal said. "But don't the titles usually get given when a monarch gets married?" Their eyes widened. "Not that I'm expecting marriage. I'm just…" They closed their mouth.

Andrew laughed. "I know, Kendal. And yes, usually. But I'm all for bending the rules when I need to. And the marriage thing is something we need to talk about later." He paused. "Actually, no. let's do this now. I want you to know everything before we announce it. I would like the two of you to marry if you want to, that is."

"Why?" Kean asked. Andrew wasn't telling them everything; he could feel it.

Andrew rested his elbows on his knees and linked his fingers, staring down at them. "You will not like my reasoning, but I won't budge on this. So you will need to decide if it's a deal-breaker." He inhaled. "I'm sixty-seven years old. You're thirty-three and thirty-one. You have a lot more years ahead of you than I do, and although I don't want to think of it, I need to. When I'm gone, you'll have each other, and I want your marriage to stand strong."

"You're not going anywhere for years to come," Kendal said.

Andrew smiled. "I hope so. I'd gladly do a ceremony for the three of us if that's something you want in the future, but if you ever decide you want to marry within this triad, it will be each other."

Kean didn't want to think about it, but Andrew was right. Plus, it might ease some concerns the public might have. Not that he cared what they thought about his love life anymore.

"Okay," he murmured, staring at Andrew. "It's not ideal, but okay."

Kendal frowned. "Fine. I'm not happy about it, but I understand."

"We're still doing this?" Andrew asked.

Kendal slapped at his arm. "Yes!"

Andrew chuckled and pulled them both to him, kissing their foreheads. "I love you."

Five hours later, they stood by a door, waiting to be led into a room where Andrew would announce their relationship. Kean's stomach churned. He hated these events because there was no telling what would happen. Too many bad things had happened at events recently, and he wished it would stop.

"It's time, Your Majesty," Randall said.

Andrew nodded. "Let's go." He glanced back at them. "Stay with Freddie and Douglas."

Kean nodded, and the doors opened. Andrew went first, stepping up to the podium, and the rest of them filed in behind him. To make it less obvious straight away that Kean and Kendal were the ones going to be in the spotlight, Randall, Brady and several bodyguards stood with them.

Andrew had explained everything to Brady when he'd arrived after his summons.

"Good afternoon, and thank you for being here," Andrew started. "I'm standing before you, yet again, because the news has targeted my family. I understand that with our roles comes some level of scrutiny, and I have no issues with that. My problem lies with gossip mongers who try to belittle us." Andrew shuffled. "Events that should be private are highlighted, poked and prodded at, and torn apart as if they are anyone's concerns but our own. This has become more and more apparent as the years go by. Before I go any further, I would ask that you imagine your home life, your work life, your relationships, the food you eat, the places you go, and so on, being open for everyone to comment on. I can hazard a guess that most of you wouldn't like it. So, why you think we do is beyond me."

Andrew cleared his throat and inhaled, the tension seeping into him, and Kean wanted to comfort him, but he couldn't. Not yet.

"I'm standing before you, yet again," he repeated his earlier phrase, "to explain my choices. Choices I shouldn't have to explain. But I'm doing it to, hopefully, stop the rumours. The people in my life don't deserve that." He inhaled again, and Kean held his breath, knowing what was coming. "I would like to introduce you to my partners, Prince Consort Kean and Princex Consort Kendal."

They stepped forward, standing on either side of Andrew but a step behind, as murmurs rose in the audience. Kean could see a mixture of responses from the journalists present, their faces showing their opinions.

"Before you cast your stones, remember this. Louisa knew what these two people meant to me, and she cared for them deeply. My feelings towards them have deepened over the past year, and I know she would want me to be happy. And with Kean and Kendal, I am. Louisa's death broke my heart, but Kean and Kendal have helped me make it whole again."

Andrew reached back for them, linking their fingers and glancing at each of them before facing the journalists again.

"*I* will take some questions now."

It was a long half an hour before Andrew called the question time to an end. Once they were back behind closed doors, Andrew pulled them to him.

"Thank you."

"We love you," Kendal said.

"I need to call my father," Kean said, dread weighing him down.

"I thought you were going to see him?" Kendal said.

Kean shook his head. "I don't want to be there."

"I'll come with you," Kendal said.

Kean frowned. "Okay."

"We'll be with you, no matter what," Andrew said. "And you'll have the guards, too."

Kean swallowed hard. It would be enough because he knew he was about to lose the only family he had left.

20

KENDAL

"Are you ready?" Kendal asked as their new guards drove them to Kean's house. Andrew had introduced Greg and Ford to them before the media frenzy, and they would be with them every day from then on.

"Not really, but it's better that I get it done now."

Kendal could feel Kean's hand shaking in theirs, and they wished they could do more than be there. They had no experience with Kean's family, so they didn't know what to expect. It made them glad for the guards to be with them if his father was as volatile as Kean implied.

Kean stared at the house when they pulled to a stop and the guards climbed out. Greg, who was Kean's guard, opened the door for them, and they climbed out, still holding hands.

"Let's get this over with," Kean said, starting for the door.

The moment they stepped over the threshold, a hard, sneering voice shouted Kean's name. Kean tightened his grip for a second before letting go completely.

"Yes, Father?"

"Get your ass in here!"

Kendal followed Kean as he entered a large, darkly decorated office. Kean stopped a third of the way to the desk.

Kean's father, Dante, narrowed his eyes on Kendal and the guards before focusing on his son again. "What are *they* doing here?"

Kendal thought he was talking about them for a moment but soon realised the man meant them and the guards.

"If you've seen the news, you know why, Father."

Dante sneered. "Don't be ridiculous, boy. This is some April Fool's joke, isn't it? The king has a plan to prank the country, right?"

Kean shook his head. "I'm leaving the business, Father. I don't want to work in construction."

Dante stood, his chair scraping back. "Like hell you are!"

The guards took a step closer, stopping at Kendal's sides.

"You'll find someone worthy to take over."

"So, you got yourself some ass, and now you want to leave. After everything we've done for you." Kean turned away. "I didn't dismiss you!" Kean kept walking.

"I need to pack some stuff," he murmured, grabbing Kendal's hand and leading them to the stairs.

The guards waited outside of the room while Kean threw some clothes and things he wanted to take with him. Kendal realised Kean didn't think he'd be coming back. Their heart broke for him. He lost his brother to drugs, his mother was lost in alcoholism, and his father wasn't a nice man at all. They resolved to be everything Kean could ever need from then on.

Kean shouldered the two bags and picked up another. "I'm ready."

"Okay."

They descended the stairs, and Dante flew out of the office, stopping in their way.

"You're not going anywhere. I've spent too much of my life making you into who you are. I'm not letting you throw it away now."

Kean stared at him. "I'm not who you need."

"Oh, you just need some royal dick, apparently."

The bags fell to the floor, and Kean slammed his hands into Dante's chest. "Shut up!"

Dante sneered again. "The man could be your father, Kean. How long do you think he'll keep you around? He'll find someone else to get his dick wet in soon enough."

Kendal didn't see it coming, but Kean's fist was smacking into Dante's cheek seconds later. Dante fell to the floor, holding his face. He glared at Kean.

"You'll regret that." Dante stood, stepping closer to Kean, but Greg pulled his gun and pointed it at Dante.

"That's close enough," Greg said.

Ford grabbed Kean's bags in one hand and Kendal's biceps in the other while Greg manoeuvred Dante into his office doorway. Ford ushered Kean past them, with Greg keeping his body between them all the time.

"It wasn't very nice to meet you, Mr Seymour," Greg said as they exited the house. He slammed the door shut, and they climbed into the car.

Kean closed his eyes and breathed as Ford drove them away from the house. "I don't know if he'll retaliate." He stretched his hand. "That bloody hurt."

Greg held something out to him. "It's an ice pack. You did well."

Kean smiled and rested it against his hand, hissing when it touched the undoubtedly raw skin.

Kendal leaned their head against Kean's shoulder. "I'm proud of you."

Kean's lips pressed against their head. "Thanks. Would it be okay to bunk with you for a bit?"

Kendal laughed. "Of course. Consider it your haven, too, as I said before."

They were quiet on the journey back, and they settled into Andrew's suite for an afternoon snack. Neither of them wanted to disrupt Andrew when he was busy putting out the fires his announcement had caused. Kendal wanted to be with him, but it was better if they left him be for now.

"I have to go in a minute," Kendal said.

Kean frowned for a second. "Oh, yes. You're having dinner with Quinn, aren't you?"

Kendal nodded. "Would you like to come? I'm sure they won't mind."

"No. You spend some time with them. They'll no doubt want you to spill all the juicy gossip, which you couldn't do if I was there."

Kendal laughed. "True. But you can come if you want to."

"It's okay, angel. I'll calm Andrew while you're gone."

Kendal pouted. "I don't want to miss that."

Kean chuckled. "Not like that."

"You can. I'm not saying you can't, but you two together are so hot."

"Thank you."

Kendal glanced at them. "And since when do you call me angel?"

"Well, I have 'my king' for Andrew, so I've been trying to think of something for you. Angel is perfect because you *are* my angel."

"So sweet," Kendal said, kissing him.

"Are you going to say goodbye to Andrew before you go?"

Kendal cocked their head. "Do you think I should? I don't want to interrupt."

"I'll think he'll be sad if you don't."

"Okay. I'll nip there now, then head out." They leaned down to kiss Kean again. "Come with me to him. He'll want to make sure you're okay."

Kendal pulled Kean up, and they wandered down the hallways to Andrew's office. "Hey, Randall. Is he free for a minute?"

Randall nodded. "He is, Your Highnesses."

Kendal paused. "That's going to need getting used to."

Kean chuckled. "I know."

They knocked, and Andrew called for them to enter.

"Hi. How did it go?" Andrew asked, rounding the desk.

"It went," Kean said. "I'm staying with Kendal for now."

"He punched his father," Kendal said, dropping Kean in it.

"You what?" Andrew looked him over. "Are you okay?"

Kean raised his red hand. "A little sore, but it was worth it."

"What did—"

"Sorry to interrupt. I need to get going. I just wanted to say goodbye before I left," Kendal said to Andrew.

"Are you coming back tonight?"

Kendal smiled. "Do you want me to?"

"Of course."

"Then I'd love to."

Andrew leaned down and kissed him. "You're taking Ford with you, right?"

Kendal nodded. "He doesn't have to stay, though, does he?"

"No. We know Quinn and his master, so you'll be fine. But call him when you're finished so he can pick you up."

"All right. See you both later."

The journey to Quinn's was a little strange. They weren't used to riding in the back of a car when they were the only passenger. Plenty of things would change from then on. How it would work, they didn't know, but so far, there didn't seem to be that much interest in them.

Quinn's house was slightly larger than their own, and lights blazed from the windows. Kendal smiled at the homely feel it had.

"Thank you, Ford. I'll message you when we've finished, but it probably won't be for a few hours."

"That's not a problem. I'll be here when you're done."

Kendal climbed out of the car when Ford opened the door for them and headed for Quinn's front door.

"Yay, you made it!" Quinn said, hugging them.

In that moment, Kendal realised they were getting better at the touchy-feely stuff. They no longer seemed to blanch whenever someone touched them, even accidentally.

"Yes, I'm not sure how often this will happen now, with security issues and such, but for today, I'm here."

Quinn shut the door and ushered them through the house towards the dining room. "We have another guest tonight, too. A friend of ours we haven't seen for a while. You'll like them."

They entered the dining room, and the second guest stood to greet them.

"Kendal, may I introduce Danny? Danny, this is Kendal, who I was talking to you about."

Kendal froze. Of all the people Quinn could be friends with, it had to be him.

"We've met, actually," Daniel said, eyes boring into Kendal. "We've played a few times over the years. I've not seen you for a while, though, Kendal. How're things?" He narrowed his eyes, and Kendal understood the subtle threat.

They swallowed and exhaled. "Everything's good, thanks. Busy, but good."

"Glad to hear it."

"Come. Sit down. What can I get you to drink, Kendal?" Quinn asked, unaware of the undercurrent.

"Just water, please."

"Seriously?" Quinn whined, waiting at the threshold of the kitchen. "Nothing alcoholic?"

Kendal smiled and shook their head, trying not to let their nerves show. "Water's good."

Quinn huffed and disappeared, and Daniel stepped closer. "Now, I don't think we need to announce any problems while we're here, do we? From your reaction when you entered, your motley crew has realised I'm not exactly who I said I was."

"Who are you?"

Daniel smirked. "That's for me to know and you to find out in due course. It does put us in a bind, though. I had planned to relax with friends tonight and try to tease information from you, but now we might have to change plans."

"Don't hurt them."

Daniel shook his head. "I wouldn't hurt them. They are actually my friends."

Kendal's stomach rolled. "Are they in on this with you?"

"No. I kept them out of it. It was nice to have somewhere to go and let off steam. I've never involved them." Daniel narrowed his eyes and grabbed Kendal's arm. "But I will if I have to."

"You'll get no problems from me," Kendal said.

He let go. "Then let's have a lovely dinner, where we discuss mutual acquaintances, and I can offer you a ride home when it's time to leave."

Kendal nodded. How the hell were they going to get out of this?

"Here we go," Quinn said, carrying a tray with four

glasses. "A beer for you, Daniel. Water for you, Kendal. And two whiskeys for us."

Quinn's master, Pierce, entered and greeted the two of them. "I'm glad you could make it. Everything's ready, so shall we sit?"

"I'm just going to wash up, okay?" Kendal said, thumbing over their shoulder towards the bathroom.

"Sure." Pierce smiled.

Kendal glanced at Daniel, who didn't seem interested in them leaving and headed to the bathroom. Once they locked the door, they fumbled through their pockets for their phone so they could call Ford back. Where was it? They rechecked their pockets, but it was nowhere to be seen. They knew they'd brought it with them because how else would they be able to contact Ford to pick them up?

Had Daniel taken it when he'd grabbed them? It was possible. Either that, it had dropped from their pocket in the car. Head bowed and shoulders slumped, they breathed for a moment, then washed their hands and returned to the dining room.

Settling into the chair next to Daniel, Kendal smiled. "Thank you for the food. It looks delicious."

"So," Quinn said a few minutes later. "I heard the announcement today. You've been keeping secrets, Kendal."

"Quinn," Pierce warned. "We talked about this. Don't push."

Kendal laughed, trying to make it sound natural instead of strained. "It's okay. I've kept secrets, but not for long. It's only really been a couple of weeks."

Quinn raised his eyebrows. "And you're already Consort? Wow."

Kendal didn't like his implications, but if the roles were

reversed, they would think the same thing, so they brushed it aside. "I love them, Quinn. That's all that matters."

"How did you meet?" Daniel asked.

Kendal pushed the food around their plate. Daniel probably knew exactly what happened if he was part of the group trying to hunt the royal family down. He was doing it to get a rise out of Kendal, no doubt. "Well, there was an incident a couple of years ago, and Andrew was there to help me through it. Kean is friends with Henry, so we met at events and things. Quinn's met him, too."

"A couple of years ago? The queen was still alive then, wasn't she?"

Kendal lifted their chin. "There was nothing between us at that point."

"Of course, there wasn't," Pierce agreed. "Daniel…"

Daniel held up his hands. "Sorry. I didn't mean it that way."

Yes, he did.

"How are you dealing with the fame so far?" Quinn asked.

"Luckily, I haven't dealt with it much yet. I still think it's going through the social channels and getting the word out and everything. Tomorrow might be a whole different board game."

"Ain't that the truth," Daniel commented, forking more food into his mouth.

"Daniel, you said you've been busy lately. What's been going on?" Pierce asked, and Kendal was grateful for the subject change. Maybe Daniel would mess up and tell him something useful.

"Just been kept on base a lot. We've had some super-secret shit going on, and it's taken time to work through it."

"You must be near the end, though, if you're allowed out again," Pierce said.

"Getting there."

"Glad to hear it."

Kendal was tense throughout the entire dinner, though neither Quinn nor Pierce seemed to sense it. At one point, a phone beeped, sounding suspiciously like their own, and Daniel apologised and switched it off before Kendal could see if it was.

Not wanting to put his friends at risk for longer than necessary, Kendal pleaded tiredness for cutting short their evening, and Daniel, as he'd said he would, offered them a lift home. Kendal agreed and hugged Quinn, then Pierce, thanking them again.

"I'm glad you're thinking like a survivor rather than trying to be a hero," Daniel said as they walked to his car. "Or would that be herox or herex in your case?"

Kendal didn't reply. Daniel opened the passenger door for them, and Kendal climbed in, frantically trying to figure out what to do. When Daniel got in, Kendal asked, "Where are we going?"

"I'm taking you home like I said I would."

"Does that mean my actual home or a place you believe should be my home?"

Daniel chuckled darkly. "This time, your actual home."

"Why?"

"We need to talk. And what better way than to talk in a fortress no one can disturb us at?" Daniel snorted at Kendal's surprise. "Yes. I know all about your security anxiety. Christian was extremely thankful when I explained what system he should get."

Kendal's heart pounded. If he knew about the security system, did he also know about the failsafe? Was it safe for

Kendal to attempt to use it? They had no choice. They had to try.

When Daniel pulled up to Kendal's house, he rounded the car and opened the door for them. Kendal tried to keep away from him, but Daniel slipped his arm around their waist. It surprised them that no journalists were present. They would've thought they'd have found out where they lived by now.

At the door, Daniel let them go. "Open it."

Kendal swallowed and opened the hatch where the security sensor lived. They inhaled and typed in the code. The light went green, and Daniel opened the door.

"Well done. Keep behaving, and we won't have any problems."

Kendal let out the breath they'd been holding and entered their house. It was no longer a home for them. Even with one step inside, Daniel had poisoned this place for them. What was it with people thinking they could take over their space and not make them annoyed?

"Do you want a drink?" Kendal asked, wanting to get away.

"Not so fast. Sit your ass down, Consort."

Daniel pulled Kendal's phone from his pocket. "When did you get that?"

Daniel chuckled. "When I grabbed your arm while we were talking earlier. You were so tense and anxious about the fact I was touching you that you didn't feel me grabbing the phone from your pocket." Daniel pressed a few buttons. "Unlock it." He held it out.

Kendal sighed and pressed their thumb to the sensor. "There's nothing on there you can use."

"Ah, but you'd be wrong there." Daniel pressed at the

screen, doing something Kendal couldn't see, then switched it off and slid it back into his pocket. "All done."

"I thought you wanted to talk?"

"Oh, but I do, Kendal, dear. I want to know all about dear old Uncle Andrew."

21

ANDREW

ndrew moved a cushion down, then lay on his side on the sofa, opening his arms for Kean to join him. The moment he did, Andrew held him tightly, allowing him to lean on him as much as he needed. Kendal had sent a message while they'd been on their way to Quinn's, giving him a quick rundown of how things had gone; therefore, he had an idea, but he wanted Kean to let it all out.

"What happened, sweetheart?"

Kean snorted. "My father was his usual self. Though usual as he was to me, not usually how he was in public." He was silent for a moment. "He said I wanted royal dick," he whispered. Andrew withheld his laughter because it wouldn't make Kean feel any better. "Maybe he's right."

"He's not. He sounds jealous."

"I kissed Henry."

Andrew's heart skipped a beat, then restarted, pounding painfully. He swallowed hard, trying to understand what Kean was saying. There was no way he would cheat on either of them, so it must've happened before.

"And?"

Kean lifted his head. "What do you mean, and?"

"There's obviously more to the story than that you kissed him." He remembered something. "Was that why you and he were estranged for a while?"

Kean sniffled and nodded into Andrew's chest. He tightened his hold. "I loved him, and I took a chance that New Year's Eve. I didn't know what he'd been going through with Charlotte and Charles. All I saw was a chance to have what I thought I wanted."

"Did he want you?"

"I thought so, at the time. He kissed me back, but then Freddie interrupted, and Henry closed up. He didn't speak to me again. It was a year later when I plucked up the courage to approach him, and by that point, he was with Robert."

Andrew pressed his lips to Kean's head. "You'd been through a rough time during that year, hadn't you?"

"I'd lost my best friend. And then my brother. Then my mother, near as dammit." Kean sighed. "When I saw Henry and Robert together, I could see it wasn't what Henry and I had. Or what I thought we could have. It made me rethink everything, and though I was sad to have lost a year of our friendship, I could see it was the right decision."

"You can't help who you care for, Kean."

"But he's your nephew."

"And I might feel differently if you'd had a full-blown relationship, but it was a kiss." Andrew chuckled. "Is it a little weird? Yes. But we're good."

Kean snuggled closer. "How can you be so accommodating all the time?"

"I've learnt, in my extensive years, that people have to bend in life. It's not black and white. There are hundreds of shades of grey around, too."

"I—"

Frantic knocking sounded, and Andrew shouted for whoever it was to enter.

"Uncle Andrew, I'm sorry for barging in," Christian said. "Kendal sent the failsafe alarm from their house."

Andrew sat upright, taking Kean with him. "Failsafe alarm?"

"It's a backup alarm. Basically, they had a secondary code they could enter to open the house if they were in trouble. Like if someone was trying to get into the house or someone made them open the house up to them. Ford is on his way to them. So are Brett and Felix. They were close by."

"Why are they at their house?" Kean asked. "They were supposed to be at Quinn's."

Christian shrugged. "I'm not sure. They have switched all the cameras off. We can assume Kendal's in trouble because of the failsafe, but we can't see what kind of trouble."

"Contact Brady, get him over there," Andrew said.

"Already done. He's on his way as we speak," Christian said.

"You're sure it's Kendal and not someone else with the code?" Andrew said.

Christian nodded. "No one has the failsafe code but Kendal. It's different from the usual one to enter the house."

"I know that code, but I had no idea there was a failsafe version." Kean started pacing.

"You know *your* code, Kean. Every person who gets personal access to the house gets given their own unique code. It's how the system works. We can identify who entered the house when depending on which code they entered."

"No wonder Kendal felt so relaxed there. It's like a fortress," Kean said.

"Does it have cameras on the outside of the house?" Andrew asked.

"One pointing at the front door and one at the back door. They're disabled, too."

Andrew's heart was in his throat, but he'd been through similar events before. "I knew there'd be issues the minute we announced this."

"Who do you think it is?"

"I don't know. Could be any one of a number of people. Including people we have no idea about."

"Quinn!" Kean said. "Let me call Quinn." Andrew nodded, and they waited while Kean dialled. He put it on speaker. "Hey, Quinn."

"Hey, Kean. How are you?"

"A little worried. Did Kendal come to you tonight?" Kean asked.

"Yes, they left an hour ago."

Kean stared at Andrew. "Who's 'they?'"

Quinn chuckled. "Sorry. We had another friend over, too. They gave Kendal a lift home."

Andrew's throat closed up. "Who is your friend, Quinn?"

"Oh, Your Majesty. Um, Danny March. We've known him for years, though he doesn't get much time off work."

Andrew dropped his head into his hands. "He's not who he says he is, Quinn. I'm sorry to tell you he's working against us."

Quinn gasped. "No! Danny's not like that. He's a nice guy. We've known him for years," he repeated.

"He might've been to you, Quinn. Same as he was to me, but he's now got Kendal, and we have no idea what he's going to do to them," Christian said.

Andrew heard muffled sniffles, and then another voice

came over the speaker. "Hello, this is Pierce. What's going on?"

"Pierce, we have some bad news. Daniel March is working for those who'd like to see us dead," Andrew said. "And right now, he's got Kendal. Can you give us *any* information about him? Anything at all."

"Fuck. Um, he's been in the Army for years. I met him when we were both Royal Signals stationed at Cawdor in Wales. That was ten years, maybe. He was transferred over to a different unit a couple of years later, and we lost touch for a while. Danny called me a few years ago, saying he worked for someone in a classified department. I didn't think anything of it." Pierce exhaled. "What's he done?" He sounded like he wasn't sure he wanted to know.

"That we don't know," Andrew said. "But it's what he might do that's worrying me. Can you think of any connection between Daniel and the royal family, even something little he might've mentioned before?"

"Not that I can think of—What?" Andrew heard mumbling on the other side of the phone, and he waited rather impatiently. "Sorry, Your Majesty. Quinn remembered Danny talking about his father turning up out of the blue. His father had never been in his life, and he lived with his mother until he signed up for the Army. Danny never mentioned it again after that, though."

"Did he mention his father's name?" Christian asked.

"Jonathon Dyer," Quinn said. "I remember because Danny said he used his middle name as his first name, and I couldn't think of many people who did that. I think it stuck with me."

"Thank you, Quinn. We'll let you know what happens. Please stay home, and if Danny turns up, let us know, but try not to be any different towards him. We don't want him spooked," Andrew said.

"We will."

They ended the call.

"Why does Daniel need Kendal?" Kean asked.

"He might not. It might have been an unfortunate coincidence that they were both invited on the same night. Maybe he saw an opportunity," Christian said, bringing his phone to his ear. "Neil, we need help."

As Christian filled his commanding officer in, a knock sounded, and Andrew's sons and their partners appeared.

"Father, are you okay?"

Andrew nodded. "Yes. Kendal might not be."

"We heard." Freddie glanced at Christian when he hung up the phone. "What's happened?"

They filled them in on what they knew. "Ford, Brett and Felix should be there now."

Christian's phone rang again. "Brett?"

"We're here. There are lights on, but the curtains are closed. Do we know if the cameras are still off?"

"They seem to be. I wouldn't put it past him to add motion sensors or something if he's had time to prepare. Otherwise, I've no idea what to expect."

"Can you get the cameras running again?" Brett asked.

"Not without Kendal's access codes. They have complete control over them for a reason. The only way we can get in now is because of the failsafe code. It activated the security access, which I've given to Brett," Christian said. "Shit!" He clenched his jaw and closed his eyes, shaking his head. "Daniel was the one who suggested the security system for Kendal's house. Fucking hell!"

"So, he knows how it works," Andrew said, his stomach churning. "Does he know about the failsafe?"

"It's not impossible for him to know about it, but it wasn't something I mentioned to him, and it's not something that comes with the system itself. We tweaked the design to add it," Christian said.

"If he knows Kendal has set the alarm off, they're in even more danger," Brett said. "We'll try to get closer and hope there are no surprises. I'll be in touch."

Kean covered his head with his arms and leaned against the wall. Henry went over to him, rubbing his back. Andrew expected to feel jealous after Kean's bombshell from earlier, but he was just glad Kean had someone to help him.

"Is Jonathon Dyer someone we know?" Andrew asked.

"Neil's looking into it now," Christian said.

"Why is that name familiar?" Freddie said. "I feel like I've heard it before."

"Kletti Pazo!" Damon suddenly said. He'd been flicking through some paperwork. "The name rang a bell with me, too. Kletti Pazo was owned by John Ernest *Dyer*."

"So there's a third person in with this?" Andrew said. "John, Ernest, and whoever this Dyer guy is."

"Could it be Daniel?" Christian asked.

"From what Quinn described, there didn't seem to be any love lost between Daniel and his father. If he's involved, I'd be surprised if he'd use his father's name," Andrew said. "Wouldn't it be too much like giving his father the credit?"

He hated this going around in circles to find answers. Kendal was in danger, and there was nothing he could do. Relying on his security team, while the best idea, didn't help his stress levels. He rubbed his forehead with both hands. He couldn't go through this again. Losing another person would destroy him. They had to get Kendal out.

"They have him!" Christian said.

"Is Kendal—"

"They're fine. Shaken, but fine."

"Bring Daniel here."

Christian shook his head. "Commissioner Thomas says you need to visit Kendal's house. He's not moving Daniel yet."

"Why?"

"Why move him when they have him in a fortress?"

Andrew could see the logic. "Okay, let's go. I want to know exactly what this asshole is about."

Thirty minutes later, they pulled up to Kendal's house. Neighbours stood on their doorsteps and driveways, talking with each other while staring at the house. The team must've made some noise when they went in. There was no point in hiding now. Colt opened Andrew's door, and he slid out, holding his hand for Kean to join him. He ignored the nosy neighbours, despite the conversations getting louder.

When they entered the house, Brady met them in the hallway. "Kendal's in the kitchen. I'll wait for you to get back."

"Thanks, Brady."

Andrew tugged Kean towards the kitchen, and Kendal threw themselves into their arms when they saw them.

"I'm so glad you're here," they said.

"Are you okay?" Kean asked.

"Yeah. He talked my ear off, and I think that's the worst thing," Kendal said, leaning back. "He sounds so normal. So sane. It was like having a conversation with the next-door neighbour."

"He didn't hurt you," Andrew asked, needing to make sure.

"No. I kept trying to get him to tell me stuff, but he's too clever."

"You shouldn't have done that," Andrew said. "You could've put yourself in worse danger."

"That's the thing, though. He could've hurt me multiple times, and he didn't. I don't know what his end game was with this, but if he had wanted me dead, I would be."

"I need to talk to him," Andrew said.

Kendal pulled at him. "Don't go in guns blazing. Just talk to him like a human being. I think you'll get more out of him."

"He held you hostage, Kendal!"

"He didn't lay a finger on me, Andrew," Kendal countered. "I'm not saying he's the best person in the room, but don't treat him like a murderer, either." Kendal reached up and cupped his cheek. "I'm fine. Forget about what he did to me and focus on what's behind all this. I have a feeling he could be the break we need."

"Stay here." Andrew stared at them until they nodded once.

Burying his anger at what Daniel had put Kendal through wasn't easy, but he could see the logic in the argument Kendal posed. He couldn't guarantee it would stay locked away, but for now, it was.

"Are you going to be okay?" Brady asked him.

"I'll be fine."

"I'm coming in with you."

Andrew snorted. "Wouldn't expect any less."

They entered the living room, where Daniel sat handcuffed. The man lifted his gaze to Andrew's but didn't say a word.

"Thank you for not hurting them," Andrew said.

Daniel's eyebrows rose. "What?"

"You heard me."

"You're seriously thanking me?"

Andrew chuckled and settled into a seat opposite. "I'd prefer to hurt my knuckles on your face, but I promised I'd be good."

Daniel huffed a laugh. "Didn't think you had it in you."

"What? To punch you or to be good?"

"Both."

Andrew studied him, the ease with which he sat as if he didn't have a care in the world. "Why did you do this?"

"It wasn't my plan. I went to Pierce's house to relax, but when Quinn mentioned Kendal was visiting, I saw it as a way to get information about you. Then that changed when Kendal saw me. I knew you'd figure out who I *wasn't*."

"I don't think that's true," Andrew said. "You've always been Daniel March. But something changed. Something made you veer onto a different path. Was it your father appearing suddenly?"

Daniel stared at him, but Andrew could see he'd surprised him. "Yes, as a matter of fact. At first, I wanted nothing to do with him. He's persistent, though. And when he explained it all, it made me think of how different my life would've been."

"So you went to his side."

Daniel shrugged. "What else could I do? My mother died, and I had no one else."

"What about your friends? Pierce and Quinn, Neil, Christian?"

"I refused to be a burden. I've seen how relationships drift apart when one person puts too much weight on another. I didn't want to lose them."

Andrew leaned forward, resting his elbows on his knees. "But following your father's plan led you here. It's led you right where you didn't want to be—on the edge of losing your friends."

Daniel's jaw firmed, and he didn't reply.

"Why did you keep calling him Uncle Andrew?" Kendal asked from the doorway.

Andrew's heart took off at a gallop. He narrowed his eyes on them and Kean, but they were focused on Daniel. He'd make them regret ignoring his order later.

"Why, Daniel?" Kendal asked again.

"Because he is. Distantly."

"How are you part of my family?" Andrew asked. "Who's Jonathon Dyer?"

Daniel chuckled, dropping his head back as he continued into full-blown laughter. Andrew's stomach rolled. He had a feeling he wasn't going to like Daniel's answer. He glanced at Kendal and Kean. They had worried expressions, too.

"Dear old dad's full name is... Wait for it... Drumroll, please..." Daniel chuckled. "Ernest Jonathon Daniel Dyer. Now known as Ernest Sutcliffe."

Andrew froze. Charlotte and Ernest had been married for forty years. "How old are you?"

Daniel smiled. "Forty-two."

"He never married your mother?"

Daniel snorted. "Why would he when he was courting a princess?" He sneered. "My mother was someone to bide time with until Charlotte said yes. It took him long enough that Mother fell pregnant with me. As soon as she told him, Father stopped seeing her. He sent money but had nothing to do with her or me other than the occasional reminder that she was to keep quiet about whose son I was."

"When did he turn up again?"

"Mother's funeral, of all times."

Andrew paused. "What did he want with you?"

"Isn't that the question of the day? I'm a pawn. Same as everyone else. I have no idea what the endgame is. All I know is that I needed to help you, and I needed to give him information. After all, it was the reason I was transferred there, so I'm told."

"And did you?"

Daniel met his gaze. "Yes."

"Will you tell us about everything you gave him and everything he told you?"

"Yes." No hesitation in his answer.

"Why?"

"Because my mother deserves a better son than I have become."

Andrew nodded and stood. "Tell Brady everything you know. No matter how small. We need this to stop, and you might just be the one to help us." He stepped closer to his partners.

"He's bloody good," Daniel said.

Andrew faced him again. "At what?"

"Being someone else. He's fooled the lot of you for forty years. He's patient, but I don't know why he's doing this. Be careful who you trust."

"We've learnt that lesson already," Andrew murmured. He slid his arms around Kean and Kendal and exited the room. "He's all yours," he told Brady. "I'm going home."

Brady nodded. "I'll keep you up to date."

"Make sure one of my team is present at all interviews, please."

"Will do."

He sighed. "Let's go home."

2 2

KEAN

When they arrived back at Windsor, worried faces surrounded them, and they threw question after question before Andrew called them off.

"It's been a long day. Kendal is fine. How about we have lunch together tomorrow, and you can reassure yourselves again that they are okay?"

"We'll be there," Freddie said, giving each of them a hug.

Kendal didn't shy away from the hugs everyone gave, which was a surprise, but Kean had noticed that they were doing better in social situations—well, with Andrew's large family, anyway.

Once they locked the suite doors behind them, Andrew led them into the bedroom. Kean expected them to snuggle up in bed and sleep, but Andrew faced them and said, "Strip."

Kean opened his mouth to argue but saw Kendal's shoulders lower as if in relief. Did they need this? The need to reaffirm the bond and that they were all still there in one piece. Because Kean wouldn't say no to it. He didn't, in fact.

He pulled his jumper off, throwing it onto a chair near the bed, and unfastened his shirt buttons, watching Kendal hurriedly stripping next to him. By the time Kean had moved onto his trousers, Kendal stood, naked as the day they were born, waiting for instructions. Kean quickly removed the last barriers and stood beside them, facing Andrew.

"Kean, lay on your back on the end of the bed, feet on the floor."

"Yes, Sir."

"Kendal, straddle Kean's knees, but don't sit down. Rest your hands beside Kean's head."

"Yes, Sir."

Once they were both in position, with Kean staring into Kendal's beautiful green eyes, Andrew said, "Kean, kiss them while I get things ready."

"Yes, Sir," Kean whispered, already lifting his head to join their lips. Their lips were soft but dry as if they hadn't had enough to drink that day, and Kean sipped at the top, then the bottom and licked across them, requesting entry. Kendal opened for him, and he slid his tongue inside, brushing along theirs, coaxing a response, which came in a low moan. Kendal's tongue chased his as he retreated, and Kean sucked on it as he would if it was something else. Kendal whimpered, pressing closer, taking the kiss deeper. Kean breathed through his nose as he concentrated on allowing Kendal whatever they needed.

"Breathe," Andrew commanded.

They pulled apart, gasping, chests heaving as they inhaled much-needed air. Andrew stood behind Kendal, mouth in a hard line, but his eyes told a different story. His eyes showed his pain. He hurt because Kendal hurt.

"Kendal, I have a suede flogger. Are you okay with me using this?"

Kendal's eyelids fluttered, and the corners of their lips curved. "Yes, Sir."

"Okay. Keep steady while I warm your skin with my hand."

Kendal's body jerked at the first smack, gentle though it was, but they pushed back straight after, searching for more, like Kean knew they would. Kean skimmed his fingers up and down Kendal's arms, the tremble in them increasing with every joining of hand to ass.

"Are you ready for more?"

"Yes, Sir," Kendal murmured. Their breath caught when Andrew dragged the flogger down their back.

"We're going for ten. Count for me."

Kendal swallowed. Kean couldn't see Andrew's movements from where his king now stood, but Kendal gasped and jerked when the flogger touched its mark.

"One," Kendal said.

"You count, too, Kean," Andrew ordered.

"One," Kean repeated.

Kendal hummed, eyes closing with the next one. "Two," they both said. "Three."

With every undoubtedly smarting flick of the flogger, they counted, and Kendal relaxed further, their arms struggling to keep themselves upright. Their cocks slipped against each other, too, which didn't help to keep Kean's arousal from rising.

"Ten," they breathed together.

"Good. Well done, my sweet." Andrew rubbed his hands over Kendal's ass cheeks, rocking them gently forward against Kean's body. "Lower down and straddle Kean's lap now."

Kean helped them because they were loose as a noodle,

and they snuggled their face into Kean's neck once they rested across him.

"Do you want more, Kendal?" Andrew asked.

"Yes, please, Sir," they mumbled, the words hot against Kean's neck.

"Colour?"

"Green, Sir."

Andrew met Kean's gaze with an arched brow. "Green, Sir," Kean added.

Andrew's mouth curled up. "Let's get you prepped them, my sweet." He disappeared out of Kean's line of sight, but he heard a drawer opening.

Kean smoothed his hands up and down Kendal's back, gently soothing them until Andrew returned. Andrew slicked his fingers and dropped the tube beside them on the bed. Kendal didn't move when fingers slid between his cheeks; he only hummed, the vibration flowing into Kean's chest. The humming turned into a moan, and Kean assumed Andrew had pressed inside. It was strange seeing it from this angle but not being able to feel or see what was happening. Hot as hell but strange.

"That's it. You're doing so well, my sweet," Andrew said when Kendal gasped.

Kendal rocked against Kean, their cocks nestled together and rubbing with every movement. He would be able to come like this given enough time, but he wanted to see what Andrew had planned for them.

"There we go," Andrew murmured. Kendal inhaled, held it, and then sighed it out again. Kean smiled at Andrew over Kendal's back. "You're almost ready for me now."

A few minutes later, Andrew pulled free and stepped back. He undressed, revealing a hard, straining cock. He opened a condom and slid it down, then slicked it before stepping behind Kendal.

"Kean, sweetheart, hold them open for me."

Kean groaned. "Fuck," he whispered. The idea of holding Kendal open so Andrew could spear inside him was far hotter than it maybe should have been. He slid his hands down Kendal's back and grabbed a handful of his ass cheeks, which were warm to the touch from the flogging. Kendal hissed but didn't object.

"Kendal, colour, please."

"Green, Sir. Please!"

"Hold on to Kean." Kendal slid their arms beneath him, holding his shoulders. "That's it. Ready?"

"Yes, Sir," they both answered.

Andrew smiled, and Kean and Kendal's cock pressed harder against each other as Andrew pushed inside Kendal. Kean couldn't see it, but he felt it when Andrew slid deep because Andrew's groin met the backs of Kean's hands. Andrew hissed and leaned down, keeping them all locked.

"Steady," he said when Kendal squirmed. "Let yourself adjust. Besides, I want a kiss."

Kendal turned their head to the side as much as possible, and Andrew kissed them, tongues tangling. It was hot as fuck to watch. Kendal writhed between them, seeking more, but only succeeded in rubbing more insistently against Kean. Andrew pulled back with a whimper from Kendal, then focused on Kean. He leaned down and captured Kean's lips, still wet from Kendal's kiss, and Kean closed his eyes, falling into it.

At least until Andrew started moving. He didn't withdraw much, if any, just gently pushed against them. Kendal keened between them, dropping their head to Kean's shoulder, and Andrew pulled away from their kiss. He stood upright, gripping Kendal's hips, and withdrew. Kendal panted against his skin, the wet heat fanning Kean's arousal along with the sounds they were all making.

"Fuck, Kendal," Andrew growled. He pushed inside again, slower than slow. Withdrawing, he hissed and exhaled, looking as though he wanted to both savour and devour at the same time.

"Please, Sir!" Kendal whined.

"Grip them a little harder, Kean. Let them feel how much we want them. How much we need them."

Kean did, and Kendal groaned into his ear. "That's it, angel. Let everything go," he said.

Andrew picked up his pace, slamming into Kendal and ensuring each movement sent Kendal and Kean's dicks rubbing together. Precome slid between them, easing their way. Kean's orgasm was streaking down his spine, pooling in his groin. He could easily come, but he bit his lip and held back, wanting to wait.

Andrew narrowed his eyes at him and then picked up his speed. Kendal moaned, squeezing Kean's shoulders as they held on.

"Come on, Kendal, my sweet. Let us love you. Come for us," Andrew said.

Kendal tightened their hold again, whimpered and tensed, and then their entire body trembled and jerked as their climax tore through them, releasing between them.

"Fuck," Kean said, glancing up at Andrew. He hadn't been given permission to come yet, but soon, he wouldn't be able to help it. "Sir?" He panted, trying to hold on.

Andrew waited, thrusting a few more times, then growled, "Come, sweetheart."

His body shook as it listened to the order, and Kendal gasped and bit down on Kean's shoulder, sending more shudders through him. He heard Andrew groan and slam deep, his groin pinning Kean's hands to Kendal's ass, and he envisaged him exploding into the condom inside Kendal.

Kean let go of Kendal's ass cheeks, rubbing gently, both to soothe Kendal and to touch Andrew. He slid his hand to Andrew's hip, squeezing gently as Andrew pulled free.

"Jeez," Kendal said sleepily. They yawned and added, "Sir."

Kean chuckled. "Yeah. Jeez, Sir. When can we do that again?"

Andrew snorted. "Not yet. I'm sixty-seven, remember? I need time to rest. You two go at it if you need to, though. I'm happy to watch." Kendal moved to stand, the stickiness between them becoming apparent and disgusting, but Andrew rested a hand on their back. "Stay for a moment." They settled back down.

Andrew disappeared and returned with a cloth and some cream. From what Kean could see and feel, Andrew cleaned Kendal and applied the soothing cream to their ass cheeks. Then they both helped Kendal to stand. Andrew wiped over Kendal's stomach and cock, cleaning them, then focused on Kean.

"I can do it. You get them into bed."

Andrew shook his head. "No, you deserve it as much as they do."

Kean stayed still as Andrew wiped them clean, dropping a kiss on his lips before returning to Kendal. The care he took of them was nothing short of worshipful, and Kean would make sure to return the favour. He stood and pulled on Andrew's dressing gown that hung on the back of the door.

"Where are you going?" Kendal asked.

Kean smiled. "To grab some snacks and drinks. I'll be back in a minute."

He fetched some fruit and yoghurt from the small fridge in the living area, two bottles of water and one of juice, then returned to find Kendal snuggled up to Andrew. Maybe others might be jealous of seeing them like that, but Kean wasn't. His heart expanded with love for them both, and seeing one give the other comfort when he wasn't there was beautiful.

"Here," he said, sitting beside Andrew on the edge of the bed. He put everything on the bedside table and put a straw in the juice, holding it to Kendal's lips. Kendal drank deeply, eyes still closed, and Kean smiled. He glanced at Andrew and saw him looking at him.

"Are you okay?" he asked.

"Perfect," Andrew said. He pressed his lips to Kendal's head when they finished drinking. "I needed that."

"Me, too," Kendal said. "I didn't realise how much I needed it until you both gave it to me."

Kean opened the lid of a water bottle and handed it to Andrew. "Drink, my king. You did well."

Kean grabbed the fruit, which had already been cut into pieces. He fed small pieces to Kendal and Andrew, occasionally taking a piece for himself, then held up the yoghurt. Kendal shook their head, as did Andrew, so he ate it himself before clearing everything away. After he'd finished drinking his water, he removed the dressing gown and slipped into bed behind Kendal, careful to keep his body away from their ass, which was bound to smart.

"Sleep," Andrew said. "We'll deal with everything tomorrow."

◆

The next day came sooner than Kean wanted, even if they didn't get out of bed until ten o'clock. They leisurely showered together and had a light snack so they wouldn't ruin their lunch plans.

By the time they wandered the hallways to the dining room Andrew and his family used when they were all together, it was almost noon. Kean heard voices before they entered, and it only got louder when they did.

"Hey, how are you all?" George said.

"And if you say the word 'fine,' I might have to kill you all," Freddie added.

Kean chuckled. "I'm good. Does that work?"

Freddie palmed his face. "Not really, but it's better than fine, I suppose." He glanced at Kendal. "How are *you?*"

Kendal smiled and reached a hand forward, resting it on Freddie's arm. Kean noticed they appeared to be more relaxed with the royals, which he was pleased about.

"I'm doing okay, Freddie. Thanks for asking. It scared me, to begin with, but Daniel didn't seem to want to hurt me. He could've done it if he had to, but he didn't want to." Kendal frowned. "I think he truly wants to stop whatever it is he was doing."

"That remains to be seen. For all we know, it could be a ruse to get closer to us. Even by being arrested, Daniel is closer than I want him to be right now," Christian said.

"You think it's a trap?" Kean asked.

Christian shrugged. "I don't know. My gut is rolling, but I don't know what to think."

"He was your friend, Christian. You can't expect to understand everything about him because he was hiding from you, too," Andrew said. "None of this is your fault."

Kean could see Christian didn't believe Andrew's words, but the man nodded and headed over to Oscar. Christian's little grabbed his hand and slid into his arms, with Christian lowering his face to Oscar's neck. It had to be extremely difficult for Christian. Finding out one of his friends was not who they said they were had to be weighing heavily on him.

"Let's eat," Andrew said.

They settled at the table with Kean to Andrew's right and Kendal to his left, and the household servers brought their food in. Once they were alone again, Douglas asked, "Have you heard the latest from the media?" Andrew shook his head, and Douglas glanced at Mav. "Do you want to explain?"

Mav cleared his throat and put down his cutlery, wiping his face with a napkin before speaking. "The results seem mixed. Some are saying they're with you, and they're happy you are being true to yourself. Others are not so happy. In my experience, it could go either way, but I think the supporters have more weight behind them."

"Any comments you've had to flag?" Andrew asked.

Mav nodded. "Several. I've passed them all to the security team for them to send to whoever deals with that side of things."

"Thank you, Mav. I appreciate your help."

Kean stared at his plate, moving the food around but not eating much. He wasn't concerned about the public's opinion, but would Andrew backtrack if support failed? He closed his eyes and shook his head at that thought. Andrew had been all in since they decided to make a go of their relationship, and Kean shouldn't doubt him now. After all, the king had just announced to the entire world that he was in a relationship with two people, and Kean couldn't demean that.

"Do you have any plans for what we're going to do next?" Freddie asked.

Andrew cleared his throat. "What we're going to do is

finish lunch and have a relaxing Sunday. Then tomorrow, we're going to carry on living and working as usual. We have people working to get this figured out, and we will work out a plan with them once we have more information."

The conversation turned to lighter subjects, but Kean kept one eye on Andrew and Kendal. Kendal seemed in high spirits, regardless of what happened to them, and Andrew was his usual accommodating, friendly self. But Kean could feel an undercurrent, and he was sure Andrew was the source. Kean studied him. Something in Andrew's tone belied his earlier words. Did he already have a plan that he didn't want them to know about? He would have to ask him later because he didn't want Andrew to carry the weight of everything when he had Kean to help.

His phone buzzed against his thigh, and he pulled it free.

DANTE: This isn't the end. You'll find out soon enough that you shouldn't cross me.

Kean swallowed hard.

"Hey, how does he get away with checking his phone when I always get told off?" George said.

Kean glanced up at him. "Sorry," he said, sliding it away again.

"Be quiet, George." Andrew covered Kean's hand. "Is everything okay?"

Kean opened his mouth to say yes but inhaled instead. "It was from my father."

Andrew tightened his hold. "Bad?"

"A threat, though, I doubt it means much. It's probably just smoke," Kean said.

"Let security know," Andrew said. "We can add him to the list of people to watch out for."

Kean nodded and turned his palm upwards, wrapping his fingers around Andrew's hand. "I will. I'm sure it's nothing, though." He wasn't sure, but he tried to put on a brave face.

Andrew smiled knowingly. "I'm sure it is nothing, but we'll just make sure."

Kean glanced at Kendal, who smiled across at him. Their attention went a long way to easing his mind, but his father was a ruthless businessman, and he wouldn't take kindly to being seen in a poor light. With Kean having declined his "birthright" at the construction company, Dante would appear to have lost his edge. They didn't need to add this worry on top of everything else they had. Unfortunately, Kean couldn't do anything about it.

23

HENRY

Henry was exhausted, and that was putting it mildly. As he studied the occupants of the table, he could see the lines of pain and loss on everyone's faces. It wasn't fair. None of them had done anything to deserve this hatred, but it was what it was. Everyone tried to keep the conversation light, and George attempted to lighten the mood with his jokes, but it wasn't as easy as usual. The toll of these attacks was visible.

Robert laid his hand on Henry's thigh. "Are you okay?"

Henry sighed and nodded, staring into the gorgeous green eyes of his fiancé and soon-to-be husband. He couldn't wait for the day he called Robert his—truly and officially his. It was only six weeks away, and although the event wouldn't be televised, it would still garner a lot of attention. He hoped with everything inside of him they wouldn't have to postpone it because of a potential attack from *them*.

That was what worried him most. Not that the wedding would be postponed, but that if there was an attack, someone would get hurt. Robert could get hurt.

They had been together for sixteen months now, and Henry still fought with his thoughts some days. Should he have brought Robert into such upheaval? Should he have painted a target on Robert's back just because he wanted him with him? He knew the answer would always be yes, but sometimes, he wished he'd been strong enough to say no and keep Robert as far from this disaster as he could.

But then he thought about his life, their lives, and he couldn't wish for it to be any other way. He couldn't imagine life without him.

"I'm here," Robert whispered, knowing the thoughts running through his head because Henry didn't keep a single thing from him. Even the bad things that had happened during his teens and beyond, Robert knew about. And it helped Henry deal with them, even though he had hoped to keep Robert from the worst of his world.

"Thank you."

"Always." Robert slid an arm around Henry's back, resting it on his chair. "Did you decide on our vows?"

Henry smiled, as he always did when he thought of their wedding day. "I'd like us to create our own if that's okay with you."

Robert's mouth curved. "I think that's a great idea. Do you want any of the official words at all?"

Henry thought about the vows he'd heard before as well as those he'd looked up when he'd been researching, and he admitted, "I like the official ones they say when we exchange rings. You know, the ones that start, 'With this ring, I thee wed?'"

Robert nodded. "I like those, too. So let's keep that for exchanging the rings and write our own for our promise. How does that sound?"

Henry grinned, his heart pounding. "Perfect."

"What about your best man?"

Henry rolled his eyes. "You know exactly who that is."

Robert chuckled. "Just making sure."

"Are you still asking Finn to stand up for you?"

Robert nodded. "Yes, and I've asked Naomi if she'd recite a poem for us at the end, as we discussed."

"I'm glad. She'll be so nervous, but I know she'll do great."

"She'll be a nervous wreck for days beforehand."

Henry chuckled. "She will."

"Did George tell you about the plans for the bachelor party?"

Henry's eyes widened. "No...?"

Robert snorted. "I'm not surprised. I have a feeling you won't like it."

Henry glared at George, who wasn't looking at him, then sighed and pouted at Robert. "What are we doing?"

"He wants a puppy party."

Henry frowned and cocked his head. "Come again?"

"A puppy party. He wants people to try being a puppy for the party. Personally, I think it's a wonderful idea. It might open doors for people they never thought of trying."

"I don't know..."

Robert shrugged. "We can talk to him about it. See what ideas he has. It might not work, and we can always veto it if we don't want to do it. It is our party, after all."

Henry leaned into him. "Six weeks," he murmured.

Robert kissed his forehead. "Six weeks."

24

KENDAL

"Thanks for coming with me," Kendal said to Kean the following day as they drove towards Kendal's house.

Andrew had been called into his office to get some work done, but he'd asked Kendal to work from Windsor for a while until they knew if Daniel had told anyone about Kendal's house and its security features. Kendal had agreed without issue. They didn't feel unsafe at home, but if it made things easier for everyone, then they were happy to relocate until they'd sorted things.

"No problem. I figured you might not be able to carry everything you needed to bring with you," Kean teased.

Kendal bumped his shoulder with a laugh. "I basically need my computer, and that's it. I can do this work from anywhere."

They pulled up to their house, and a swarm of reporters crowded the car. Kendal was glad for the tinted windows, but it wouldn't stop them when they had to get out. They took out their phone and checked the cameras in the house.

"Everything seems clear," they told the guards.

"Wait here until we clear a path for you," Ford said, climbing out of the passenger side. "Move!" he ordered to several people, blocking Kendal's door from him. They pushed away, allowing Ford to stand beside the car.

Kendal braced themselves for the questions that would be thrown at them the moment the door opened.

Kean grabbed their hand. "I'm with you every step."

Kendal smiled at him. "Right back 'atcha, but why a king, Kean? Why did we have to fall in love with a king?" They laughed.

"We like a challenge?" Kean chuckled.

Ford knocked on the window, advertising he was going to open the door, and did so. The noise rose drastically, and Kendal winced before climbing out with Kean in tow. Ford and Greg surrounded them as they worked their way through the heaving crowds.

"Kendal! Kean! What's it like being with a king? How does it work? Who's on top? You can't legally get married, so what's the plan? Can the king get it up?"

The last question had Kean's hand tightening on Kendal, but Kendal wrapped his hand around Kean's arm and yanked him forward, knowing he was seconds away from blowing. Greg opened the door, having been given the entry code, and Ford slammed the door closed behind them.

"Well, that was fun," Kean snarled, staring through the door as if he could see the reporters with a look that could kill.

"We'll call a couple more guards to come for the journey home, I think," Greg said.

Kendal shook their head. "I wouldn't bother. I'll be quick, and we can get back." They led the way to their office.

"I need to figure out where I'm going now that I'm not entering the construction business," Kean said, frowning.

"You enjoy business, don't you?" Kean nodded. "Then why not continue in the same vein and see if anyone at Windsor has an idea for you? Did you enjoy working alongside Damon before the kidnapping?" They entered the room, mentally listing what they needed.

Kean nodded again. "I did. I've helped him with some other bits as well since, but it's unlikely to be a full-time position."

"Do you want to finish university?"

"Not really. They're not teaching me much I don't already know."

"I can almost guarantee someone will have an idea for where you can work. There'll be plenty of positions within the royal family if you want to stay close to them, or they'll have connections if you want to go further afield." They grabbed a bag and unplugged their computer. "There are even things within the author world that you can do, but it might not be as fast-paced or interesting for you, but it's something to look at. There are so many options open to you." And Kean would be so good at any of them.

"Yeah, I suppose. I guess I need to think about where I want to go before deciding where to look."

"As I said, ask around. Even if you don't work at Windsor or with the royal family, there are plenty of people there you can ask for advice." They shoved everything they could think of needing into the bag and zipped it up.

"It's weird. I know what I don't want to do, which was to be part of my father's business, but I don't know exactly what I *do* want to do."

Kendal reached for his hand, twining their fingers

together. "Sometimes, you have to start with what you know you don't want to do and work from there."

"Thanks." Kean leaned forward and kissed them. "I think I'll speak to Damon and see what advice he can give. He's worked with the auditing and other stuff for a while now. Maybe he can shed some light on my predicament."

"Good idea."

Ford and Greg waited at the bottom of the stairs. "Are you ready to walk the gauntlet?" Ford said.

"Let's do it," Kean said after checking with Kendal.

It was just as bad heading back to the car, but they soon settled inside and headed out. They supposed they needed to get used to it. It was only the second time the cameras had been focused on them, the first having been when they arrested Daniel, but it would take some time to relax around them.

Back at Windsor, Kendal settled into the suite, and Kean disappeared to speak with Damon. Within minutes, there came a knock, and Kendal called for them to enter. It was weird thinking they had the power to let someone in or not to the king's suite.

"Your Highness, His Majesty has an office for you. If you'd like to follow me," Randall said with a smile.

Kendal lowered their eyebrows. "He does?"

Randall nodded. "You may change anything about it you want."

Kendal stuffed the items they'd already taken from the bag back into it and rose. "I'm sure it's fine how it is. I wasn't expecting an office. I was just going to work here."

Randall smiled again, leading the way down the hallway. "His Majesty said you might say that, but it's really not a problem. We have several rooms dedicated as offices for anyone who'd like to use them. This one is close to where we're located, so you won't be too far away should you need anything."

When they entered the brightly lit room, Kendal smiled. It was larger than his own, and the decoration was more in line with royalty—more expensive—but it was nice. Two armchairs sat next to a coffee table in the centre of the room, but it had a heavy, decorative desk which dominated the space. Kendal pulled a face at the uncomfortable-looking chair.

"Your Highness?" Randall asked, stepping forward.

Kendal wrung their hands. "Is there any chance of getting a more comfortable chair, Randall? I don't think I could spend a lot of time sitting in that."

Randall chuckled. "Of course, Your Highness. I will find something more suitable if you can give me a few minutes."

Kendal waved their hands. "Oh, I don't mean right now. It can wait. Just whenever you have the time. Or I can find something if you tell me where to look."

"It's not a problem at all, Your Highness. It will take barely a few minutes. Make yourself at home while I see to it. There is a coffee machine over there, which also makes tea and hot chocolate. There is a small fridge beneath it with everything you might need—I hope—and the drawer holds some snack items should you get peckish."

"Thank you, Randall. This is perfect."

"I will be back, Your Highness." Randall turned away.

"You don't have to call me that, you know. Kendal is just fine."

Randall's lips curved, and he bowed his head. "Thank you for the offer, Your Highness."

Kendal chuckled when Randall exited, saying nothing further, but by the end of his sentence, Kendal assumed it wouldn't happen. Now they knew how Andrew felt when people wouldn't use his first name.

They rested their bag on the desk and made a cup of tea to take back to the desk while they set everything up. The desk had built-in sockets on the underside of it, which helped tremendously with Kendal's short laptop cord, and was large enough to hold all Kendal's paperwork without any hanging off the edge like they usually did at home.

A knock sounded, and Kendal called for them to come in. Randall entered and unlocked the second door, and two people carried a large chair between them. Kendall could see already that this chair was a lot more comfortable than the one they currently sat on. They moved away from the desk, and the chairs were switched before the two people carried the old chair from the office. Randall closed the second door behind them and then stood on the threshold.

"Is there anything I can help you with, Your Highness?" he asked.

Kendal hid their smile at the use of their title. "No, thank you, Randall. Don't worry about me. I'll figure everything out. I know you're busy with Andrew."

"I'm here to help you, as well, Your Highness."

Kendal stared at him. "And I refuse to bother you because you have enough work. If I need something desperately, I will find you. Otherwise, I will figure it out myself. You're not my PA."

Randall tilted his head. "Do you need a PA, Your Highness?"

"I am a PA, Randall."

"I know. But sometimes, a PA needs a PA."

Kendal studied him, noticing the dark circles under his eyes. They made a note to mention to Andrew that Randall needed another person to help him. "That's true. At the moment, though, I'm fine. Thank you for asking."

"I'm just a call away should you need anything, Your Highness."

"Thank you, Randall."

Randall bowed his head and retreated, closing the door behind him. Kendal chuckled and settled in the chair, humming when it cushioned them rather than holding them aloft. Their ass wasn't smarting as much as it had done the previous day, but there was still a slight ache whenever they sat wrong or for too long.

Kendal blew out a breath, took a sip of tea and logged on to the computer. They had several emails to catch up on, authors to check in with and enough work to last them several hours.

A knock at their door interrupted them a couple of hours later. George popped his head around the door.

"Busy?" he asked.

Kendal smiled. "As always, but always ready for a break." They stood. "Would you like a drink?"

"I wouldn't mind a coffee if you can spare the time. I'll get them, though."

"I'll have tea, please. No sugar, just a splash of milk."

Kendal let George make the drinks, sensing he needed to do something before getting to the reason he was there. They settled into one armchair and waited for George to take the other.

"Is everything okay?" they asked.

George nodded slowly. "I wanted to check that you were all right. I know a lot has happened quickly, and I want to make sure you're okay with it all."

Kendal smiled. "It *is* a lot, but I'm good, thank you. It'll take a while to get used to everything, I think, but it's worth it."

George sat forward, leaning his elbows on his knees, so reminiscent of his father. He ran his hand around the rim of his cup. "Mother would've loved you for how you treat Father," he whispered.

Kendal's heart cracked for the boy who'd lost his mother under such horrific conditions. "I'm not trying to take her place. Neither is Kean."

"I know!" George snapped their gaze to them. "I didn't mean it like that. I just meant she would approve. Not that you need her approval or anything." He rubbed his forehead. "I'm messing this up," he mumbled. "I mean—"

Kendal leaned forward and placed their hand on his forearm. "George, it's okay. I understand. I loved Queen Louisa. Absolutely adored her. From afar, obviously." They chuckled. "I am honoured that you believe she would approve. I want Andrew to be happy, whatever that means for him."

"He is," George stated, the truth visible in his eyes. "He loves you both. He lost that look when Mother died, and I didn't believe he would ever get it back...until he let his feelings show for you and Kean." George leaned forward, grasping Kendal's hands. "I'm so grateful to you for taking a chance with him. There are so many things in this life that we have no control over. Privacy, for one. But we do control who we admit to loving. And to do that in front of the entire world is amazing, especially when you're the king. He could've easily hidden away, but he's strong."

"Don't tell him I told you this, but it's because of you. His children and his nephews. He saw how strong you all were during the trials of your relationships, and he stood up for you then. He told me, if you can be strong enough to reach for what you want, then he can, too." Kendal smiled. "Don't dismiss how much he loves and admires you all."

Tears brimmed in George's eyes but didn't fall. "Thank you."

Kendal sat back, taking a sip of tea and allowing George time to calm down. After a few minutes, they said, "So, you're a narrator. Have you done any books I might know?"

And with that, they turned to lighter topics, and Kendal had an amusing break from work. When George left, around an hour after he first arrived, Kendal settled back at the desk to finish some more tasks. It felt like no time had passed when another guest arrived.

Andrew rounded the desk and leaned down to kiss Kendal before resting his ass on the edge. "How has your day been?"

"Busy," Kendal replied. "You?"

"Same." Andrew shifted. "I've had some information from Brady. You know the shooting?" How could they forget? But they nodded, anyway. "The assailant, Jeremy Blatch? He was Daniel's cousin."

Kendal frowned, working through the connection. "From Daniel's father's or mother's side?"

Andrew smiled as if in approval. "Father's."

"So Ernest has more family."

"He does. As far as we knew, he only had his father, who passed away four years ago."

Kendal glanced down, trying to follow a thought they'd had. "Four years ago," they murmured. "Four years ago was…2020." They glanced up at Andrew. "When in 2020?"

"I'm not sure, to be honest. Why?"

"Wasn't Freddie's helicopter crash in 2020?" Kendal asked.

Andrew stared at him for a long second. "It was…" He stood and fast-walked to the door. Kendal followed. They strode down the hallway to Andrew's office. "Randall, when did Ernest's father die?"

Randall didn't look shocked at the abrupt entrance and random question. He pressed a few keys on his computer, clicked a few things and said, "10 March 2020."

Kendal covered their mouth, understanding the significance of the date, but Andrew pushed on with another question. "When was Freddie's helicopter crash?"

Randall clicked a few more things. "24 July 2020."

"Louisa is the key," Andrew murmured, stalking from the office.

"Thank you, Randall," Kendal said as they hurried after Andrew. "Andrew?"

"I need to talk to Brett."

"Isn't he still on leave?" Kendal asked, struggling to keep up with him.

Andrew faltered a step before continuing. "I'm going to have to ask him to come back."

"Why?"

Andrew stopped, and Kendal hadn't been expecting it, so they carried on a few more steps before halting themselves. They turned to him, waiting.

"Did you understand the significance of the dates?" he asked.

Kendal swallowed. "10 March is when Queen Louisa died. But I'm not sure about July."

"24 July was the day Louisa's mother died in 2019."

"I don't understand."

"Ernest is focusing on Louisa, it seems. But I don't know why."

Kendal shook their head. "But the car was supposed to have George in it."

Andrew faltered for a second. "They must've known or heard about the swap."

"Hey, there you are," Kean said, his voice trailing off when he stopped beside them. "What's happened?"

Andrew appeared lost in his thoughts, so Kendal brought Kean up to speed on Andrew's thoughts and their findings.

"It seems legitimate. I can't think of a reason, but the dates match if they knew about the swap. It's possible, especially with Aaron and Tobias working for Andrew at the time. Louisa might've mentioned to or around them."

Kendal's stomach rolled. "So what does it mean?"

"It means there's some connection between Louisa and Ernest we're not seeing," Andrew said.

"We can dig deeper into his background. Maybe there's something else he's hiding," Kean said. "Maybe Daniel might know something."

"We need to work out Daniel's family tree. See who else might be around that we don't know about," Andrew said.

Kendal couldn't believe someone had been so focused on Queen Louisa that it was seemingly the catalyst for such horror.

ANDREW

Once Andrew had briefed Brett and settled Kean and Kendal in the suite, he wandered off to speak to his security team. They wouldn't like what he had to say, but at least he was warning them in advance. He was putting them in danger, true, but he refused to let them go into it blindly.

"No. Absolutely not," Dominic said.

Andrew had promoted Dominic into Simon's position once the new guards had arrived. He'd taken to the role well, but he didn't have Simon's finesse of talking to him yet.

"I'll let that slide because of everything that has happened, but you will do as I say. I'm going, with or without you."

He turned and exited the room, glancing over his shoulder when Dominic called to him.

"Will you allow us to make a plan before you leave?"

"Can you make a plan within the hour?" he asked.

Dominic glanced at the team, then nodded. "We will."

"Then, yes. You have one hour. If you're not at the door when I arrive, I'll go alone."

He left them, probably cursing at him, and headed to his office. There were a few things he needed to put into place before he left. Just in case.

An hour later, he strode down the hallway to the entrance doors, pleased to find the guards present, all eight of them. None of them looked happy about the situation, but they were there, nonetheless.

"I can't guarantee she won't harm me, but she won't kill me while she's with me. I don't believe she's strong enough to do that."

Dominic sighed. "We all have serious objections to this, but it's our job to protect you, no matter where you go. Please listen to us and be careful, Your Majesty."

"I will."

They climbed into two cars and set off. It would take just under an hour to get to Kensington Palace, and he filled the entire journey with thoughts of Kean and Kendal. He hadn't told them he was leaving; they believed he was in a meeting. It was better this way. They would only worry. He'd be back before either of them was any the wiser, and then he could put up with their anger and reprimands.

The guards at Charlotte's home tried to deny him access, but Andrew ordered them to open the gates. Once they parked in the driveway, the guards from the first car exited and fanned out, studying their surroundings. With a nod from one of the team, Dominic opened the door for Andrew.

"Thank you, Dominic."

He strode for the door, a household staff member opening it for them immediately. Two guards settled in front of him, two at his side and two behind, with the other two on lookout. He didn't need to say a word to anyone because the household staff member waved their hand towards the stairs.

"This way, Your Majesty." As if they had been expecting

him. That wasn't possible, though, because it was a spur-of-the-moment thing. Well, kind of spur of the moment. He had thought about it a few days ago, but then, when everything happened, it got pushed aside.

Dominic opened the door of the room the household staff led them to, and three guards swooped in to check the room before Andrew entered.

He raised his eyebrows when he saw Charlotte sitting on a chair, holding a glass loosely between her fingertips. Her head rested back against the chair, but her gaze followed him as he settled into the chair beside her.

"Charlotte. It's been a while. How are you?"

She snorted and sipped her drink. Whiskey, if he wasn't mistaken. "Just peachy, brother."

Her hair was tied into an updo, with tendrils falling around her face. She wore a white blouse with small black pots tucked into navy blue tailored trousers and cinched with a thin black shiny belt. But what struck him the most was that she was barefoot. He couldn't remember the last time he'd seen her without shoes. Maybe as a child, but not since.

Andrew glanced at Dominic, who had a frown on his face as he stared at Charlotte. There was something wrong. He'd get the information he came for and leave.

"Did you know about Ernest?"

Charlotte shook her head, lifting the glass lazily and sipping at it. "No. Forty years he played me for a fool." She huffed a laugh. "But by god, he was good in bed. It could almost be worth it." Her voice slurred.

Andrew leaned forward. "When did you find out?"

She glared at him. "When you told me about the law. Ernest and John were always talking about the history of the monarch whenever we were together. The torture our ascendents used on the unrighteous. They were fascinated. I just thought it was a hobby. An interest." She waved her glass as if to make a point. "They played me."

Dominic and Colt stepped forward. "Your Majesty, she appears…"

Andrew waved them off. She was either drunk or high, or both. He couldn't decide which.

"And do you know what the worst thing is?" she mumbled. "He made me believe it." She leaned forward, grabbed the glass decanter from the table in front of her and sloppily filled her glass. "I have my beliefs, Andrew, but I was willing to ignore it all until he whispered in my ear." She gulped some more alcohol.

"It's not your fault, Charlotte," Andrew said.

She snorted. "No, it's not." She slammed back the rest of the drink and stared at him. "It's yours."

Andrew frowned. "Mine?"

"He used me to get to you."

"Do you know what he wants?"

"He wants you to suffer."

He couldn't figure it out. "But why? What does he have against me?"

Charlotte shrugged. "Everything. His life should've been different."

"Different, how?"

She drank some more. "I don't know. I just remember him saying that over and over."

Andrew sighed. "Did you know about Daniel?"

Charlotte sneered. "My husband's firstborn? Not until recently. He was happy to throw that in my face, though."

"What?"

"That Albert was weak and had defected, and Charles had got caught and arrested. Whereas his son was still working diligently for his cause. It's my genes that are the problem, it seems."

She was mumbling more and more, her head rolling on the back of the chair instead of her lifting it. Her eyes were bloodshot, her cheeks pale, and sweat beaded on her forehead.

Andrew glanced at Dominic. "Do you think she's taken drugs, too?"

"Either that or she's been drugged." Dominic lifted the decanter and sniffed, then studied the glass, pulling it closer. "Someone has added something to the alcohol. There's white powder around the top that stuck to the wet sides." He stuck his finger in it, putting some on the tip, and held it out for Andrew to see. "Could be anything, but taking her behaviour into consideration, I'd say some sort of relaxant, maybe."

Andrew rubbed his mouth. "We need to get her a doctor."

Charlotte chuckled. "It's too late, Andrew dear. You took the bait. Now we both pay the price," she finished in a whisper.

Andrew's heart raced. He'd made a huge mistake.

Dominic shouted, "We need to leave! NOW!" He grabbed Andrew's arm and headed for the door.

"We need Charlotte!" he called as Dominic dragged him alongside him.

"Colt will get her." Dominic grabbed the handle and yanked on the door. It wouldn't budge. "What the fuck? Evan? Anna? Can you hear me?" Silence. "Fuck," he mumbled, turning to study the room.

Colt lifted Charlotte's now unconscious body into his arms and stared at them. "What the fuck is going on?"

"They've fucking ambushed us. They knew you would come here, Your Majesty. It's a fucking trap," Dominic said. "We need to find a way out of here."

He let Andrew go and headed for another door that should've opened into a bedroom if Andrew's memory served him correctly, but that door refused to open, too. The third door held a bathroom with no windows.

"How did they know I would come?" Andrew said.

Colt laid Charlotte on the chaise lounge. "Have you been trying to contact her, Your Majesty?"

Andrew nodded. "I've left messages, but she's never replied."

"They've probably been screening the calls," Colt said. "If I hadn't heard from my family after a certain length of time, I would have gone looking for them. They must've assumed you'd do the same."

Andrew rubbed a hand over his face. "I'm sorry to you both. I shouldn't have come. I should've listened."

Despite the gravity of the situation, Dominic laughed. "Simon always said you never listened to reason."

Andrew smiled. "I listened; I just didn't always agree."

Dominic stood with his hands on his hips, staring around the room. "What's their plan? To hold us until they get here? I don't understand."

"Andu..." Charlotte murmured, her head rolling on the cushion. "Go... Expos..."

"Expos?" Dominic said. "What does she mean?"

Andrew moved closer. "Charlotte?" He touched her cheek. "Charlotte. Wake up for me. What do you mean, expos?"

She sighed, and he could see whatever she had taken or been given was pulling her under. He didn't know if it was something she would survive or not.

"Explo...sion," she mumbled.

Andrew stared at her, dread filling his limbs.

"Fuck, we have to go!" Dominic grabbed him, dragging Andrew to the bathroom. "Get into the bath."

"What?"

"Don't argue, Your Majesty." Dominic sighed. "Please, just get into the bath."

Andrew climbed into the porcelain tub, laying down with his knees bent, and Colt lay Charlotte with him. It was a squeeze, but he put his arm around his sister and held tight. As much damage as she had done, she was still his sister. He loved her, even if he didn't like her. She would pay for her crimes.

If they survived whatever this was.

As soon as he thought the words, he heard a boom, and Dominic came flying back towards him, and the ceiling rained down, knocking into him.

26

KEAN

"I still can't believe you had never seen *Pitch Perfect*," Kean said, pressing his lips to Kendal's temple. He loved having them in his arms, cuddled up while they watched a film. When they had watched films before, at Kendal's house, they had never cuddled, but they always sat close. It was so much better to be able to hold them.

"Hmm. We'll add the next ones onto the list," Kendal said, yawning. They twisted their wrist to look at their watch. "I wonder what time Andrew will finish. He's been gone two hours already."

"Must be some meeting." Kean kissed their lips. "Would you like a bedtime snack?"

"I'd love—"

Insistent knocking on the door interrupted Kendal. "Come in!" Kean shouted.

Freddie came in, and it was the first time in a long time that Kean had seen him flustered. "Kensington Palace has just exploded. Where's Father? I'm not sure if he knows yet."

Kean frowned. "He's in a meeting. Has been for two hours. I'm assuming it's in his office."

"Okay, I'll check in with him."

"We'll come, too," Kendal said.

Kean wiped the tiredness from his face and joined them on the trek to Andrew's office. They rounded a corner and bumped into Nick, one of Andrew's guards. He'd been injured in the shooting and had been relegated to planning and desk work until he was fighting fit again.

"Hey, Nick. How are you doing?" Freddie asked.

"Can't complain, Your Highness. Where's the fire?"

"We're looking for Father," Freddie said. "I'm hoping he's in his office."

Nick winced, and Kean tilted his head. "Nick," Kean said. "He's not in a meeting, is he?" Nick met his gaze but said nothing. "Where is he?"

Nick sighed, his shoulders lowering. "He went to visit Charlotte."

Pure terror shot through Kean, and Kendal grabbed for his hand. Kean shook his head. "Say again."

"He went to visit Charlotte," Nick said. "We didn't agree with him, but he pulled rank. Said he'd go alone if we didn't accompany him. In the end, he had eight guards with him. Not sure how long they'll be."

Kean grabbed Kendal when their legs crumpled, and tears started pouring down their face. Kean wanted to do the same, but he kept his composure for the moment.

"Freddie?" He tried to get the prince's attention, but he was frozen. Kean tucked Kendal into him and reached for Freddie, gripping his forearm. "Freddie?"

Freddie stared at him, eyes wide, as if he couldn't believe what they'd just been told. Kean could understand it. He was feeling the same, but there was no reason for Nick to lie to them. He had to keep his cool until they knew more information.

"What's the matter?" Nick said.

"Did he go to Charlotte's home?" Freddie asked, voice cracking.

Nick frowned and nodded. "Yes."

Freddie closed his eyes and leaned against the wall.

"What's wrong?" Nick demanded, standing taller and looking at them all.

Kean swallowed. "Freddie just came to tell us that Kensington Palace exploded. We were coming to tell Andrew about it."

He watched his words register with Nick. The guard scrambled for his phone and dialled, eyes darting everywhere. He hung up and dialled again. Same thing. He hung up and dialled again. "Fuck. No one's answering."

Kean grabbed his phone and dialled Andrew. It rang and rang, no voicemail at all because Andrew didn't have it set up.

"Freddie?" He got the prince's attention. "Get a message to everyone. Tell them to meet us in the security room as soon as possible. We have to find information."

It snapped Freddie out of his fugue state, and he pulled his phone out. His fingers flew over the screen. "I have sent a group message out." He dialled and held it to his ear. "Commissioner Thomas, sorry to… Yes… I know… Can you let me know as soon as you have anything, please? Thank you." He hung up. "Brady already knows. He's on his way there now."

"Okay. Let's go." Kean started walking, holding Kendal in his arms. He didn't want to think about what could've happened to Andrew. He needed to be strong for Kendal and everyone else, and the only way to do that was to ignore the thought that Andrew wasn't coming home to them.

Nick led them into the security room, where several guards milled around. "Brett, have you heard?"

Brett nodded, his mouth in a fierce line. "I swear to god, these assholes are going down. No offence, Your Highnesses."

"Definitely none taken, Brett," Freddie said. "We have everyone coming here for an update. The rest of them don't know yet."

"I shouldn't, but I hope it got some of those treasonous bastards," Brett said. "Is Andrew on his way?"

Kean stared at him. Shit, he didn't know about *that* part.

Nick cleared his throat. "Brett... Andrew was at Kensington Palace."

Brett frowned. "When?"

"When it blew."

Brett stared at Nick, as frozen as they had been when they received the news. "What?" he whispered when silence descended in the room.

Nick nodded but said nothing.

Brett sank into the seat behind him and put his hands over his mouth, staring at nothing. He visibly pulled himself together and swallowed. "Do we know anything?"

Freddie stepped forward. "Brady is on his way there now. We can't get hold of Father or his guards."

Brett closed his eyes and exhaled, then stood. "I'm sorry, Your Highness, but you're acting monarch in his absence," he told Freddie.

Freddie nodded, though Kean could see the pain crossing his expression. "What do you need?"

"At the moment, the only thing I need from you is the promise you will not go off half-cocked whenever we get information. We need you to survive."

The words were harsh, but Kean understood where they were coming from.

"Understood. You have my word." Freddie stepped to the side when more people entered the room.

Giving the news to the rest of the family was not something Kean had ever expected himself to have to do, but he would stand up and do his duty, even though the ceremony to make them Consorts had not yet taken place. He wanted to take some of the burdens from Andrew's family. He settled Kendal into a seat and stood beside them with a hand on their shoulder.

"Everyone! Can you settle down a moment, please?" Kean waited until the door was closed, and he could hear a pin drop. "I'm the bearer of bad news, unfortunately. Kensington Palace exploded a short time ago." He paused while shocked words rippled through the occupants of the room. "We have just found out that…" He cleared his throat, swallowing the lump that wanted to stop him. "We've just found out that Andrew was in attendance when it did."

"No!" George shouted, pushing through the people and stopping in front of Kean. "No. He can't have been."

Kean's heart broke all over again. The whole family had been through so much already. "We don't have any news on them at the moment. Brady is heading there now—or should be there by now, I don't know. We can't get hold of anyone, but we're hopeful. Andrew's guards are resourceful."

George rubbed his head. "Why are they doing this?"

Kean turned to Brett. "Can we get an update on everything that we've found out lately? Let's get everyone up to speed. Maybe someone will see something we haven't."

Brett nodded and settled in front of his computer. "Give me a few minutes. Can someone grab a hell of a lot more chairs, please? I can't move all our stuff right now, so we're going to have to squeeze in."

It took around fifteen minutes for enough chairs to be located and moved, and by that point, Princess Victoria and Prince William had arrived with their families, too. Kean settled into a chair beside Kendal, who had barely said anything.

"Kendal, how are you doing?"

"I'm pissed," they stated without fanfare.

Kean chuckled despite the seriousness of the situation. "I am, too. We're taking them all to hell."

"We need to be looking for him. For them," Kendal said, lifting watery eyes to him.

"People are looking for him. The best we can do is figure this out. Then, when he comes striding through the doors, we can kick his ass and tell him how kick-ass *we* are."

That gained a small smile, and Kean hugged them.

"Right. Let's go through everything we've got," Brett said. "Daniel March gave us some information about Ernest. Apparently, Ernest was going after Charlotte for at least a year before they even met properly. Ernest had let slip to Daniel that he had briefly met her at an event one year and then focused solely on her. It didn't stop him from playing around, though, hence Daniel. Daniel's mother, Anne, kept quiet about everything because she didn't want to cause issues for her son. His mother had never mentioned anything about any other family. It was only after she passed away that Ernest came calling. At first, Daniel ignored him, but Ernest mentioned his sister. Ernest's sister that is." Brett paused. "We don't have much information on her, but we're getting it. We've requested birth certificates. From what Daniel could tell us—because he's never met her—she married a man from the Army, and they had Jeremy, who was the shooter from the other week."

"Did we ever figure out why Jeremy did it?" Douglas asked.

Brett waved his hand back and forth. "Daniel said it was because he had terminal cancer. He had nothing left to lose. That was why we couldn't find any financial incentives. For some reason, Jeremy Blatch was willing to give his life on the off chance he killed the king. But we don't know why."

"Did you find any connection between Ernest and Queen Louisa?" Kendal asked.

Brett shook his head. "Nothing yet. We have Her Majesty's family tree, and there is nothing on there about Ernest. We need a bit more information before we can complete Ernest's family tree."

Freddie cleared his throat. "So, we believe the death of Ernest's father was the catalyst?"

"I think so."

Henry shook his head. "That doesn't make sense. Charlotte, Charles and all the rest of them were hurting all those men for years before Ernest's father died." Robert slid his arm around Henry's back. Henry, unfortunately, had seen one such atrocity, and it had caused him years of pain.

"He could've been working up to it?" Brett said. His laptop chimed, and he checked it. "Jeremy's birth certificate. Fantastic," he mumbled, clicking a few things and reading. "Jeremy's father was called David Edward Blatch, and his mother was Nora Joyce Dyer. Jeremy was thirty-seven years old. They lived in Kent at the time of Jeremy's birth." Brett glanced at them. "We'll get searches started for David and Nora to see what comes up. But we're a little closer to figuring out who Ernest actually is."

"Have we heard or seen anything from John?" Christian asked.

Felix took this question. "No. We have checked his home; he's not there. The staff said he hadn't been for several weeks. We don't know where he is."

"Has someone checked Clarence House or Highgrove House?" Damon suggested. "They're the ones I wasn't given access to." He was sitting next to Freddie, holding his hand.

"We're still trying to get access," Felix said. "From what His Majesty last told me, Commissioner Thomas was sending out his men to search both premises. I had expected to hear from one of them today or tomorrow. But nothing, so far."

"Do we know where Ernest is?" Kean asked.

Kieren shook his head, taking over. "He's disappeared, too. We've tried facial recognition in some places to see if we find them both, but so far, it's not worked."

"Is it me," Douglas said slowly, "or are things happening faster now? Like one after the other. There was always time between other 'events,' but these past couple of weeks, there's been the shooting, then Daniel, and now an explosion."

Brett nodded. "It does seem to be escalating. Either John and Ernest are fed up with waiting, or we're close to stopping them. I'd prefer the latter, but who knows?"

"Why was Andrew there?" Kendal asked.

Kean glanced at them, then focused on Nick, who seemed to be the only one who might have an answer. Nick sighed.

"He's been trying to contact her for days. It just kept going to voicemail. After Daniel showed up, he wanted to know if Charlotte knew about Daniel and about what Ernest had planned." Nick grimaced. "He insisted on checking on her."

"He should've done it at a neutral location," William snapped.

Nick nodded. "True, but there was no way of knowing if she was getting the messages or not. Or if someone else was going to intercept it. At least by him showing up unannounced, we thought he would be safer."

Freddie's phone rang, and he answered. "Commissioner?" He listened, and his shoulders lowered, and his head bowed.

Kean's stomach churned, bile rising as he waited for news. It couldn't be the end. It couldn't. They'd barely found each other.

"Thank you, Commissioner." Freddie blew out a breath and lifted his head. "He's alive."

Rumbles flowed around the room, lifting in volume as the relief of the news sank in. Kean's chest loosened a little, but it wouldn't completely until he could see Andrew and make sure he was in one piece. He studied the occupants of the room. Smiles graced most faces, though William and Victoria appeared gaunt. It had been a long couple of years for them all, but Kean hoped they were closing in on John and Ernest and that they'd get their comeuppance sooner rather than later.

He tightened his hold around Kendal and kissed their head. "How are you doing?"

"Getting angrier by the minute."

Kean smiled. "You're a hellcat, aren't you?"

Kendal bared their teeth. "And don't you forget it." They turned to Freddie. "I want to see him."

"He's being brought here as soon as Brady says he can," Freddie said. "Brady wants to keep Andrew's presence quiet and out of the media where possible. At the moment, Andrew is secure, and no one knows he's there."

"I have first dibs on kicking his ass," Kendal stated.

"Second!" George shouted.

"No, Kean gets second," Freddie said. "Then it's me. I'm not ready to be King."

Damon slid his arms around his fiancé. "Yes, you are, but I hope you don't have to be for a while yet."

"What else needs looking into?" William asked.

The room settled down again, and Brett exhaled. "Neil and Gia are still working through Daniel's files, but none of us believes they'll find anything. He's too careful. We're basically at the waiting-for-information stage now. I'll be requesting marriage certificates for Jeremy's parents, which will then give us Ernest's parents, in theory. We're waiting on the searches from Brady for the two houses. We have people interviewing staff and friends of both John and Charlotte to see if they have anything for us." He spread his hands. "I don't know what else we can do at the moment."

"Thank you, Brett. And everyone," Freddie said, scanning the room. "You've been great, and we appreciate your support." He stood, clapping his hands on his thighs. "And we'll even give you a pass at Andrew when he's well enough." He winked.

A ripple of laughter went around the room. Kean helped Kendal to their feet, and the entire royal entourage left the security team to their jobs. They trailed down the hallway to the receiving room in silence, everyone settling into seats.

"Andrew has a lot to answer for," Victoria said as William handed her a glass with golden liquid in it.

Eddie went to the coffee machine and started handing out hot drinks to everyone who wanted one. Kean had a coffee as he needed the hit of caffeine, and Kendal had a tea, though they opted for a decaf version.

"I wonder if he even saw Charlotte," Damon said.

Kean leaned back and closed his eyes, resting his mug on

his thigh. Exhaustion filled him, but he couldn't rest until he knew Andrew was in one piece. He knew what he'd been getting into when he agreed to a relationship with Andrew, and his gallivanting off on a suicide mission, was not it. He didn't care if Andrew was their dominant; when the man got home, Kean would have a lot to say about it.

27

GEORGE

George settled himself into an armchair in the corner of the receiving room, away from everyone else. He couldn't be drawn into the conversation right then. He needed to wallow in his pain, and he couldn't do that when people were talking. Staring out of the window into the gardens, he breathed. Even that took effort. He'd lost his mother in a car bomb and had almost lost his father in an explosion. He wasn't sure how much more he could take.

Arms slid around his back and under his knees, and he was lifted before someone sat in his chair and cradled him against their chest. George closed his eyes, not because he didn't want to see Timothy, but because he didn't want him and Eddie to see the pain undoubtedly filling his gaze.

Timothy pressed his lips against George's forehead, and Eddie rested his head in George's lap. It was a position they had taken many times, and it helped soothe him. Being surrounded by those he loved was everything he needed at that moment, and both of them knew it. They didn't try to soothe him with platitudes; they were just there. Holding him together. It was that, more than anything else, that helped his words come.

"I'm going to destroy them. I swear to god."

"We all are," Timothy said. "They will not get away with this."

"We're close. I can feel it," Eddie added.

And even that wasn't a platitude because George felt it, too. Their attacks had increased, and though they appeared to be focused solely on his father at that moment, he knew they were getting desperate. The more people they arrested in connection to the treasonous parts of the family, the more information they were piecing together. It took time granted, but they were getting there. Soon, there would be nowhere for them to hide.

George's fingers played with Eddie's hair as George rested his head against Timothy's shoulder.

"I want our ceremony to be before Christmas," he blurted. "Not too close, but close enough to wipe away some of the pain from what happened last year."

Timothy squeezed him. "How about November? We need to make sure we don't hit anyone's birthdays."

George nodded and smiled. Of course, he'd been thinking about it. Timothy was a planner. "Any day you'd thought of?" he said, peering up at him.

The corner of Timothy's mouth curled. "18 November."

"Any reason?"

"It's between Henry's and Kendal's birthdays and not too close to Christmas."

George chuckled, glad they'd helped him find some humour after such an awful event. "Done."

"Don't you want to check it doesn't clash with anything?"

"Does it?"

"Well, no. Not that I know of. But you might want a different date."

George kissed his cheek. "It's perfect for me. Eddie?"

"Same here," he said in a tired voice.

"I'll let everyone know," George said.

Happy to have a date set, he focused on the view from the window again. It helped distract him, along with ideas of how he wanted the ceremony to go until his father arrived. And when he walked through the doors of that receiving room, a weight lifted from George he hadn't realised was holding him down. Just seeing his father in one piece, albeit a little bruised and battered, was the balm he needed to patch the cuts in his soul.

They would do this. They would find them and bring them down. They had to. There was no alternative.

KENDAL

As everyone waited for Andrew to return, Kendal sat on the sofa, working through their thoughts. Angry was a benign term for how they were feeling, but it was the only one they would permit themselves to use in polite company. Truthfully, their insides churned and roiled while their lungs battled for air and their heart raced for a finish line somewhere. Even though Andrew was safe, Kendal's brain couldn't process it until they saw him. Understandable.

The problem Kendal had was that they wouldn't be able to forgive Andrew straight away. Granted, it wasn't his fault the place blew up, but it was his decision to not tell them and Kean where he was going. If it had ended differently, they would've never had the chance to say anything to him.

For most people, that might make them more inclined to forgive and forget because the person was alive and well. Andrew knew, though, that there were dangers all around, and he still chose to leave without telling hardly anyone about it. If things had turned out badly, no one would have known he was in the rubble of that building until they potentially found his body. Andrew would've just disappeared.

And that pissed Kendal right off.

They were supposed to be a team, a triad working together to live their best lives under difficult circumstances, but instead, Andrew went off "half-cocked," as Brett had called it earlier to Freddie.

Therefore, Kendal waited patiently on the sofa, minding their own business and ignoring the lighter conversation that now surrounded them.

Their eyes focused on the door when everyone stood, but they didn't move. They saw Andrew enter, and the air trapped in their lungs slowly dispelled. He had a few scrapes, dried blood on his clothes and messy hair, but he was in one piece.

Andrew hugged those who greeted him, shaking hands with others, and then Kean was in front of him. He punched Andrew on the arm, then dragged him in for a kiss. Kendal rose, slowly making their way over to them. When they came up for air, Andrew focused on Kendal. He held out his hand. Kendal took it and rose on tiptoes to kiss his cheek.

"I'm glad you're okay," they said, then let go and walked out of the room.

"Kendal!" Andrew called.

Kendal stopped but didn't turn to look at him. "Yes?"

"Are you okay? Where are you going?"

Hardening their resolve, they faced him and slid their hands into their pockets. "I'm going to see if Brett needs any help with information gathering," they said, ignoring the first question.

Andrew stepped forward, but Kendal stepped back in time with him. Andrew paused, eyebrows lowered. "What's wrong?"

"I can't do this right now, Andrew. I'll be back later."

Kendal turned and walked away, though they wanted to throw themselves in Andrew's arms and never let go again. But that wouldn't solve the tumultuous emotions swirling inside them. They needed to work through them before they could explain them to anyone.

When they arrived at the security team's base, they knocked on the door. Felix opened it, eyebrows shooting up.

"Your Highness, is everything okay?"

Why did everyone keep asking that?

"Yes, everything's fine. Andrew has returned in one piece. I wondered, though, if you needed some help with the family tree or locating other information?" They smiled and cleared their throat. "I need to keep busy for a while," they explained when Felix opened his mouth to no doubt decline.

Felix snapped his mouth closed again and glanced over his shoulder. "Sure. Come in."

Kendal crossed the threshold and found half a dozen people working at computers. Ford jumped up and crossed the space between them.

"Your Highness. Is everything okay?"

Kendal gritted their teeth, swallowed the answer they wanted to give and nodded. "Yes. Just here to work."

Ford frowned. "I thought His Maj—"

"He has. He's with his family." Kendal looked past Ford to Brett. "Would you like another pair of eyes?"

Brett licked his lips but nodded. "Sure. We're still waiting on the marriage certificate for Jeremy's parents, but we want to look further into Daniel's mother and her family. We don't want any more surprises."

"Understandably." Kendal glanced around. "I have some connections through work, which I may be able to use to get information through social media. Although you've probably already got that through Mav." They weren't sure how much help they could give them, but they needed something to do.

"He has provided some, yes, but we welcome any information you can find." Brett handed them a piece of paper. "This has a list of all the people we're looking into and the information we already have on them. Pick whichever you want and go hunting." Brett smiled.

Something inside Kendal loosened. Brett had been trained to see more than the naked eye, so they were sure he understood what Kendal needed without them having to say anything, and they couldn't be more grateful for the distraction.

"Where would you like me?"

Brett pointed to a laptop in the far corner, and again, Kendal was grateful that he knew what they seemed to need. They settled themselves down and studied the paper and attached photographs. Daniel March. Anne Denison. Jeremy Blatch. David Blatch. Nora Blatch, nee Dyer. Ernest Dyer. Charles Sutcliffe. Juliet Sutcliffe, nee Mountford. Arthur Sutcliffe. Isla Sutcliffe, nee Bonner. Elizabeth Sutcliffe. Ian Sutcliffe, nee Trenton. The list went on with all known and potential suspects in the treason plot. Kendal exhaled and picked Anne Denison, as Brett had mentioned wanting to know more about Daniel's mother.

They accessed the internet and started a general search for the name to begin with. There were a lot of results, and Kendal got to work checking each site and the information on it. Every time they found something they weren't sure if it was related or not, they saved it into a new internet folder to find again later. Then they focused on social media. They didn't expect Daniel's mother to be on there because it was more for the younger generation, but they might get lucky.

They had no idea how long they worked for, but Ford

brought them tea regularly and a snack of fruit at one point, too. When Kendal finally pulled their gaze from the screen, they stretched their arms to the ceiling, hearing their back click in several places. They chuckled when two guards blinked at them with wide eyes.

"Sorry, I'm getting old."

"If you're getting old, Your Highness, I have no hope," Brett said, heading towards them. "How are you doing?"

"Good. I've found a couple of things from my searches. Anne Denison was born in Catterick to an Army Sergeant father on the Army base. And..." Kendal exhaled. "Ernest Dyer was stationed at Catterick for two years when he was twenty-five years old. He married Anne Denison the following year."

"They were married? How did you find this?" Brett said, rounding the desk.

Kendal snorted. "People put all sorts of photos up on social media now, reminiscing about times gone past. Someone put a photo up of their wedding, tagging Anne in it. Now, she didn't have a very active page, but she was still on there. And there are some people older than the rest of them who could be parents, but I don't have names."

"Please tell me he was still married to her when he married Charlotte?"

Kendal shook their head. "Sorry, no. They divorced after a year."

"Then how did Daniel turn up?"

Kendal hummed. "Well, it just so happens... Anne Denison, who reverted to her maiden name, moved shortly after Ernest left the Army, which was at the same time as the divorce. Do you want to have a guess where she moved to?"

Brett met their gaze. "Edinburgh."

Kendal nodded. "Edinburgh. Where Ernest started

working as a teaching assistant just before he met Charlotte."

"Jesus Christ. '*Oh, what a tangled web we weave when first we practise to deceive.*'"

Kendal smiled. "I love that quote."

"It's so true in this case," Brett said, then sighed. "Okay. You've done enough tonight—or should I say, this morning—so get some rest. You're welcome to come back at any point to help. You've been invaluable."

"I've enjoyed it." And they had, and it wasn't just because they needed an escape.

"Great minds must think alike," Brett said.

Kendal frowned at them and saw their attention on the other side of the room. Andrew and Kean stood in the doorway, looking a lot more unsure of themselves than Kendal had ever seen them. Andrew had changed clothes and looked a lot less grimy than he had. They glanced at Brett.

"Thank you, Brett. I appreciate it."

"You're always welcome." Kendal left the desk as it was and headed for the door, but Brett called after them. "Did you happen to log which websites you found this information on?"

"It's all in the folders titled 'Assholes.'" Laughter rang out behind them, and Kendal reached Andrew and Kean with a smile on their face. "Hello, my liege. Hello, honey." They closed the door behind them, hiding them from the security team.

Kean grinned. "Are we in a competition for who can make the best nicknames?"

Kendal tilted their head. "I don't know, are we?"

"Are you ready to leave?" Andrew asked.

"I'm ready for bed."

Andrew worked his jaw and squinted at them. "With or without me?"

Kendal slid their arms around Andrew's neck. "With, of course."

Andrew's arms banded around them, and his face rested against Kendal's neck, so they could feel the enormous breath he let out. "I wasn't sure you were coming back to us."

"Of course I am. We made a promise to each other. One which I intend to keep." They pulled back and pointed a finger in Andrew's face. "But that does not mean we are on good terms right now. I'm pissed at you. Extremely pissed, and it will take a lot of grovelling to make me not pissed."

Andrew smiled. "Understood."

Kendal lifted their chin, waiting for what they knew they both needed. Andrew lowered his mouth to Kendal's, and tingles spread from their lips to the rest of their body. Their mind spun, and they tightened their grip on him. Too soon, Andrew pulled back.

"I hear you've been busy," he said, breathing heavily.

Kendal blinked and licked their lips. "Uh-huh. I found out that Ernest was actually married to Daniel's mother, but not when Daniel was born."

Andrew's eyes widened. "He must've been hiding a lot of things because I know for a fact Father wouldn't have been happy about that had he known. He was not one for having his children marry divorced people, and he would've checked. Thoroughly."

"Either Ernest is good at destroying evidence, or he had someone help him," Kean said.

"How did you know where he'd been?" Andrew asked as they started walking towards their suite.

"I didn't. I was looking into Daniel's mother. A picture

came up of a wedding, and I recognised Ernest. When I realised that, I went looking at the service records. I couldn't find anything, so I checked the ancestry websites. They have a lot of service records on there, but not always new ones. I couldn't find his record there, either. I started checking through social media for Army groups stationed in Catterick and found photos they'd uploaded. One said something about newbies, and there was a photo of Ernest."

"You're amazing. I didn't realise you were so good with computers," Andrew said.

Kendal waved him off. "I'm not brilliant, but I know where to look sometimes. Authors have a lot of random information they might need, so research is often something I'm roped into doing. I enjoy it."

"I second Andrew. You're amazing," Kean said, threading their fingers through Kendal's.

"Thank you, honey."

They entered the suite, and they said goodnight to the guards who had been following them. It was getting easier to forget they were there with how quiet they were. Even their footsteps had been silent.

Kendal settled in the corner of the sofa, tucking their legs beneath them and pulling their jumper over their legs. They peered at Andrew. "We need to talk."

Andrew blew out a breath as Kean laughed. "The dreaded words in any relationship," Kean commented in a droll voice, settling in the opposite corner, leaving the middle for Andrew, who glared at him.

Kean held his hands up. "Hey, I'm not the one who went off alone."

"I wasn't alone," Andrew growled but sat in the middle and faced Kendal, the cut just beneath his eye making Kendal boil a little more. "Let me have it."

Kendal sighed, dropping their gaze and picking at a lump on their jumper. "It's not that you went, Andrew. Although that was not the best idea. It was that you went without telling us."

"You would've tried to change my mind."

"Yes, we would've tried to change your mind. But we would've supported you if you still wanted to go. You didn't give us the option, which makes me wonder about the balance in this relationship."

Andrew leaned forward, covering Kendal's hand. "I didn't want you to worry."

Kendal tilted their head. "So you just let us worry when we thought you were dead, and we'd had no chance to say goodbye?" They refused to pull punches. Andrew had to see that they needed to be involved; otherwise, they wouldn't work.

Andrew closed his eyes, his shoulders lowering, his body sinking into itself. "I'm sorry. I thought I was doing the best thing."

"Did you do the same to Queen Louisa?" The question was sharp, but they needed the answer.

Andrew's gaze met theirs, and they could see the pain in them. "No, I didn't."

"Then don't do it to us," Kendal said. "We're by your side, through thick and thin, no matter what. Understand?"

Andrew rubbed his hand over his beard, cleared his throat and said, "I'm sorry." He didn't try to make any further excuses for what he'd done, which Kendal was grateful for.

"I know."

Kendal uncurled their legs and knelt up. Andrew sat back, giving them room. They rested one knee between Andrew's thighs, which Andrew raised an eyebrow at—he probably thought Kendal was going to knee him or something—swung his other leg over towards Kean and placed that knee between Kean's thighs. That way, he was straddling them both, so to speak. Resting his hands on each of their shoulders, he glanced between them.

"I'm not doing anything but sleeping tonight, and maybe all of tomorrow, because I'm exhausted, but I love you—both of you—so much that the idea of losing you is excruciating. I know, though, that there is every chance that it might happen. I went into this with my eyes open, knowing the dangers. You made sure of it, Andrew. But what I can't do is pretend I'm okay with lies and secrets. If that becomes the norm, I'll walk. I'll have to. Whenever any of us walk out of that door, we know there's a chance we might not come back. I don't want to make every exit a sombre event, but I want to be able to tell you how much I love you every time you leave and every time you return."

Andrew pressed his lips to Kendal's cheek. "I understand, and I'm sorry I made you feel this way. I shouldn't have. There is so much uncertainty in this life that I want you to know I love you. Every minute. Every hour. Every day."

"Bloody hell. You've left no words for me," Kean said. "Other than I love you."

Kendal leaned forward and kissed Andrew, then Kean, but ended up breaking off to stifle a yawn. "I love you. Now, let's go to bed." They climbed off their laps and paused. "But I reserve the right to check you over from head to toe in the morning."

Andrew chuckled. "Permission granted."

"Question, Kendal?" Kean said. Kendal glanced over their shoulder as they headed for the bedroom. "Why do you still call her Queen Louisa? Andrew has said we can drop the 'Queen' part?"

Kendal smiled. "Because she will always be my queen,

and she deserves every ounce of respect if she had to put up with *him*."

Andrew swatted their ass, and they yelped as heat flowed through them. They glared over their shoulder. "I'm too tired for that. Stop winding me up."

"You started it," Andrew said.

"No. I told the truth."

Andrew grabbed for them, but Kendal danced out of reach, laughing. "Payback is a bitch," Andrew murmured.

"Bring it on." Kendal paused. "Just not tonight."

Kendal grinned and slipped into the bathroom to wash up. Despite the seriousness of the situation and Kendal's words to Andrew, the weight on their shoulders had lifted. They were glad they had brought it up and told him of their fears because it would only fester inside them if they let it.

As they settled into bed between Andrew and Kean, they thought about helping Brett. They were glad to be able to do something, even if it was just something small. They hoped they could do some more, too. They had more than enough work at their normal job, but they could easily find a few extra minutes here and there to research. Organising and research were two things they loved doing, and the only tiring thing about it was staring at a screen all day.

As far as they knew, they could relax for a while. No events were coming until Damon's birthday towards the end of the month, and Kendal would like it to stay that way. The following weekend was Easter, and they wanted to do something special, even if it was a little ridiculous, but they thought the family would enjoy it. A large Easter egg hunt in the vast garden of Windsor would be great fun. If the weather held, maybe they could have a barbecue like George and Damon loved doing. And add in some other foods that the rest of them like; cheesy Doritos for Douglas, cheesy chips for Mav, chocolate spread and breadsticks for Freddie, something Indian for Damon, love hearts for George, pizza for Timothy, an unlimited supply of coffee for Eddie. Plus, of course, bourbon for the three of them.

As plans swirled around their head, they felt settled and at home for the first time in a long time. And it was only then they realised they hadn't felt the need to check the cameras or check their security measures. They truly were settled. And it was all thanks to the two people surrounding them.

29

ANDREW

"Good morning, Leonard. How is Charlotte doing?" Andrew asked, cradling the phone between his ear and his shoulder as he signed each form Randall handed to him with a cursory glance over it.

"Good morning, Your Majesty. I have some good news and bad news, I'm afraid. We haven't been able to identify what Princess Charlotte had in her system as yet. We're still doing tests, and I hope to have something in a few hours. Unfortunately, during the early hours of this morning, she slipped into a coma. Now, I say unfortunately, but this isn't always a bad thing. Sometimes, the body needs this type of rest to heal, so we're not concerned, especially as her vitals are strong."

Andrew sighed, wishing everything would go back to the way it had been a few years ago. What he wouldn't give for Charlotte to be throwing a tantrum about something benign instead of in hospital after everything she, John and Ernest had done. If it turned out she had been poisoned or drugged, then the finger pointed heavily at Ernest. Whether he did it himself or just ordered it didn't matter. Depending on what they found in her blood would signal whether Ernest meant it as a way to distract them only or a way to get rid of Charlotte entirely.

"Thank you for letting me know, Leonard. Please call me as soon as you have the results or her prognosis changes."

"I will, Your Majesty."

"The guards will remain at her door for her stay."

"I would expect no less, Your Majesty."

Andrew ended the call and slumped back in his chair.

"Bad news, Your Majesty?" Randall asked, cradling the paperwork to his chest.

"Charlotte's in a coma, and they don't know what drugs are in her system yet."

"I'm sorry, Your Majesty."

"Thank you." Andrew scratched his beard. "Oh, while I remember. I told Kean to speak to you about positions available within the businesses. He's no longer following in his father's footsteps, and I feel he would make an excellent addition to the royal companies. He might work well alongside Damon, but he also might prefer something different."

"I'll speak to him and find out what he's interested in. I'm certain we'll have something to suit him."

"I have no doubt." He sighed. "Can you send the statement that George created, please? I've had a read of it, and it seems perfect."

"Of course."

Randall disappeared, and Andrew faced the window, staring out at the gardens. Although both Kean and Kendal said they forgave him for disappearing on them, it would take him a long time to forgive himself. Kendal had been completely right when they said he treated them differently than how he treated Louisa. It hadn't been on purpose. He hadn't realised he'd done it. But he had, and now he had to find a way to make it up to them.

It wasn't that he didn't think they were as capable as Louisa, far from it. Their abilities were just as important and merged well with what he needed for him and the role of king. The problem was that he wanted to shelter them from the negative side of his position because of everything they had already been through. Kendal had been abused by a club member, and Kean had been kidnapped. Both were directly and indirectly related to him and although his ego wasn't large enough for him to say it was solely *because* of him, it almost was.

But he realised too late that he needed to let them be the people they needed to be, and he needed to support them. Nothing less. It wouldn't be an easy lesson, and he would undoubtedly have to beg for forgiveness again—maybe more than once—but he would try. They deserved it.

He faced his desk again, remembering the Easter event they had planned for that weekend. He called through to Randall.

"Randall, could you please cancel my attendance at the Easter event this weekend? I don't think it's such a good idea to be out and about at the moment."

"I'm sorry, Your Majesty. I forgot to mention I had already changed it. Prince William requested he take your place. I should've checked with you, but I mistakenly assumed he had already run it past you. I'm sorry."

Andrew chuckled. "That sounds like something William would do. It certainly wouldn't be the first time. It's okay, Randall. It's worked out fine. Maybe contact Brett and ask him to ensure William takes extra guards with him."

"I can ask him right now, Your Majesty. He's here waiting to see you."

"He is? Okay, send him in, and I can ask him, don't worry. You're inundated with wedding plans, I'm sure."

Randall cleared his throat. "Just a few things, Your Majesty. Nothing that won't get done."

"I have every faith in you, as always." Andrew replaced the receiver, and then a few seconds later, Brett knocked at the door. "Come in."

"Good afternoon, Your Majesty," Brett said, closing the door behind him.

Andrew looked at his watch. "Afternoon already. Where does the time go?"

Brett snorted. "I have no idea, but if you ever find out, please let me know. I'd love a few more hours to my day." He settled into the chair in front of the desk.

"So, what do you have for me?"

Brett fidgeted, which was unlike him. "I wasn't sure whether you wanted anyone else at the meeting. I do have a few things that I've found. Do you want me to wait?"

Andrew waved him on. "No, tell me, and then I can pass on the information if I need to."

Brett nodded. "Well, Kendal was a great help in finding out some things that we hadn't."

"They told me what they'd found." Andrew chuckled. "Hidden talents indeed."

"Definitely. I won't ever turn down their help."

"I'll let them know."

Brett glanced at the papers in his hand. "Kendal found out that Ernest and Anne had married, then divorced within a year, but it seems they were still 'together' when Ernest moved to Edinburgh. Kendal also found a photograph which showed two sets of what appeared to be parents. We believe them to be Ernest's and Anne's parents, but we've not confirmed that yet."

"Did you find out who Jeremy's parents were?"

"Yes, David Blatch and Nora Dyer. They were married—"

"Wait, give me those names again." Brett glanced at him, then repeated the names. Andrew stared to the side, trying to figure out which name he recognised. "Nora Dyer. I know that name."

Brett raised his eyebrows. "Can you remember where from?"

Andrew filtered through his memories, flicking through his ancient mental address book. "Holy shit!" he said suddenly, eyes fastened on Brett. "Nora Dyer was who I was supposed to marry before I met Louisa! My father had arranged our marriage without my consent, but I was going to go ahead with it because I couldn't find anyone I could tolerate and thought I had no other option. Then I met Louisa, and I declined Father's arrangement."

Brett's eyes widened, and he stared down at the paper, his finger tracing something. "Would that be enough to piss the family off enough to do something like this?"

Andrew frowned. "I didn't—don't—know much about them, but what I remember was them being very easygoing. The complete opposite of my father, which was maybe why he chose them. Easy to manipulate. Nora was softly spoken but a little standoffish at times."

"Nora Dyer is Ernest's sister," Brett said. "Do you think he took offence to it? His life would've been drastically different if you had married her."

Andrew thought it through. Ernest would've been the queen consort's brother had Andrew married Nora. Although that might not have come with a title, Andrew probably would've given him one, anyway. Especially if they were close siblings. But even if he didn't, the status elevation itself would've made sure Ernest lived comfortably and would want for nothing.

"He probably wasn't happy about it. He is, what, five or six years older than her."

"Eight, actually. A surprising difference that we looked into. When Ernest was born, it was usual to have kids closer together."

"Same as we were. Ernest is older than me, which is another thing Father wasn't happy about."

"Well, the reason for it was because Jonathan and Elenora Dyer suffered three miscarriages between Ernest and Nora."

Andrew's heart broke for them. He and Louisa had been graced with three healthy sons, but not everyone was given that. "They would've coddled her, potentially."

Brett nodded. "I can imagine they would."

"The family must've had a high status if we were to be married, but I can't remember what it was. And I certainly don't remember Ernest at all. I would've remembered him if I'd met him."

"Jonathan Dyer was the Earl of Scarborough. Ernest received the title upon his father's death. It could be why Ernest requested the transfer to Catterick. Closer to home. And from what I gather, he was away in the Army during this time," Brett said.

"If it was such a snub, why didn't they do anything about it until now?" Andrew mused. "It was forty-odd years ago."

Brett shrugged. "I can't answer that yet, Your Majesty."

Andrew smiled. "I didn't expect you to. Thank you, Brett. I'll pass this on to everyone and see if anyone has questions or, even better, answers."

They said goodbye, and Andrew settled back in his chair. He'd asked Randall to request everyone's presence, and once they settled, Andrew went through everything Brett had told him.

"So, you were supposed to marry Ernest's sister but didn't, and Ernest set his sights on Charlotte...because she would give him the status he was denied?" Freddie surmised.

"That doesn't surprise me any longer," Christian said. "After everything that's happened, starting a treason plan forty years prior seems possible."

"But why did it take until his father died to do something more than sit in the background and whisper in Charlotte's ear?" Douglas asked.

Henry sat forward. "Would his father have been for or against Ernest's plans if he knew about them?" He glanced at Andrew.

"I can't remember a huge amount about Jonathan, but from what I do, he seemed a pleasant enough man. Father said he was fine about breaking off the arrangement; he mentioned something about not being able to help falling in love."

"He probably didn't want any harm to come to anyone," Patrick said. "Could Ernest have kept this quiet until his father's death because his father wouldn't approve, and then afterwards, he had free rein?"

Andrew raised his eyebrows. "That sounds plausible. Ernest wouldn't want to go against his father, though I'm sure he would've if he'd needed to. Maybe he was worried he wouldn't get his Earl title, though why he would worry about that when he received the prince title when he married Charlotte, I do not know."

Andrew's phone rang, and he apologised to his family and answered it. "Brady?"

"Andrew." His voice sounded grim. "I won't sugarcoat this for you. We found a body within the rubble of Kensington Palace."

Andrew's heart skipped. "Who was it?"

"We don't know for definite, but we think it's John."

Andrew closed his eyes, holding the phone closer to his ear. He bowed his head. "How? I'm assuming it wasn't from the explosion."

"No, it wasn't. The body has a gunshot wound to the forehead."

As much as he didn't care for what John had been part of, he hadn't wanted him dead. "I'm assuming it wasn't a suicide."

"Not likely with the position of the bullet wound."

"Thanks, Brady. Let me know when you've formally identified him."

Brady hesitated. "You're so sure it's him?"

"Ernest wouldn't want any hangers-on. He planned on getting rid of Charlotte and me through the explosion. It wouldn't leave many people in his way. Especially not many who knew he was involved."

"It makes sense in an evil sort of way," Brady agreed. "I'll let you know as soon as I know something."

"Thanks."

Andrew hung up the phone and sighed, facing his family. "Brady suspects John is dead. They found a body in the rubble with a gunshot wound to the head. I'm waiting for Brady to confirm, but he thinks it's him." He glanced at Christian, who stared at the floor.

"Ernest's cleaning up," Damon said. "Makes sense. He didn't expect Charlotte to survive the explosion either."

Christian stood, pacing. "Does he know she didn't?"

Andrew studied him. "I don't know. Leonard called this

morning to say Charlotte is in a coma, but he's convinced she'll wake soon. But I haven't told anyone else."

"Can we use that to our advantage?" Christian asked.

"In what way?"

"Could we announce she's dead and let Ernest continue with his plan? Then when Charlotte wakes, she can be a thorn in his side?"

"That would work as long as he didn't see us leaving Kensington Palace. He'll know I'm alive for obvious reasons, but if he didn't see Charlotte with us, then we might get away with it."

Christian shook his head. "Even if he did, you can say she died at the hospital."

Andrew blew out a long breath. "Do we really want Ernest to continue?"

"Do we have any other choice?" Freddie said. "We have no idea what his plans are unless Charlotte wakes and tells us. And it's likely she might not know, either. This might backfire, but it seems to be the only option."

Andrew stared at Christian. "Get an idea together of how you think this would work. I'll speak to Brady about it, and then we can go from there. If it ends up being too dangerous, we'll figure something else out." Christian nodded and sat again. "Does anyone else have any information or questions or…anything?"

"Has the law been finalised?" Henry asked.

Andrew paused. "I don't know. Hold on." He picked up the phone. "Randall, do we have any information on the law yet?"

"No, Your Majesty, but I can follow up on it."

"Thank you. Please do."

Andrew hung up and said, "No, but Randall's going to check. Why do you ask?"

"I don't know if this will make sense, so I'm just going to blurt it all out. If the law has not been passed, then if they'd succeeded and we died, the throne would go to Arthur, I believe, or maybe Uncle William. I'm uncertain about who. That doesn't benefit Ernest much unless Arthur is completely under his thumb, which I don't believe he is. Christian?"

Christian exhaled. "I don't know, to be honest. We barely spoke, especially the last few years, but what I saw was Arthur as more of a minion than a leader."

Henry nodded. "So, how does that help Ernest in any way? To gain any kind of title, he would've needed John, I would've thought."

It hadn't escaped Andrew's notice that his family no longer called John, Ernest or Charlotte their uncle or aunt, and he couldn't agree more.

"If the law has been passed," Henry continued, "the throne would go to Albert, which still wouldn't help Ernest at all."

"Maybe it has nothing to do with titles at all. Maybe it is just revenge," Douglas said. "Ernest making those he thinks wronged him suffer for it."

"If that's the case, then he's even more dangerous," Andrew said. "And unpredictable."

"But where is he?" Damon asked.

"That, we don't know." Andrew rubbed a hand over his beard.

"Did we get anything else from the video feed?" Freddie asked.

"All the people who we identified as being in contact with Charles more than once are being looked into and interviewed," Andrew said. "So far, they all seem clean."

"Has anyone spoken to Charles lately?" George asked.

"Not that I know of," Andrew said.

George raised his eyebrows. "It might be worthwhile. He might know nothing, and he might not talk if he does, but maybe we could lean on the Charlotte 'being dead' thing and push for information?"

"Is he likely to go against his father?" Patrick asked.

"He might if they mention how much his father preferred his firstborn." Andrew stared at the group. "Charles would hate that, and he might talk if he believes it'll pay Ernest back."

"Who wants to do the honours?" Freddie said with a smirk.

Several hands went in the air, and Andrew chuckled at the eagerness. "I think I should do it," Andrew said. Everyone groaned. "Okay." He sighed. "Maybe Damon should." Damon lifted his head. "I'm sure you have plenty to say," he murmured.

"Damn right, I do."

George put his hand up as if they were in school. "Can I go, too?"

"Do you know what? Fight it out amongst yourselves. I'm going to see my better halves."

Andrew stood but paused when George called him. "Don't you mean your better thirds?"

If Andrew could've reached him from where he was, he would've clipped his ear. Instead, he just glared at him. "Have a good day, everyone. Let me know what you decide."

He exited his office, leaving them to discuss who got to interrogate Charles, and headed for Kendal's office. He wasn't even sure if either of them would be finished, but he wanted to see them all the same. Plenty of work awaited him if they still had things to do, so it wasn't a problem. After knocking on Kendal's door and finding it empty, he had high hopes they'd be in the suite.

Five hours was far too long away from them, especially with everything he'd learnt that day.

30

PATRICK

"I want to go," Patrick said when the door closed behind Uncle Andrew.

"I think we all do, but who is most likely to get information from him?" Freddie said.

Patrick didn't care. He wanted to see Charles squirm beneath their questioning, writhe in the pain of "knowing" his mother was dead. He wasn't a bad person, but he wanted that man—if he could call him that—to hurt, and he wanted to be the one to do it.

Kieren slid an arm around Patrick's shoulders, tugging him closer and leaning in. "You don't want to do this, Patrick."

Patrick moved back away, dislodging Kieren's arm. "Yes, I do."

"You're angry. We all are. But you won't get anything from him. He would want to taunt someone, and you wouldn't listen."

Patrick gritted his teeth. Kieren was right, but it didn't make a difference. He wanted to do it.

"I think Damon and Christian should go," Douglas said. "They have had more dealings with him. He'd react most if they were the ones to break the news."

Patrick leaned back, crossing his arms, but said nothing. They were right. They all were. He wanted someone to rail against. Someone to hurt, and Charles was there. He couldn't squash the need, though.

"Come on," Kieren said, standing. "We agree. We're going to head out. Let us know if you need us," he said to the rest of them.

Patrick stood, stalking to the door and going through it without even checking Kieren was with him. He exited the office and turned left, aiming to go home, but Kieren grabbed his arm and tugged him after him to the right, towards the security room.

"Where are we going?" Patrick asked.

"Training."

Patrick's stomach swooped, and his heart rate increased in preparation. They strode for the training room, and Kieren held the door for him. In silence, they changed into clothes that were always readily available and headed for the mats. Kieren stopped on the mats and faced Patrick.

"Hand-to-hand." Patrick exhaled and stopped in front of him. "You take it out on me." Patrick shook his head, but Kieren nodded. "Yes. Let the anger go. It clouds your judgement and stops you from seeing the big picture."

Patrick clenched his jaw, eyes downcast. He was right, but Patrick didn't have to admit it.

"Go."

Kieren came towards him, and Patrick reacted, blocking the punch. They moved around the mats, blocking, punching, kicking, until sweat dripped from them, and their lungs complained. When Kieren knocked Patrick to the floor, he stayed there, chest heaving, staring at the ceiling. Kieren crawled over him, legs and arms on either side of him, and Patrick cracked his first smile since the meeting.

"I remember this position," he said.

Kieren's cheeks, flushed from the exertion, deepened in colour, but his eyes heated. "Me, too."

Patrick slid his hands up Kieren's sweat-soaked T-shirt to his nape and pulled him down. Kieren went to his elbows and stretched his legs out alongside Patrick's so they were touching everywhere but their lips. Which Patrick would rectify shortly.

"Thank you," he said, staring into those blue eyes he loved so much.

"You're welcome. Feeling better?"

Patrick nodded and tugged on Kieren, bringing him closer. "Kiss me."

"Yes, sir."

Kieren lowered his head and brushed their lips together. Patrick's anger had diffused as they'd trained, which Kieren had known, and despite wanting to hang on to it, it wasn't healthy. They needed clear minds to work through the problems being thrown at them, and anger wouldn't do that. As Kieren took him apart with his lips, Patrick felt himself being put back together again as well.

Charles had already received what he deserved, life imprisonment, and now someone else would take on the task of getting as much information from him as they could before dropping the bombshell that, actually, Charlotte wasn't dead. He hoped they'd be able to get a photo of Charles's reaction because that would be priceless.

And something he could put on a dartboard and use as target practice.

31

KEAN

"Why didn't you call me? I would've come to the meeting," Kean said, standing in front of Andrew with his hands in his pockets.

Andrew had just disclosed everything he'd found out and what they had discussed at the meeting. Kean was a little annoyed he hadn't been asked to attend.

"I thought you were busy with Randall. I'm not keeping anything from you. I've told you everything we spoke about." Andrew stepped closer, and Kean fought to step back. He trusted Andrew, but he thought they were a team.

"I want to speak with Charles, too," he said. He wasn't saying that to be awkward; he truly wanted to face him again. He'd not seen Charles since he'd been rescued, and he needed closure.

Andrew inhaled, then exhaled slowly, and Kean knew he was pushing down his need to say no. Kean waited, and Andrew finally said, "I wish you wouldn't, but I understand why you need to. I'm sure we can arrange for you to accompany whoever is going."

"Give him a punch from me, eh?" Kendal said, face hard and unforgiving.

Kean's mouth curved at the thought, but he nodded at them. "Will do." He studied Andrew. "I'll be okay."

Andrew slid his arms around Kean, and Kean sank into the embrace, burying his head against his king's shoulder, the heat of him seeping into the areas Kean needed to warm. Those areas that had chilled at the idea of Andrew not wanting him at the meeting. It was irrational, but he couldn't help it. Andrew's mouth pressed against his temple and skimmed down his cheekbone to his mouth. Kean lifted his head, wanting more. He opened, and Andrew's tongue slipped inside. Their tongues tangled, and Kean's hands tightened against Andrew's back. Andrew gentled the kiss, brushing his lips across Kean's but retreating when Kean pressed forward, needing more.

"If you want to go, we need to see who's going with you." Andrew dropped another kiss on Kean's lips, then pulled away again. "Come on."

Andrew held Kean's hand and beckoned to Kendal. They headed to Andrew's office, but the family weren't where Andrew had left them.

"Randall, where did everyone go?" Andrew asked.

"They went to their respective rooms to get ready, Your Majesty."

"Did they say who was going?"

Randall nodded. "Princes Damon and Christian."

"Thanks." Andrew turned to Kean. "You'll be in good company. Let's go find them."

Freddie's room was closest, and Andrew knocked and entered when called to. Freddie sat on the sofa with a laptop balanced on his lap, but he looked up when they entered and smiled.

"Hey, I wasn't expecting to see you." He stood, placing the laptop on the coffee table. "What's going on?"

"Kean's going with them," Andrew said without preamble.

Freddie glanced at him with raised eyebrows before nodding. "Okay. Damon's just getting changed…"

"I'm here," Damon said, entering the room. "Hey."

"Kean's coming with you," Freddie said.

Damon smiled at Kean. "Glad to have you. The more to annoy him, the merrier."

"This is going to be fun," Kean said, waggling his eyebrows.

They laughed, then sobered. Andrew slid his arm around Kean. "I want you safe, though." He glanced at Damon. "All of you."

Damon nodded. "We have plans in place. Guards are coming with us in addition to the ones at the prison. We'll be covered."

Andrew said no more, and he, Damon and Christian were on their way quicker than Kean expected. When he asked why it was such a rush to get there, Christian explained it was because they didn't want the news of Charlotte to leak out before they could use it as bait for Charles. If he found out before they got there, he wouldn't say a thing. There was still the chance he wouldn't cave, but Kean believed he would. Charles would see his father killing his mother as a slight against them and then throw in the firstborn child, and Charles would see red.

The prison was as heavily guarded as Kean expected it to be, but he was glad for their extra protection all the same. The grey, sombre buildings were nothing to write home about, and it definitely wasn't a holiday spot.

The room they were shown into was as gloomy and sterile

as the rest of the place, but there was one chair bolted to the floor in front of a table, which was also bolted down, and three chairs on the opposite side of the table that were free to be moved. Christian moved the three chairs a little further away from the table and then took a seat in one. Damon and Kean followed suit, and they waited in silence while their personal guards settled against a wall around the room. A knock sounded to advertise that the guards were bringing Charles in, and Kean held his breath. He wasn't sure how he would react to seeing Charles again, and he wanted to steel himself against it, so he didn't show any fear or negative emotions that Charles could turn against him.

Charles appeared the same as always, except he was a little more gaunt, but his piercing blue eyes and black hair from the Sutcliffe genes were still going strong. A smirk curved his mouth as the prison guards chained him to the table and chair. They were taking no chances with three royals in the room with him, apparently.

"Well, well, well. To what do I owe this pleasure?" Charles said when the prison guards had left.

"We have news for you, Charles," Christian said, his voice pitched low and sombre, making Charles narrow his eyes.

"What's that then?" Charles appeared mostly unaffected, but he couldn't keep completely still.

"Kensington Palace blew up," Damon said.

Charles chuckled. "And?"

"Your mother was inside," Kean finished.

Charles went pale, and he slumped back in his seat. He stared at the tabletop. Kean let himself bask in the man's sorrow, even though it wasn't something Kean ever thought he would do—he wasn't a mean person—but Charles deserved all the pain they heaped on him.

"We have reason to believe that your father is to blame. John was shot and killed, his body being buried in the rubble of Kensington," Damon said. "Does this sound like something Ernest would do?"

Charles didn't reply.

"What about your father's illegitimate firstborn?" Christian asked. "It must gall you to think he prefers his illegitimate child to you."

Charles's jaw clenched, and Kean could see they were getting to him.

Christian continued. "From what we've heard, Ernest has been boasting about Daniel and how he never let him down, whereas your brother defected from Ernest's cause, and you ended up, well, here. Daniel has never let him down. So we heard."

"Father would never say that!" Charles shouted, causing their guards to snap to attention.

"Oh, but I think he would. After all, if his legitimate children couldn't do as they were told, he had no choice but to turn to someone who would."

Kean bit his lip to stop the smile from spreading. Christian was brilliant at twisting things to sound worse than they were. "I can't believe you were so gullible to believe your father wanted you to be his second." Kean shook his head and chuckled.

Charles glared at him, his cheeks flushing, replacing the paleness. "You know nothing!"

"Then enlighten us, Charles. Tell us exactly how much of an asshole your father is," Christian said, leaning forward. "Tell us everything about him so we can make him pay for killing your mother."

Charles snorted. "As if you want to help me."

Damon shook his head. "We don't, really. But the enemy of our enemies can help bring them down."

Charles studied them, and Kean could almost see his brain working through the options—of which Charles had none. If he wanted revenge, he'd have to enlist their help, and to do that he would need to divulge everything.

"I didn't know about Daniel until he came to visit me last week," Charles began. He settled back in his seat. "I'd interacted with him at the club, but I didn't know who he was. I didn't believe him at first, even though he looked similar to Father."

"What did he want?" Christian asked.

"He wanted to know if I would help him stop the 'madness,' as he called it."

"And what did you tell him?"

"To go fuck himself." Charles chuckled. "I wasn't having anything to do with him." He sighed. "Father started disappearing for several days at a time without telling us where he was going. This was a couple of years ago. I was curious where he was going, so I had him followed." He shook his head. "Didn't do much good. Father found out and smacked me around a bit when he got back. He's always been the one in charge. Mother was happy with our little tête-à-tête with the men we chose from the club. Originally, she had no plans to go further."

Kean's stomach swooped. He knew about those "tête-à-tête" meetings because Henry had explained what went on.

"When did things change?"

"After Grandfather died. Father's father, I mean. We went to his funeral, but Father was stone cold. I'd never seen him like that. After that, he was a stranger. It was like someone had taken over his body. I caught him giving Uncle John orders for an event, but I said nothing. Afterwards, though, I studied him, watching what he did as well as listening to what he said. He was always bringing things into a conversation with Mother. Little bits that she would initially brush off, then she brought them up herself, and Father agreed it was a good idea. But the ideas were his all along."

"Did you know his final plan?" Kean asked.

"No. I knew Uncle John was a pawn, though. Everyone was. Including me. I don't know what his end game is—I doubt anyone does but him."

"Why didn't you stop it?" Damon asked.

Charles snorted. "Because I didn't want to. I wanted you gone. I wanted a chance at the throne, and I trusted Father to lead us in the right direction. Besides, you're abominations."

Kean held his breath to push down the need to punch the man. He might get away with it because Kendal told him to do it. He was a lot more confident now he'd seen Charles taken down a few pegs.

"How did you recruit people?" Christian said.

"The club. Perfect breeding ground for 'paths of all kinds."

"Paths?" Kean asked.

"Psychopaths, sociopaths, and so on." Charles grinned.

"How did you choose?"

"It's not hard to see which men were into the more hardcore elements of BDSM. You know, the consensual non-consent stuff, sometimes, breath play or high-level impact play. Those kinds of things. Drop a few specific hints, and they're putty in your hands. Everyone is looking for their next 'high.' And it doesn't take long for them to need more, and by that point, you have enough material to blackmail them into doing the jobs for you."

"Who?" Damon asked.

Charles laughed. "Do you need to ask?" They stayed silent, and Charles shook his head. "Talon, Harvey, Vincent, Tobias, Aaron, to name a few. Need I say more?"

"So you believed the idea was to have Charlotte on the throne? What are your thoughts now you know he killed her?"

Charles gritted his teeth, but Kean could see he was considering Christian's words. They kept silent, waiting for Charles to speak.

"Well, the plan had always been to kill Uncle John. He was too much of a liability. But Mother shouldn't have been in the firing line." Charles shook his head, his jaw clenching repeatedly. "I can honestly tell you I have no idea. Father only ever mentioned getting Mother on the throne. If he had a secondary plan, I wasn't privy to it."

They asked a few more questions, and then Christian stood. "Thank you for the information."

They headed for the door with their guards, and Charles spoke again before they exited.

"Will they let me attend the funeral?"

Damon smirked and shook his head. "She doesn't need a funeral yet. The hospital is doing all they can to keep her alive."

Kean saw the confusion, shock, and then anger register on Charles's face before he struggled to stand, his chains rattling as he fought them.

"You assholes! Let me out of this! You fucking shitheads! I'll make you pay."

Christian chuckled as they closed the door on Charles's tirade. "That was fun."

Kean couldn't agree more, but had they stirred up a hornet's nest?

When they arrived back at Windsor, Brady was sitting with Andrew and Kendal in their suite, sipping coffee, or in Kendal's case, tea. Andrew stood and greeted them, leaving a lingering kiss on Kean's mouth before returning to his seat.

"Everything okay?" Kean asked, taking a perch next to Kendal.

Andrew sighed. "The body was John."

Kean reached across and squeezed Andrew's forearm. "I'm sorry."

Andrew sent a small smile his way. "How are you after seeing Charles?"

"Lighter," Kean admitted.

"I'm glad."

"We found out some information," Damon said.

They spent the next hour talking about what Charles had told them, which wasn't a huge amount, while the rest of the family joined them once again—it was becoming a regular occurrence, and one Kean didn't mind at all.

They'd wanted to know Ernest's endgame, but Charles had no idea. They knew a bit more about how they recruited and how their victims were chosen, but not much else.

"And we have no idea where Ernest is now?" Freddie said.

Damon shook his head. "Charles had no idea. Ernest hasn't visited him since he was in prison. He's had no contact with him at all."

"What about Albert? Would he have any idea?" Douglas asked.

"They barely kept him in the loop with anything, even from the beginning," Andrew said. "He doesn't know anything." He glanced at Brady. "Did you get into the houses? I forgot to ask with everything that's happened."

Brady nodded. "We did, and it surprised us to find nothing except for potential evidence of wrongdoing. There had been a lot of things that had been moved around. We could see the marks across the floors where furniture had been moved, and when we moved some rugs aside, there was damage to the floors underneath. We've taken samples to see if they're blood stains, so we need to wait for the results."

"Other than that, there were no signs of foul play?" Andrew asked.

"The household staff weren't the most...dedicated. Some were willing to talk, and we're currently interviewing them. Hopefully, they'll have something juicy for us."

"And the others?"

"They're being held as associates to Charlotte, John and Ernest until we've had time to investigate."

"Sounds like we're finally getting somewhere with their structural hierarchy," Kean said.

He couldn't believe how convoluted Ernest's plan seemed to be. If what they thought was true, and he'd been holding the grudge since Andrew declined to marry his sister, then that was forty years' worth of planning. Did he have a plan before he even married Charlotte, or was it weaved and sewn over the years until it all came together?

At least now, they were getting somewhere. The foundations of the plan were coming apart, and it was leaving Ernest with not much left to lean on. Or so they hoped. But it also left them with a potentially desperate man. A potentially *angry,* desperate man. And one who might look around and decide he had nothing left to lose. If that happened, who knew what he'd take the chance of doing.

"Okay, enough for today. It's getting late," Andrew said. "Get yourselves fed and rest up. We have plenty more work ahead of us."

Kean said goodnight to several of the family, then headed

for the bathroom to run a bath. He'd just started the water when Andrew entered and turned off the taps again.

"We'll do that later, but first, I want you both naked and on my bed. I find I have need of you."

Kean smiled and strode for the bed. "Your wish, our command."

Kean and Kendal stripped, not making it a striptease this time, and then they were gloriously naked, awaiting Andrew's next command.

"Kean, lie on your back like you did the other day. You're taking the same positions but with a slight difference."

"Yes, Sir."

Andrew undressed and grabbed a pillow from the bed and the necessities from the bedside table. He stood between Kean's thighs, slid his arm beneath Kean's back and lifted him, sliding the pillow beneath his ass. Kean raised his eyebrows but said nothing.

"Kendal, please straddle him."

"Yes, Sir."

When Andrew positioned them where he wanted them, he said, "I'm going to prepare you both."

Kean met Kendal's gaze and smiled. If it ended up anything like last time, they'd all be satisfied. Kendal's mouth dropped open, and Kean glanced over their shoulder to see Andrew focused between their legs—between both their legs. Kean would love to be inside Kendal as Andrew slid inside him, but that could wait. He was curious about what Andrew had planned for them.

Kendal gasped, their arms and legs trembling, their eyes closed tightly, and they tried not to rock back against Andrew's ministrations. Then Kendal sighed, and Kean felt the slickness against his hole. Andrew took no prisoners. He slid one finger inside, then two, scissoring and rotating them to stretch him. Three fingers. Four and Kean winced and bit his lip.

"That's it," Andrew growled. "Now open for me. One at a time."

Kendal rocked forward as Andrew slid inside them, and Kean stopped them by joining their lips in a soft kiss.

32

KENDAL

The pressure as Andrew slid deep inside them was immense, but they wanted everything he gave them. And everything Kean gave them, too. As Kendal lost themselves in Kean's kiss and Andrew's claiming, they let their mind float and just felt. The first time they had made love this way, it had blown Kendal's mind, and they waited for it to happen again. But they knew Andrew had something planned to make it even better. They couldn't wait to find out what.

"That's it," Andrew crooned. "You're taking me so well, my sweet. Bear with me for a moment." Andrew kissed their back and withdrew, drawing an unexpected whimper from them.

They felt Andrew still between their legs, but they didn't know what he was doing until Kean pulled his mouth from Kendal's and gasped. Kendal glanced down between their bodies enough to see Andrew sliding into Kean.

"He feels good, doesn't he?" Kendal asked Kean.

Kean nodded and bit his lip, his eyes at half-mast. "So good."

When Andrew slid completely inside Kean, his torso rested against Kendal's ass, keeping them connected. But then Andrew slid his fingers inside of Kendal again, and they gasped, too.

"He's inside us both," Kendal murmured, eyelids drooping.

"Not exactly how I want to be, but I have plans once I have the necessary equipment," Andrew growled.

Kendal's channel spasmed at the idea. Would Andrew do what they thought he might?

"You both feel amazing surrounding my cock. I'm glad I don't have to choose."

He removed his fingers, slid his arms beneath Kendal's chest and dragged them upright. As Andrew slid into Kean, he pressed against Kendal, snapping his hips forward to nudge against Kean's cock. All three moaned, and Kendal dropped their head back on Andrew's shoulder, allowing him to guide them where he wanted them to be. As he began a continuous rhythm, he encircled their shafts, and Kendal's heart raced as heat pooled in their groin. It wouldn't take them long to fly—they were finding it easier to achieve release with Kean and Andrew than they ever had before. It seemed they didn't need the impact play as much as they initially believed, although they still enjoyed it.

Andrew slid free of Kean, pressed his cock head against Kendal's entrance and slammed deep.

"Yes! Oh, fuck, yes!"

Andrew set a faster beat, jerking them off as well as sliding deep into Kendal. He repeated the action of slipping into Kean and back into Kendal again, keeping their arousal heightened. Then Andrew rested Kendal back onto Kean's prone body, removing his hands.

"Come for me, my sweet. Come for me, sweetheart," Andrew hissed, slamming his hips forward.

The command alone sent Kendal close to the edge, but what sent them over was feeling Andrew releasing inside Kendal, then pulling out and sliding into Kean and continuing his release. It was the perfect way to claim them both at once.

Kendal lay their sweaty head on Kean's chest, their cheek immediately sticking to the man, and breathed through the contractions still wracking their body. They doubted they would ever get enough of this. The three of them together. They knew Andrew was concerned about their age gap, and in truth, so was Kendal, but not enough for them to stop their relationship. They couldn't imagine not being with them now.

"You should see what I see," Andrew groaned, and Kendal realised he knelt behind them. "Watching my release slide out of you both at the same time is better than I ever believed it would be."

Andrew sounded tired, though, and Kendal knew it wasn't just his body. His mind and his spirit were, too.

They jumped when Andrew's tongue lapped at them but sank into the feeling of being looked after. Presently, Kendal didn't feel the need to return to the club, and he was sure Andrew wasn't bothered about it. Kean was a little different. He might want to visit as he'd never spent a lot of time there, and Kendal would, eventually, be able to join him fully. They'd have to discuss that at some point. The same with the living arrangements. They would have to go back to their own homes soon. They couldn't just move into Windsor from the beginning. Could they?

When Andrew finished his ministrations, Kendal rose on shaky legs and stumbled to the bathroom. They turned on the taps and started a bath. It wouldn't be a long one, but it might heal some of Andrew's aches. The physical ones, at least.

Kean came up behind them and slid their arms around them. Before, it would've freaked Kendal out, but they were getting used to being touched and held now, even when they weren't expecting it.

"Our king needs respite," Kean said.

"Our liege needs sleep."

"Great minds." Kean kissed their cheek. "I'll get him in here."

"Good luck."

It had taken nine days to get the results from Brady about the two houses because of Easter, and during that time, Andrew had been pulled in so many directions, he was exhausted every time he finally came to bed. They both tried to do everything they could to ease the weight of his work, but it wasn't easy, but they'd known that going into the relationship. But it was more than that. Kendal could see the burden of Andrew's family's treason was worse than his workload, even as he put up a good front whenever anyone was around. Occasionally, Kendal found him staring out of a window, mind elsewhere, and they couldn't do anything to help.

When Brady finally came to them with answers, everyone piled into Andrew's office once more. Kendal and Kean settled in the chairs in front of Andrew's desk while Andrew settled against the edge of his desk between them.

"The stains on the floors of both houses were blood. We don't yet know whose, but hopefully, we will eventually. Though we don't always know who is missing if they're not reported," Brady said.

"Can we cross-reference those who have not attended the club for a while?" Christian asked. "Some may just not attend any longer, but some might be people who would not be missed, hence why they chose them."

Andrew nodded, scratching at his beard as he did when he was thinking things through. "We can certainly ask Clarice to collate a list for us. We won't have their DNA on file, but we might get some information from their files or their families."

"Would Charles not corroborate anything?" Kendal asked.

Kean and Damon shared a smile. "Not with how we left things," Kean answered. "We've burnt that bridge now, I'm afraid."

Andrew tutted, but his mouth curved. "Were you mean, sweetheart?"

Kean flushed but threw his shoulders back. "We all were, but no less than he deserved."

Andrew chuckled and squeezed his shoulder. "I'm sure you were more polite than I would've been." He focused on Brady, his smile dropping. "What else did you find?"

Brady shifted in his chair. "I swear, Andrew, I'm going to buy you new chairs if you don't replace these soon." He shifted again and sighed. "We didn't find anyone at the properties other than staff, but there was evidence that someone had been there recently. Whether it was Ernest or John before he died, we don't know. Most staff aren't talking yet."

"Probably too scared for the repercussions, though, I think," Freddie said, "with Ernest being the only one left, he wouldn't be too worried about what his staff said. He would be on the offensive now."

"I agree," Brady said. "You need to stay close to home, Andrew. Everyone should. Minimise the chances of his plans working. Whatever they may be."

Andrew didn't reply, his attention on the floor. Kendal watched him, waiting for whatever he was trying to piece together in his head to finish. They saw the moment he did.

"Where's his sister?"

Kendal's heart lodged into their throat. No one had contacted her as far as they knew. Was she in on it as well? Was she waiting in the wings to help Ernest finish his plan? Or did she know nothing about it?

"We believe she's still in Yorkshire," Brett said. "We've had someone speak to her, but she mentioned not having seen or heard from Ernest since their father's funeral."

"Did you believe her?" Christian asked.

Brett nodded. "The interviewer did. I stand by their opinion."

"Can we check up on her and make sure she's still where she's supposed to be?" Christian said, and Brett nodded.

"So, if she's not involved, Ernest is all on his own now. True?" Andrew asked. Everyone nodded. "What will a man do when he has nothing left?"

"Anything he can," Brady answered, staring at Andrew with a grim expression. "That's why I want you close to home. He can't get in here without being seen, and everyone here knows who he is."

"I don't like being imprisoned, Brady."

"It's for your own good, Andrew."

They stared at each other as if in a battle of wills, and Andrew capitulated with a sigh. "Fine. But not long. If it takes too long to find him, I'm going back to normal, no matter what."

Brady stood, wincing. "Maybe you'll have time to look online for new chairs."

He waved and exited. It must've encouraged the others because they stood, too. Kendal rose and kissed Andrew's cheek. "I'm going to get some work done."

Andrew drew them into his arms and hugged them tightly. "Don't work too hard."

Kendal pulled their head back and smiled. "I should say the same to you."

Andrew dropped a kiss on their lips, then pulled Kean to them. "We need some assistance," he murmured.

"Oh? Why's that?" Kean said, leaning against him.

"Kendal's leaving us. We need to make sure they don't stay away too long."

Kean grinned. "I'm sure we can do that."

"On that note, see you later!" Freddie shouted, and footsteps raced to the door. Kendal laughed and kissed Andrew and Kean in turn before pulling away.

"See you soon."

They left the warm embrace and headed out of the door, stopping when they saw Randall with his head in his hands.

"Randall, what's wrong?"

Randall shot upright, shaking his head. "Oh, nothing, Your Highness. Everything's just fine."

Kendal raised their eyebrows and settled opposite him. "Now, you can do that with Andrew, but not with me. What's wrong?" Randall opened his mouth, ready to argue. "And if the next thing out of your mouth is an excuse rather than the truth, I will have words with Andrew about you being tired."

Randall gaped at them, then sighed. "Planning two

weddings is taking a lot longer than I thought," he murmured, lowering his head.

Kendal's heart broke for him. "You can ask for help, Randall. No one would deny you aid should you need it. You have a lot on your shoulders."

"I haven't struggled before, Your Highness," Randall protested.

"Because you haven't had two weddings and a king and everything else that we've all put on you. You're only one person, Randall."

Kendal turned back to Andrew's office. "No! Please!" Randall said, coming around the desk.

"Relax. I'm not telling him you can't work. Trust me."

Randall stopped complaining and lowered his shoulders. "I wouldn't blame you if you did. I'm not capable any longer."

"Of course you are. Don't talk silly."

Kendal left him for a second, entering the office with barely a knock and finding Andrew and Kean locked in an embrace. They smiled and closed the door again, not wanting anyone else to see them.

"Sorry to interrupt," they teased. "I need you to hire a PA for Randall. Immediately."

Andrew stood straight. "Why? What's wrong with him?"

"Nothing. He's more than capable of doing the work, but he's been given too much. He won't tell you, no, so I am. Find someone for him. Now. Otherwise, he won't be fit to do anything soon." They lifted their finger. "And if you tell him I told you that, you won't touch me for a week."

Andrew gaped at him for several seconds and then reached behind him to pick up the phone. "Portia? You know how you said you wanted a change of pace? Well, how about being a personal assistant?" He listened with a small smile.

"Good. Randall's office as soon as you can." He ended the call and then held out his hand. "I should've thought about it. Thank you, Kendal."

Kendal stepped into his embrace, smiling into his chest when Kean's around looped around them, too. "You're welcome. You're busy enough without trying to make sure everyone else is okay, too. It's all right to lean on us."

"I'm an old man, Kendal. I can't change my spots now," Andrew joked, and Kendal chuckled at his attempt to lighten the mood.

"You're keeping up with us in bed. That proves you're not as old as you believe yourself to be," Kean said, sliding his hand lower to cup Andrew's groin.

Andrew hissed and narrowed his eyes. "Not now, sweetheart."

Kean pouted, which looked hilarious with his strong features, but Kendal loved the playfulness. They needed every inch of happiness and fun they could grab.

"Right. Let me talk to Randall; otherwise, he'll think I'm sending him to the gallows," Kendal said.

"Tell him Portia will take on a new role as his assistant. She has the same level of clearance as he has, so there shouldn't be any problems," Andrew said. "She used to be Louisa's assistant but couldn't face working too close right after her death."

"Understandable." Kendal kissed both their cheeks and returned to Randall, who paced in front of his desk. He snapped to attention when Kendal stepped out of the office. "Portia is your new personal assistant."

Randall's shoulders lowered further. "Okay. I'll get my things." He headed around the desk, looking forlorn.

Kendal frowned for a moment, then sighed. "Randall, sit down, please." He did so immediately—a built-in need to obey orders, possibly. They made sure to enunciate every word. "You are not fired, Randall. Portia is going to be helping you. She is *your* personal assistant. She will do whatever you tell her to do. She will not take orders from Andrew unless you are not around. She takes orders from *you*. Clear enough?"

Randall's eyes darted around the room as if he couldn't understand what Kendal was saying. His gaze finally settled on Kendal. "An assistant? My assistant?"

Kendal nodded. "Maybe she could start by helping you with the weddings from hell." They chuckled when Randall gasped, a hand going to his chest.

"They're not hell, Your Highness!"

Kendal waved a hand. "I'm joking, Randall. Trying to loosen you up a little." They turned to exit the office but paused and faced Randall again. "Just make sure you learn to delegate because I will check on you." They waved a finger at him just as they had at Andrew.

"Yes, Your Highness."

The slight smile on Randall's face was enough to know they'd done the right thing. They headed back to their office and settled in to go through their emails and messages. Being a personal assistant themselves, they knew the weight they carried, even though their weight wasn't fraught with life-threatening issues. At least, not at the moment.

After checking in with their three authors, one of whom had just woken up on the other side of the world, they set to work. The most time-consuming task, which they always did first, was advertising or promoting the books. They had to visit different social media platforms to post about the books, and although a lot of it was copy and paste, it took enough time to make sure the graphics and wording were right for the group they were in.

Once that was done, they set about answering the most important emails first, then scheduling information on the relevant author's calendar. Then they looked ahead in the calendars to see what was coming up and made a list of the items that needed to be completed before those events began. They sent emails to the relevant people and added tasks to the calendars.

For some, it might seem tedious, but for a perfectionist like Kendal, that type of job fit them like a glove—or a crown, in this case. They chuckled. What were the chances of them ever wearing a crown? They might be considered Prince Consort, but they'd never need a crown to do their duties.

Would they have duties as a Prince Consort? They hadn't asked Andrew, but maybe they needed to. They might have to schedule time in their day to do that as well as their job. Hopefully, it wouldn't impede on their author time, though they were sure they could juggle it all. The thought made them remember they hadn't asked Kean about the job they'd been speaking to Randall about. They'd have to ask them when they spent time together that night. Randall would've found him the perfect job. Kendal knew it. And if they knew Kean at all, they would understand how impatient Kean was to start, too.

Hours passed, and they managed to complete their task list for the day with barely any issues cropping up. They signed off with the authors, letting them know to message them if any fires needed putting out, but they didn't have any regrets when they logged off the computer. They also had no concerns about anyone finding out who they were. They used a pen name as a business, and only computer-savvy people could find out their real name. Kent Worthing wasn't original by any means, but it was better than the alternative he'd been called as a child—Ken-doll got old fast.

They chuckled to themselves as they got ready to leave the office. It hadn't been something they'd thought about recently, and they certainly had no plans to share the name with anyone. Even Andrew and Kean. They would undoubtedly have too much fun with it.

33

ANDREW

It had been years since Andrew had watched *The Lion, the Witch and the Wardrobe*. The last time must've been when George was a kid, and though Andrew had forgotten a bit of the storyline, he enjoyed watching it. They were just setting up the second film when the phone rang. Andrew frowned at it but rose to answer.

"Hello?"

"I'm sorry to interrupt your evening, Your Majesty, but I've realised I've forgotten to complete one set of paperwork that needs your signature," Randall said. "Would you mind coming to the office to sign it, please? I wouldn't usually ask, but it's the papers for the Chancellor."

Andrew rubbed a hand over his face and sighed. "Of course, Randall. I'll be there shortly. Although...why are you still working? I thought you'd gone home?"

Randall cleared his throat. "I had, Your Majesty, but I'd forgotten something, and when I got back to my desk to collect it, I found the paperwork."

"All right. I'll be there in a few minutes."

"Thank you, Your Majesty. And I'm sorry again."

"It's fine, Randall."

Andrew hung up the phone and exhaled. "I'm going to have to miss the start of this one. Randall needs me to sign some paperwork before he leaves for the day."

Kendal frowned. "I thought he'd gone home?"

"I did, too, but he said he'd forgotten something. I shouldn't be long. These papers are important, so it needs doing sooner rather than later."

"Hurry back. We promise not to eat all the popcorn," Kean said, shoving another handful in his mouth.

"I'll believe that if there's any left when I get back," Andrew joked.

He headed for the door, his guards standing at attention when he emerged. "Sorry, Colt, Dominic. I'm needed at the office for a quick job. It shouldn't take long."

They strode down the corridors to the office, and Andrew entered, leaving his guards at the door as he always did. He glanced around, not seeing Randall. His assistant would usually wait in the foyer office for him. The man had seemed frazzled that day, even with Portia's help, so maybe that made for the strange behaviour.

Andrew opened the door, immediately spotting Randall sitting in his chair behind his enormous desk, hands flat on the surface, no paperwork in sight. Andrew didn't close the door, a shaky feeling of betrayal working its way through him as he faced his most trusted assistant.

But that feeling only lasted a few seconds until the door slammed shut behind him, and an icy sensation pressed against his nape. Andrew glanced at Randall.

"I'm sorry, Your Majesty," he whispered, eyes filling with tears.

"I told you to stay quiet," a deep, calculating voice snapped.

Andrew exhaled quietly and sent a small smile to Randall. He wasn't sure how they were going to get out of this because the bullet from the gun would hit him a lot quicker than his guards could get to him if he shouted. His best bet would be to keep Ernest talking until someone came looking for him because he was taking too long.

"What do you want, Ernest?" he asked.

"What do I want?" The gun—which was what he assumed it was—pressed harder against his neck, pushing him forward slightly. "I want you gone. I want the entire Sutcliffe line to disappear. Is that too much to ask?"

"Why?"

Ernest snorted. "Why, he says. For god's sake, Andrew. I sometimes wonder why you're on the throne at all."

The gun left his nape as Ernest walked around him until they were face-to-face. It never wavered in his hand, no trembling, no uncertainty, just plain brutal resolve.

"Sit, brother-in-law, and let me tell you a story." Ernest motioned to the sofa next to Andrew, and he sat, Ernest taking the sofa opposite and resting his gun on his knee, though still pointed at him.

Now that he could see him, he saw the edginess in his eyes, the dark flush to his cheeks and the relaxed demeanour of his body. He hadn't changed much over the years, and despite being older than Andrew himself, he hadn't allowed his grey hair to grow out. He still dyed it to its original colour. He was a little thinner than Andrew remembered him being the last time he'd seen him at the charity event, but what worried Andrew the most was the steadiness of his hand. Ernest had no qualms about what he was planning to do. A desperate man making a last-ditch effort that might just work.

His desk chair squeaked, and Ernest narrowed his eyes on Andrew but spoke to Randall. "One wrong move, Randall, and you know what will happen."

The squeak subsided, and Andrew wanted to look at his assistant to see what he was doing.

"Would you like a drink, Ernest?" Andrew asked instead.

"Do you know? I think I will, actually. Randall, get me a whiskey. And get Andrew a bourbon, and then sit back down."

Randall did as Ernest asked, handing him a glass filled halfway with the golden liquid, then handing one to Andrew.

Ernest swirled the glass, then sipped, making an agreeable sound. "I appreciate you giving me the finer things in life, I must admit, Andrew, but having to spend so many years pretending to love your sister was almost more than I could bear. But I held on, knowing my time would come and enjoying bending your family to my will in the meantime." Ernest chuckled, the dark sound filling the room, and Andrew wanted to punch him.

"What did we ever do to you?" Andrew asked, feigning ignorance.

Ernest studied him as if trying to figure out whether he knew the answer to his own question. Then he shrugged. "You were supposed to marry my sister. I would've been elevated to a better station than what I ended up with."

"You're a prince, Ernest. What could be better than that?"

"I'm a prince because I married a princess." He slammed the glass onto the coffee table. "If you had married Nora like you were supposed to, I would've had a title of my own right rather than given to me because of someone else."

Andrew didn't understand what the difference was. A title

was a title. And technically, he would still have only been given the title because of his marriage to Nora.

Ernest huffed. "I can see it in your eyes that you don't understand. Those who were born into privilege rarely see what common-born people do. If I had a title, I wouldn't have to bow to anyone. They would bow to me because they wanted me happy. Where I am now is that people bow to me only because Charlotte is my wife. If she wasn't, I would have nothing."

Andrew still wasn't sure he understood, but Ernest believed it. That's all that mattered. He waved around them. "Then what is all this for?"

"I told you; I'm telling a story." Ernest picked up his drink again and finished it in one gulp. "Once upon a time, there was a boy who had big dreams. Bigger than Earldom, but to gain what he wanted, he needed his sister to marry the future king. Unfortunately, that heir fell in love and broke a sacred agreement between their families. The boy was angry, and he raged at his father to seek justice, to demand what was their due, but he refused. His father was a romantic at heart and believed in love itself. The boy, however, did not. He believed in fate, and he knew he would get what he so rightly deserved one day.

"It took a lot of finagling to get himself right where he needed to be—next to the princess he could woo—lots of research, studying, improvising his resume, but he got there. She didn't fall for his charms straight away, though. He worked at her, wooing her gently but steadily, and eventually, she gave in to him. He'd succeeded."

Ernest clenched his jaw. "The problem was, he couldn't be happy about it because he wasn't given the title outright. It came with conditions. Mainly giving the princess an heir. He did his duty—twice—but received nothing but weak impersonations of him. He wanted an army, and he got disappointment instead. The anger from his sister's disgrace festered inside him, and he, once again, sought his father's counsel. But yet again, his father denied him retribution."

The story wasn't much different from what they'd guessed, which pleased Andrew. He was glad they'd seen behind the curtain of his greed and anger. But the crucial question was, what was his endgame?

"It took too many years for his father to pass kindly into the night, and to pass the time, he played a game. He titled it, 'What does it take to turn a royal rogue?' It started slowly, and as the years passed, it grew into something he'd never imagined. Something fierce. Something binding. Something disastrous for the royal family. And he couldn't have been happier. One sad night, the boy was freed from his father's hold, and he could do as he pleased. And what pleased him was to make the royal family suffer the injustice wrought on his family.

"Slowly, methodically, the boy took apart the foundations of the royal family. He shook their belief in themselves. He moulded those closest to him into shells of their former selves. All without lifting a finger. He had a way with words, you see."

Anger built inside Andrew, but he refused to show it. If it was the last thing he could do in this life, he would take this man with him.

Ernest sighed. "But the game had to end for him to finish his forty-year-old plans. With every small win the royal family gained, the boy won something, too. He won the pain and suffering of those within his household. And with every minor loss the royal family felt, the boy won, too. The pain and suffering of the royal family. No matter what he did, he won. Because the royal family was at war with each other, and it was pure bliss for the boy."

"That's why you were so willing to let your pawns be captured and arrested," Andrew said.

Ernest glared at him and continued as if Andrew hadn't spoken. "He would've loved to see what became of his game if he had continued with it, but he needed people to take the fall. He needed to step back. To hide for a short time. Who would've thought to hide in the very place the royal family thought they were safe? The boy did. And within the walls of the castle, he stayed for five nights and days until the royal family was relaxed and unprepared for the final stake at the king's feet."

"I'm assuming you mean this moment," Andrew said, throwing his drink back and grimacing as he swallowed. "There's only you left, Ernest. What is your plan? If you assassinate me, you won't get out of here alive."

Ernest chuckled again. "My seconds are numbered. I know that. I'm not stupid. I don't care if I die."

Andrew swallowed down the fear those words sent through him. A man without a future was more dangerous than anyone else. It was why Jeremy had been willing to kill him; he was already dying. But Ernest was *willing* to die.

"Why? Why do this if you end up dead in the end?"

Ernest growled and kicked the coffee table, sending it into Andrew's shins. "Weren't you listening? I just told you my story."

"From what I gathered, you threw a hissy fit when you didn't get what you wanted." Andrew knew he was playing with fire, but he needed Ernest to lose control. He needed just a moment of that hissy fit to escape, and Andrew could turn the tide in their favour. He hoped.

Ernest gritted his teeth, and his nostrils flared. Andrew

couldn't ever remember the man raising his voice or glaring at someone with the immense hatred he was shooting at Andrew right now.

"That 'hissy fit' has caused more lasting damage to this royal family than any of your ancestors." Ernest stood and turned away.

Andrew glanced at Randall and mouthed, "Shout at three," at him, holding up three fingers, just before Ernest turned back around again.

"You have lost so many people in this family, and you didn't see any of them coming, did you? Including several people I guarantee you don't know about. Good luck finding them."

He had him there. He didn't see the death toll being what it was, but it would stop here. Ernest would spend the rest of his life in prison.

"Number one," he glanced at Randall, then back again quickly, "was Louisa. It was only recently I realised the connection. You were going after her all along. Hitting where it would hurt the most."

Ernest nodded, a smile creeping across his face. "Pure genius. And if we hadn't had insider knowledge, we wouldn't have had the bounty. You have Tobias to thank for that."

Andrew's heart ached, both for the loss of his wife and for the loss of the guard whom he thought was a close friend. "Number two was Miranda. Tying up loose ends. She was working to help us, but it was too late to save her."

"Was Christian as distraught as I'd hoped he'd be? Not only to find out that his father and mother were part of this but that his siblings were, too. It was so easy to steer their minds in the right, sorry, wrong direction."

"John was…three."

As soon as he said the word, Randall screamed at the top

of his lungs, and Andrew leapt over the back of the sofa. He heard Ernest's gun discharge, but nothing hit him or Randall.

"I wasn't finished—"

The door slammed open, and Andrew's guards entered, taking in the situation immediately. Ernest got off another shot, hitting Dominic in the shoulder, but both Dominic and Colt opened fire on Ernest. When the sound died down, Colt stayed where he was, and Dominic slipped through the room. Andrew tried to stand, but Colt held him down. He waited impatiently, then Dominic returned, and Colt helped Andrew to stand.

"He's dead, Your Majesty."

Andrew blew out a breath. "Thank you, both. Your reflexes are immeasurable."

"Are you hurt?" Colt asked.

"No. Well, my eardrums a little. Randall can shout when he wants to." Andrew chuckled. He glanced over to where Randall sat on the floor, resting against the wall, with his knees pulled up to his chest. "Get yourself checked out immediately, Dominic. That's an order."

"Yes, Your Majesty. As soon as cover comes."

Which it did as soon as he'd said the words. Along with Kean, Kendal and a host of other family members. Andrew hugged Kean and Kendal.

"I'm fine, but I need to see Randall. Give me a minute."

He stepped closer and knelt in front of his assistant. "I'm so sorry, Your Majesty. He just came out of the wall. I didn't know there was a secret doorway. He startled me and then pulled the gun. I wasn't sure what to do, but he gave me no choice. I'm sorry." Randall's voice gave, and he sobbed into his hands.

Andrew grabbed Randall in his arms and held him as he cried, soothing him as best he could. It would take time for him to believe that Andrew didn't hold any grudges against him. If he'd been in a similar situation, he would've done the same. Self-preservation was important. He glanced across at Ernest's body, wishing he'd had time to find out what he had planned. He hoped it wasn't something that would come back to bite them later on. He needed his family safe. By cutting off the snake's head, he hoped it would stop any others from surfacing, but it was a conversation he would have with Charlotte when she woke. There was a lot of information she did have that could be useful in ensuring the entire network was closed down. He just had to hope that Ernest hadn't hidden something else from them.

He handed Randall off to Brady when he arrived, and Kean and Kendal grabbed hold of him again.

"We were getting worried when you hadn't come back. We were coming to see you when the screaming and gunshots started," Kean said.

"I have never been so scared in my life," Kendal said. "Don't ever do that again."

Andrew chuckled. "I don't think I have much choice over that, but I will do everything in my power to ensure I'm not put in danger again. Is that okay?"

Kendal pouted. "I suppose it'll have to do."

He received hugs from his entire family, all wanting to check he was in one piece. He let them all fuss over him, then told them to go to bed. He would arrange breakfast for them all the following day. A late breakfast. Because he had plans for Kean and Kendal that didn't need to be discussed with the family present. They all needed reassurance, but Kean and Kendal needed him the most. And he needed them.

They would discuss everything over the next few days and get everyone involved to clean house so to speak. And he wouldn't hide the stain within his family. He would show the world that even family—even the royal family—is not free from corruption and pain.

But that was for another day. That night was for sleeping with his arms around the two people who loved him for who he was. No matter the age gap. No matter the burden. Kean and Kendal were his future, and it looked bright. Just as Louisa had predicted.

34

DOUGLAS

Douglas hugged his father so hard he thought he'd break him, but he couldn't help it. How many brushes with death was the man going to survive before his luck ran out? If everything went well now, it would be his last assassination attempt because Ernest was dead.

That sounded so good; Douglas thought he might cry. Charlotte was in hospital where she couldn't hurt anyone at the moment, John was dead, Ernest was dead, Charles was in prison, as was Daniel, plus all the other assholes who tried to mess with them.

It was over.

Andrew agreed to a late breakfast with them the following day and left with Kean and Kendal. Douglas was so happy his father had taken the chance with those two people because they were perfect for each other. Douglas slid his arm around Mav, waved to everyone and left, too. He didn't want to dissect anything at that moment. He needed to breathe, and what better way to do that than be with the man he wanted to spend his life with.

"Where are we going?"

"To bed."

Mav chuckled. "I wasn't expecting that."

"I want to feel you all around me, Mav. I was to begin this new chapter with an orgasm or three from us both."

Mav's cheeks heated, and he brushed his hand against them, but Douglas hid his laugh. He loved it when Mav got embarrassed. Douglas inhaled and exhaled as they wandered through the hallways to his suite. He would've taken them home, but he didn't want to go too far just yet. There would be time for them to spread their wings again now the threat had been taken care of.

They'd be able to relax further at the club, not looking over their shoulders for a hint of a threat. It was a good time to be free, and Douglas couldn't wait to share it with Mav.

"How do you feel about a spring wedding?" he asked.

Mav stumbled, but Douglas had hold of him, so he righted him straight away. "Um, yeah."

"Good. Spring is a time of birth and new beginnings. Sounds fitting to me."

Mav tucked himself closer as they drew near the door. "Me, too."

"I'll let you break the news to Randall."

Mav hit his chest and pulled away, laughing. "Meanie."

He could get used to this feeling. The feeling of having no extra burdens placed on them, not having to wonder if stepping outside the door will be the last time they do. It was wonderful.

As he closed the door behind Mav, slamming him against it and taking his mouth, Douglas vowed to make the most of every second he had.

35

KEAN

Five months later

The idea that Kean would be in front of hundreds of cameras was only mitigated by the fact that it wasn't his wedding. He would be near the front and arriving with Andrew, who was obviously the king, but he wouldn't be the sole focus of the event.

Freddie and Damon were tying the knot, and the world was in upheaval. Some had protested that the wedding was taking place at Westminster Abbey when "a gay marriage should not take place in a building of such holiness." Others protested that the wedding should not take place at all. But still, more were happy for them, and Kean chose to focus on those supportive people rather than the ones trying to tear them down.

Arms slid around his waist, and he automatically smiled

when Kendal's cheek rested against his shoulder blade. He covered the slim fingers with his own and squeezed.

"Are you okay?" they asked.

"A little nervous, but all good," Kean replied. "You would've thought I'd have got used to it by now, but I haven't."

"I think there's so much to this royal life that we can never truly 'get used to it.' I think only people born into the role can understand exactly what it entails."

Kean nodded. "So true." He inhaled and sighed it out. "Let's go, yeah?"

Kendal slipped in front of him and hugged him again. "Yeah. Let's go get them married."

Kendal gave a little squeal and a shimmy, leaned up and kissed him, then grabbed his hand. If someone had told Kean that Kendal would be this open and relaxed in such a short time, he would never have believed them. They had been so torn up by what had happened to them, but they had fought every step of the way to get back to their new normal, and Kean was so proud of them.

They headed to the door, meeting with Andrew just as he came back from speaking with Douglas and George.

"You both look fantastic," Andrew said. "Going somewhere nice?" He winked.

Kean laughed and kissed his cheek, and Kendal slid an arm around Andrew's waist. "Nah, just round to the corner pub. You?"

Andrew slipped an arm around Kendal, leaning them back and kissing them, then pulled them back up again, laughing. He repeated the action with Kean, who had never expected it, and kissed him, too.

"I'm going to see my son get married. Would you like to come?"

"Ooh, who could decline an invitation to a wedding?" Kendal said, joining in the fun.

They all laughed, and Andrew sobered a little. "I can't believe the day has come."

"It'll be done before you know it," Kean said, and a bit of him hoped it would. He didn't want to make a spectacle of himself. And truthfully, he was worried about what his father might do. He hadn't heard from the man since that last threatening message, but with him being part of the royal entourage, it might bring him out of the woodwork. Dante hadn't had any communication with him after Henry's wedding, but that didn't mean he wouldn't with this one.

"That's the problem. I want to memorise every moment. I know I have three sons, but they only marry once...usually."

"I don't think you have to worry about that. They've found their forever partners. I'm certain of it," Kendal said, smoothing a hand over Andrew's chest.

"I am, too," Kean said.

Andrew chuckled. "Well, if you both think they're all good, then I definitely need to remember everything."

Kean tugged them towards the exit. "I don't think you need to remember everything."

"Why?"

Kean winked at Kendal. "Because this is being immortalised for the world to see over and over again on the internet. Whatever happens today will never be forgotten. Any embarrassments will be forever out there for all to see."

Andrew hummed. "Bloody hell. I didn't trim my beard this morning, either."

Kean laughed, the lighthearted feeling settling inside of him. He'd had more happy days than ever before, and he never wanted it to stop. Having spent so much time with Henry, he'd already known how unique this family was, but to formally be a part of it was a wonderful experience, and he knew every other partner felt the same.

"This is the biggest wedding since you married Louisa," Kendal said as they wandered towards their guards.

Andrew stayed silent, then said, "You're right. There have been other weddings, but no heir weddings."

"I'm glad they chose this day to marry. Uniting Freddie's love for his mother at the same time as tying himself to Damon is pure beauty," Kendal continued. "It's something my authors have written about many times over. But this is real life."

"Have you told them about you yet?" Andrew asked once they settled into the car with their guards at the helm.

Kendal shook their head. "I'm keeping them separate. At least for now. I might not be able to do it for long, but for as long as I can get away with it, I will. I don't want it to change how they feel about me, and it will."

"I doubt it," Kean said. "They know how good you are at your job. Who you are and who you're with shouldn't change that."

Kendal side-eyed him. "You haven't been immersed in the author world for several years. Trust me when I say that *everything* is relevant, especially when it isn't."

Kean couldn't say he understood, but Kendal knew what they were talking about. And Kean knew they weren't hiding things because they were ashamed, and that was the main thing.

"So, can you go over the plan again?" Kean asked, his nerves returning full force as he saw the crowds of people lining the roads.

Andrew slid his arm around his shoulders. "When the car stops, the guards will open the doors, and we will climb the steps of Westminster Abbey, greet the Dean and continue down the aisle to our seats. I won't leave your side, don't worry."

Kean tried. He really did. Andrew and Kendal kept up the conversation, and Kean stared out of the window at the waving crowds. Now and then, Andrew nudged him to wave back, which he did, and then the car arrived. Butterflies churned in his stomach, but he slid out of the car after Kendal, with Andrew going out the other side. Bells pealed, and a fanfare sounded. They rounded the car and met Andrew at the bottom of the steps. They turned and waved to the people who had spent so many hours waiting to see them. After a moment, Andrew grabbed Kean's hand—as if he thought Kean might run off—linked his free hand with Kendal's and started up the steps.

At the top, Andrew let them go to shake hands with the Dean of Westminster. They spoke for a few moments and started down the aisle. No rushing on their part, though. They couldn't be seen rushing to their seats. They had to let everyone see them and interact with certain government and commonwealth representatives, as well as greet the foreign royal family members who had attended.

It was a monumental event, and Kean had more respect than ever for Randall and Portia. Although lots of stuff had to be delegated, they did most of the organising and were the ones overseeing everything on a higher level.

Freddie would already be there with Douglas and George, who were standing up as his best men. And as soon as the king and his consorts were seated, Damon would start his brief journey from Clarence House, where he had stayed the previous evening with Christian, who was standing up for him. Damon's parents had been invited, but they refused to attend. As far as everyone in the family was concerned, they were no longer Damon's parents. If they couldn't see past their fears to see how happy Damon was, they weren't worth breathing the same air.

As for Charlotte... She had not been invited to the wedding, for obvious reasons. She was healed from her injuries after the explosion, but her mental health was not faring so well. She now stayed out of the limelight as much as possible, especially as some groups of people called for her to be sent to prison. Kean agreed, but Andrew had decided on psychiatric help instead. It wasn't Kean's call to make, but he would support Andrew's decision.

They continued down to their seats, which were set to the side of the High Altar, past around two thousand guests. In another reshaping of history, when they sat, the king was not in the prime spot right on the end of the seats. Andrew had refused. He wanted Kean and Kendal on either side of him, and although many people had warned him against it, he got his way. As always. With a hand at Kendal's lower back, Andrew led them to their seat, following in after them, leaving the normal "prime" seat for Kean. Something he struggled to accept, but he'd ceded to Andrew's wishes.

They were barely seated before the music changed, signalling Damon was on his way. They made idle chatter between them, talking to other family members while Kean tried to keep his nerves from showing. He dreaded hearing what the TV presenters would narrate about the event. Well, not about the event, but about him.

Freddie, Douglas and George arrived from St Edmund's Chapel, where they had been waiting. They bowed to Andrew, Kean and Kendal—another thing Kean couldn't get used to—then stood at the High Altar, waiting. The music changed once again, letting them know Damon had arrived and waited at the door to enter. They couldn't see him yet, but he would take the same route they had.

When weddings had taken place previously, the brides had returned after the wedding to place their bouquet on the Grave of the Unknown Warrior, the only grave that was never walked upon but around instead. In another slight change—the number of which was steadily growing—Damon had opted to bring a small bouquet of forget-me-nots to place on the grave as he passed on his way to Freddie. Kean loved the meaning behind it, and he would've chosen a similar option had he been in Damon's place.

A hush descended over the guests, and Damon stepped into view, Christian striding beside him. Damon and Freddie had chosen to wear formal suits instead of Freddie wearing his uniform, and Damon looked amazing in the dark, almost midnight blue colour. There was a shimmer to it as he walked past the sconces. Christian was in a black suit, as were Freddie, Douglas and George. There had been discussions about the colour of Damon's suit. Many of the "professionals" had suggested he wear a white suit, but everyone had shot that down straight away, especially Damon. Kean was glad they got their way because the suit was amazing.

Damon reached Freddie, smiles on their faces as their gazes never left each other. Christian handed Damon over officially, then settled into his seat next to Oscar. Freddie and Damon stepped up to the High Altar, and the song ended. They turned to the framed picture that had been set up to one side of the altar and bowed to the image of Freddie's mother, Louisa, then faced the front once more.

"Welcome, one and all, to the celebration of Frederick and Damon's marriage," the Dean of Westminster started.

Kean listened intently to every word, knowing he needed to retain this information for when—if—he and Kendal decided to follow Andrew's request and get married themselves. It was a long ceremony but a beautiful one.

"Repeat after me," the Dean said.

"I, Frederick Alexander Andrew, take thee, Damon Philip, to be my wedded husband, to have and to hold from this day forward, for better, for worse; for richer, for poorer; in sickness and in health; to love and to cherish, till death us do part, and thereto I give thee my troth."

"I, Damon Philip, take thee, Frederick Alexander Andrew, to be my wedded husband, to have and to hold from this day forward, for better, for worse; for richer, for poorer; in sickness and in health; to love and to cherish, till death us do part, and thereto I give thee my troth."

The Dean retrieved the rings from the cushion. "Repeat after me. With this ring, I thee wed; with my body, I thee honour; and all my worldly good with thee I share."

Both men repeated the words, sliding the ring onto their fingers, and then they knelt in front of the Dean as he led them through a prayer. When they stood, Freddie and Damon moved over to the seats and settled in while Patrick rose to recite a reading for them.

Kean loved the entire ceremony, even if it was a little longer than he wanted to be sitting in a chair. When the Dean said they were going to sign the register, he, Andrew and Kendal stood and followed Freddie and Damon into the Shrine of St Edward the Confessor, which was the room all registrations took place in. It gave them a moment of privacy from the cameras. As the door closed behind them, Kean relaxed, and Kendal rubbed a hand over his back.

"If I can ask you to be seated," the Dean said. He stood behind the table and gestured to the two seats in front for Freddie and Damon. Both settled in, and the Dean took them through the papers they needed to sign. Once they had, they rose from the chairs, and Andrew took their place. He signed beneath Freddie and Damon, then rose and gestured for Kean and Kendal to sit.

Kean frowned. "Why do we need to?"

"Because you're my partners," Andrew said with a smile.

Kean didn't understand, but the Dean pointed to the box they needed to sign in, one signature beside the other. It felt far too official for Kean to be putting his signature to something so important, but he did as he was told.

Once that was completed, they all stood, and the Dean asked if they were ready to leave. They collectively took a breath, then nodded. As they left the room, the entourage followed Freddie and Damon down the aisle, walking at a sedate pace so their guests could see them as the newly married couple.

When Freddie and Damon exited Westminster Abbey, the roar of the crowds was immense, and Kean was sure the cameras had recorded the undoubtedly wondrous expression on his face. Even though he was several years younger than Freddie and Damon, he felt a need to be there for them, to offer his shoulder should they need anything.

Freddie and Damon waved to the crowds as they climbed into the car that would take them in a slow procession to Buckingham Palace. Andrew, Kean and Kendal would follow them in a second car, with Douglas and Mav in a third and George, Timothy and Eddie in the fourth. Kean had almost had a heart attack when he saw the lineup of the cars in the plans. He'd been so scared about having so many royals in one indefensible place, but they reassured him as best they could. He didn't lose the concern completely, but he knew they had done this hundreds of times. For events and weddings and coronations—they had it down. And now that the threat of Ernest and his wildly crazy plan was gone, they could go back to almost normal. Well, as normal as possible after finding three more prisons and seventeen tortured victims, who were now receiving the best care possible after being in Charlotte, Charles and Ernest's clutches for far too long.

"How are you doing?" Andrew asked him, and Kean sent him a smile.

"I feel better now I'm away from so much scrutiny."

"You'll get used to it. I promise." Andrew kissed his temple.

Kean and Kendal shared a look and a smile, remembering their words from earlier that day. Andrew would never understand why it was so difficult for them, even if they tried to explain it, but it didn't matter. Andrew was perfect the way he was, and they didn't need him to change.

"One final newsworthy event left, then we can hide away for the rest of the day."

One final, huge event.

As they all stood side-by-side, on the balcony of Buckingham Palace, waving to the crowds, Kean was glad he wouldn't get used to it. He didn't want to turn into an Ernest, believing he should have more than he had been given. It would never happen.

Freddie and Damon kissed on the balcony, and the public went wild. A sea of people lay as far as his eyes could see, flags and other items waving in their hands as they celebrated the wonderful occasion.

Andrew slid his arms around Kean's and Kendal's shoulders, glanced to each side of him, and said, "On the count of three. One, two, three."

On the three count, Andrew lowered his head and brought Kean and Kendal closer, kissing them chastely for the world to see. Kean was so surprised; he'd kept his eyes open and had seen Freddie and Damon, and Douglas and

Maverick kiss, too. When they separated, he glanced around them, noticing the Sexy Sixteen were standing at the forefront, and all the princes wore smiles, and all their partners wore surprised expressions.

"Did you just get all of us to kiss at the same time?" he whispered to Andrew.

"That I did, sweetheart. That I did."

Kean and Kendal burst out laughing.

"I can't wait to see what social media says about this," Kendal said.

"*'The Sexy Sixteen are at it again,'*" Kean murmured. "*Causing ripples wherever they go.*"

"How about '*The Balcony of Love,*'" Andrew said.

"Oh god, no!" Kendal said, hiding their laughter behind their hand. "Let someone else choose a title."

"Mav!" all three of them whisper-shouted to their right.

36

KENDAL

Seventeen months later

Kendal roused to the gentle tugging on their cock. They blinked, letting themselves slowly wake as pleasure flowed down their spine towards their groin with every suck of Kean's talented mouth. They peered at Andrew, who lay beside them, stroking his cock at a leisurely pace. He hadn't noticed Kendal was awake, so they got to appreciate the sight of the man without him knowing. He hadn't diminished in personality one bit since they'd started on their journey together, and Kendal loved that about him. He hadn't changed to fit them, and they hadn't changed to fit him. Naturally, there was some compromising, but it worked well.

Kean gave a stronger suck, and Kendal glanced at him, smiling when Kean met their gaze. He pulled off. "Good morning, angel." Then he went back to sucking, taking Kendal's arousal higher.

Andrew leaned closer, cupping Kendal's chin to bring their face up to his. "Good morning, my sweet. Did you sleep well?"

"I did. And I woke even better."

Andrew smiled and lowered his mouth. Their lips sipped at each other, their tongues tangled, and their teeth nipped while Kean wreaked havoc with their cock. They felt themselves nearing the edge and pulled back.

"Please!" they moaned, lifting their hips for more.

"Kean, flip and eat them."

Kean pulled off, grabbed Kendal's hips and flipped them until their stomach met the bed, and they got a mouthful of pillow. They laughed and pushed at the pillow while Kean dragged them to their knees. Immediately, Kean's mouth fastened on their pucker, and they bucked, needing more even as the sensations overwhelmed them.

"That's it, my sweet. Let Kean take care of you."

Kendal reached a hand out, seeking Andrew and finding his slightly furry chest. They ran their fingers over the hair, needing Andrew as much as Kean.

"Come on. There we go."

Andrew's hand smoothed across Kendal's back, leaving goosebumps along the way, and Kendal closed their eyes and concentrated on the dual sensations. Kean's tongue speared inside them, and they gasped, pushing back. Kean slowly loosened them, and then slick fingers found their entrance. Kendal wanted more. They wanted Kean.

"Enough, Kean. Inside them now." Andrew's voice brooked no argument.

"Yes, Sir," Kean said.

A slight pause before Kean slid inside them was the only

warning they got. Kendal moaned long and loud as Kean's cock rubbed against their insides. He withdrew and slammed forward several times until Andrew told him to stop. Kendal whimpered, reaching back to keep Kean inside.

"Slip deep, stay there and pull them upright," Andrew said. Kean complied, and Andrew lowered to his elbow right in front of Kendal's red, straining shaft. "Now go."

Kean withdrew and thrust forward, holding Kendal's hip for leverage. Kendal dropped their head back onto Kean's shoulder and groaned as Kean's cock hit their prostate with unerring accuracy. They rocketed higher when Andrew's hand wrapped around Kendal's dick.

"Let go, my sweet. Let us have you."

Andrew's crooning words took Kendal over the edge with unsurprising ease. Unsurprising because it had happened so many times. Kean's teeth scraped along Kendal's shoulder, the indication he was going over, and Kean gripped them harder as he held himself deep, shuddering through his release but keeping Kendal upright.

Kendal was a hot, floppy mess when they came down from their ultimate high. Kean helped lay them down beside Andrew and dropped down beside them.

"Wow," was all Kean said, his breathing still elevated.

"Uh-huh," Kendal replied.

Andrew chuckled. "I would've thought you two would have more energy."

"Nope. Done for," Kendal managed.

"You can't be completely done. We have a busy day, hence why we woke you up so early."

Kendal opened one eye and fixed Andrew with a glare. "How early?"

"With enough time to get ready."

Kendal blinked a few times, then smiled and sat upright. "It's our wedding day."

Andrew smiled. "It is."

Kendal threw themselves into Andrew's arms and gripped him. When Andrew and Kean had proposed to Kendal, it had been a surprise because it came on the back of George's ceremony with Timothy and Eddie. At the after-party, Andrew and Kean had backed them into a corner and asked them to marry them. Kendal had immediately said yes, knowing that officially they would marry Kean, but they would have a similar ceremony to George's for themselves, either before or after.

That time had come, and they'd arrived at Sandringham House the previous day. Kean and Kendal's official joining would happen at St Mary Magdalene Church, with only a few important guests. Freddie, Douglas and George and their partners, plus William, Victoria and their families, would be the only people attending. They were not making a big deal out of it, and they had tried, as much as they could, to keep it out of the news. They'd even gone so far as to say a friend of the family was getting married. It hadn't worked. So, although they had figured out Kean and Kendal were getting married, they wouldn't be getting a lot of photos, as there would be a tunnel tent erected over the entrance to the church, keeping everything quiet. And dry. Because it was just typical that they predicted rain on their wedding day.

"How long do we have?" Kendal asked.

"A lifetime," Kean said.

Kendal kissed his cheek. "Come on."

By the time they were ready, they had put up the tunnel tent over the entrance to Sandringham. They didn't mind sharing their wedding with the world, but they wanted to keep some of it for themselves. They climbed into the blacked-out car under the cover of the tent and headed for the church. Kendal was so excited about the day. Although they couldn't marry both men, they were happy to be able to marry Kean and then have the triad ceremony to include Andrew afterwards.

At the church, they entered the vestibule and waited for everyone to join them. Their guests headed into the church to wait, and Andrew kissed them both before sliding their arms into his.

"Are you ready?" he asked.

"Always," Kendal said.

"And forever," Kean said.

The music started, and Andrew led them down the aisle to where the priest waited. When they reached the altar, Andrew kissed both their cheeks and joined their hands and encouraged them to continue forward. It felt wrong to do it without Andrew, but it was how it had to be. And although Kendal didn't like it, they understood.

"We are gathered here today to witness the joining of Kean and Kendal. This ceremony is slightly shorter than our usual ceremonies, but it is nonetheless binding." He focused on Kean and Kendal. "Please step forward." They did, Kendal with their heart pounding and butterflies in their stomach. "Please repeat after me."

"I, Kean Seymour, do take Kendal Lawson to be lawfully wedded husband, to have and to hold from this day forward, for better, for worse; for richer, for poorer; in sickness and in health; to love and to cherish, till death us do part."

"I, Kendal Lawson, do take Kean Seymour to be lawfully wedded husband, to have and to hold from this day forward, for better, for worse; for richer, for poorer; in sickness and in health; to love and to cherish, till death us do part."

Kendal glanced behind them to Andrew and smiled. Andrew returned it, and they faced forward again.

"Please repeat after me as you slide the ring on their finger."

"With this ring, I do wed; with my body, I do honour; and all my worldly good with you I share." Kean slid the ring onto Kendal's finger.

"With this ring, I do wed; with my body, I do honour; and all my worldly good with you I share." Kendal slid the ring onto Kean's finger.

"By the power vested in me, I pronounce you husbands. You may kiss."

Kean and Kendal faced each other and smiled, leaning forward to kiss chastely. Cheers sounded behind them, and they laughed. They turned to their guests and waved, hands still joined. They stepped down and paused, waiting for Andrew to join them, but he waved them on. Kendal's stomach churned, and they glanced at Kean and shook their head. They both stared at Andrew, eyebrows raised, until Andrew laughed and stood, sliding his hand into Kendal's.

"We're three, and no paperwork will change that," Kendal said.

"Okay, okay," Andrew said. "Sorry. I thought you'd like to bask in the wedding feeling."

"We're not finished yet," Kendal said. "Hurry up."

Andrew chuckled again and walked beside them down the aisle. They headed into a side room to sign the registration paperwork, then exited the church into the cars and aimed back for Sandringham again. The entire event had only lasted around half an hour, a much quieter affair than most royal weddings, for sure. The drive was only a few minutes, and when they arrived, they went straight through to the back garden, where a marquee had been set up to keep them away from prying aerial eyes.

Kendal hadn't seen this because they'd kept it a secret from them, and when Andrew and Kean led them into the white fabric tent with their eyes closed, they laughed at the absurdity of it. But when they opened their eyes, they were blown away by the twinkling fairy lights, pale yellow roses and splashes of green and blue—Kendal had insisted on having all their favourite colours represented at their joining.

"It's beautiful. Thank you," they said to them.

"Don't thank us. We just told Randall what we thought you'd like, and he went with it," Andrew said.

Kean laughed. "Don't be so modest. You declined several options before settling on this one."

Andrew's cheeks darkened. "It needed to be perfect."

Kendal kissed his heated cheek. "It is."

They had placed seats in a semi-circle around a slightly raised dais at the front, and they were filling with their guests. Having the ceremonies one after the other made it easier for their friends and family to stay in their outfits, after which they could get changed before the party.

"Are you happy?" Andrew asked them.

Kean rested his cheek against Andrew's chest, and Kendal did the same. "I am ecstatic."

"Me, too. Are you?"

"I love you both so much," Andrew said. "I'm so happy."

Freddie came up to them and smiled. "It's time." He squeezed Andrew's shoulder.

"Thanks." Freddie returned to his seat, and Andrew pulled away, grabbing their hands and threading their fingers together. "Let's make history."

"We already are," Kendal said, their heart bursting with love for these two people.

Soft classical music played as they walked down the chair-made aisle. Kendal saw all the people they loved, including the security guards and household staff, that had been a big part of their lives. Kendal remembered when they'd invited Randall. He'd been overwhelmed and promptly burst into tears at the invitation. They had reassured him they truly wanted him there because he was a close friend. They knew Brett had tried to decline, but Andrew hadn't let him. Or anyone else who declined because they didn't believe they belonged there.

Since the treasonous events had finished almost two years ago, they had become even closer to those surrounding them daily, and they'd made a bond with them all. Andrew hadn't wanted the same thing to happen again, and even though Tobias had broken their "bond," Kendal had surmised that it had been a pretend bond and not a true one. Whereas the relationships they had cultivated since were based on true respect and friendship.

They reached the front, and Kean and Kendal stepped to the side to make a triangle. The officiant stood behind them.

"Welcome to one and all. We have been invited to this wondrous occasion to celebrate the joining of Andrew, Kean and Kendal. The joining of people is not to be taken lightly. These vows are binding and meaningful. These three people have chosen each other, and they wish to celebrate this with you." The officiant opened his hands to the side, and Kendal couldn't help but smile. "Andrew, Kean, Kendal. Please let your guests hear your promises to each other, one at a time."

Andrew smiled. They'd decided ahead of time who was going to go first.

Kendal inhaled. "Andrew, Kean. You are everything I never realised I needed in my life. You have been rocks through a time of deep unsettlement, but I truly believe it is because of you that I am who I am today. Without your support, your faith, your love, I would be a shadow of myself. With those things, I am flying." They licked their lips and bit the bottom one before continuing. "I love you. There are no fancy words needed for how I feel. Plain and simple, I love you. With everything I am."

Kean cleared his throat. "Some people believe in fate. Others don't. I believe we were brought into each other's lives when we needed to be there. Initially, I thought we didn't stand a chance. It was impossible for two people to want me as much as I wanted them. But then I began to believe in the power of us. We had a rocky start, but we conquered our fears and took a chance that reaped multiple rewards. I will never regret a moment. I love you. Forever and always, my liege and my angel."

Andrew exhaled slowly, rubbing his fingers over the back of their hands. "I had the greatest gifts given to me at a time when I believed all hope was lost. At a time of immeasurable pain and upheaval, I thought I was alone. Then you came into my life, refusing to take no for an answer, and I chose to listen to what my heart was telling me." He chuckled. "It helped a little that Louisa had told me to do the same." Kendal squeezed his hand. "Life may never take us in the direction we were expecting, but life will continue, and I am overjoyed that you want to spend your lives with me. Your humble servant." Kean snorted. "I love you more than I ever thought possible."

"Please repeat after me altogether," the officiant said, handing them each a ring. "With this ring, I make a promise to you both. I promise to love you, to support you, to cherish you and to uphold your beliefs. When there is strife, we will work together to find peace. When there is anxiety, we will work together to find calm. This is my promise to you both."

They repeated the words, and Kendal couldn't keep from smiling. The butterflies had turned into a raging heat of excitement, and they couldn't wait for the last words they knew were coming.

"By the power given to me, I can happily pronounce you joined as a triad. Congratulations."

The officiant bowed to them, and Andrew pulled them into a hug and a three-way kiss that had become easier over the years. Everything felt so natural, and Kendal had never been happier.

"Ready for a party, angel?" Kean said with a wink.

"That is Princex Consort Angel to you." Kendal lifted their nose but ruined it by laughing. They brought their hands up to cup each of their spouses' cheeks and kissed them again. Though they then got distracted by the ring on their finger.

It had taken them a long while to decide what they wanted their rings to look like, but they'd finally found a design they were happy with. Each ring was the same gold band, but the gems inset into them were different. Kendal had one shimmering golden gem and one ocean blue gem. Kean had one ocean blue and one emerald. Andrew had one golden and one emerald. The same colours as each of their eyes—or as near as they could get.

"You'll have time to study that later," Kean said. "Let's party!"

"Hold on. We have to have the photos taken first," Andrew said. "It won't take long."

Kendal didn't care how long they took as long as they stayed together. They glanced across to the side, smiling at the photo they'd brought of Queen Louisa. Although it had been almost three years since her death, Kendal had refused to let Andrew stop talking about her. She was a huge part of their lives, and she had been a wise woman. One he was sure had psychic gifts. Andrew had shown them the letter from her, and Kendal had to read it several times before they understood just what she was implying. She truly was the most perfect person they had ever known, and they silently thanked her every night for letting Andrew know it was okay. Few people got that chance, and they believed it was her words that had given Andrew the courage to stop fighting their love. To choose them. They would forever be grateful to her.

Kendal glanced around the room at the number of guests they'd invited. Initially, it had been a small party, but as they worked through those people who were close to them and meant something, it had grown bigger and bigger, but Kendal was happy they were there to share their lives—even if some were missing who should've been there.

Life wasn't a straight path. It wasn't easy. It wasn't even a gentle ripple in a pond. It had hills, valleys, mountains, hurricanes, waterfalls, sandy beaches, riptides and every other naturally occurring element within it.

Life was living and believing in their path.

Life was love.

The most perfect element of all.

Read on for the description of the first book in the new Guarding Royalty series, Protecting his Past, which might just feature a very handsome bodyguard, who has secrets, and a certain personal assistant, who thinks he's too old for love.

For a taste of the free short story you get if you sign up to my newsletter...

PROTECTING HIS PAST

His secrets catch up with him, but luckily, protection is in his blood.

Dominic has big shoes to fill. His promotion to the Lead Protection Officer for the king came at a price no one wants to think about. However, its something he is very aware of. When his past comes calling, he has to make even more split second decisions, and he's terrified of the potential consequences. Not for himself, but for those he cares about and protects. Including a certain PA who's never too far from his thoughts.

Randall has been the King's personal assistant for many years. It's long hours and extremely busy, but he loves it. Even after being held prisoner by a twisted man hell bent on revenge, it didn't diminish his love for the job or the people he works for. But he never imagined falling in love. Especially with someone ten years younger than him. But love is love, right?

When Dominic's secret comes to light, he has to shore his defenses against those people who would use it against him.

And the harder he falls for Randall, the more chinks in his armour appear.

How can he keep everyone safe when the clock is ticking?

Protecting his Past is a kinky, age gap romance with a handsome bodyguard, who has secrets, and a personal assistant, who thinks he's too old for love.

ABOUT ELOUISE EAST

Elouise East writes sweet and steamy connections in gay romance. She also touches on taboo stories under the name Elouise R East.

Books that tell the stories where friendship and family are the focal point - be it blood family or chosen - are very important to her. That's why she includes a variety of personalities, talents, ages, situations and abilities as she believes a story or character needs. She wants her characters to be real, to be relatable, to be free to have whatever views they tell her they have. And trust her, most of the time, she does not have *any* say in the matter!

Her characters come to life on the page for her as well as her readers. Their stories unfold in front of her as she writes, and she has very little input into how they want to be shown. Just like real life, the lives of her characters change with every choice, every interaction and every conversation. And she wouldn't have it any other way.

She writes books that are emotionally realistic, even if liberties are taken with other aspects of the stories. She doesn't know any other way to write. It comes from deep inside.

Who is she? A single parent to two children living in the UK. An avid reader who still tries to devour every book she can get her hands on. A student of learning about any subject that takes her fancy. An author of books she would read herself. And a romantic at heart who loves anything cheesy.

Who's joining her on her journey?

Stalk her here… ;-)
Website : https://elouiseeast.com
Newsletter : https://elouiseeast.com/newsletter
All links : https://elouiseeast.com/links

Out of the Frying Pan

Smokescreen

Breathing Fire

<u>Crush</u>

Love Conquers

Instant Desire

Primary Seduction

Deep Down

A Crush for Christmas

Life Support

Covert Strength

Love Scene

Lawful Attraction

Crush Box Set 1-3

Crush Box Set 4-6

Crush Box Set 7-9

<u>Just A Little Crush</u>

First Kiss

He's Behind You

A Special Love

<u>Standalone</u>

Treehouse Whispers

Star-Crossed

Protecting the Thief

Sizzling Chauffeur

ELOUISE R EAST (TABOO)

Dark & Divergent

Forbidden Temptation

Too Many Secrets

Collide

When Fantasies Collide

When Dreams Collide

When Pleasures Collide

When Cravings Collide